What people have
Steve Nallon's

'One of our best impersonators h
– stories full of wit, character and
of Steve's characters.'

Rory Bremner, BAFTA winning comedian and satirist

'*"It's What She Would Have Wanted"*... compelling and page turning – a delicious ghostly thrill of the witty and the twisty.'

Helen Lederer, actress, comedian and author of best sellers such as *Not That I'm Bitter, Coping with Helen Lederer*, and *Losing It*.

'In Steve Nallon's *The Ghost Light* we have a supernatural whodunnit told from the perspective of the theatre's 'ghost light'. The story delighted me (as a seasoned theatrical, familiar with all the parlance), but Nallon's or rather the ghost light's 'guide' to theatrical terms makes the more arcane elements accessible to all readers. The plot is clever and as satisfying as an Agatha Christie with adroit character sketches that give a head nod to J.B. Priestley's world of weary actors in *Lost Empires*. Nallon's engaging writing style draws you in much as any good performer does on stage. Encore!!'

Jessica Martin, actress, singer, illustrator, graphic novelist and author of *It Girl* and *Elsie Harris Picture Palace*

'These ghost tales are vivid, grotesque, funny and curiously believable. Compelling reading for the young, old and in-betweens... *The Oath of Aesculapius* is a lovely, twisty, gothic horror story about a dining club – think Bullingdon – where rich men eat rich food and – hallelujah! – get their just desserts.'

Jonny Maitland, *Tonight* television presenter and author of the play *The Last Temptation of Boris Johnson*

'FABULOUS. Fascinating tales. Fascinating writing. Fascinating wit. Steve Nallon has a HIT... Needs to be a show, Netflix are you listening?'

Christian Dion, Television Celebrity Psychic

'"A picture is worth a thousand words", but with Steve Nallon's *For The Hell Of It*, his words evoke a thousand pictures. Beautifully written, thought provoking and original, the script feels like an adaptation of a literary classic.'

John Henderson, BAFTA and Emmy winning director

'Steve Nallon's homage to M.R. James captures both the wit and horror of that master's ghost stories – with their thoroughly decayed country houses, cobwebbed churches, and lonely windblown inns on the Norfolk coast, where the most terrifying of fellow guests emerge from oil paintings and cracked mirrors. I hope the old master materialises at least briefly in Steve Nallon's shaving mirror to gently bestow on him a solemn but generous nod of praise.'

William Palmer, award winning novelist and author of *The Contract, The India House, Four Last Things, The Good Republic, The Island Rescue* and *In Love with Hell*

'*The Ghost Light*. I loved this so much. I've worked with these people. I know them. I've met many Dereks in my life. The whole thing gave me a warm feeling as I read it. Having toured in many whodunnits over the years, I think Steve Nallon has caught the whole "world" so well... I highly recommend it.'

Denise Silvey, casting director for T*he Mousetrap*, the longest running play in the world, which had its first performance 6 October 1952

'I enjoyed reading *The Ghost Light* very much... I have believed in ghosts ever since I slept in a theatre on my first day of employment! Frightening! Don't dabble with the ghost light!'

Ian Talbot OBE, West End theatre director of Agatha Christie's *The Mousetrap*

'This collection of stories stands alone as a perfect amalgamation of dark British humour and truly chilling classic horror. It uniquely shows the creativity of an author who has excelled in a range of fields – giving it a voice of authority and authenticity that makes it impossible to put down!'

Matthew Cuss, Horror YouTuber and education consultant

'Steve Nallon's *"It's What She Would Have Wanted"* is funny, relatable and spookily familiar – finding the funny in death is no mean feat and Nallon has done it – read this and take heed, it could well be you one day!'

Arabella Weir MBE, actress, writer and author of the international bestseller *Does My Bum Look Big in This?*

'Two unpromising angelic visitors and a melancholic young man for whom Christmas evokes only sad memories unite in *Under The Mistletoe*. Steve Nallon tells a festive tale that is witty and warm, delightfully combining the familiar and the unexpected. I can't think of another writer who would make a connection between mistletoe and syphilis.'

Revd Simon Buckley, Rector of St Anne's Church, Soho

'A ghost story told with wit and imagination from Steve Nallon, whose ability to impersonate political and show business personalities is matched by his writing skills in inhabiting the characters in this paean to *Carry On* films. A genuine knowledge of the films and fondness for the usual suspects pervade this yarn. Noted for her warmth, sense of fun and lover of all things (and people) camp, how the mischievous Miss Jacques would have loved *Visiting Hattie*.'

Andy Merriman, author of *Hattie Jacques: The Authorised Biography*

'As well as being one of Britain's best and best-loved comedy performers, by all accounts Hattie Jacques was the personification of kindness. There was always a saucy tinkle at play too, and in this beguiling short story Steve Nallon not only captures her bewitching, compassionate nature, but hints at the playful sexiness that beats within the heart of her greatest performances. Reading *Visiting Hattie* is like a warm hug. Much like watching Hattie Jacques.'

Robert Ross, author of *The Carry On Companion*

'I love a ghost story that gives you a chill as you reach the conclusion – almost as if something has passed over you – and *The Ghost Light* delivers it beautifully!'

Neal Foster, Actor/Manager, Birmingham Stage Company

'*The Return of the Handbag* – The ghost story meets the comedy sketch; Nallon's Thatcher voice rings from every page like a live performance.'

Jenny Lecoat, screenwriter, novelist and author of *Hedy's Girl* and the movie *Another Mother's Son*

'*The Ghost Light* is charming. Immensely readable and written with warmth and humour about our ridiculously precious thespian world!'

Graham Seed, British character actor with *The Archers*, *I, Claudius*, *Victoria Wood: As Seen on TV* and *Brideshead Revisited* among his many credits

'What if Maggie Thatcher is haunting Number Ten as a ghost? Or all ex-PMs are? In this imaginative fantasy, Nallon brilliantly constructs the chaos it would cause if the lady is for returning. And very funny *The Return of the Handbag* is, too.'

Nigel Nelson, political pundit and former political editor of *The Sunday People*

'These are absolute GENIUS! Perfectly formed, individually wrapped treats, to be consumed by the fireside, a large sherry in hand, the fingers of long branches scraping across a window. A mixture of Wodehouse, Conan Doyle and fresh Nallon, these spooky tales chill and thrill in equal amounts.'

James Dreyfus, *Gimme, Gimme, Gimme* and *The Thin Blue Line*

'Just when you thought it was safe, she's back. A shiver will run down your back when you learn of the return of Mrs T in ghostly form. Be afraid. Very afraid.'

Iain Dale, LBC broadcaster, writer and editor of the award-winning book *The Prime Ministers*

'With a fine grasp of character and idiolect, Steve Nallon conjures up worlds with a great sense of authenticity and an even greater sense of imagination... Steve has an uncanny ability to find fresh and disturbing images – of life and death – in what we think are familiar worlds.'

Alistair McGowan, BAFTA winning comedian and actor

Screenplay Film Festival Awards

FOR THE HELL OF IT

Best Original Screenplay
Cleveland Film Awards

Best Screenwriting
MEI International Film Festival

Best Screenwriting and
Best Feature Screenplay
Athens International Film & Art Festival

Best Horror
Kookai International Film Festival

Best Unproduced Script in Feature
Hollywood International Golden Age Festival
Nashville Independent Filmmakers Festival

Best Feature Script
Rameshwaram International Film Festival
2 11 17 International Film Festival

Award Winner in Best Screenplay
Scream Queen Shockathon

Scariest Story (Runner Up)
Film Basement Horror Film Awards

Screenplay Finalist
Cambridge Script Festival and
13Horror.com Film & Screenplay Contest

Honourable Mentions
Sci-Fi & Horror International Festival
BAFF – Big Apple Film Festival

To Alan
Best wishes,
Steve Nallon

STEVE NALLON'S GHOST STORIES

Twelve Spooky Tales
of Supernatural Strangeness
and Weirdly Wonderful Goings On

With illustrations by
Scott Brooker

Scratching Shed Publishing Ltd

Steve Nallon is a writer and actor. He began his performing life with his own comedy act on the Northern Working Men's Club circuit in Yorkshire back in the 1970s. After gaining a degree in Drama and English at the University of Birmingham, Steve became a founding member of the television series *Spitting Image*, where for over a decade he voiced many of the programme's most iconic characters, including Margaret Thatcher, Alan Bennett and The Queen Mum. Steve's acting work now ranges from theatre, film and television, to video games, radio drama and audio books. As a playwright and comedy writer, Steve has a considerable body of credits to his name, including plays and series for BBC radio, three one-man theatre shows and the satirical book *I, Margaret*, which he co-wrote with Tom Holt. In 2022 Steve's novel *The Time That Never Was*, the first book in a new young adult book series called *The Swidgers*, was published by Luath Press, and the second in the series, *The Time They Saved Tomorrow*, came out in 2024. *Destination Time Travel*, an exploration of the story tropes of time travel tales written with British Film Institute archivist Dick Fiddy, was published in 2023. Over the years, Steve has contributed to numerous periodicals such as *The New Statesman* and *Musical Stages*, and is a much sought after speaker on the lecture circuit and in university colleges for his insightful and amusing talks.

Social Media: *@SteveNallon*

Growing up in a haunted house, **Scott Brooker** is no stranger to the weird and supernatural – talking of which, he first met Steve in 1984, when a ghastly career as a character designer and puppet-maker began upon joining the *Spitting Image* team in an old banana warehouse in London's Docklands. Since then, he has designed and/or made many characters for television, film, ads and theatre, including the Peperami sausage, Rattus from CBBC's *Horrible Histories*, and the woefully under-rated *The Harry Hill Movie*. Thanks to Steve, this is Scott's first foray into the weird and supernatural world of publishing...

Instagram: *scottbrookerart*

In Memory
of Mum and Dad

First published by Scratching Shed Publishing Ltd in 2024
Registered in England & Wales No. 6588772
Registered office: 47 Street Lane, Leeds, West Yorkshire. LS8 1AP
www.scratchingshedpublishing.co.uk
ISBN: 978-1068618963

A catalogue record for this book is available from the British Library.

Printed and bound in the UK by
CPI Group (UK) Ltd, Croydon, CR0 4YY

Contents

The Collection

(I've tried to avoid outright spoilers in this introduction, but it's impossible to write about any story without giving something away, so perhaps it might be best to read the tales first 🙂)

I AM ONE OF THOSE ACTORS who can't be myself. This goes back to childhood because when playing out I much prefered to invent people rather than be me. And perhaps all that constant pretending explains my preference now for writing stories in first person character voices. I like first person as well because it allows the writer a bond with the reader that's direct and intimate, plus for a ghost story collection, the different tones of voice, from the comic and endearing to the austere and macabre, offer something of a variation.

Traditional first person is seen as restricted in that a character narrator can't usually go inside someone else's head and know how they're feeling, but this can be an advantage in mystery stories such as *The Ghost Light*, where the theatre's ghost light is very much the outside observer keeping his distance. However, the narrator of *Under the Mistletoe* is supernatural – a famous diviner of dreams, in fact – and so he does have the power to go inside hearts and minds. *Visiting Hattie* is narrated by the spirit of Kenneth Williams, and, since Adam and Calvin are fans of the *Carry On* series, it seems right enough that Kenny has a way into how the couple think and feel. But that idea doesn't stretch to the ghost of Lady Thatcher in *The Return of the Handbag*, who is only ever concerned with herself. Besides, Mrs T wasn't exactly known for her empathy when alive.

First person can become a bit of a jigsaw puzzle when it's the narrator's job to piece together different narrative elements. This is the case with *The Portrait of a Looking-Glass*, which uses the structure of M.R. James's *Count Magnus* as its model. James in turn was probably influenced by the tales of Sheridan Le Fanu, such as *Borrohomeo the Astrologer* and the cases of Dr Hesselius that make up the collection called *In a Glass Darkly*, which use found documents in the narration of the story.

The Oath of Aesculapius is different again in that, as with one of those Russian dolls, it's a story within a story within a story – and specifically an armchair after dinner ghost story. A journalist is the narrator of *The Final Fake*, so you'd expect he'd be able to tell a good yarn and not reveal the twist until the end, even though he knows from the first line what it is. As for *Who Fed the Cat?*, well, that's more complicated as it's a first person narrator who uses the second person 'you', for the narration, or whatever you want to call it, as he directly addresses a police officer named in the tale.

Of course, not all the stories in the collection are written as first person narratives. *'It's What She Would Have Wanted'* is told through an exchange of emails, *The Strange Case of The Unaccountable Shadow* is presented in diary form and the story of *For the Hell of It* is written as a screenplay. Yet the point is they all have individual character voices and these I would often act out as I did as a child.

Only, nowadays, I write down what they all say – and that becomes the tale.

The Oath of Aesculapius

An Armchair Ghost Tale to Warm (and Chill) Your Heart.

The idea for this tale came about when I was reading Rudyard Kipling's *They*, which has the line, 'The Doctor was a man of some humour, for I remember he claimed my car under the Oath of Aesculapius, and used it without mercy.' Out of curiosity I checked to see whether such an action was legal, but discovered that there is no actual law which states a doctor, nor indeed a police officer, has the right to commandeer a private motor vehicle. However, since I was keen to include a ghost-on-the-road scenario in the collection, I thought the concept of a doctor waving down a car owner in order to take an injured patient to hospital was an interesting starting point for a tale. Yet as I developed the idea it became clear the story wouldn't be enough on its own and so, as I was also keen to have an armchair ghost tale, the Oath of Aesculapius scenario became the story within the story.

SEND **'IT'S WHAT SHE WOULD HAVE WANTED'**

SUBJECT A Modern Tale of Ashes to Ashes and Dust to Dust

Years ago a friend told me about his very possessive and controlling mother and, as he did so, the image came into my head of her bringing an ornament to his house, putting it centre position on the mantelpiece and saying, 'This will look very nice here.'

I never did anything with the thought, but it came back to me as I was preparing this collection and I developed it into a tale about the inability of a mother to let go. The original ending was more sinister, but friends said it left an unpleasant taste, so I rewrote it to be less about power and control and more about acceptance and understanding. The story concept of the willing surrender of a character's want which I talk about in *Thoughts on the Ghost Story* doesn't apply in all the tales in this collection but it does in *'It's What She Would Have Wanted'* – and I am grateful to friends who persuaded me to make that the apex of story.

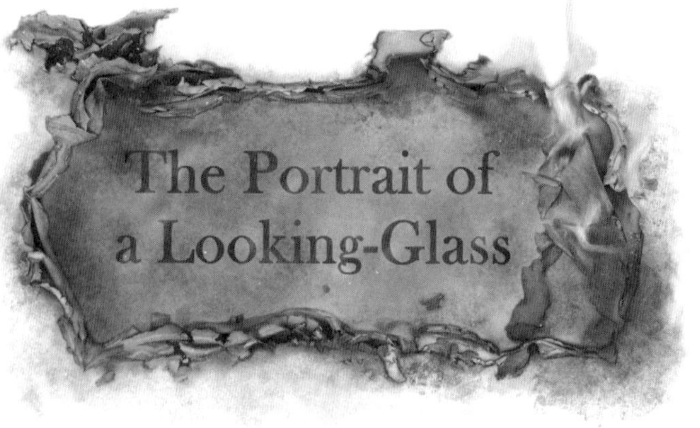

A Homage to the Master of the Ghost Tale, M.R. James.

I gave up on my first attempt at writing a homage to The Master. I played with an ancient artefact scenario where a tallow candle when put in some sort of supernatural candlestick holder would give off a light that could reveal the presence of ghosts by their shadows. And as that candle flickered, the ghostly shadow developed a malevolent corporeal life all of its own. But frankly the problem was that I couldn't make the story about anything other than a magical candlestick holder and so instead I worked on plan B, a haunted portrait and its looking-glass companion.

M.R. James aficionados are likely to recognise steals from *The Mezzotint*, *Lost Hearts* and *A View from a Hill*, plus there is the obligatory Jamesian comic servant with his many mispronunciations. There are also references to people with connections with Aldeburgh (or Seaburgh in his stories). However, in a way the tale is really about Montague Rhodes James himself. The main character is called Rhodes and there are historical events, notably the letter to *The Times* concerning the bones of St Edmund the Martyr, which identify the narrator specifically as M.R. James.

It's all very meta – 

Of course there's more to any writer than how one individual reader perceives her or him through their writing. And from that point of view I doubt I've got James right, in that my way of seeing him won't be the same as anyone else's. However, I've tried to distil an essence as I see it and if *The Portrait of a Looking-Glass* can cause the reader some 'pleasing terror' my purpose in writing the tale will have been attained.

VISITING HATTIE

A Titillating Tale of Spooky Seductiveness as Told by the Ghost of Kenneth Williams.

An actor friend called Adam Trembath from Cornwall, who stays at my house when working in London, told me after a visit to the bathroom that he found it very difficult 'to go'. 'Why?' I asked. 'Because Hattie keeps looking at me,' he replied.

I should explain that on the wall of my bathroom is an array of black and white publicity photographs of favourite comic actors from the *Carry On* series, including Frankie Howerd, Kenneth Williams, Charles Hawtrey and, of course, a grinning Hattie Jacques. When Adam told me of his bashful bladder in the presence of her mischievous smile I was in the early planning stages of these stories and so, perhaps not surprisingly, his experience developed into *Visiting Hattie*. And in my house a 'visit to Hattie' has now become the 'spend-a-penny' euphemism for a trip to the loo. Ooh, Matron!

I should mention here two excellent books which proved invaluable when writing *Visiting Hattie*. The first is Andy Merriman's beautifully written *Hattie: The Authorised Biography of Hattie Jacques* (2008), and the second is Robert Ross's meticulously researched *The Carry On Companion* (2002), which *Carry On* star Jack Douglas called 'The Carry On bible'. And I have no doubt that fans of Hattie and the *Carry On* series would enjoy reading both!

THE FINAL FAKE

A Tale of Lies and Truth...
but not necessarily in that order.

We had to read the *Book of Samuel* at school – such is the nature of a Jesuit education – and I never forgot the story of the Witch of Endor. I noticed, in various ghost tales, that Miss Endor occasionally received a passing mention, notably in Robert Louis Stevenson's *Thrawn Janet* and E.F. Benson's *Negotium Perambulans*. However, perhaps she was due for, and deserving of, a more starring role. But how and where?

Years ago I had planned to do a one-man show about people who made their living by pretending to be somebody else – including imposters and fraudsters. Part of my research included the John Stonehouse trial, which revealed the fascinating tale of a Member of Parliament in the 1970s who faked his own death and created an alternative identity in Australia. Re-reading the research I could see how the Stonehouse trial could work as the opening scene of a tale about how to expose phoney clairvoyants who take on the voices of the dead. Of course the Witch of Endor in the Hebrew Bible was consulted by Saul not just to listen the spirit of Samuel but to actually conjure him up from wherever he was. But exactly how and where all this fits into *The Final Fake* would be to reveal the ending. And I suspect Miss Endor certainly wouldn't want that!

THE RETURN OF THE HANDBAG

TOP SECRET

As told by The Infamous Lady Herself

One of the questions that came up when Lady Thatcher died was what sort of gravestone to give the former Prime Minister.

One wag suggested, "A very, very heavy one!"

Well, it wasn't quite heavy enough: The Lady is for Returning! But what sort of ghost story should it be?

It's not unknown in tales for a hauntee to become a haunter. This is the case with the judge in Sheridan Le Fanu's *The Haunted House in Westminster* and its prequel *An Account of Some Strange Disturbances in an Old House in Aungier Street*. You might add the recent horror hit *Talk to Me* (2023) and the television movie *The Stone Tape* (1972), both of which are discussed in *Thoughts on the Ghost Tale*. Anyway, when my friend Ninia Benjamin insisted that I write a Mrs Thatcher ghost tale, the idea came to me of Lady M not only being a ghost now haunting Downing Street but when alive being the one who was haunted. Such a scenario would, I thought, be an intriguing way of looking at the end of her tenure in Number Ten, when it was clear to even her closest colleagues that she was becoming increasingly detached from reality.

To discover more about the potential haunter PMs of the past I read *The Prime Ministers*, edited by the political broadcaster Iain Dale. And what an odd set of misfits they turned out to be! Yet there was much comic potential in their personalities and the lives they lived.

I also did some research on the history of Downing Street and began to realise what a peculiar place it is. Incidentally, transforming the store cupboard into an alcove was at Mrs Thatcher's own request when the house was undergoing one of its many refurbishments. And that alcove became the place of Lady Thatcher's return in my story. As she famously said herself, 'It's a funny old world.'

The Unusual Memoir of a Victorian Institution

As a child I enjoyed Anna Sewell's *Black Beauty* not because I especially liked horses, but rather because I loved the idea of an animal telling his own story. I'd also liked those descriptions in Dickens where houses are seen as people. I particularly remember this from *A Christmas Carol*: 'They were a gloomy suite of rooms, in a louring pile of building up a yard, where it had so little business to be, that one could scarcely help fancying it must have run there when it was a young house, playing at hide-and-seek with other houses, and forgotten the way out again.'

Well, then, why not combine those ideas and let a house tell its own tale? And since characters in stories often have a lacking of some sort or other, why couldn't our Victorian manor house be in want of a ghost? And when one unexpectedly arrives after the building is refurbished as a conference venue, where the first event is a symposium on 'images of spectrality', as academics insist on calling spooks, why not have it that the visiting ghost was murdered? And that's how *'I Was Once a Haunted House'* turned into a kind of whodunnit.

The word 'haunt' comes from Old French *hanter* (in the sense of 'to frequent a place'), which is of Germanic origin and is related to 'home'. And the ever present frequenters of house-proud Claverley Manor are rats. And here I have Bithia Mary Crocker's *Number Ninety* to thank for the story potential of those ever present rodents

('It was all imagination, I assured myself – or rats! Rats were capable of making such curious improbable noises!'). In fact, '*I Was Once a Haunted House*' developed into my tribute to the whole gothic nineteenth century tradition. You don't need to know any of the Victorian tales which are referenced in the short lectures delivered at 'The Ghosts of Many Worlds' symposium, but if I had to point you to just one it would be Margaret Oliphant's *The Open Door*, which for me has all the elements of a classic Victorian ghost story. And Ellen Glasgow's *The Shadowy Third* would be useful too as it plays an important role in the plot of '*I Was Once a Haunted House*'.

The Strange Case of the Unaccountable Shadow

The Startling Diary of a Worried Mother

My friend Gemma Ross and I were chatting one day about home devices. Gemma was saying how scary it is that you can now have a hidden camera and microphone placed in the house and are able to check in to see what's happening from anywhere in the world. That's fine for when you're away on holiday, but unnerving if you happen to be a house-sitter.

Unnerving is always a good starting point for a supernatural tale and as I was keen to have modern technology at the centre of one of the stories in the collection, I began to develop the scenario of a paranoid mother who through a hidden camera secretly watches the home tutorial sessions that take place between her son and his teacher. However, as she watches from an upstairs room, the mother notices an 'unaccountable shadow' – a phrase I came across in a H.R. Wakefield tale – only it isn't there when she comes down and examines the room itself. I should acknowledge here a debt to Edith Nesbit's *The Shadow*, one of her finest tales, which also features a lurking and unexplainable shadow.

But what would be the text taught in the tutoring session which the mother watches via the camera? Why not *The Strange Case of Doctor Jekyll and Mr Hyde*? It's now a set text at GCSE and there are parallel themes. The terms that story theorists use when a well known tale or myth underpins or provides background to your own are 'mythical infra-narrative' or 'textual infra-narrative', both of them ugly phrases, as many academic terms often are, but nevertheless they can be an effective literary tool. It's a technique, for example, that Ruth Rendell uses in *A Bad Heart*, which is discussed in Appendix I, *Thoughts on the Ghost Tale*.

Unreliable narrator has in recent years become something of an over-used and certainly over-hyped term. You could argue the mother in *The Strange Case of the Unaccountable Shadow* is unreliable in that there's the question of whether what she sees is real or simply a manifestation of her paranoia? Except, as with the governess in Henry James's *The Turn of the Screw*, what she sees is the truth to her. And what the mother sees certainly looks real enough in Scott Brooker's brilliant illustration.

I've known Scott for over forty years and I know he wouldn't lie.

Would he?

FOR THE HELL OF IT

The Troubling Tale of Seven Little Sins.

Gemma pointed out when we'd got to story ten that there wasn't an outright horror story yet. Yes, a few of the ghost tales had elements of horror *in* them, but relatively little was out-and-out gross-out. So could I perhaps write a schlock horror yarn with lots of broken bones, lashings of Kensington Gore and high scoring body count?

I'd always enjoyed the Universal movies of the 1930s and '40s, notably *Frankenstein*, *Bride of Frankenstein* and *The Old Dark House*, all directed by James Whale, plus the Hammer films made at Bray (and later at Pinewood) and the Amicus horror pictures produced at Shepperton in the 1950s and '60s, yet I'd never been a particular fan of the slasher movie. However, I'd recently seen Demián Rugna's *When Evil Lurks*, Jordan Peele's *Get Out*, Danny and Michael Philippou's *Talk to Me*, Mark Jenkin's *Enys Men* (Cornish for 'Stone Island') and Elizabeth Banks' *Cocaine Bear*, all modern takes on the horror movie and I'd admired each in different ways. So I said to Gemma that I'd try to think of a story with lots of spilt guts and splurting claret resulting in horrible deaths, but which also had a point to it.

Next morning I woke up with the image of a severed head washed up on a beach and the group of thirty-somethings who discover it. Perhaps it was from an old storybook I'd read of the legend of Blackbeard's ghost, where his chopped head is hung from the bowsprit of the ship. Or perhaps it was Caravaggio's *Salome Receives the Head of Saint John the Baptist*, one of the many religious paintings I saw every day on the walls at school. Either way it was good to know that lurking childhood memories were now paying off.

I also recalled how William Golding's *Lord of the Flies*, another influence from my schooldays, had a beach setting and the parable nature of that paradise story began to colour the one forming in my mind. The more I thought about it, the more I realised the best way of presenting the tale would be in a screenplay format. Not a shooting script with 'Fade to', 'Cuts to' and the rest, but rather a story that is primarily written as visual images, action and dialogue, which activates, as it were, the camera inside the reader's imagination. Nowadays the writing style of a screenplay specifically aims to set the tone of the movie and sometimes even offers a sense of what the audience might be thinking, feeling or sensing. In this way the modern screenplay is similar to what John Steinbeck in his foreword to *The Pearl and Burning Bright* called 'the play novelette', which for him was a hybrid form somewhere between a play and a novel – in practice a speech drama that was easy to read. And that was my intention with the screenplay style of *For the Hell of It*.

The branching structure of *For the Hell of It* owes much to *Theatre of Blood* (Harbour Productions) and, to some degree, the omnibus or portmanteau movies *Doctor Terror's House of Horrors* and *Tales from the Crypt*, both made by Amicus Productions. I should add that the maze is probably a borrowing from *The Shining*, and the presence of the aggressive seagulls almost certainly comes from seeing Hitchcock's *The Birds* at an impressionable age. One scene though in *For the Hell of It* was inspired by an actual dream I had, where a falling barbell bar in gym brushed by my knees and could so easily have broken them. It's not a barbell bar in the story, but the fear of something landing on that crucial joint is, to borrow Stephen King's phrase, a pressure point moment of horror in the tale.

However, I'd say the biggest influence on it is my Catholic upbringing and Jesuit education. There's even in the screenplay a small but heartfelt tribute to the traditions of my old school of St Michael's College in Leeds. But how exactly has all that theology seeped itself into this supernatural story? Well, it's been said that the horror genre more than any other explores the sheer unfairness and injustice of life. That's true, and that's the case with *For the Hell of It*. Yet at the end – and a horrible and bloody end it is too – there is at least some hope and possibility of spiritual redemption.

Not many supernatural horror movies offer you that.

Who Fed the Cat?

A Feline Tale of Sound, Taste, Smell, Touch and Sight.

I noted as I was reading the ghost stories of E.F. Benson how cleverly Edward Frederic makes use of nearly all the human senses in his tales. Certainly far more than any other writer. As he writes in *The Terror by Night*, 'Some ghosts are seen, some heard, some felt, and though I know of no instance of a ghost being tasted, yet it will seem in the following pages that these occult phenomena may appeal at any rate to the senses that perceive heat, cold, or smell.'

But why should a spirit, if it wants to reveal something to the living, simply not communicate by speaking? Ah! Suppose the ghost can no longer talk properly. Suppose its larynx has been damaged, perhaps as a result of a gunshot wound through the neck. That means the ghost would have to make themselves known by the other senses. And that's essentially what the murdered woman has to do in *Who Fed the Cat?*

Scott Brooker's illustration for *Who Fed the Cat?* was, unlike the other stories in the collection, created before I wrote the actual tale itself. His femme fatale in the casket was so startling that I realised I would have to find a writing style to match. Dashiell Hammett, Raymond Chandler and Damon Runyon obviously came to mind. Although the narrative style of *Who Fed the Cat?* may seem pastiche, there is a logic for it being so – but that, dear reader, is the final twist of the tale.

THE GHOST LIGHT

A Theatre Ghost Story of Murder and Vengeance

I'd wanted to include a theatre ghost tale in the collection and the inspiration came during the Covid lockdown when I saw dozens of images on social media of ghost lights standing centre stage in theatres.

I should explain that a ghost light is a theatre tradition whereby an exposed lamp mounted inside a wire cage on a stand is left centre stage when a theatre is unoccupied and in the hope that one day all the lights will be switched on again. The ghost lights I saw on Instagram postings by friends looked so lonely, and my natural propensity for turning inanimate objects into living personalities led me to the idea that the ghost light could be the storyteller.

I've been lucky enough to have toured many and various theatres in Britain and The Chertswood is an amalgam of several of them. Likewise the characters of the director, the stage manager, the principals (meaning the main actors) and the understudies. All professions have their archetypes and I've tried to capture some of those from the theatre world in this story.

An Angelic Tale of Wonderment and Weirdness.

Charles Dickens's novella *The Haunted Man and the Ghost's Bargain: A Fancy for Christmas-Time* is a sort of back-to-front version of *A Christmas Carol*. Whereas in *A Christmas Carol* the spectres revive the Christmas memories of Scrooge in order to bring about his reclamation, in *The Haunted Man*, Redlaw, a gentleman suffering from melancholia, what we today would call depression, encounters a doppelgänger spectre who at the beginning offers him the opportunity of having all his sad memories wiped away. This should, argues his ghostly twin, bring to an end his depression. Well, it's an intriguing theory, but it doesn't quite work out as easily as that.

Under the Mistletoe is very loosely based on the idea of a depressed man having his sad memories removed, but other than that premise there's little that connects it with the Dickens story. I have, however, consciously borrowed from two Christmas angel movies, namely *The Bishop's Wife* and *It's a Wonderful Life*. I know I'm supposed to prefer *It's a Wonderful Life*. It's a better film, I agree, but I prefer the festive charm of *The Bishop's Wife*. If you've never seen it, find a copy and give yourself a Christmas treat!

MY BELIEF IS THAT A STORY is simply a game of pretend that goes on in your head and heart.

For me, stories are a form of play that prepare you not only for life when you are a child, but which also help you to deal with the continuing problems that experience so often throws at you as you get older. Yes, ideally a tale should be about something, and I'd say my themes range from loneliness and redemption to the joys of sex and food. But whatever they are about, my primary aim with these stories is simply to tell an entertaining yarn.

And when making them up – or pretending them in my head – my watchwords have been plot, character, humour... with, I hope, a surprise twist or turnabout at the end.

I've certainly been inspired by the many classic ghost stories I've read over the years, but the scenarios of the majority of the tales originate from somewhere in my mind, be it an image, a phrase, an idea, a half-remembered incident. It's what Stephen King talks about in his foreword to *Night Shift* as the 'sludge' that never gets filtered away. All I would add is that when your storyteller 'radar' is on high alert, your brain somehow spots the potential in the memory sludge and whatever that is begins to turn itself into something worth finding.

I don't think all ghost stories have to be creepy or even scary. I've always enjoyed, for example, those quirky playful tales of Oliver Onions such as *The Ether Hogs* and *The Mortal*, which tell the tale from the perspective of the ghost. Sometimes, like him, I just want to make the reader laugh and smile. But if there are those stories which freak you out along the way, well, I'll take that too.

Anyway, I hope you enjoy them!

Steve Nallon

STEVE NALLON'S GHOST STORIES

The Oath of Aesculapius

An Armchair Ghost Tale to Warm (and Chill) Your Heart.

AN AFTER DINNER GHOST STORY IS best told with a log fire blazing, for the enchantment of the naked flame, that prize stolen by Prometheus from the gods, imbues all about it with the power to take the listener into a world beyond dreaming. However tonight there were no roaring flames, not even the waxy glow of a candle. The proprietor of The Silver Turul, that well-known Hungarian restaurant in the beating heart of Soho, was adamant that our private dining room was subject to the same Health and Safety laws as the tables downstairs, where the plebeians sat.

'Our insurance is not covering for naked flames. Except in kitchen. Candles make fire risk. So no candles.'

I didn't arrive until the dinner was underway, but that's what I was told the catering manager said.

Our dining club – The Bacchanean – was made up, exclusively so, of college friends of old and we met about three times a year, as close as we could to the first day of term of our *alma mater,* Baltram College, Oxford. Tonight's meal would mark Michaelmas.

The summer had been exceptionally hot and even now, in October, the weather was still unseasonably mild. Perhaps that explained the high turnout. The menu included shrimps, mussels and oysters, all especially shipped in, or rather driven in, that morning from Cornwall. The entrée was followed by a wild boar goulash, enriched with paprika and caraway seeds, and, in memory of many a hall meal, spotted dick and custard for pudding. It was our first time at The Silver Turul and the Hungarian chef had to be given the recipe for this uniquely British pile of sweet sticky stodge.

It was a black tie affair as always, but relaxed and joshing too, as you might expect from men who had roomed together and shared the unholy pranks of youth. We even still used our nicknames from our university days. 'Perry', the founder of the dining club, had been given his nomenclature for his liking of expensive champagne. 'Cheesy' was so called because he shared his surname, 'Morbier', with a village in Franche-Comté which produced a rare cheese made from cow's milk. 'Mouse', not surprisingly, was the shortest in our group and the joker of the pack. One of the more vulgar etymologies came about because at college one chap always had prophylactics in his top pocket, or 'rubbers', as we called them then. As a result he was nicknamed 'Pencil'. If you follow my meaning.

As you might guess, the humour during dinner was ribald and unrepentantly dark.

'...so the doctor, having told the lady that she only had six months to live, then says, "But you could try having a mud bath." The lady suddenly cheers up and asks, "Will it cure me?" The doctor replies, "No, but at least you'll get used to the dirt."'

Mouse, who told the joke, had himself been a doctor until, like many of us, becoming seduced by the silver shilling of the corporate world. 'Bluebottle', christened such for winning three sporting 'blues' for Oxford in rowing victories over Cambridge, spoke for us all when he said, 'I am now rich enough to commit what follies I please and connected enough not to suffer the consequences.' 'Yes,' replied Pigleg (real name Trotter), 'it is my experience of the world that it is far more important to find a good lawyer than a good wife.' Yet what might be thought 'good' in Pigleg's domain of international finance is unlikely to be the same as in yours. And perhaps that includes our skewed attitudes to our lusty natures. 'Sex,' pronounced Perry, 'is like fox hunting – the pleasure is in the pursuit. And, as ever with the hunt, all the more joyous when you're riding on someone else's land! Ha! Ha! Don't you agree, James?'

That question had been aimed at me. I smiled but didn't answer. I should say, incidentally, that 'James' isn't my real name. I became known as that because I was the only undergraduate with wheels. And since the aristocracy had a habit of calling their chauffeurs 'James' no matter what name their mothers had given them, 'James' is what I became.

The meal itself had been a delight. Except, as I say, I had arrived late and so missed the first course.

'Yummy, they were,' said Perry, 'and so they should be because I own that part of the coast. Didn't let them go to waste, so I ate yours too. Serves you right for missing assembly. Naughty James! Five hundred lines. Ha!'

The wild boar goulash, however, was faultless and the beers and wines were exceptional. In our day we were all 'heavy lifters', but nowadays it was quality over quantity. I felt the cook had done a reasonable job with the pudding, but some thought it ruined by having crème brûlée instead of Bird's custard powder. In honour of our friend we had Morbier as the only cheese, which, along with some figs flown in from Spain, concluded the meal. The dining club never had chocolates, for they were considered effeminate and suitable only for the fairer sex or 'those boys who think boys *are* girls', as Pencil put it.

Stomachs were now fuller, cheeks redder and grins wider. The absence of candles, however, still riled our founder. Perry, the sort of man who always entered a room voice first, wouldn't shut up about his 'right to do as I bloody well please' and the nonsense of all those 'retard regulations'. To hear him go on you'd have thought the Bolsheviks had taken over and wiped their arses with the Magna Carta. But Perry, a schemer by nature and bad loser by temperament, had come up with a plan to have the last word on the subject.

'Gents,' he said, rising from the table after the final slice of

Morbier had been eaten, 'the servant class has been dismissed, the door is closed to the outside world–'

'Sporting the oak!' spouted Pigleg, reminding us of the college slang we used all those years ago.

'Indeed! And we will soon have our customary ghost story to bring our splendid evening to a close. Sadly, there are traitors at the gate and we have witnessed a flagrant attack on the freedom of the flame. I have, however, my gold lighter and if candles cannot accompany our ghoulish yarn, then we shall have in their stead smouldering leaves. For what are fraternity and liberty without cigars!'

The questionable legality of lighting up was raised, but Perry would not be put off his stride.

'*Novus ordo seclorum*, as our friends across the pond would say: "New order of the ages". Well, at least for tonight. Do we here present in the room declare unilateral independence from our sovereign state? All those in favour say "Aye".' There was a unanimous chorus of 'Ayes' from the dozen or so gathered, which included a Member of Parliament who, before an embarrassing resignation following an 'indiscretion' late one night with an ancient object in the British Museum, had in his time been a prominent cabinet minister.

'The "Ayes" have it, the "Ayes" have it,' declared Perry, to the loud accompaniment of fists banging tables. He then reached for his briefcase and took from it an ornate mahogany box. 'The old man used to say that he who is careful in the choosing of cigars has the advantage over the indiscriminate fool of smoking his down to the last.' Cigars were passed round and lit. There being no ashtrays, the members simply let the burnt flakes of tobacco drop on to the carpet below.

'Jackets off, gentlemen,' Perry announced, 'and let us now retire from our table and gather the armchairs around the unlit fireplace – boo! hiss! – for our brandies and the telling of the evening's spooky story.'

The armchair ghost tale had been a feature of our evenings for three decades now and, for many members, a tradition from days at school. My own prep master on a Sunday evening after vespers would tap his mortarboard in the direction of a few select pupils, usually those who had done well that Saturday at rugger or cricket, and this would be the sign to join him in his rooms, where, lit only by candles, he would indulge us in a fiendish tale.

'Boys,' he would say, 'never forget those words of Tennyson: "You are bones, and what of that? / Every face, however full, / Padded round with flesh and fat, / Is but modelled on a skull." For remember, we all become ghost stories in the end.'

That would certainly be true tonight.

By now the armchairs and Chesterfield sofa had been rearranged in a half circle, and, in the absence of candles, the electric light had been dimmed to that of a hazy dusk. But before we could sit down for our tale, and this evening it was I who would tell it, there were the brandies to be poured. Perry, however, was dissatisfied with the bottle left by our hosts. He pronounced it inferior and produced from his briefcase a vintage of his own. As for the one offered by the restaurant, well that 'camel spit', he said, was fit only for cooking and cleaning carpets.

'And what a ghastly rug it is,' he added, promptly emptying the entire contents of the bottle all over the thick black weave beneath his feet, patterned with swirling twists of yellow and orange. 'Looks like a bloody nest of snakes.'

We were not as riotous as in our youth, but given our behaviour tonight I thought it unlikely that The Silver Turul, as with many a restaurant of yesteryear, would welcome us back in a hurry.

Perry then poured himself a brandy from his own bottle, a fine and very expensive champagne cognac, before passing it to the next man. When glasses were full, our founder offered the toast.

'Gentlemen, I give you our traditional toast. To our four loves: The Bacchanean, Baltram, boating and most of all bedding!'

We then made ourselves comfortable in our seats for the telling of the tale.

'I hope it's not going to be one of those stories where there is someone who's dead but the person telling it doesn't know it yet,' said Bluebottle. 'There are too many like that.'

'Or there's an old aunt who lives in Timbuktu who comes to you in a vision covered in blood and the next day you get a telegram saying how it was at that very moment that she was eaten by a tiger,' said Pigleg.

'Ha! I wouldn't mind if she were leaving me her dosh,' grinned Mouse. 'With the first guinea I'd send a reply telegram thanking the tiger.'

'And don't let there be some sucker who encounters a spirit, falls in love with her, only then for the spook to want him all to herself and so the poor chap's doomed to a living death,' said Pencil.

'I think you'll find that's what's called "marriage". Ha! Ha! Ha!' quipped Mouse, laughing a little too loudly at his own joke.

'I liked the one we had the night of Trinity. About that opera singer who had her lungs burnt out in a fire and whose ghostly screams were mistaken for a top C,' said Bluebottle.

'That wasn't Trinity, that was Hilary. And I should know because I told it!' said Mouse. 'Ha! Ha! It's giving me tingles just thinking about it now. By the way, whose turn is it tonight?'

'Mine,' I replied.

'Oh good,' said Perry. 'James is one for the classics. Victorian governesses and phantom men in redcoats and all that.'

'Not this year.'

'What's it called, James?' asked Pigleg.

Odd. I hadn't yet given it a title. I thought for a moment.

'*The Oath of Aesculapius*,' I said.

'Ah yes, but better known as the Hippocratic oath,' said Mouse. 'I took it myself.' Yes, I do remember the day Doctor Mouse took his oath. Yet, as my tale is revealed, perhaps you'll come to understand why I believe my friend, today a company director in the corporate world of pharmaceuticals, failed to keep to the spirit of that promise. Not that any of it matters now.

'Does your tale involve a sawbones?' asked Perry.

'Yes,' I said.

'Spoiler! Spoiler! Spoiler!' cried Pigleg.

'I hope it isn't going to be a long-winded epic,' remarked Perry. 'Look at Cheesy over there. He looks almost asleep. You still with us, Cheesy?' Cheesy didn't reply, but nodded his head and gave us what we took to be an attempt at a smile.

'I'm not sure how long it's going to be, because I'm not sure if it's even finished yet,' I went on. 'You see, it's a true story. And it happened to me tonight. On my way here in my pride and joy, my Austin 1951 Somerset. That's why I was late.'

'Oooh, I'm intrigued,' said Perry. 'Never had a true ghost tale before.'

'There's no such thing,' said Pigleg. 'Just a bit of fun and nonsense, that's all.'

'Perhaps you'll change your mind when you hear it.'

Perry stood up for a moment, unusually for him, a little unsteady on his feet, and said, 'Enough chit-chat,' then pointed at me and added, 'Five, four, three, two, one – begin!'

I was ready. Well, as ready as I could ever be.

'As most of you know, I moved out to the countryside a few years ago. Little place called Great Milton. Perfect for commuting if needs be, because it's close to the M40. Only tonight my Sat-Nav was telling me the M40 was closed and the A40 was chokka, so instead it was recommending the country lanes via Marlow. On top of that, with it being so unseasonably warm, there was a terrible thunderstorm overhead.'

'Less of the weather and the road map and more of the tale!' snapped Pigleg.

'Why do ghost story writers make the best lovers? Because they always put in a mysterious twist at the end! Ha!' laughed Mouse, enjoying a joke he had told many times before.

Such interruptions and banter were commonplace. However, tonight they became fewer as my story unfolded.

'It's both a map and a tale with many turns and twists,' I said in response.

'You sock it to 'em, James,' said Bluebottle.

'I will if you all let me. The rain was coming down in stair rods and, as you know, there are many dangerous bends on those old country lanes. One especially tricky corner is a hell hole for accidents and so when I approached it I wasn't that surprised to see a figure waving me down to stop. Which I did. It was a middle-aged man, like us, in dinner jacket and black tie. Except of course he was soaked to the skin. I thought, well, if he is a highway robber he is at least wearing his best. The first thing he said to me as I lowered the car window was, "I'm a doctor. It's my wife. There's been an accident. We need to get her to a hospital. I know a route you can take."

'I'm usually a good timekeeper. I even left home very early in the afternoon because I had planned a get together with a friend before our dinner. But with the traffic chaos, and now this detour, that meeting was looking less and less likely. I'll be honest with you, I listened out for any other cars coming. Why did it have to be me? Couldn't someone else do it? But it was odd because, as I thought about it, there hadn't been any cars on the road for the last half hour. And that was also strange because if the M40 was closed then why weren't the back lanes busier?

'Anyway, I asked the doctor if he had tried phoning for an ambulance. He said yes, but no surprise when he told me he couldn't get a signal. I hadn't one on my phone either; telecommunications-wise half of Oxfordshire is in a black hole. The doctor by now was getting agitated and insisted we take his wife to the hospital pronto. Well, there would be blood stains on the back seat, but it'd be my good deed for the day. Don't do many of those.

'Still seated in my car, I drove it slowly round the bend and it was there that I saw the terrible state of things. The accident hadn't been his fault. A fallen tree had blocked part of the road and it looked to me as if he had swerved to avoid it but in doing so gone into a hedge. The airbag on the driver's side had opened but his wife's, in the passenger seat, had not. I parked close alongside the hedge. "I'll put up a warning sign where you flagged me down," I told him. "I keep a large red warning triangle in the back. My wife, Jes, bought it."

'"Yes," the doctor replied, in an oddly reflective tone, "I think that will prove most useful." He was so calm, blasé almost. So unnerving. But then again that's the nature of doctors, I suppose.

'As I approached his wreck of a car, I saw that his wife's external injuries weren't as bad as they might have been. Cuts and bruises everywhere, but no bones were broken as far as I could tell. "I'm concerned," said the husband, "that there may be internal bleeding. That's why we must get her to the hospital as soon as we can."

'I looked once more at the body slumped in the seat. The doctor appeared to sense what I was thinking. "If you're worried about moving her, I shall take full responsibility. I'm a doctor. I do know what I'm doing. But I'll need your help, of course." As it happened, his wife was still partially conscious and able, to some degree at least, to move herself into the back of my vehicle. "The nearest hospital is in Marlow," said the doctor, settling himself in beside his wife. "That's about fifteen minutes away. When we're nearer I'll check for a signal and ring, so they will be ready for us. And thank you for doing all this." He then smiled and added, "You know, in my time I've turned many a taxi driver into a midwife."

'We drove on in silence for a while. Well, except for the odd cry of pain from his wife. "It might help if we have some music. To keep my wife awake," he said. I nodded and put on the radio.

She didn't do it,
But I believed she did.
She didn't do it,
But I thought she might.
She didn't do it.
Though I knew she could.
And all on a Saturday night.

'"Ah," said the doctor. "The Excluders. A 60s revival of the 90s. Good tune, I always thought."

'He was right, but it was the wrong song, the very worst song, for me to hear tonight. "Would you mind," I said, "if we listen to something else? Classical music?" "Of course," replied the doctor, "it's your car."

'I pressed the preset. Chopin was playing, Jessica's favourite.

'The doctor then suddenly said, whether to me, his lady or even himself I wasn't sure, "The Oath of Aesculapius. As originally worded began: *I hereby swear by Apollo the physician, and Aesculapius the surgeon, as well as Hygeia, Panacea, calling upon all the gods and goddesses as my witness, that I will keep, observe and carry out this oath to the very best of my ability and judgement*. You then vowed to hold the man who taught the art – and they were all men in those days – as dear as your own father, and, if requested, to teach the doctor's sons what you had learnt. Pass on the gift and do so freely and without charge. Turn left at the crossroad, if you would. My wife took that ancient oath too, for she is also a doctor. We promised to administer only that which benefits the patient and not what would cause them harm. The physician must never seduce the sufferer, be they man, woman or slave, and whatever is overheard in the house of the sick should never be repeated beyond those walls. The oath ends, *If I keep and carry out this vow, fulfilling its obligations, may I then thrive and prosper and go on to live in the estimation of posterity. However, if I were ever in breach of my oath may the reverse fortune fall upon me*. There's a right turn coming up, take that."

'"My wife and I," the doctor went on, "both broke our oaths. Yet we are second chancers. In middle age, through the intervention and endowment of someone I now look back on as a friend, we found a new path and a more honest way of living. Life – and death – can give that to you sometimes."

'This was all very interesting, but what I wanted to know was did he have a signal. He checked, but said not. The steam from their wet clothes was so badly misting up my windscreen and rear view mirror that I had to slow down for a while. Even so, I thought we must be approaching Marlow by now, yet I hadn't seen a road sign for miles. "These country lanes have so many twists and turns and they all look alike, don't they?" I said. "Yes," the doctor replied, "but no need to rush now. My wife is dead. No pulse." I didn't know how to respond, except with those words people always say – "I'm sorry."

'Suddenly, I am thinking of Jes, at the house alone. Those walls have become her fortress, as the steel frame of my car has become mine. I know that right at this moment she is crying and realise all I want to do is hold her and never, ever let her go.

'"There is a difficult bend coming up," says the doctor. "Take it carefully and you'll be fine. For at heart you are a good man." Then I see it. My fluorescent triangle warning of danger. The one I placed ahead of that bend. As I turn the corner, I see flashing blue lights. Two bodies are being carried on stretchers into the back of an ambulance. Both heads are covered by sheets but an arm falls and I see that it's a man in a dinner suit. I slow down, but a policeman waves me on. I look in my rear view mirror. The mist has cleared and I see two faces glowing with a divine light and eyes that sparkle like iridescent stars. "The direction you take in life, as on a country road, can unexpectedly change," says the doctor. "And in death I have become the physician of your soul. Your medicine: to know that what you hold most dear can be taken from you in an instant."

'"Yes," I say, softly.

'His wife then speaks: "May the kindness you showed me tonight be the beginning of a new life. And now we both ask you, if, in the hour of your own death, you would be willing to endow another with the gift we have given you." "Yes," I say again. "Good," says the man, "Remember this oath. Oh, but may that be many years hence. Now go to your dinner, my friend. You'll be late, of course, but you may well thank us in the hours ahead."

'And that, gentlemen, is the reason I was delayed. For I met two ghosts on the road.'

The room stayed silent. Well, until Perry spoke up in his usual foghorn way.

'James! I'll be frank with you, my boy, it wasn't a terrible tale but I think we all guessed well before the end that they were spooks. And Bluebottle doesn't like those tales where there's somebody who's dead but you don't know it yet. That's what you said, wasn't it?'

But Bluebottle didn't reply.

'And to be honest I feel a bit cheated,' Perry went on, 'especially all that guff about it being true. I wasn't going to say this James, but we all know the real reason you were late. "Planned a get together with a friend before the dinner." Do you take us for fools? We all know you're having an affair. Bridget. Yes – we even know her name. And you used our dinner tonight as a cover to leave good wife Jessica at home, come into town, stay over in a nice hotel and get a bit of nookie on the side. Nothing wrong with that. We've all done it. But this cock and bullfrogs story about corpses talking! Predictable, moralising claptrap – and all rather a bit of a bore. Ha! Look, you've even sent Mouse and Pigleg to sleep.'

Perry was getting genuinely angry. 'Well, bugger that for a game of soldiers,' he went on, 'I think I'll have myself another cigar and an extra brandy.'

He took out his gold lighter and flicked. The fuel must have been depleted for the flame was very low, certainly not enough heat in it to light up a cigar. But Perry, of course, was never one to be denied his pleasures, so withdrew from his wallet a fifty pound note, put it to the flame and soon had the intensity he needed.

I protested at the waste.

'Oh, James! Have you never read the economic theories of Adam Smith? Value is based on rarity, so the fewer notes there are, the more those I have left will be worth. Ha! Ha! Ha!' At which he threw the burning remnant into the air without a thought.

Suddenly, a blinding flash of blue light, blazing with a bewildering intensity and existing only for a moment but it is long enough. The gift of Prometheus to mankind, stolen from the gods, explodes throughout the room, somehow releasing the demons of Hell; for what I see next I still dare not believe to be true. Fork-tongued serpents, coloured yellow and orange, rise from the floor curling and twisting in their multitude. These vipers now entwine themselves round the body of our club founder, who squeals like a pig but can offer no resistance. Their pointed fangs bite into his skin and pierce his flesh with a ravenous and vicious appetite.

Now these thin devil dragons move on to the next victim and all are devoured to the core so that all that is left are bones and skulls dressed in white shirts and black ties. Yet I remain untouched and somehow immune. The monsters have now done their worst and they fall back to the floor from whence they came before re-burying themselves in the black earth. And for a while all becomes silent.

A reticent knock at the door. Then another. A few moments later a waiter enters. What he sees are a dozen or so dead men in chairs, a body on the carpet whose face is frozen in a scream of agony, and myself, a lone figure standing among corpses.

IN YEARS TO COME I WILL no doubt rationalise what I have witnessed tonight. Or believe I witnessed. Reason will tell me that on that lonely country lane I simply passed an accident and saw two blood soaked bodies in a car. At that moment I thought of Jessica and how I might lose her. Our marriage crisis and the conflicts within me suddenly came into sharp focus. In that second I knew I had done her wrong and said aloud, 'I'm sorry'. My feverish brain then imagined that I had stopped and helped the injured. My unexpected but sincere act of contrition turned them into spirits of redemption who, in death, offered me a final act of compassion in exchange for the help I gave them. But the whole thing was just a mental aberration. Projections of a guilty conscience. Those deserted lanes weren't real and the man and wife weren't angels. As for turning it all into a ghost story, well, any psychologist would tell you that remorse sometimes needs a public confession and tonight that was helped along by too much red wine and rich food.

Oh, and that blue flash which opened the gates of Hell was simply the flame from the fifty pound note meeting the alcohol vapours from the spilt brandy. And those thin devilish snakes. My mind went into overdrive there and turned the harmless squiggly pattern of the black carpet into Dante's inferno. My friends were not eaten by serpents, they died of natural causes. Well, one cause. Toxic phytoplankton. In the unusually hot summer, algal blooms had thrived and so been eaten to excess by filter-feeding shellfish. If this natural poison is then consumed by humans there is no antidote. Symptoms begin an hour or so after ingestion. First come pins and needles, then muscular weakness in the legs, and finally death through respiratory collapse. Mouse's tingles weren't a remembrance of his ghostly tale, but rather the oncoming of paresthesia. Perry's unsteadiness was not the drink but the early stages of paralysis. And poor Cheesy wasn't smiling. Oh no, he was trying to open his mouth to warn us, only that breath he took was almost certainly his last.

The Bacchanean was for those of us who believed we had been born to lead the pack. Yet over the years we became slaves to our ambitions. Our financial propriety had the morals of a slot machine and our carnal desires had hardened into salacious vice and unrepentant deceit. So then, why was I the only one to survive? Because by chance I hadn't eaten those oysters? Perhaps. That's the line the newspapers will report and it's what reason and logic dictate. But it isn't the truth. Something not of my knowing and beyond this world had given me a second chance. We all make promises to ourselves when we are young. Oaths and vows. But along the way we break them because that's what happens in life. And it's those lies that we tell others, and ourselves, that eventually take their toll, leaving us empty of hope. Yet, tonight a dream, if that's what you want to call it, gave me a belief in myself again.

And that, my friend, is the unexpected twist to end this tale that I didn't see coming.

SEND

'IT'S WHAT SHE WOULD HAVE WANTED'

SUBJECT

A Modern Tale of Ashes to Ashes and Dust to Dust

Sent: Sunday 12 January 18:06
From: sonia@toomfly.ork
To: fiorenza123@wikkerbox.stat

> Hi Fiore –
> It's happened again 🙁
> John's mother! One day she'll be the death of me. Janet came round this morning with another of her 'gifts'. Today it was a hideous ormolu carriage clock in the shape of a harp with two baby cherubs lolling about either side blowing their trumpets. Lumbering us with all this senseless kitschy bric-a-brac. Fiore – I'm at my wit's end! I mean, our living room is beginning to look like the front window of the local Kitty Rescue charity shop.
> Of course, Hubby John doesn't see any of this as a problem. And why should he – he grew up with his mother's clutter. If 'grew up' is the appropriate phrase. I wish I could make John understand that this is our home now, not an extension of the maternal nest. But all I get is, "Oh, but she means well." Hmm – and that's debatable too.

And it's not just the goodies themselves, it's the fact that it's Janet who decides where they should go. In my own house! Oh but she's clever. Always waits until John is in the room before she stands up and gives the whatnot its pride of place. Today she had the nerve to move one of our wedding photos from the mantelpiece and replace it with her less than heavenly tacky tick-tock. "Oh yes!" she says, "That will work very nicely here, won't it John?" Silly question to ask, because John has never disagreed with mummy in his life. And the problem is I feel as if I can't say anything either. You see, she helped us so much when we got married last year. The deposit on the house and so on. Oh but doesn't she like to remind us!!! Maybe that's why Janet thinks she has the right to interfere the way she does. But that money came from what John's father left in his will, so I see it as much John's as hers.

But what really worries me is what's gonna happen when his mother downsizes? BECAUSE SHE IS INCAPABLE OF EVER THROWING ANYTHING AWAY!!!! Every side-table, window sill and glass cabinet (four at the last count) all littered with her gaudy chintzy knick-knacks. I've always said you can tell a person's character by the books on their shelves. Well, a psychiatrist would have a field day in her house! Endless porcelain figures of historical characters like Elizabeth the First, Catherine the Great, Boudica, Mary of Teck, Queen Victoria, (no kings, notice!) And then there's the weird stuff like this ceramic apple with a worm that squiggles in and out if you wind up the key at the back and a bluebottle ashtray where you have to lift the wings to stub out your cigarette (and Janet doesn't even smoke!). Not that any of the ornaments are ever the colour they're meant to be. Oh no! It's all green mice, purple and pink zebras and turquoise Labradors. The thought that one day we could end up with this bizarre menagerie is driving me crazy –

Assistance pleeeeeeease!!!!

Luv,

Sx

PS Thank Heaven for small mercies! I've just discovered the chime on that awful gaudy harp clock doesn't work. Yippee!!!

PPS I don't want to be mean but I can't help thinking sometimes that the whole problem would go away if mummy ever started playing her harp for real – if you know what I'm saying – lol!

Sent: Monday 13 January 08:06
From: fiorenza123@wikkerbox.stat
To: sonia@toomfly.ork

> Darling Sonia –
> Oh dear! Bound by a rock and a hard place is nothing compared to being caught between a husband and his mother. My everlasting sympathies!
> Advice? Well, what about moving some of these trinkets and gewgaws to the spare room? If I ever come to stay, I'd only be sleeping there – and I do that with my eyes closed! – so I'd never even have to look at the stuff. Lol!
> Better still, hide it all in a drawer and only get it out when she comes round. Men tend not to notice what isn't there, if you know what I mean, so perhaps Hubby John would be none the wiser. Or is there so much of it that even a man could tell the difference?
> And if it's really getting to you, what about accidental breakage? Except that might be difficult with that lovely thick carpet of yours.
> Oh, I'm at a loss as to what to suggest but I'll put on my best thinking cap. And even wear it to bed!!!
> Hugs,
> Fiore
>
> ---

Sent: Thursday 16 January 21:58
From: sonia@toomfly.ork
To: fiorenza123@wikkerbox.stat

> Hi Fiore –
> Your suggestions are fab 🙂 – oh but if only life were that simple…
> For one thing, Janet never warns me when she's coming round, so if the doorbell goes right this minute (and it's now ten to nine at night!) it would almost certainly be her 😐 And there's something I haven't told you yet... Janet persuaded John to give her a key!!!! (I KNOW. I'M AN IDIOT!!!)
> But you'll be proud of me for at least putting in one line of defence. Well, not so much 'putting in', as 'taking out', because yesterday I dragged

down the mattress from the spare room, drove it to the tip and dumped it. My way of saying, "Okay you can have a key, but you ain't moving in!" I know Janet too well – overnight would become a weekend and then that weekend would turn into a week. And then we'd never be rid of her!

Hold your horses… I've just heard the doorbell

DISASTER! THE WORSTEST EVER!!!!

I am now the proud owner of a Marie Antoinette Toby Jug!!! Who knew the world ever had or wanted such a thing?!? Marie Antoinette!!??!! Zut alors! But at this rate it will soon be me who's losing her head. LOL!!!

Pray hard! It's my last hope!

Luv,

Sonia

PS And Janet even brought round one of her small side-tables so the Queen of France can have her very own resting place! Mon Dieu, aide-moi!

Sent: Friday 16 January 08.06
From: fiorenza123@wikkerbox.stat
To: sonia@toomfly.ork

Sonia –

Bull by the horns! Simply tell her to stop giving you all this stuff. No more room at that inn and all that.

(Tough) love,

Fiore

Sent: Saturday 17 January 12:04
From: sonia@toomfly.ork
To: fiorenza123@wikkerbox.stat

Oh Fiore! You're right, but Janet lives in the world of Janet. She never sees anything from my point of view. And as I've said, the same goes for Hubby John. The two of them have this strange way between them sometimes. Last week she gave us this black lacquered box that has a lid with an inlaid painted red rose that's now sitting on the coffee table next to a pink giraffe coaster set. "It's a 'Useful Pot'. For putting things in", she says to John in a baby voice which makes him laugh. Am I missing something? "It's a keepsake," she then says to me. I wanted to say, "If it's a keepsake, keep it yourself! The clue is in the name." But I don't and I know why…

Bestest –

Sonia

PS It's curious, but she also has a collection of cups and saucers (bizarrely all from different sets because none match – how did that happen!?!) and all have red roses on them – yet she won't have real roses in her garden, only rhododendrons.

Sent: Tuesday 28 January 16.09
From: fiorenza123@wikkerbox.stat
To: sonia@toomfly.ork

Darling Sonia –

I won't bore you with how this came about but I was having a chat with a gardening friend of mine and oddly enough the subject of rhododendrons came up. Anyway, my green-fingered friend, who's very 'astral' and 'New Age' and believes 'auras' and the like, said that she has this theory that a person's psyche gravitates towards flowers that reflect their own nature. Guess what! The rhododendron bush has sap that is poisonous and its roots tend to out-muscle any plant that comes near. No wonder your mother-in-law loves that horrible weed so much! I don't mean to make fun here, because Orla – my gardening lady – has a rule that she won't work with rhododendron owners because of their 'invasive toxicity', as she puts it. That's going it a bit strong but maybe she has a point.

Incidentally, Orla describes herself as a 'white witch'. Not sure what your policy is regarding spells and such, but would you like me to ask her advice re trinkets and bric-a-brac??????

Hugs,

Fiore

PS So you know why you didn't say, "If it's a keepsake, keep it yourself!" – what was the reason exactly?
PPS The nectar of a rhododendron contains diterpenes called grayanotoxins. Thank goodness for Wikipedia!

Sent: Tuesday 4 February 15.15
From: sonia@toomfly.ork
To: fiorenza123@wikkerbox.stat

Hi Fiore –
Who knew about rhododendrons! Poisonous, eh? Maybe I should put some of those grayanotoxins from her bushes in her tea… ha! ha! Talking of things green, we have a landscape designer coming round next week. I'm going to suggest roses (WHITE!!!).
Luv,
Sx
PS No spells please. At least not for now. Keep that as an emergency option!!!!
PPS Well, maybe just a little one… I've always wondered what Janet would look like as a toad!
PPPS You asked why I didn't say, "If it's a keepsake, keep it yourself!" Truth is, deep down, I'm a bit frightened of her. And you're the first person I've ever admitted that to.

Sent: Wednesday 5 February 08.01
From: fiorenza123@wikkerbox.stat
To: sonia@toomfly.ork

Hi Sonia –
Bizarre but I woke up in the night and suddenly remembered where I'd heard "It's a 'Useful Pot'. For putting things in" before. It's from an A.A. Milne story. For his birthday, Eeyore gets given a burst balloon from Piglet and an empty jar that once contained honey from Pooh Bear. But Eeyore is happy enough – if Eeyore ever can be happy – because he

keeps putting the burst balloon in the pot. I'm betting his mother told that story to Baby John when a boy and it became a sort of private joke between them.
Big Hugs –
Fiore x

Sent: Wednesday 5 February 08.10
From: sonia@toomfly.ork
To: fiorenza123@wikkerbox.stat

Perhaps that's where Janet got her idea for useless presents from!!!

Sent: Saturday 8 March 19.04
From: sonia@toomfly.ork
To: fiorenza123@wikkerbox.stat

FIORE –
I FEEL TERRIBLE.
ALL THE THINGS I SAID ABOUT JANET.
I DON'T KNOW HOW TO SAY THIS... BUT SHE'S DEAD!
I'LL EMAIL AGAIN LATER WHEN I KNOW MORE.
SONIA XXX

Sent: Saturday 8 March 23.55
From: fiorenza123@wikkerbox.stat
To: sonia@toomfly.ork

Darling – SO sorry to hear your news. Difficult times – thinking of you – Fiore xxxxxxxx

---

Sent: Tuesday 11 March 20:08
From: sonia@toomfly.ork
To: fiorenza123@wikkerbox.stat

> It was a heart attack at home. Poor John. He's completely lost.
> Won't be able to email for a while. Muggins has volunteered to organise the funeral.
> As ever,
> Sonia
>
> ---

Sent: Monday 17 March 03.03
From: sonia@toomfly.ork
To: fiorenza123@wikkerbox.stat

> Hi Fiore –
> The guilt is piling up and kicking in. All that talk of poisoning and spells and her playing her harp – and now she's gone for real.
> But there's a job to be done and I've got to do it. Currently I'm contacting all her friends. Her address book is the size of the Encyclopaedia Britannica! John is taking care of the paperwork and dealing with solicitors. All straight forward enough as John as the only child is the sole beneficiary. We'll get the house – and all that's in it (DON'T GO THERE – NOT YET!) – but John says that he's going to wait until after the funeral to find an estate agent.
> Much to think about.
> Sonia x
> ---

Sent: Tuesday 3 April 16.08
From: sonia@toomfly.ork
To: fiorenza123@wikkerbox.stat

> Hi Fiore –
> Funeral is tomorrow.
> John is now making noises about keeping Janet's house and even

> moving in. I think it's madness I just couldn't cope. She'd be in every room
> Yours in despondency -
> Sonia
>
> --

Sent: Tuesday 3 April 20.08
From: fiorenza123@wikkerbox.stat
To: sonia@toomfly.ork

> Darling Sonia – Try not to worry. It's going to be a big change for John, but I'm sure he'll see it from your point of view eventually.
> Triple Hugs!!! I know you need them xxx
> Fiore xxx
>
> --

Sent: Thursday 5 April 09.01
From: sonia@toomfly.ork
To: fiorenza123@wikkerbox.stat

> Hi Fiore –
> Funeral was yesterday. Good turnout and quite a number of Janet's friends made it. Discovered she went to the Westchester Preparatory College for Girls. Who knew? Seems her parents scrimped and saved to send her there. So difficult at a funeral to talk properly, but I had the impression these ladies – the indomitable generation – had a lot more to say than they did…
> Luv,
> Sonia
> PS John hasn't mentioned the house situation for a few days. My plan is to let it lie and then start dropping hints about a visit to the estate agents in a week or so.
>
> --

Sent: Monday 14 April 07.02
From: sonia@toomfly.ork
To: fiorenza123@wikkerbox.stat

> Hi Fiore – John's having a meltdown! JANET'S ASHES HAVE GONE MISSING! The crematorium gave them to him. A simple plain mahogany urn. I know, I was there. But now he says the urn isn't in the drawer where he left it. Poor John's under a lot of stress. Perhaps he's just forgotten and put it somewhere else.
> Need to be strong and take him in hand…
> Sonia
>
> --

Sent: Monday 14 April 08.02
From: fiorenza123@wikkerbox.stat
To: sonia@toomfly.ork

> I'm sure Janet will turn up somewhere! She always did before!
>
> --

Sent: Monday 14 April 08.06
From: sonia@toomfly.ork
To: fiorenza123@wikkerbox.stat

> Just thought! Maybe it was Mrs Dornton who moved the urn from the drawer. Unlikely, I know. Her cleaning day is Thursday, but did she change her days this week and I didn't listen properly????
>
> --

Sent: Monday 14 April 08.14
From: sonia@toomfly.ork
To: fiorenza123@wikkerbox.stat

> No, Mrs Dornton couldn't have moved Janet's ashes because I've just rung Mrs D and she said she has that flu that's going round and so hasn't been out the house for days.
>
> --

Sent: Tuesday 15 April 15.17
From: sonia@toomfly.ork
To: fiorenza123@wikkerbox.stat

> Hi Fiore –
> The strangest thing. That urn with Janet's ashes has turned up as you said it would. But guess where? Remember I told you about that Marie Antoinette Toby Jug and how Janet brought a small side-table to put it on? WELL, NOW THE MAHOGANY BOX HAS TAKEN OVER THAT EXACT SPOT. And poor Marie Antoinette has been relegated to the window sill! But here's what's weird… I didn't move it or put it there and John says it wasn't him either.
> Bewitched, Bothered and Bewildered,
> Sonia ☹
>
> ---

Sent: Tuesday 15 April 22.09
From: fiorenza123@wikkerbox.stat
To: sonia@toomfly.ork

> Don't stress yourself! There'll be a simple explanation! There always is with these things! – Fiore
>
> ---

Sent: Wednesday 16 April 09.11
From: sonia@toomfly.ork
To: fiorenza123@wikkerbox.stat

> Now it's getting beyond weird.
> Janet's urn has disappeared from its pedestal! She was there at ten past eight – and I know that was the exact time because the news on Radio Four had just finished and that's when I switch over to Radio Two. Believe me it was there an hour ago – BUT NOW IT'S VANISHED!!! AND THERE'S BEEN NO ONE IN THE HOUSE EXCEPT ME!!!!!!
> Don't call the men in the white coats just yet – I suppose it could just be my mind playing tricks….
>
> ---

Sent: Wednesday 16 April 11.08
From: sonia@toomfly.ork
To: fiorenza123@wikkerbox.stat

> Am I going mad? The good news (ish) is that the mahogany urn with Janet's ashes has returned – in the kitchen next to the recycling bin. But the bad news (VERY! at least for my sanity) is that when I opened the box it was empty! WHERE'S JANET NOW?!
>
> --

Sent: Wednesday 16 April 14.08
From: sonia@toomfly.ork
To: fiorenza123@wikkerbox.stat

> Just noticed that that black lacquered box with the red rose on the lid has moved from its place on the coffee table and is now on the mantelpiece – next to Janet's harp clock.
> Fiore – I'm too frightened to lift the lid. I know her ashes are going to be in there. IT'S HER! JANET!!! 👻 SHE'S DOING ALL THIS!!!
> 👻 👻 👻 👻 👻 👻 👻 👻 👻 👻
>
> --

Sent: Wednesday 16 April 15.09
From: fiorenza123@wikkerbox.stat
To: sonia@toomfly.ork

> Sonia – calm down. Don't be silly. Open the box! Nothing's going to be in there. Holding your hand as you take a big breath… Fiore
>
> --

Sent: Wednesday 16 April 15.29
From: sonia@toomfly.ork
To: fiorenza123@wikkerbox.stat

> **THE ASHES!!! JANET'S ASHES ARE IN THE BLACK LACQUERED**

> **BOX – I KNEW THEY WOULD BE – AND AS I OPENED THE LID THAT HARP CLOCK BEGAN TO PLAY '*WE'LL MEET AGAIN*'... SHE'S BACK!**
>
> --

Sent: Wednesday 16 April 16.02
From: fiorenza123@wikkerbox.stat
To: sonia@toomfly.ork

> I don't know what to say – except what you need me to say and that is **I DO BELIEVE YOU**.
>
> --

Sent: Wednesday 16 April 16.04
From: sonia@toomfly.ork
To: fiorenza123@wikkerbox.stat

> Could you ask your astral friend Orla for help???? Advice??? Spells???? Seances!!! Exorcisms??? Anything!!!!!!
>
> --

Sent: Tuesday 22 April 10.01
From: sonia@toomfly.ork
To: fiorenza123@wikkerbox.stat

> Okay. Life can be unexpected sometimes, but we live with it. And in situations like this Miss Practical Me takes over.
> This is my morning:
> I remove the black lacquered box with inlaid red rose from the mantelpiece, carry it carefully to the kitchen and place the said black box on top of the breadboard. I then leave the house, shut the door, wait thirty seconds before re-opening said door, and then return to the kitchen to check the breadboard. No black lacquered box. I next walk calmly into the living room and there I see the aforementioned black box on top of the mantelpiece next to that ghastly harp clock.
> I am not mad. I do not know if it's Janet's aura or her ghost or her spirit

> or her psyche or whatever you want to call it but Mother has decided to take up residence in my house. As I always said she would. And the fact that she's dead hasn't stopped her doing it.
> However, she's met her match. I'm not going to let her beat me. And I've told her that myself. I lifted the lid of the lack lacquered box and said to those ashes, "I have no intention of being out-muscled by a spook!"
>
> ---

Sent: Tuesday 22 April 18.02
From: fiorenza123@wikkerbox.stat
To: sonia@toomfly.ork

> Orla says that if Janet has a strong reason to be there, you have to give her a far stronger reason to leave - Fiore.
>
> ---

Sent: Tuesday 22 April 23.08
From: sonia@toomfly.ork
To: fiorenza123@wikkerbox.stat

> Makes sense. But what would that be? I'm stumped ☹
>
> ---

Sent: Wednesday 23 April 00.06
From: sonia@toomfly.ork
To: fiorenza123@wikkerbox.stat

> No I'm not. I've just had an idea 💡
>
> ---

Sent: Thursday 22 May 22.06
From: sonia@toomfly.ork
To: fiorenza123@wikkerbox.stat

It's been all quiet for a while on the Janet front and let me explain why. A week or so ago I organised an afternoon tea for her friends to celebrate her life. I extended the dining table (the one with the side leaves) and brought in extra chairs. About a dozen came in all.

There were smoked salmon sandwiches, cucumber with ham, cucumber without ham, plus pasties, cakes and dainties. For crockery I 'borrowed' Janet's collection of cups and saucers with all those painted roses. And in the centre of this afternoon feast I placed the black lacquered box, with the lid slightly open.

You see, I concluded that the main reason his mother wishes to reside in my house is to oversee everything I do, because, quite frankly, I've never been good enough for her son. An unnerving eye, certainly, but one I've now come to understand so much better.

The thing is, those who listen and watch from beyond the grave have no choice but to listen and watch everything. And that's why I invited round as many of her friends as I could for that tea party.

We hadn't had much of a chance to talk about Janet at the funeral but as the Early Grey flowed (and after six o'clock the sherry!) these ladies began to let slip what they all thought of her. Nothing cruel or unpleasant. Janet wasn't in any way a bad person, but as they chatted away I began to see how much her parents' decision to send her to a private school had impacted on her life. For one thing, her mother and father weren't at all well off, and had scrimped and saved to get her there in order for their daughter to 'better herself'. Socially more than academically. And that's what happened. She found in that set a husband from a wealthier world.

What we never had as a child, we often make up for when we become adults. And so it was with Janet. All those porcelain figures were to prove to herself, said one of the ladies, that now she could afford and possess nice things. And as her friends chatted away, it became clear that's how she sometimes treated her son. John belonged to her and so she could never quite let him go. Especially after the death of her husband.

The ladies drinking their tea and nibbling on their dainties wouldn't have noticed this but as they talked about Janet and her ways that lacquered box began to lose its gleam. And by the time we were on the sherry, a perceptible hairline crack had appeared. Yes, I thought, it's always painful to hear home truths. Even if all that's left of you are ashes.

When the last of her friends had left, I tidied up the cups and saucers on the table and noticed that the black lacquered box had disappeared. Only this time I wasn't in the least concerned. Nor was I at all surprised when I found it, with the lid completely open, on the table near the back door in the kitchen – and I'll explain why in a moment.

But what of Hubby John? Well, the morning after the tea party, John woke up and said that he'd had a very odd dream. He'd found himself in his mother's house, only it was empty. In the dream he'd gone round every room to find her, but she wasn't there and every wall, ceiling and floor were blank.

After breakfast John announced that he had decided to sell his mother's house and that everything in it could be given to one of the local charity shops. The Kitty Rescue perhaps. As for Janet's ashes, he said, he thought it would be macabre to keep them in the house. He'd noticed that the landscape gardener had delivered some roses in pots and left them by the back door, so why not scatter his mother's ashes on the roses that were being planted later that day. And I said, "Yes, but why don't we keep one of her vases. And every summer, when those roses bloom, we can bring them into the house and give them pride of place."

Then John thought for a moment and said, "Yes. I think that's what she would have wanted."

Yours and forever after,

Sonia x

A GHOST-STORY OF AN ANTIQUARY

The Portrait of a Looking-Glass

A HOMAGE TO
MONTAGUE RHODES JAMES, LITT.D.
FELLOW OF KING'S COLLEGE, CAMBRIDGE

LONDON
HUMPHREYS AND POYNTER
DOLLS HOUSE
MARTIN'S CLOSE
WESTMINSTER
2024

The Portrait of a Looking-Glass

THIRTY YEARS AGO A CHANCE COLLISION between the rotating spokes of my bicycle and the advancing legs of a recently appointed Fellow of St. James's College has, by a subsequent obligation, now led to the writing of this story. The details of our accidental concurrence need not detain the reader, for it bears little on the tale I am to relate. It is enough to say that no permanent damage was done to either party, aside from a slight scuffing to my Dutch Bible tied with manila rope to the front bar of my bicycle, and a repairable tear to the gentleman's ankle turn-up, which was the fashion of college men in 1895.

Apologies from both parties were immediately forthcoming, and following these there were various versicles[1] and polite exchanges concerning the weather. Following our encounter it appeared that the gentleman was not in a hurry to continue his journey but inclined instead to further conversation. I discovered his name was Rhodes, a name familiar to me and one with a growing reputation in Cambridge. Was he the same Rhodes who had recently published a history of St. Edmund the Martyr? Indeed he was. It was a book I had read with some relish, and in an opinion I shared with him, the most distinguished history of the saint since the French monk Abbo wrote his life of the martyr, *Passio Sancti Eadmund*, in 986. Aside from a shared interest in medieval history, it transpired that Rhodes and I had much else in common. We were both Suffolk men and in the Long[2] we each took our holidays either on the Suffolk coast or the Broads.

It will not be irrelevant to my purpose to describe the gentleman I knew in those halcyon days before the Great War. Rhodes was small-made with black hair, with a nervous untempered brow and light grey eyes that could not be said to be pleasing. He was of the heavy whiskered-race, and his smile, when it was possible to perceive it, would often give place to a look of concern that seemed possessed of some private fear. Even on the day of that first encounter, I noticed his laughter was strangely hollow, and his mood was apt to sudden alteration.

In the following months, the status of our acquaintance became such that I was obliged to accept his opinion that he had made me his confidant. An incident had troubled him, he said, and he was perishing to get it off his mind, yet whenever Rhodes raised the subject of 'the looking-glass', he would in the next second become his own interrupter and abruptly change the conversation to remarks concerning the latest college appointments.

I was in no great taking to be acquainted with the story he wished to tell, for it appeared to cause him much anxiety and fretfulness. I must be forthright with the reader and reveal that melancholia in others has never been conducive to my own disposition. However, later that year, on the eve of All Hallows, I heard a desperate knocking on the window panes of my college rooms, and, pulling back the curtain, saw the disquieted face of Rhodes peering up at me. I admitted him, despite the lateness of the hour, and that night he told me his story.

That was in the year of our Lord 1895. The year is now 1925 and it is enough to know that following the delivery of a box of papers and a sealed letter to my address, I am now at liberty to write and complete the tale that Rhodes began those thirty years ago. I shall do better, I believe, to keep back the particulars of recent events until I have told of the circumstances which led up to them. However, the reader will not be far out if he guesses that the box of papers came from the Rhodes residence.

Two boxes, one large and made of copper (to judge by the green patina), the other mahogany and as small as a snuff-box, were put into the hands of my housekeeper two days ago by the driver of a hackney cab. They came, he said, from a gentleman who had not obliged him with a name. Inside the smaller box was a key that with a simple turn unlocked the larger. Once opened, I saw that is contained an assortment of papers and books, including diaries, journals, private correspondence, drafts of letters unsent, news cuttings from *The Morning Chronicle*, an astrological Almanac dated 1880 and an unusual vellum parchment with uncial[3] writing in Latin. In short, a jigsaw puzzle of disparate pieces in requirement of affiliation in order to beget a complete and coherent narrative. Further to this jumble of notes and jottings I can reveal that the sealed letter delivered with the boxes had made me the plenary author of the story they told.

I would ask the reader to accept my undertaking that what follows is the story of Rhodes and the looking-glass and its accompanying portrait as best as I can elicit it. Where an original source is apposite, I will present it, and where a word-painting is needed to set the scene, I hope the reader will grant me the latitude of an inner eye. Elsewhere I shall epitomize events in such a way as might allow the reader into the mind and thoughts of Rhodes concerning his encounter with that devilish mirror and the accursed oil painting.

Writing as I am now in late October, with a bleak autumnal wind battling against the outer shutters of my window casements and the noise of London trams clanking their way along on steel-grooved girders, I find it hard to summon up the feelings that will put the reader in the locale and footing of a bright and tranquil morning on the Suffolk coast in 1894. Rhodes had taken the first Great Eastern train of the day from Bishopsgate to Ipswich and then the branch line via Melton and Wickham Market to Seaburgh. Burnstow-on-Sea, further up the coast, had been the exclusive sojourn of his childhood holidays and so the coastal retreat of Seaburgh was new to him. The primary purpose of his stay was to visit the church of St. Edward's in Seaburgh and there to consult the church records to discover whether there was any evidence missed by previous generations concerning the cult of St Edward that grew in East Anglia following the death of the saint. The conquering Vikings had destroyed all records of his reign but historians live by hope and curiosity in equal measure. Besides this, Rhodes was fain to hold in his hand one of the coins minted by Edmund kept at the church that archaeologically gave proof that he had indeed succeeded Æthelweard as King of East Anglia.

The train journey to Seaburgh. As the steam engine enters a clearing through a wood, Rhodes can see on either side of him sinewy Scotch firs, standing in untidy formation. From his window seat he looks down to the sandy soil along the tracks and notices a small rabbit scrabbling for its life, only for it to be caught in the claws and mouth of a stoat. Rhodes adjusts the railway-rug on his lap and then casts his eyes upwards to the thin line of blue sky between the top of the firs, yet even here twisting branches and their needles knit together to form heavy green clouds of hanging thunder.

Coming out of the clearing in the wood there is a sudden expanse of gorse-covered land that stretches across the horizon. Through the window on the other side (for this is a branch train and so without a corridor), Rhodes catches sight of a distant line of trees, beaten sideways by the commanding winds that come in from the sea, and beyond these are the remnants of two Martello Towers,[4] relics of the Napoleonic Wars, which tell Rhodes and his fellow travellers that the coast is almost upon them. These landmark towers are now in decay but they bring to Rhodes's mind thoughts of his fishermen forebears who would have seen them in their glory before the ravages of time took their toll. Yet nothing stays the same forever. Or so he thought.

Rhodes had engaged a room at The Slaughden Inn, which, upon inquiry, he discovered had a reputation for a good table. The inn was by the sea but it was some distance from the main town and so easier on the pocketbook than its rivals The Globe Inn, The Bear Inn and The White Lion. The inn was solidly built but its timber frames and greying limestone plaster gave it an antediluvian countenance and the fractured light now flickering in its diamond shaped thick hobnail glass windows made it appear that this old tavern was being forced to squint at the brightness of the midday sun.

Rhodes stepped over the patches of rough grass among shingle that led to the inn's ancient oak door. He turned the wrought iron handle, entered, and found himself on a stone floor in a hall of dark wood panelling, with a staircase leading up to the upper storey. Even though the morrow was November, no fire was lit. Rhodes smelt the air. Stale tobacco smoke still lingered from the night before, but there were no fellow-lodgers to be seen. He put down his bags and made a clearing of his throat to summon attention. As he waited, Rhodes noted a grandfather clock in the corner and next to it a barometer, upon which hung a pair of binoculars. On the walls were several heads of the taxidermist craft, including those of a fox and a wolf, and a dozen or so brasses on leather could be seen hanging on the panelling along the staircase that led to the upper floor. However, the solitary feature of interest to the visitor was a hurdy-gurdy[5] which sat on a small table and which, as Rhodes lifted it into the air, produced an impromptu though somewhat discordant tune.

A moment later a figure emerged from the parlour and made it known that he was Mr Grimes, the innkeeper. Rhodes put down the hurdy-gurdy and subsequent to the usual exchanges Grimes, a thin man with a red complexion and bristling moustache, dressed in the habiliments of servitude, took the bags belonging to Rhodes and beckoned his guest to follow him upstairs. As Grimes and Rhodes began their ascent, the visitor then noticed another figure behind the parlour door, uncomely in appearance and with a choleric expression. Upon further exposure he saw it belonged to a formidably stout woman. The reader would be correct in the assumption that she was the innkeeper's termagant wife.

Grimes, a smartish fellow full of talk, was inclined to make himself agreeable and when Rhodes stopped at the first turning on the staircase to study on the wall panel a Queen Anne house captured on a framed mezzotint,[6] Grimes, too, halted and rested the bags he carried on the next step.

'Ah, the great 'ouse. Razed to the ground by fire some nineteen winters ago. It was the year of grace 1875 and, if my recollection be *bona fonda*, it happened this very night of All 'Allows Eve. Since that time it 'as been common land with Lammas rights,[7] yet there ain't from a man with two legs to a sheep with four who will venture where that great 'ouse once stood. All that remains now are the broken pillars that 'eld the iron gates, yet, though they be mossed and lichened, no 'orse will step through them. Not one 'oof. But, as the engraving do show, 'twas a great 'ouse, and much deserving of the epifit. 'Twas owned by an earl, the 'copper earl' folk called him, on account of the tan of his 'air. Lived for many years in the great 'ouse by hisself, with neither chick nor child for company, yet he travelled often to distant lands, black pilgrimage some say, and after one visit returned with an Italian gentleman of the Babylonish church.[8] Most 'ereabouts keep a close tongue and are not likely to say what they think true if there be a stranger nearby, but in whispered talk they believe the Italian, who wore a black cloak and cowl, practised wicked arts and was guilty of perfitiness sin. Mrs. Grimes, the better spouse, who saw once beneath the 'ood, said the Italian had wicked eyes. He was one, she thought, who might spend the 'ours of the owl flaying a man alive and then eat 'is 'eart for breakfast.'

Rhodes asked about the fire.

'Oh, no one knows 'ow the blaze started, a visitation some say, but no bodies were ever found among the ashes. 'Im being an earl, and people measuring a man by the length of his fork, peelers[9] were brought in on a coach from London to the make inquiries. Ponds were dragged, questions asked among bagmen,[10] tramps, the railway people, absconding sailors and even travelling players with their painted cloths. But no. The copper earl, he 'ad disappeared like the night fox at dawn. If you desire my private thoughts, I'm of the opinion he threw up the sponge and done away with hisself. Yet it physicks[11] me to this day why, if he has long since gone to his account, no cadaver has ever been found.'

Grimes's story was then interrupted by a loud voice calling from the wife in the parlour and the keeper answered, 'My dearest, I'm in the endeavour of conducting the gentleman to his room.' Grimes then looked down the staircase, uttered a coarse oath beneath his breath, picked up the bags from the step above and continued the short journey upwards.

The room Rhodes had been allocated was plastered and painted grey, but it was well-lighted, with two windows set apart both looking out to sea. 'There's some dodge of opening the casement on the left,' said the keeper, 'but, to be sure, it's Mrs. Grimes who is the expert, for it yields to her strong arms alone. Yet with winter almost most upon us, I doubt, sir, you will be wanting as your evening companion the sea fog that comes in at night.'

Rhodes took in his temporary abode. Beneath his feet was a small carpet, but the rest was bare floorboards. In the furthest corner was an iron bed, with mattress, bolster, yellowish-linen and a patch-made counterpane. Beneath the tall frame lay a small truckle bed, hiding like a child in the shadows. In the nearest corner was a wardrobe, and beside it a marble-topped wash-stand with the necessary bedroom china and soap. Next to this was a small table upon which stood an oil lamp, a candlestick, tapers and a tinderbox. Rhodes was pleased to see that between the two windows of the wall there was a knee-hole desk, upon which lay pencils, an inkwell and a few sheets of wood-pulp paper. He had requested a room where he could pursue his writing and when he looked up from the desk saw that his inspiration would be a portrait in oil of a most elegantly dressed gentleman, with long flowing black hair. His tailcoat was a vibrant green, with an edging of silver-gilt embroidery and expensive lace could be seen in the jabot[12] and in the cuffs. His breeches were a deep red and his stockings a sumptuous cream. He would be called, in the parlance of the 1890s, a dandy. The gentleman had been painted in the opulent chamber, hung with rich velvet curtains, and on the wall of the mahogany panelled room Rhodes now noticed a looking-glass.

It was then that Rhodes's gaze was drawn, as if by something unknown, from this oil to the decorative overmantel[13] of the fireplace. The frame of this mirror had the exact same ornate carvings as the looking glass in the portrait of the gentleman. Rhodes had been unable to distinguish the nature of the design in the oil, but now, as he moved closer to the substantive original above the fireplace, he saw the sculptor's art had fashioned the wood into the phases of the moon. Rhodes tapped the aged and slightly tarnished glass, looked again to the oil, and then inquired of the keeper how he had come to possess this peculiar pairing.

'Well y'may hask, sir. Together with the mezzotint you saw on the stair, that portrait of the fine gentleman and the overmantel were the only survivors of the great fire at the great 'ouse. As I recall the matter, the lumber-room, adjacent to the old stables, was untouched by the wreckful flames. Folk who stay 'ere say they find these 'curious cousins', as the better spouse calls them, most alluring. See 'ow in the painting the looking-glass is angled on the wall of the fine gentleman's chamber in such a manner as to show no reflection of the said fine gentleman. It ain't sixpence to me, but I say, as I look at that glass in the oil, that if there be a reflection at all it should be of ourselves. We who stand and admire the hartistry of the hartist. And I've noted that to guests fifty times, if I've said it once.'

Rhodes then asked if the keeper knew the origins of these unusual companions or the name of the gentleman in the painting.

'Begging your pardon, sir, I couldn't say. But don't you be worrying about the looking-glass. I've never seen nothing in it worse than myself, as the saying is, and I trust neither will you.'

Rhodes inquisitive nature had let loose a maggot in his mind and he now asked Grimes how far were the remains of the great house, for, he added, a walk was what he now required after so many hours on the train.

"Well, sir, if you have an hinclination to take the air, and it's wise of a man to consult his 'ealth daily with a country walk, it's two miles if you take the path through the woods but four if you walk the lane, which, being market day, will be the busier. But mark the hour of your return, for they do say that at twilight in a wood folk meet persons walking who should not be walking and who by rights should be at rest and giving thanks to the mercy of the sexton's blade. Yet those of a scholard brain say that we see only what we fear and it's the nervish mind that turns bushes into men of bloody bones and thorny branches into the faces of the rawhead.[14] Tt-tt! If you desire my private thoughts, the wood's as little 'azard to life as a Fifth of November mask or a child's penny picture book. Yet perhaps, sir, it would be incumberent of you to make your way back before dusk, for there's nothing like the sun to keep off ghosts. I thought, meself, I saw one once. A mighty ghost it was! But on the lighting of the candle it revealed itself to be Mrs Grimes, wearing nothing but her shift.'[15] There was at that moment another and now louder call from below. 'Speak of the – oh, begging your pardon, sir. It's at such moments as these that I think of my dear brother who, when in little more than muffin-cap and leathers, took the Queen's shilling[16] and left Seaburgh for the navy. Settled in the New World and there lives a fine life as a grocer. Oh, yes, a happy man indeed. But here 'tis well gone noon and I 'av' not yet 'ad m'morning pipe.' Here Grimes plunged into family reminiscences that need not trouble the reader, but before he left, Rhodes made Grimes the necessary observance. 'Oh, thank you, sir. Much obliged, I'm sure. We had rain this morning and my barometer tells me, and it's as sure as any horacle of the Greeks, that the afternoon and evening will be chilly, but with the moistness in the air we should expect a night fog. I can offer as refreshment from your constitutional a cider cup or a posset[17] to give warmth from the cold. If you do choose until after twilight to make your return, and were I a betting man, I'd put a crown-piece on you needing the stronger brandy and water.'

After the innkeeper left, Rhodes unpacked his travel bags and being a methodical man put his possessions and materials in apple-pie order. As he placed his books upon the desk, his eyes again were drawn to the oil. It would be easy to be dismissive of this daub, for it was not in any manner the equal of the masters such as Titian, Quentin Matsys or Raphael, yet it had a mesmerising quality of its own, and Rhodes's eyes were compelled to linger on the face of gentleman in the portrait for some considerable time. As for the looking-glass and its carvings of the cycle of the moon, this too had intrigued him and Rhodes next went over to the fireplace to examine the overmantel more carefully.

The frame was made of ancient cedar and Rhodes speculated that by nature of its age and design it probably came from the Levant.[18] Surely, he thought, this does not belong in a coastal tavern but in the Wentworth Collection at Cambridge. As Rhodes stared at the glass, he became more and more drawn to it in a way he did not understand. *What's this? Stay! There's someone else in the mirror!* he thought. Rhodes quickly turned his head, but the room was empty. No, it must have been a trick of light, for when he looked again into the glass there was no one to be seen in the mirror but himself.

Rhodes went back to the desk and set down a detailed transcription of what Grimes had told him of the great house, the disappearance of the earl and the mysterious figure of the Italian priest. Unlike most scholars, he had a peculiarity in his preference for blue ink. However, from my perusal of his notes made that afternoon (discovered in the copper box now sitting on my own desk) I can see that the ink in his pen ran dry and so he had cause to use the inferior brown iron-gall ink provided by The Slaughden Inn and it is in this ink that Rhodes first writes of that puzzling looking-glass and the beguiling portrait.

When Rhodes had completed his writing task, he put on his great-coat and buttoned it to his chin. He then picked up the parish map of the area brought with him from London and pocketed it. Before leaving the inn, he again closely studied the mezzotint of the Queen Anne house hanging on the staircase wall. *What a handsome dwelling,* he thought. A great house indeed. Only then a large hairy spider emerged from behind the wooden frame that enclosed the image and so, with some necessary haste, Rhodes made his way down the stairs and outside.

Before setting out on his journey to its ruins, Rhodes consulted his map and noted that if he were to make his way there through the woods he would pass the church of St. Edmund's and so resolved that this would be the direction he would take.

Upon reaching St. Edmund's, Rhodes observed that it was an unexpectedly large church made of local dark grey flint and to its side was a graveyard, sheltered by yew trees. He saw too that the flint on the church had been knapped[19] so smooth that the surfaces of its walls and tower had become almost effulgent in the low afternoon sunshine, which with its bright rays caused momentary coruscations in the shining glass of the lattice lead windows.

Unfortunately, the porch door was locked and the only other living creature thereabouts was a hen who, no doubt, had escaped from a nearby barn. Yet the visit would not be wasted, for Rhodes now made his way to the graveyard. (I note from his diary that Rhodes often carried a compass which, I would conjecture on this occasion, was to avoid his walking over grounds on the north side of the church. We who were born in Suffolk know the people of East Anglia still cling to the old ways with the belief that murderers and the sinner who self-slaughters should be buried in ground where there is the least amount of sunlight.) Rhodes wrote some of the names he saw on the gravestones in his notebook (I conjecture here that his purpose was to look them up in the parish register the next day, had his intended meeting with the vicar gone ahead, which, of course, it did not). These were Ager, Hambling, Mothersole, Britten, Sydall, Worby, Burscough, Whistlecraft, Crome and Dennistoun (née Anderson). Rhodes then resumed his walk towards the woods.

The reader has perhaps observed that Rhodes was superstitious in his avoidance of the north side of a church, but did not succumb to idle talk of bushes becoming goblins. Not to delay the reader any further in this portion of the story we may assume that on his path through the woods Rhodes did not anticipate, nor indeed encounter, any tree sprites or bogeymen.

The next section of the narrative I offer (in part) as I heard it from Rhodes himself on the night of All Hallows Eve when he rattled on the windows of my college rooms. To aid the reader, I should add that the manner in which he spoke of the Queen Anne house he had seen earlier in the mezzotint, by then uneven ground, overcome by nettles and its trees stubbed up, was as if he were in a living dream.

'When my path through the woods came to its end, there, a furlong or so beyond, was where the great house once stood. I walked towards the stone pillars, still standing proud, and placed myself where heavy iron gates once hung. And there I let my fancy bring it all back to life. From the surrounding high stone wall, two lines of noble oaks, green and luscious, guide the eye along the drive, where a pack of Springer Spaniels chase a fox. In the yellow gravelled open courtyard, a pair of footmen stand aside a coach, awaiting their master's departure. Behind them is the great house, so refined and pleasing to the eye. A square, red-brick dwelling, detailed with light stone and neatly cut masonry quoins in the corner walls, with a sweep of steps leading to the carved stone door-case. Three lines of precisely positioned sash windows, flush to the brickwork, accentuate the perfect symmetry of the design. A pediment[20] crowns the top, but then I see at its point a gilded cupola in the shape of a crescent moon. On no house of its kind before have I ever seen such an ordainment.'

Here I remember Rhodes pausing and becoming agitated for several moments before recovering and then continuing.

'The hour is past four in the afternoon, for the sun is declining in the heavens, and there, above the hip roof in the reddening sky, is my first sight of... of... the new moon. It is like a spell, for, without thought, I step across the threshold of the gated pillars. It is only the moon, yet somehow it is blinding and I must look away. Except what I descry as I lower my head is its very reflection in a puddle of fallen rain. A sudden shadow seems to fall upon me and when I raise my head, my vision of the great house has dissolved in the ever-dimming twilight and the overtaking darkness.'

It was at this point in his narrative that Rhodes became so disturbed of mind that I am now unable to recall in detail what he said. I labour under a disadvantage as a narrator in that I become nonplussed when encountering outcries of emotional fervour. In short, I am that placid bachelor who is the Edwardian fruit of a Victorian tree. The particulars of Rhodes's disjointed ejaculations cannot therefore be dwelt upon, but the reader should be made aware that Rhodes, from that moment on at the location of the ruins of the great house, felt the presence of a dark shadowy figure, which, he believed, without the evidence of his eyes, was now following him. However, I will hold back from any further revelations as to the veracity of Rhodes's claims until the end of the narrative. What can be said at this stage is that Rhodes departed the scene with some alacrity and made his way back to The Slaughden Inn via the lane and was at pains to walk those extra miles at his top speed. Needless to say that had the innkeeper laid his bet on Rhodes needing a brandy and water on his return he would have been a crown-piece the wealthier.

While you might count to forty, Rhodes sat alone in his room with the stillness of the dead. The sky outside the windows, over which the shutters had not yet been placed, was now jet black, yet he had not yet lit the lamp; the flame of a single candle on his desk was his only illumination. But that was all he needed, for Rhodes's eyes were fixed and unblinking on the oil painting on the wall between the casements. Statues and portraits offer those who have departed this life the service of a permanent memorial, yet the more Rhodes stared at the figure in the painting, the more alive it appeared to be. *What is that aroma?* he thought, for suddenly he could smell the sweet summer scent of roses. Yet such a thing was not possible in late October. It was then that his eyes fell on a specimen table in the background of the painting, upon which sat a large bowl of freshly cut roses.

The senses can play jests on the mind and at once Rhodes bethought himself that the extravagant long-haired gentleman in the painting chamber was not unaccompanied and that a friend lurked in the wavering shadows of the drapes – the very same gentleman seen earlier inside the mirror. 'No! It must be the sallow light of the lamp,' Rhodes said aloud to himself. Yet by now fancy had ascendancy over reason and Rhodes became convinced that this companion was advancing towards the frame of the picture and, as he neared, was revealed to have ginger hair, an aristocratic countenance and the enticing smile of a libidinous libertine.

It so happened that as Rhodes had been staring at these living oils, a beam of light from the new moon had emerged from behind a cloud and begun slowly to make its way across the floor towards the edge of the fireplace. Inch by inch it crept along and as it did so Rhodes's sense of foreboding grew to unbridled fear. He turned from the painting, only for his eyes to meet the looking-glass, which by now had the light of the moon smote full upon it. Its luminance was hypnotic and possessing and his mind became one of anguish and confusion, for the lustrous light revealed within the mirror the impossible world of that luxurious chamber depicted in the canvas oil on the wall. Aghast, Rhodes then descried that the two gentlemen were beckoning, with wanton gestures, for him to join them. Somehow the moon's radiance had transmuted the looking-glass into a gateway to ignominy and wretchedness.

It has been said that in the darkening hours we begin to see that which we fear. If this be so then Rhodes at that moment was living with the vexatious terror of coming face-to-face with all his inner perplexities and inversions. Yet, with whatever firmness of mind he has remaining, Rhodes now turns away from the looking-glass but what he sees in its counterpart in the brush-work oil are arms reaching into the frame *of their own mirror*, which now shows within it Rhodes and his room at The Slaughden Inn. As these arms stretch forward they grow longer and more hirsute than ever was known in human form. From behind him, Rhodes suddenly feels the touch of fingers upon his shoulders, like the groping tentacles of the devil-fish.[21] He resists, but these hands are strong and begin to pull his body towards the enchanted looking-glass. Again he resists but, as he does so, sharp long nails clasp onto his neck, like the teeth of dogs who bite on bones, and a grip with the strength of talons takes hold of his shirt, so much so that a portion of his sleeve is rent off.

Rhodes perceives that the faces of the men have become shameless creatures of the night with rapacious wants and needs. By now his back is pressed hard against the fireplace, but stretching an arm to one side he feels no glass within the frame of the mirror, for it has transmuted into an open portal to a licentious and feral world.

The long arms of these gentlemen display inhuman strength and begin to lift Rhodes from the floor into air, when suddenly the room is consumed by shadow. The beast-like clench of their bristly knuckles loosens and Rhodes falls to the ground.

What saved my friend that night was the fog that came in from the sea, so dense against the window that it broke the bewitching light of the moon upon the looking-glass. Yet for a while the figures in the painting lived on; for Rhodes, as he lifted his head, saw the copper earl glaring at him and clasped in his hands were the rags of a shirt-sleeve. Crawling in haste to the casements, Rhodes raised himself up and pulled across the shutters to lock out any further glow from that lunar globe at the zenith of its potency.

Rhodes spent the remainder of that night and most of the next morning hidden under the iron bed frame on the small truckle bed. The groping hands that had preyed upon him lived on his mind's eye, giving him a thousand remembrances. He waited until the sun was at its height before daring to turn the painting on the wall around and remove the overmantel from its position above the fireplace before placing it, glass down, on the carpet. He noticed that attached to the back of the looking-glass was a vellum parchment, which he removed, and which I now hold in my hands. The words there written are in Latin:

> *Patientes sint ei qui petant immortalitatem libidinosam; nam nocte umbrarum luna cum plena coniuncta, patefacietur per speculum via arcana ad terras corporis voluptatis aeternasque.*

My Latin is no longer what it was, yet I can offer the reader this rudimentary translation: 'Patient be those who seek a libidinous eternity; for when the night of shades is conjoined with a new moon, there shall be laid open through the mirror a path to lands of undying carnal pleasure.'

It has been said that a withered heart makes an ugly ghost and it is my belief that that night Rhodes had a spiritual quietus, for the events at Seaburgh were a contamination that became the plague of his life. There is no glamour in madness and his continuing *delirium tremens*[22] indicated that what he saw, or believed he saw, was what led him forever after to be a man who took a candle to every corner.

What portion of his tale is true and what is a counterfeit of the mind is not, perhaps, for us to judge. I would only ask the reader to forebear indulgence in any speculations concerning astrological divination, esbat[23] witchcraft or Tartarean Orphicism,[24] the veracity of which can never be established. However, I can disclose a postscript to the incident at The Slaughden Inn and it is that the looking-glass and the portrait were later stolen from that hostelry, for in the copper box I found a local news-letter with a report of the theft that Rhodes cut out and kept. It would be my conjecture that it was the Italian who stole these, and that the figure in black at the site of great house was that very same man.

After that night in 1895 when Rhodes related his story, exchanges between us became limited to matters of academia. It was unfortunate that our collegiate friendship became strained when, in 1901, the

Archbishop of Westminster, Herbert Vaughan, received relics from the Basilica of Saint-Sernin, which were believed to be the bones of St Edmund the Martyr and which were intended for the high altar of Westminster Cathedral. Rhodes expressed the strong opinion that they were genuine, while I and another, in a letter to *The Times*, wrote of our doubts as to their authenticity. In this matter Rhodes never became an alienated adversary, but since that controversial and public dispute we had no further correspondence, that is until I received the delivery of the boxes and sealed letter a few days ago.

I undertook to lay before the reader Rhodes's tale as best I could. Yet the word-painting I have offered so far is but the first act, for I discovered the apex of his story in the sealed letter, with the words of Isaiah,[25] '*Secretum meum mihi secretum mihi vae mihi*' – 'I have a secret, I have a secret, woe is me' – written in red ink on the envelope, the contents of which I hereby present to the reader.

'He comes for me! He comes for me! In two days time, on the night of All Hallows Eve, there is to be a new moon. Yet I shall not live to see it, for, by my own hand, I must end my life. It grieves me that my bones shall lie on the north side of the church, but I dare not risk again that wanton entrapment I encountered those three decades ago. *Quid multa*?[26] I therefore ask you, my friend of old, to share my tale that it may be a warning to the curious. The choice of how you tell my story, be it in words of your own making or by those notes and diaries of mine I now give you liberty to share, I trust to you. *Experto crede*.'[27]

I spent many hours reading and deciphering his writings, for his hand was not always steady. I took up my own pen this morning to write this narrative and lay it down as dusk now approaches on this All Hallows Eve.

A moment.

My housekeeper has just knocked on the door of my study to inform me that a gentleman in a black cloak waits downstairs. He claims to know me, and she says, though his English is comprehensible, some of his words are unfamiliar to her, for they are in the Italian tongue.

Notes

[1] Versicles. Short sentences spoken by the minister in a church service, to which the congregation gives a response. Used here in the sense of back and forth.
[2] The Long. The extended academic summer holiday.
[3] Uncial. A script written with rounded unjoined letters found in European manuscripts of the fourth to eighth centuries and from which modern capital letters are derived.
[4] Martello towers. Small defensive forts often found on the coast built during the 19th century.
[5] Hurdy-gurdy. A string instrument that produces sound by a hand-crank-turned, rosined wheel rubbing against the strings.
[6] Mezzotint. A print made from an engraved copper or steel plate. The surface of the metal was scraped and polished to give areas of shade and light. The technique was a popular method for the reproduction of paintings from the seventeenth century onwards.
[7] Lammas rights. Land which, between Lammas day, 12 August, and 6 April, commoners had the right to use for pasture following the harvest, even if they did not have any other rights to that land. Lammas rights often had the effect of preventing building developments on agricultural land or areas set aside of pasture.
[8] Babylonish church. Pejorative term for the Catholic church or the church of Rome.
[9] Peelers. A slang term for a police constable. The first modern professional police force, the Metropolitan Police in London, was formed by Sir Robert Peel in 1829.
[10] Bagmen. Travelling salesmen or commercial travellers.
[11] It physicks me. 'To physic' means to treat or purge with remedies, but here Grimes uses the word in its colloquial sense of 'I can't work out how...'
[12] Jabot. A ruffle of cloth or lace that falls from the collar down the front of a dress or shirt.
[13] Overmantel. An ornamental structure over a mantelpiece, often of carved wood and usually including a mirror.
[14] Rawhead. Samuel Johnson in his *Dictionary of the English Language* (first published in 1755) defined 'rawhead' as 'the name of a spectre, mentioned to fright children.'
[15] Shift. A long loose-fitting undergarment worn by women.
[16] Took the Queen's shilling. Meaning he joined the Royal Navy.
[17] Posset. A warm drink made of milk curdled with wine or ale, and sometimes spiced.
[18] Levant. Historical term for the geographical, cultural and archaeological area of land bordering the Mediterranean Sea, which includes present-day Israel, Jordan, Lebanon, Syria, the Palestinian territories and most of Turkey.
[19] Knapped. Shaping a piece of flint, so as to make a flat-faced stone for building walls.
[20] Pediment. Triangular section on the front of a classical building, typically above a portico.
[21] Devil-fish. Generic term for a fearsome or formidable fish, but in this context a cephalopod, that is a mollusk with muscular sucker-bearing arms such as a squid or octopus.
[22] *Delirium tremens*. A psychotic condition involving tremors, hallucinations, anxiety, and disorientation. From the Latin, 'trembling delirium'.
[23] Esbat. In pagan worship there are lunar cycles known as 'esbats'. And esbat is also a term for a witch's coven.
[24] *Tartarean Orphicism*. Tartarean, from Greek mythology relating to or characteristic of Tartarus, that is hellish and infernal. Orphism, a mystic religion of ancient Greece that originated in the seventh and sixth centuries BC, based on poems attributed to Orpheus, where individuals rid themselves of part of their nature by means of reincarnation.
[25] *Isaiah* 24:16.
[26] *Quid multa*? Roughly equivalent to the English phrase 'Need I say more?'
[27] *Experto crede*. Meaning 'Leave it to the expert'.

VISITING HATTIE

A Titillating Tale of Seductive Spookiness – as told by the Ghost of Kenneth Williams.

(A glossary of the polari words and phrases used by Billie Blooming, one of the characters in the story, can be found in Appendix II.)

HATTIE JACQUES ONCE REVEALED TO ME that she wasn't too keen, to use her exact words, 'on those men who were very narrow at the equator'. Even I took a moment or so to realise precisely what it was she meant. And it may take you a lot longer, perhaps even the time it takes me to relate this story. Yes, you may be one of those poor souls we call *homo innocentes* – that's your actual Latin – who are pure of thought and guiltless in the ways of sin. However, I suspect most of you know how to boil your onions and have already worked out Hattie's cryptic meaning. Nevertheless, I shall withhold the more vulgar details until we get to the very end of my tale. If you pardon the expression.

I suspect as well, there are those of you wondering how it is that I, Kenneth Charles Williams, am able to offer you this ghostly missive at all. Well, the truth is, I have been given a *temporarius ostracismus*. No, that isn't what they do to cats. To put it in a more secular parlance, I have been granted a brief sojourn among those who still draw breath. Oh, but my dear friends, do not be fooled by my eloquence and erudition, for I must warn you, the yarn I am to tell is a gruesome ghost story, a spine-tingling tale of terror and delight, and not only that, but it gets a bit kinky too.

So now, without a further delay, impediment, obstruction, encumbrance, hitch or hindrance, I shall commence.

It all began once upon a dark and foggy night. A whirling mist moves stealthily among the shadowy trees, enveloping the wood in a haze of obnubilation and mystery. There under its branches are three companions, sitting in their open automobile. The Old Queen is dead – Victoria I'm talking about, you common lot – for this is the Age of Edwardian Invention. The men are lost and fearful, only they suddenly see a light flicker in the distance and their hopes are raised. As they drive their motor vehicle through a clearing they discover that the illumination comes from a large, lonely house, half hidden by the swirling vapours of the night.

The driver, dressed in the Edwardian fashion of heavy tweed coat and hat, stops in front of the forbidding iron gates and the three men cautiously step out of their automobile onto the damp and gritty sod. The youngest, and most handsome, notices a sign to the side of the gate telling him this ageing country manor is a Rest Home. Strange, though, that it should be hidden in such sepulchral seclusion.

The three gentlemen walk across the courtyard to an unwelcoming entrance, for above the door is an ugly demonic stone gargoyle, with sharp pointy toes and a tongue protruding from its fiendish mouth, as if in warning to stay away. But our companions live in a rational age and they do not believe in devils and spirits. At least for now.

One of the gentlemen tries the bell, but to no avail, for it is old and broken. The man in tweed instead hits his fist three times upon the ancient timber door.

Footsteps are heard echoing within, but then they come closer and the door creaks open. A tall, pale faced man appears. The butler, it seems. Oh, but how drained of life he looks, bloodless, with dark and empty eyes. One of the men asks if it would be possible to see the master of the house, only for the butler to inform them, in a voice as if from the grave, that the master of the house is dead and has been dead these fifteen years. The most timid of the men takes off his bowler hat, perhaps in respect for the deceased, only then the butler informs the gentlemen that he will, nevertheless, enquire if his master will see them.

It was at that very moment that Adam first reached his hand across and put it onto Calvin's own. And who wouldn't, for that's one of the scariest moments in *Carry On Screaming!*. Calvin's other hand, I think, would have joined in, only it was embracing a large bucket of popcorn bought in the cinema foyer. Even so, Calvin was thrilled to high heaven that Adam had made the first move and in return Calvin now let his loving thumb and fingers intertwine with Adam's in such a way that one could no longer tell whose was whose.

Calvin had, it should said, considered grabbing Adam in the opening scene of *Carry On Screaming!* – that fearful moment when the creature abducts the beautiful girl. The two young lovers, Doris and Albert, had come into the woods to do what those in love do. But Doris was suddenly frightened. Not of Albert, for who in their right minds could fear Jim Dale? No, Doris – played with great subtlety, I thought, by the ever lovely Angela Douglas – sensed a presence in the bushes. Someone – or should that be some *thing* – was watching them in their courtship. Albert, in a fluster of frustration – which Jim Dale always performed to perfection – went forth to make sure all was well, but it was then that the hairy monster came forth to take the girl. Oh poor Doris, she tried to scream – oh, how she tried and tried – so very trying, but alas, it was no use. The creature had her!

Yes, in that precise moment, Calvin's own hand had hovered over Adam's, only at the last, Calvin hesitated, and grabbed what became a gob full of popcorn instead. Not that it mattered, for now Adam's warm hand was exactly where Calvin wanted it.

Cupid's arrows pierce lovers who come in all shapes, sizes and preferences. And, as you have no doubt worked out, Adam and Calvin were the sort of men who, in the parlance of the day, licked the other side of the stamp. The love dart was shot the instant they revealed their shared admiration and affection for the *Carry On* films. And now, as the pair watched *Screaming!*, Cupid smiled, for their hearts – and soon mouths – would become as one. Yes, my friends, they had entered that empty cinema on a wet Wednesday in April as men alone in the world but they left together with love in their souls and popcorn, nougat and four caramel bars in their tummies. But that wasn't quite enough, for they stopped off at the sweet counter in the foyer and added some chocolate fudge, four marzipan fruit boxes and two portions of banana marshmallows with hot melting raspberry syrup.

As they looked at the poster of *Carry On Screaming!* they agreed it was one of the most brilliant of *Carry On* films, yet it couldn't possibly be top of their list. That, they decided, had to have in the cast their favourite comedy actress, that mistress of merriment, the wonderful and dearly beloved Hattie Jacques. But which *Carry On* would it be?

The human heart. What an utter mystery it is. For as the hot red syrup dripped from their lips, their two voices spoke as one.

'My favourite is *Cabby*.'

They then laughed like a symphony of joy at their synchronicity.

'Ha! Ha! And of course, *Cabby* was Hattie's favourite too!' said Adam.

'Oh, and her best. It's both funny and moving,' replied Calvin.

'And feminist in a way. Her pink cabs are so much better than Sid's boring old black ones.'

'Talking of cabs. I was thinking, shall we, er, get one back to my place? I've a number for a gay taxi service called OVER THE RAINBOW.'

It cannot have been the first time that a pink or black cab, or indeed one with every colour in the spectrum, had taken two lovers on a journey that would end in intimacy. And without, I hope, being too prurient, one can say that Adam and Calvin enjoyed a ride that night that lasted long into the morning. But something they said in the back of the car would come, dare I say, to haunt them. Adam, you see, thought it was a shame that Hattie had died in her prime. She loved life and food and men so much.

'Oh, if only she were with us today. Wouldn't that be wonderful? I'd love to meet her.'

'Me too.'

Oh, but gentlemen, be careful what you wish for. You never know who might be listening...

The nuptials of Adam and Calvin were memorable for three reasons. First, the betrothed went down the aisle to the opening theme music to *Carry On Loving*, which got everyone laughing and cheering straight away. Second, there was no wedding cake. Instead the caterers, FILL YOUR FACE, provided an abundance of choice desserts. Chocolate mousses, jam roly-polys, apple and butterscotch pies, blueberry and almond pies, lemon cheesecakes, walnut and date cakes, carrot cakes, gingerbread men, truffles, doughnuts, strawberry crumbles, ginger sponges, macaroons, muffins, Danish pastries, toffee éclairs, Bakewell tarts, Malteser tiramisus, scones (or if you're from the North, 'scuns'), honey crème brûlées, lemon cheesecakes, oh, and I haven't even mentioned yet the accompanying custards, sweet sauces and double cream helpings. Ah yes, and the many ice sorbets to cleanse the pallet and obligatory marzipan fruits for after. It was an array of delights to satisfy the taste buds of any persuasion. And there were quite a few persuasions about that day.

The third notable feature of the nuptials, and the most pertinent to our story, was the range of wedding gifts, all of which had a *Carry On* theme. Let us begin with the set of coffee mugs, each embossed with a caricature face of the *Carry On* stars Sid James, Joan Sims, Hattie Jacques, Kenneth Connor, Charles Hawtrey, Jim Dale, Barbara Windsor, Peter Butterworth, Bernard Bresslaw and, of course, myself, Kenneth Williams. These were simple cartoon-like drawings in black and white, not the minimalist genius of Matisse perhaps, but each instantly recognisable. And the selection, I believe, was not entirely random for we were what I called 'The Top Ten Teeming with Talent', who had clocked up more leading appearances in the *Carry On* canon than any of our fellow celluloid thespians.

Next among the array of bestowals was a set of cushions, again with the same familiar characters imprinted on the cotton fabric, only I have my doubts, however, whether Jim Dale would have been particularly enthused had he heard one guest observe coarsely, 'Oooh! I could sit on his face all night!' My own visage was, of course, among these colourful soft furnishings, but at least I was spared the threat of an expansive and very flabby bum.

In addition to these endowments there were signed photographs of June Whitfield, Dilys Laye, Esma Cannon, Jack Douglas and Leslie Phillips, all in very tasteful sepia. Barbara Windsor, however, was represented by a rather common plastic toy that nodded its head, and whose brassiere, when the figure's arms were pulled back, pinged itself across the room. On seeing this contraption in operation, one gentleman among the guests observed, 'Oh, that's how you take a woman's bra off, I've always wondered!'

Among those gathered that day was a man named François de Maël, who you could tell instantly, given his mauve silk jacket and orange velvet trousers, had an overwhelming gift for design. His wedding present to the couple was two large teddy bears in the personas of Adam and Calvin that François had created himself. 'Calvin Bear', much like his alter ego, bearded and well fed, had been dressed as Henry the Eighth, no doubt as a homage to Sid James in *Carry on Henry*, though given that monarch's attitude to marriage, I wasn't sure that this particular motif had been quite thought through. 'Adam Bear', the slightly thinner of the two husbands, but only very slightly, had been dressed in a dark suit and a Fez. An unfortunate lady had made the mistake of asking the designer why 'Adam Bear' had been 'kitted out as Tommy Cooper'. With eyes to half and mouth to lemon, François de Maël informed the erring guest that 'Adam Bear' had not been 'kitted out' as that lumbering magician but rather his 'couture' had been fashioned as Kenneth Williams in *Carry on Spying*. I, myself, would have been proud of the withering scowl on the face of François as he passed this information on to that poor ill-fated and now very red-faced guest.

Everyone's favourite person at the wedding was Billie Blooming, a man, shall we say, of generous proportions and equally abundant good humour. Billie made his way around the room saying to all and sundry, given the opportunity, and more often than not creating it for himself, that he had 'dragged himself up for the wedding of the year' as Lady Puddleton, the character Charlie Hawtrey disguises himself as in *Carry on Again, Doctor*. And this role had afforded him two bites at this cherry. For the morning ceremony at the register office, Billie's attire had been the relatively subdued blue twin-set, familiar to anyone with knowledge of the film. However, we are now at the reception, and so, like the caterpillar that becomes the butterfly, Billie had transformed himself into Lady Puddleton's glorious outfit of effervescent pink feathers. Billie Blooming indeed. And given his considerable size and following a 'zhoosh up of the riah', Billie now looked like the nesting habitat of an entire flock of flamingos. At a wedding there is always the unspoken battle for sartorial supremacy between the mothers-in-law. Which matriarch will surpass the other in elegance and resplendency? But alas, both Adam and Calvin's dear mamas came very distant seconds to Billie's expansive panache and chic.

I cannot help myself. I must say it. With all the food, the presents and the guests, Adam and Calvin's wedding was, with the pun fully intended, a right Carry On.

Haaaaaaaaaaaaaaaaaaaaaah!

Yet something was missing. The couple had dropped heavy hints that they were in search of a little addition to what Adam and Calvin euphemistically called their 'smallest room'. A space was going begging on the wall just above 'the porcelain throne', and although there was no need to 'go potty' and 'splash out', unless you were 'very flush', it would, nevertheless, be so 'convenient' if someone could bestow upon them a portrait of their beloved Hattie Jacques, to be positioned there in pride of place. Yet among their many and various presents there was no such picture. But then, right on cue, the pink feathers of Lady Puddleton squawked.

'Sweethearts!' said Billie. 'Pin back your aunt nells and let me tell you about this nuovo bijou lattie that has just opened in Soho. It's run by this omee-palone called Percy Pickwick, who we all call Pee-Pee. Nanti pots and a naff shyker, but a heart of oro.'

Now Adam and Calvin were familiar with every shop in Soho, or at least those within spitting distance of Old Compton Street. However, the 'lattie' of which Billie spoke was situated in a shady cul-de-sac just off Beak Street and to Adam and Calvin that might as well have been on the Isle of Skye.

'It is a bona botega that sells your classic cinema memorabilia. Oh yes, he has the lot. *Strangers on a Train*, *Dark Passage*, *Eyes Wide Shut*, *Let the Right One In* and *Hello, Dolly!*. And Pee-Pee tells me he's got his lills on an old cassa full of photographs of British movie stars – every eek of the silver screen! – and he's promised that if among them is the lovely Hattie Jacques then he will – nanti dinari, keep it in your handbag – set it aside as my wedding regalo to you both. Heartfaces, I sense Hattie will be there, for as you know, your Auntie has always been a bit on the mystic. Mother's gift to me. Oh yes, she used to cackle with Joan of Arc every day, well, at least until that regrettable incident with the fire extinguisher. Here's the address of Pee-Pee's lattie,' Billie added, handing Calvin a card. 'And now, my pretties, Auntie must fly! For my feathers are in for a bene ruffling this noche. And his name is Rocco. Oh, what a dish!'

The great mystery of those 'in the life', or, as my mother's generation used to say, 'a bit so', is why it's so often the effeminate omme-palones who find bosom companions in a vigorous and virile men. Charlie Hawtrey was a flicker of a flame yet he attracted the most muscular of moths. In fact, he got through so many sailors he could have commissioned his own navy. And so it was with Billie Blooming. Large, camp, frivolous, and as dizzy as a goose in May, yet he always ended the evening with the nearest scaffolder, bricklayer or fireman. Or indeed any butch omi who looked as if they possessed a tattoo or heavy goods licence. No hoofers or crimpers for Billie. And never assume which is Arthur and which is Martha, or, putting it in theatre parlance, who's Front of House and who's Stage Door. It so happened that particular evening Billie had found himself a footballer, the said Rocco, who, by joyous coincidence, had been attending a sports dinner in the same hotel as the wedding reception. I say 'had been' for Rocco and his new teammate Lady Puddleton had now gone off into the night to explore no doubt what I believe is called the off-side rule.

We can assume the honeymoon of Adam and Calvin was blissful and triumphant, for the couple returned very tanned and full of joy and blossom. And, it must be admitted, several pounds heavier than when they left. They did not reveal their destination, and as you know, I am not one to indulge in idle gossip or let slip the intimacies of others to all and sundry. And we shall therefore move on to the next port of call in our tale: The Cinema Shop.

Along one side of that shady cul-de-sac just off Beak Street, there was a barbers, with a spiralling red and white cylinder fastened to its lintel, next to it a locksmiths, with a giant brass key protruding from a brace, and, at the end, The Cinema Shop, with a clapperboard mounted somewhat precariously above its entrance.

As Adam and Calvin opened the door, a bell attached to the frame inside shook and clanged, and the jingle-jangle alerted the proprietor's attention to their presence, for a bald-headed man, with tufts of hair sticking out behind his ears like stuffing from an old mattress, immediately popped up from behind the counter.

'Ah! Adam and Calvin! The happy couple, I presume. Oh, but my dears, I'm sorry to report there is no Hattie! No Hattie at all. Oh such a shattering disappointment. But my dears, it would be my delight to show you the photographs that have come into my hands from that golden era of British comedy...'

Percy Pickwick, for it was he, went on to explain in infinitesimal detail that the 'old cassa', of which Billie Blooming had spoken, was in fact a dilapidated leather suitcase that had been found in a store-room once rented by the Anglo Amalgamated Film Distribution Company, the original financiers of the *Carry On* series. Anglo Amalgamated, he explained, had been absorbed into EMI. Pee-Pee even offered dates and share prices, but frankly Adam and Calvin, despite their firmly-fixed smiles, weren't really listening, for their passion was for the stars and the films, not the men with cheque books. However, if for some perverse reason you are interested in historical minutiae of the British film industry, may I suggest you look up Anglo Amalgamated on something which, I am reliably informed, is called Wikipedia. Though of course, those of us with a good education and memory never had need of such nonsense.

The salient point of Pee-Pee's prattle was that it was most fortuitous that a suitcase containing publicity photographs from that era had been uncovered, after many decades, in a dusty and forgotten room at Elstree. Of course, such an oversight would never have happened at Pinewood Studios, which, like many an actress over forty, is in a state of constant renovation and refurbishment.

Percy Pickwick was acutely aware, as he lifted the worn and battered case onto the counter, that he had dashed the hopes of Adam and Calvin, and so he tried to make amends. There was, he said, a rare photograph of Charles Hawtrey without his wig, a picture of Joan Sims on a camel, Bill Owen in stripped pyjama tops but no bottoms. Or maybe they should just open the leather suitcase and have a rummage for themselves?

Percy Pickwick then spun the case round so that the lock catches were now directly in front of Adam and Calvin. The two men pressed down on the brass fittings, but they were stiff and wouldn't budge.

'Oh, my dears,' cried Pee-Pee, 'no, no, no, a little tickle is all you need to tease it open – as the Bishop said to the curate in the vestry! Ha! Ha!'

Instructions were closely followed and the suitcase obligingly unlocked and snapped opened. But that was just the start of it, for then the lid suddenly sprang up all by itself, as if by magic.

At that moment did a bell ring? Adam and Calvin could have sworn they heard a tinkle-winkle-jingle-jangle from somewhere. Yet when they turned round towards the door, there was no one to be seen. But that moment of enchantment was soon forgotten, for when they returned their attention to the suitcase their unbelieving eyes saw what can only be described as a miracle.

Hattie Jacques! There she was! Resting on top of her fellow luminaries. And looking gorgeous, as she always did.

Oh, but this was no photograph. No indeed, my friends, for what they were seeing was something much more exquisite and enticing than that. A beautiful colour pastel drawing. It was, and there's no other word for it, Fantabulosa!

Percy Pickwick was at first baffled by this unexpected and unaccountable manifestation, for he assured Adam and Calvin that it certainly wasn't there yesterday. Despite his wittering ways, Pee-Pee was a level-headed man of good sense, and he soon came up with the feasible explanation that the drawing must have stuck to the sticky side of some photographic paper, perhaps a publicity shot of a smirking Sid James or playful Peter Butterworth, and had come loose when he put the suitcase on the counter.

Pee-Pee then noticed that the portrait was signed 'V'. 'V', he suggested, was almost certainly Alex Vetchinsky, a production designer on *Carry on, Sergeant*, who was known always as 'Vetch'. No doubt he had been asked to draw a sketch of Hattie and somehow it had found itself among all these old photos. Yet Adam and Calvin knew better. Yes, perhaps it was a commission, and yes there may be logical reason for its not having been found, but all that mattered was that their wish had come true. Hattie was theirs and the pair would give her a homely welcome.

Percy Pickwick, of course, was aware of the financial worth of this drawing, but he valued his word more, and so this mysterious sketch of our beloved Miss Jacques was handed over to the adoring couple with cheery alacrity.

'And what a portrait it is. I do believe Vetch has captured her very soul.'

Yes... and Adam and Calvin were soon to discover that never a truer word had been spoken...

Leonardo de Vinci's *Mona Lisa* and Alex Vetchinshy's *Hattie Jacques* could be said to have several characteristics in common. First, the sultry enigmatic smile, and second, the uncanny ability of the eyes to follow you around the room, which, in Adam and Calvin's case, was their downstairs lavatory. Yet they began to feel that those penetrating orbs of Hattie's were observing them even when their backs were turned to wash their hands in the basin.

Now as you might have guessed Adam and Calvin were a particularly social couple, whose friends were constantly popping by. As a result, the two men always had a bottle of good wine in readiness for any visitors, and for those who were abstemious, an assortment of teas and light refreshments, plus, of course, numerous accompanying cakes and fancies. The conversation and beverages would flow, and hours go by, which meant that bladders eventually needed to be emptied. Besides, visitors had become curious to see Hattie, for the portrait had been much talked about. Yet, one or two who had a call of nature had been genuinely perturbed by Hattie's constant scrutiny. And the position of the drawing, on the wall looking down as it seemed, at your waist, didn't help matters. But it wasn't just her eyes. Several gentlemen remarked how, as they prepared themselves for use of the necessary, Hattie's smile had seemed to widen. Most disconcerting, they said. And these were prudent and sensible men. One even worked at John Lewis. The haberdashery department, so I heard.

'It was Hattie's expression as I unzipped myself,' said a regular drop-in-er, 'for her face went from hope to disappointment. A look I've been familiar with all my life.' 'I've done my fair share of cottaging,' said another, 'but I never expected to have Hattie Jacques stood next to me, giving me the eye.' 'I simply couldn't go,' said one poor chap, 'I suppose I'll have to hold it in till I get to the bus station.'

And all this could not be laughed off as a joke, for it was now very clear that their downstairs lavatory was most definitely haunted. Adam and Calvin had no choice but to allow their guests to use their en suite upstairs. Oh, but me dearios, that was when their problems really began.

Peculiarity has been a constant in my life, yet even I was a little surprised by the events that followed. Remember Calvin's teddy bear? The one dressed as Henry the Eighth? Well, one evening Calvin came home to find that the said King Henry had been placed on all fours with his posterior in the air, and with a daffodil protruding from where daffodils do not grow.

Here some expositional information may be required for those of you unfamiliar with the entire *Carry On* canon. You see, in *Carry on Nurse* – one of my favourites – a rather troublesome patient, referred to as The Colonel, is expecting to have his temperature taken with what he believes will be a small rectal thermometer, as was the custom in those days. Only Hattie Jacques, as Matron, discovers that her naughty nurses have in fact used the stalk of that charming spring flower.

Calvin smiled when he saw the daffodil, and, in anticipation of an amorous night, prepared himself for whatever ingression Adam had in mind. Yet when Adam returned home, he was nonplussed. It was not he who had inserted the daffodil. However, Adam did want to know why the cushions of Charles Hawtrey and Bernard Bresslaw had been sewn together at the mouth, so that lips, and presumably tongues, were now in constant exchange. Calvin denied he had done any such thing. No latter day Pandarus was he. Yet the excellent stitching did not lie. So who else could have done such a thing when house had been locked all day? There was no sign of forced entry, except, of course, with the daffodil, and only Adam and Calvin had keys.

The argument was heated, voices were becoming raised, and that's when the itching began. Shoulders first. Then down the spine. Now round the chest and soon in the small of the back. And then, merciful heaven, lower... oooh... and under... ooooooooh! That bit certainly needed a scratch. And another... ooooooh! And another!

'*Carry on Teacher*!' the two gentlemen cried in unison, as they grappled beneath the elastic of their unmentionables. Itching powder had been a prank in *Carry on Teacher* played on the pedagogues, myself among them, resulting in a dance of Dionysian frenzy. But we were simply acting, the agitation in the nether regions of Adam and Calvin was real. Lashings of calamine lotion were applied and eventually all became calm. And in that serenity they realised who the culprit was. Not pupils this time, but the lady teacher herself. Hattie!

Now despite the smallness of the smallest room and the largeness of the two large men, both Adam and Calvin managed to squeeze themselves inside and confront her face-to-face. As they began to chastise poor Hattie, her normal smile soon became a frown, and when the men came straight out with it and accused Miss Jacques of these silly pranks, she closed her minces and refused even to look at them.

Oh dear, something had obviously upset her, but what could it be? At that very moment the doorbell rang – *Ding-Dong!* – and Adam and Calvin remembered they had invited Billie Blooming and his new beau, Vince, a carpet fitter from Kidderminster, round for tea.

Billie had the gift of finding a new companion on a weekly, and occasionally daily, and not infrequently, hourly basis. However, Vince had lasted a fortnight, which for Billie was the equivalent of a golden wedding anniversary. Unfortunately Vince was running late, but would be with them shortly. Billie then apologised profusely for his uncharacteristically dull attire.

'Wednesday, sweethearts! Well, a girl's hemline got to show some rispetar for midweek. Nishta gildy. Think Bette Davis in *Little Foxes*. Oh, but your Auntie's had a long day on her lallies, so off with the sling backs, vogue me up and mine's a Vera.'

Billie from time to time had had employment as a spirit medium, and it was he who had predicted and indeed facilitated Hattie's arrival in Adam and Calvin's lives. Perhaps he could explain these strange phantasmical transgressions.

As Adam and Calvin sat round a large pot of Earl Grey tea, with that accompanying large gin for Billie, the homely couple began to tell their guest what had happened and their suspicions as to the offender. I say 'began' for they never completed their testimony. You see, just as Calvin was pointing out the very neat stitching between the lips of Charlie Hawtrey and Bernie Bresslaw, a more incongruous couple one could not imagine, the bra on the plastic model of Barbara Windsor suddenly, and seemingly of its own free will, flew off and up into the air. The novelty plaything had been given pride of place at the centre of the kitchen table, but now the model was semi-naked and so the arms of Miss Windsor reached across her chest to protect her modesty. Meanwhile, the spinning brassiere hovered about, as if deciding where to land – and eventually chose the top of Barbara's head. Yet the bra continued in its tailspin and the cups, though not designed for this usage, became as if the blades of a helicopter, and as a result, the whole body of Miss Windsor rose into the air like an ascending goddess and then began to fly and dart about the room.

Billie clapped and cheered at this remarkable psychical phenomenon happening right there in front of his eyes.

'Oh, Duchess Gloria! Oh, so very bold. Not since mother's lungo chats with Mary Queen of Scots, brought to a premature finir by an unfortunate incident with a meat cleaver, did I riguardar such wonderments.'

'Don't encourage her,' said Adam, firmly.

'Hattie is being very mischievous,' added Calvin.

'Oh, but osservar, ducky, how she's making Barbara Windsor flutter about like a little sparrow in charper of a nest.'

However, the couple were more interested in why it was that Hattie had suddenly taken on these poltergeistian tendencies.

'Sweethearts,' said Billie, now on his third gin and sixth cigarette, 'your spirits rarely intend to harm or scare us vivo omees. No, what they bisogno more than anything else is attention. And Hattie is a lively dolly spectre. With molto needs. It was just the same when mother invited the ghost of Eleanor of Aquitaine to come and stay. Very demandar, she was. And tutto in Franglais! *Fais ci, fais ça*. Huh! But nishta ever contentar that dona. Eventually I had to take to the veil, as Eleanor herself had done in 1202, as it was the solamente way I could get her to take note of y'Auntie.'

It was then that the doorbell rang – *Ding-Dong!! Ding-Dong!!* – and Bird Barbara's soaring heights came to an abrupt end with an emergency landing on the cushion displaying her very own cleavage.

'Ah, that will be Dexter – no, Vince. Dexter was that weekend in Maidenhead. A place most appropriate, given his inexperience. Oh but wait till you park your yews on Vince. Bona bod, a very manly Alice. Oh and his stimps and thews! And vada at the larder! Bonaroo cartso!'

Vince it turned out was indeed a strapping soul who would make anyone's chips sizzle. *Ding-Dong! Ding-Dong! Ding-Dong!*

'Great to meet you guys,' he said, 'but I'm desperate for a pee.

Would you mind if I quickly used your loo?' Adam and Calvin looked at each other. A penny suddenly dropped.

'It's the second on the left.'

The second on the left was not of course their private bathroom upstairs but the small closet where the famed drawing still hung. Forgive the vulgarity, but the word 'hung', in its more lascivious meaning, leads to a significant development in our story. You see, Vince was born, shall we say, in a very good year for cucumbers. In fact, Vince was quite exceptional in that department. Indeed, of stallion proportions.

Now when I began this tale I said it would be gruesome. Well, as Vince looked into Hattie's eyes what he held in his hand grew-some-more, for Vince was one of those gentlemen who, shall we say, walked both sides of the street. Never had there been a more instant and mutual attraction between the two worlds of spectre and spirit and flesh and blood. Oh yes, spines were undoubtedly tingled across the divide of the quick and the not-so-very dead.

Now as you know, I am not one to be prurient and I have never been desirous of salacious discourse. What occurred between Vince and Hattie is their secret. But, by the look on Vince's face when he came back into the kitchen, whatever happened must have been quite Heavenly, I can tell you. Adam and Calvin immediately rushed to the second on the left to see how the lady herself had reacted. Oh, my word, how wonderful! Hattie was smiling again.

As I have been relating this most singular of stories, it has occurred to me that there is a possibility, however absurd it may be, that their may be those amongst you who are disadvantaged in not knowing the unique place that the *Carry Ons* have in British cultural life. And even those who do, might have limited knowledge of the heroine of our tale, beyond her fourteen appearances in the film series. A moment of digression is therefore required and brief excursion of social and intellectual enlightenment now follows.

The critics, a haughty and often snobby breed, saw the *Carry On*s as a little below stairs, commonplace and insignificant, and yet we clicked with the public. And still do. We were neither cynical nor profound, we simply offered warm-hearted fun, in a world of gloom and despondency. Our comedy was childish, in the best possible sense of being child-like. And children love the *Carry On* films because they're silly, but so is life, and so are people. And I should know! Besides, being silly is one of life's greatest joys.

It has often been said that Art is a lie in search of its Truth. The Truth we told in the *Carry On*s was – and is – that the British dislike officialdom and enjoy nothing more than watching self-important busy-bodies falling flat on their faces and so those who run our institutions are there to be made fun of.

The early *Carry On*s in black and white sent up the army, the police and, of course, the various medical professions. If time allowed I would share my own experience of cold fingers which ventured where even angels dare not look. Yes, the plots of *Sergeant*, *Constable*, *Doctor* and *Nurse* were very much the same. New recruits aren't up to the job and those in charge despair at their incompetence. Yet, being British, in the end, we pull together and win the day. Even when the series became burlesque and parody, decamping to foreign lands such as ancient Rome, the palace of Versailles and even the dusty saloons of the American Wild West – where I gave one of my greatest performances as Judge Burke – we always took with us that mockery of pomposity that is so distinctly and uniquely British.

Those of us who lived our life on this septic isle, as I called it in *Round the Horne*, have learnt to accept the painful truth that Englishmen are often scared of sex. Kenny Connor's entire career was based on the principle. I cannot speak with any personal experience, but the *Carry On*s worked on the assumption that women were far more keen on 'rumpy-pumpy', as my mother Louie always called it, than were men. The comedies of Aristophanes, which obviously I have read, proclaimed a similar view of the female libido. Yes, the *Carry On*s have been accused of being sexist, and I will acknowledge that the producers found every opportunity in the plot for women to be discovered in a state of undress, be it a keep-fit class, changing rooms, communal showers or even a harem. However, it was always we men who were made the idiots of circumstance. My own trousers went up and down more often than a fiddler's elbow, and more than once I was subjected to the ignominious indignity of nudity. In *Carry on Constable*, Leslie Phillips, Kenneth Connor, Charles Hawtrey and I had to run around as naked as the day we were born, though I do remember Charlie was none too keen on showing his bum. I told him, 'Don't see why not. It always pays to advertise.' Not that he ever went without.

Yes, there was much ribaldry. In the bar at Pinewood Studios we even had a double-meaning cocktail, because if you asked for an 'Innuendo', the barmaid would give you one. Those familiar with the Greek language, as I am, know that the word 'comedy' comes from *komos*, a dance of revelry. And the films often incorporated such mayhem in their closing scenes, be it a bun fight, the wrecking of a house, a chaotic car chase, a battle with swords, custard pies, or, for me, the inevitable dunking in some disgustingly viscous liquid.

The cast, the only repertory company in cinema history, were blessed with cartoon faces and idiosyncratic ways of speech. Sid James was once described as looking like 'a relief map of the Himalayas' and on cue my own nostrils could flare up to become almost triangular in shape. And Charlie Hawtrey, with his etiolated stature and epicene voice, walked and talked as if created for the theatre by the comedy gods themselves.

As for Hattie Jacques, ahh! What a wonder she was. A large lady with a heart in size to match. The camera loved her, and, when seen on the big screen, the world became smitten too. In life, Hattie was everyone's ideal sister or auntie. As for her persona in the *Carry On*s, well, her make-believe character became truly iconic. I bet you both ends of the bedpan that if you were to ask the British people for the most recognisable woman from the world of medicine, Florence Nightingale might well come out on top, but Hattie Jacques would be a very close second... Oh, Matron!

But the Hattie I knew was no battleaxe. Her real name was Josephine; she became 'Hattie' when somebody remarked on her physical similarity to Hattie McDaniel, the buxom house servant in *Gone With The Wind*. Oh, she was so caring and generous. And at Christmas her table groaned under the weight of her festive delights. What fun we had!

As has been said, Hattie loved life, food and men. Her dark sexy eyes always flashed with oysters and wine. And it happened that she found attractive those gentlemen who looked as if they'd be the one driving the getaway car. But there was more to her than that. In the war, Hattie had medical training and during an air raid even delivered a baby girl in a public phone box. She worked as a welder, and the pontoon bridges that Hattie helped build were among those used on D-Day. And it was the war, I think, where one could be snatched from this earth in a breath, that gave Hattie her a special love of life.

And I say all this because that is why Hattie came to Adam and Calvin. Theirs too was a house of joyous humour, never cruel or vicious, and like her they celebrated life and what it had to offer. Including handsome men, such as those Billie seemed to find on every corner. The sort who pull up a tree and do justice to a meat pie. And often these chaps were, as Billie put it, 'Tommy Two-ways' who 'only occasionally liked to catch the second bus home.' And always born in a good year for cucumbers – and even occasionally a prize-winning marrow. Oh, the perfect match for Hattie.

And so it came about that Billie, whenever he had a new friend, would take him to meet Adam and Calvin. This fellow would then be plied with tea, wine or beer, and eventually the full bladder would make it necessary to visit Hattie in the smallest room. Exactly what took place was never revealed, but they always came out happier than when they went in.

Another brainwave of Billie's was for Adam and Calvin to have regular evenings screening *Carry On* movies. And some supper to go with the jollity. Fish, chips, sausages, onion rings, bacon, mushrooms – oh yes – we're frying tonight! And on such occasions, said Billie, Hattie's portrait should be brought out to sit among yer manjari munchers and share their love and the affection.

Ah well. My time with you, like this story, is now near its end. I must return, as we say in the theatre, to the 'bar upstairs'. Yet, as this tale has shown, we 'carry on' in your memory. And so every time you giggle at my puerile nonsense – infamy, infamy... they've all got it in-for-me! – I'll be with you. Each of us – Sid, Charlie, Joan, Peter, Barbara, Bernie, Kenny, Hattie – will all be in spirit at your elbow, as you enjoy the earthy pleasure of laughter.

THE FINAL FAKE

**A Tale of Lies and Truth...
but not necessarily in that order.**

I'VE ALWAYS HATED CHEATS. AS a young journalist covering the John Stonehouse trial at The Old Bailey way back in 1976, that contempt for swindlers and fakes grew into a long and lasting loathing. Of course all politicians are liars, it goes with the job, and, frankly, it's sometimes necessary, but John Stonehouse, Member of Parliament, Privy Counsellor and former Government minister, was something else. He wasn't just a bad apple, he was the whole goddamn orchard.

The details of his nefarious life you can discover for yourself with a quick search on Google, but, in short the strapline of the story would be 'Faker leaves clothes pile on beach in shark scare con.'

Yes, this is the guy who, on 20th November 1974, left his trousers and passport on a sandy coast in Miami in the hope we'd all think he'd gone for a swim and been eaten by Jaws. In truth – if you can call the world Stonehouse lived in any sort of truth – he meticulously planned his disappearance, fraudulently transferring funds to a new identity, one Clive Mildoon, with the intention of beginning life afresh in Australia with his mistress. And the con very nearly worked, for obituaries were even published in several London newspapers, including my own, *THE CHRONICLE*. However, after suspicions were raised, police in Australia, who at first thought 'Mildoon' was the runaway aristocrat Lord Lucan, arrested Stonehouse and our faker was deported back to Blighty. You can see why the trial kept the name Stonehouse above the fold, as the old broadsheet editors used to put it, for weeks on end in that summer of 1976. Fleet Street, or whatever you care to call it now, has always depended on the old adage that fact is stranger than fiction. Yet none was ever stranger than that of John Stonehouse. Except, perhaps, the peculiar yet true tale I am about to tell.

In a way my part in the story begins in the press gallery of Number One Court at The Old Bailey. My fellow journos, middle-aged old soaks to a man, couldn't believe my luck. There I was, a rookie twenty-two year old, covering arguably the most infamous trial of the decade. My editor at *THE CHRONICLE*, the legendary Tim Timothy, was aware I came from the Black Country, as was every journo who frequented in El Vino's. These men, and they were all men, as no woman was allowed into the bar of that rakish watering hole, knew I was proud – and loudly so – of my Walsall roots and background. It was my good fortune that despite his arrest, John Stonehouse had chosen not to resign his seat as Member of Parliament for Walsall North and so was technically my MP as in those days I was still registered to vote at my parents' home in Birchills, which, if you could see past the smoke and fog, was in sight of the Walsall canal. Tim, who everyone called 'Titan Tim', for he was as tall as the gods, called me into his office and said that he thought a constituent covering the Stonehouse trial would give the story a greater sense of betrayal.

THE CHRONICLE in those days was the pioneer of personal reporting and most articles had an endnote, a line or two about why the writer was qualified to say what they had. In me, then a young chippy grammar school upstart who could spin and weave a fair bit of good copy and still get it in by deadline, Titan had certainly chosen the right dog to tear apart that sneaky weasel, yet I don't think even he had bargained for the vitriol of my pen. My reputation on Fleet Street grew. And not only there, for it seemed some of the daily reports I'd filed were now being picked up by the international press.

It was on the day of the verdict that Elga Gumma sat herself next to me in that crowded press gallery. Forgive an old stinker, for it was the 70s and sexism was rife, but I'd be lying if I didn't tell you that Elga's seductive bends and curves received more eyeball attention than Stonehouse himself. The ladies fashion then was for white cashmere and boy, oh boy, how it clung to Elga like a lover's embrace. It was as if a magic spell had been cast on every seasoned hack of Fleet Street, for hands began to caress the empty air just imagining. Even Old Charlie, Sheriff of the Court, who hadn't cracked his face since God was a boy, was smirking like a man possessed. Moreover, he didn't even stop Elga from unwrapping her sandwich in a place where for Old Charlie even eating a KitKat was on a par with treason.

'I love you Roast Beefs,' Elga said in her charming Scandinavian accent as she chewed on a mouthful of pink meat.

It took a moment before I realised she was actually talking to me.

Crikey. What to say?

'Er, well, it's the French who call us English *les rosbifs*. You mean your 'roast beef' sandwich.'

'Yah,' she replied, laughing. 'I love my roast beefs. My roast beefs sandwich.'

More 70s sexism I'm afraid, but in those days I truly believed I could read a woman just by her smile. And Elga's pleasing grin, with teeth as perfect and white as her cashmere, was easily as enticing as that of Bardot or Monroe. And she had this habit of teasingly covering the bottom row of her teeth with her lower lip, giving her, I thought, a look of enticing innocence.

Elga was, she explained, covering the Stonehouse story for her Swedish newspaper. It was my copy, she told me, that had inspired her trip to London, and she'd especially asked the Sheriff of the Court to point me out.

'I like you English men,' she whispered in my ear, for the court was now convening for the verdict, 'but not zat one,' she added, looking towards the dock where Stonehouse now stood.

'*Kvacksalvare*, we say in Sweden.'

I wasn't sure what she meant, but could make a reasonable guess.

'Cheat. Crook. Charlatan. Con artist,' I said.

'Yah, all these. You have muchly too many of those kinds in England now. You have saying I think – "*Pull wool over eyes.*" Not good thing. Eyes are for seeing.'

Elga was right. What had ultimately got me as I watched Stonehouse conduct his own bizarre defence during those sixty-eight long summer days (anyone of that era will tell you it was one of the hottest years on record) was the fact that everything about him was so very clearly a charade. Yet no one had seen through it. The smart suit, the silk lilac handkerchief edged with a thin lace braiding – I never trusted anyone wearing that colour from that day on – had duped us all. 'Pull wool over eyes', he certainly had.

But why hadn't we seen past the smoke and mirrors? Maybe the bigger the lie, the more flamboyant the Emperor's clothes, the more willing we are to believe. Even during the trial itself, Stonehouse had attempted the magician's trick of distraction, but he had found his match in the judge, Sir Edward Eveleigh, who, no doubt, had come across his sort before. Sir Edward put it well when he sent down Stonehouse saying, 'You falsely accused others of cant, hypocrisy and humbug when you must have known all the time your defence was the embodiment of all those things. You know that you are not an ill-fated idealist.'

I'd already written most of my copy for *THE CHRONICLE* – I mean, it was plain Stonehouse was as guilty as a cat with a mouse in its mouth – and so when the verdict came in I was in no rush to get out. Besides, and I'll be honest here, I was unable to stand up. If you know what I mean. What testosterone crazed twenty-two year old could have?

Elga. Wow, what a beauty she was. And when not speaking, she would hum. Not a tune I recognised, but somehow she made you feel you'd known it all your life. And she had this playfulness I found unbelievably attractive. Constantly tugging away at my red tie, making it dance up and down like a finger puppet of the Devil himself. What else could I do but give it to her, and in return she offered me one of her beef sandwiches. I normally don't eat meat – a preference based on taste and texture rather than virtue signalling

– but that day my vegetarianism lapsed as quick as a wink. You see, Elga wasn't the sort of woman a man said no to. Ever.

The meat, I remember, was a little on the rare side, but I managed to keep smiling while I chewed and then swallowed. As I ate, Elga kept asking me questions. Where did those steps in the dock disappear down to? What place would Stonehouse be taken? And would he be kept there or go straight to prison?

I was glad at that moment for the extensive research I had done on The Old Bailey to give a historical touch to my news copy. In my reading I had discovered, for example, that there had been courts on the site ever since the Elizabethan era.

'Oh, there's a hive of cells underneath this building,' I explained, with something, I wasn't sure what, still dripping down my chin from that sandwich. 'And below those there are ancient ruins. In fact, hidden away, if you dig down deep enough, there's even an old tunnel where the river Fleet still flows.'

Elga then said something odd.

'There is no hidden place deep enough for sinners to truly escape.'

I must have thought little of it at the time. I mean, why would I? Besides, as Elga said this, she lifted her leather bag, white again as was the fashion, onto her shapely legs, which gave my wide eyes an excuse to look down to where I had not previously dared.

'I have for you this,' she said, reaching inside her bag and taking out a clipping from an old copy of *THE CHRONICLE*. 'You English. Not good. Too many *Kvacksalvarns*.'

In my vanity I thought the article might be one of my own reports, but no, it was a feature on a lady called Doris Stokes, who at the time had a growing reputation as a spiritualist. Again you can do your own online search, but in brief, Miss Stokes went on to become Britain's best known clairvoyant. Her homespun wisdom and friendly armchair manner won over many a convert. But definitely not our Elga.

'You are the man. You should write of this lady. And Stonehouse. And of all *Kvacksalvarns*.'

I was young, it was true, but whereas the rich can afford to waste life opportunities, those of us from backgrounds not so privileged often get only the one chance. And this was mine. I could see it straight away: *CHEATS*. All in caps. With the words '*SUNDAY TIMES* bestseller' above and my name below. And I would use my growing reputation on Fleet Street to do it.

The next day, at the suggestion of Elga, I took the idea to the publisher Saunders and Saunders. The top honcho there was a splendid old girl called Eileen McGuffrey, a well-fed figure of a woman with a peculiar liking for Battenberg cake. And she had three slices on the go when we met. Miss McGuffrey loved the concept, she said, for it came straight out of the zeitgeist, but, she thought, *FAKES* would be a better title. *CHEATS*, she argued, like the trained lawyer she was, suggested criminal intent, and may be difficult to defend in court, whereas *FAKES* were simply those who weren't what they seemed.

'Besides,' she added, with pink and yellow crumbs falling from her mouth in every direction, 'with *FAKES* you can have some fun chapters too. Leaven the bread. Or cake! I should offer you a slice, but this one seems to be my last. I simply don't know where they all go!'

Well I did. But I didn't care. I was never much of lover of fancies. Besides, I was offered something that satisfied my appetite much better. A contract.

My investigation into all things fake began in the animal kingdom. Who knew there is a hoverfly that developed black and yellow stripes to make it look like a wasp so as to avoid being eaten by birds who didn't want to get stung? Or carrion flowers that emitted an odour like rotting flesh to entice flies and beetles? And we had human fakery in the form 'Enhancement Underpants', which added a bit of frivolity. An advert in my own newspaper led me to a costume designer called Maureen who'd made a small fortune from male readers wanting to buy a pair. 'Can't see the point in wearing them, myself,' she said. 'Gives you the look of a double-garage, but inside it's still a bike.'

The old joke in theatre is that acting is about honesty – and once you learn to fake it, you're in. But one thesp turned out to be a double faker. After a nod and a wink from a blind bat, I found myself in a bar with an old actor called Norman Shelly, who claimed it was he and not Churchill who had delivered those famous wartime broadcasts on the wireless. And Norman brought along a 78 shellac disc to prove it. Yes, it was certainly Mr Shelly on the recording, but the dates didn't add up. Perhaps as he grew older he began to believe he really did stand in for Churchill. Of course, we didn't include his story in the book and I make a point of mentioning this because if I'd been taken in myself, it would have undermined the whole project. Ironic, that, when I think back now.

Of course, *FAKES* is out of print now but in December 1977 it did reach number three in the non-fiction *SUNDAY TIMES* bestseller list and helped pay for my first divorce. Remember this was the post-Nixon era and trust was at an all time low. However, what truly drove up sales, and certainly garnered all the media attention, was the chapter on communicating with the dead.

Clairvoyants are simple tricksters. And I say that because some of their deceptions are blindingly obvious. The Fox Sisters, the most famous spiritualists in America in the nineteenth century, used apples tied with string to create those eerie bumps in the night. But you have to give credit to their knack of cracking the joints between their bones to fabricate noises from 'the other side'. Sorry to disillusion you folks, that ain't uncle Earl saying '*Howdy!*', but cavitational gas popping in the ligaments of a fraud's foot.

Apple cores and big toes aside, most ruses of the spirit medium come from the psychological bag of fakery. Begin with something that could apply to anyone – '*Lavender.*' But is that the plant, the perfume or the colour? Wait for your answer. '*Oh,*' says the victim, '*auntie had a lavender bush in her garden.*' Now you're in. And here's a manoeuvre we all know: making the boss think your idea was really theirs. Psychics do the same when they give you the impression that what you've just said came from them. '*Now that lavender bush in your auntie's garden...*' '*It's still there.*' '*Yes – and that's where she goes when she thinks of you.*' Cue hankies and tears.

And have you ever noticed how mediums always talk in fits and starts? Have those who've 'passed over' suddenly developed a stutter? No, it's a trick to buy time. '*She had a friend called Bill... or Jill... or*

Will... or Phil?' Then they see a smile of recognition – '*Yes, Phil. Definitely Phil.*' Again, you're hooked. And they get away with it because the sad truth is if people want it enough they will buy into anything.

Yet what really got my goat with these mountebanks was how they would take advantage of loss and grief. That's the connection with the Stonehouse swindle, because, as the judge Sir Edward Eveleigh observed, we're not dealing with misunderstood romantics here but rather sharp-eyed vultures. And the more I read of their chicanery, the more my mission became to pull back the curtain and reveal those psychics for what they truly were: not just frauds but downright monsters. And my publishing house felt the same. They didn't just want an entertaining chapter of historical curiosities, they sought blood, and were willing to invest money to get it. And they got their payback. Big time.

The Trap is Set

The lady who came up with the sting was my editor, Aubrey Winters. She refused to take credit for it at the time. Only later did I understand why.

Miss Winters was an American ex-pat who made her home in England after the war. Her specialist areas in publishing were travel, cookery and, curiously, archaeology, which had been her subject at Oxford. Whilst an undergraduate she had even developed a correspondence with the Edwardian ghost story writer, and expert in dead men's bones, M.R. James. Well, until James worked out that Aubrey wasn't the name of a man but a woman. That cloistered schoolboy needn't have worried she wanted him for his body as Miss Winters made no secret of being what she euphemistically called 'a confirmed spinster'. Nowadays, we use different words, but in truth Aubrey defied any category or lexicon. To me she was a one-off. Which seems an odd thing to say now, as I look back.

Unlike today, where boys and girls in publishing look no older than readers of Enid Blyton, those who ran the ship in the 70s were men and women who had had, as people used to say, 'a good war'.

And that was often code for a job in Counter Intelligence. Of course, that generation never spoke of what they did in the 1940s, and the Official Secrets Act forbids that anyway, but every line on their faces told you they had seen both life and death at close quarters. And such was Miss Winters.

Fluent in most European languages, including many of their ancient antecedents, she would quote Milton as if he were an old friend. But my abiding memory on meeting her is the constant swirling smoke that came from the never-ending supply of French cigarettes that rarely seemed to leave her mouth. I've said before that I believed I could tell a woman by her smile, well, in Miss Winters's case, the constant smoke had turned her teeth a tarnished bronze, but the smile itself was wide and generous. A top tooth was chipped and somewhat triangular, but 'Fang', as she unceremoniously named it, was never hidden, for there was no vanity in the lady at all. In fact that tooth soon became for me her most alluring feature. Especially when she licked it with her tongue, as she did as she outlined her ruse.

'Kid,' she said – oh, she loved calling everyone 'Kid', especially men older than herself – 'You'll catch more flies with honey than vinegar. What we must do is give these Tomb Tommys what they can't resist: an authentic ghost.'

'But Miss Winters,' I replied – I never dared call her Aubrey to her face – 'there's no such thing as an "authentic ghost".'

'Ha! I know that! But I'm in publishing, and if people read it in a book – *Beholding the bright countenance of truth in the quiet and still air of delightful studies* – they'll take it as fact. What's the name of that Victorian guy? Wrote those railway guides that men who can't get it up at night read in bed?'

'Bradshaw.'

'Yeah. Him. Dig out something similar, only a "History of Stately Homes" or whatever. We will find a house and then move a ghost in. Next we invite those Death Dannys to the haunted honey pot. Take recording equipment, they love all that, and when they start channelling or whatever with our fictitious ghostly tenant we'll have proved they're a Freddie Fake.'

'But you can't just take an old book and put a pretend ghost in it.'

Miss Winters intake of breath now became so startlingly violent that her lips acted like bellows and set her roll-up completely ablaze.

'Why the Hell not? Gee! You'd have been no fun in the war! "Can't". We weren't even allowed to think the word. Haarr! Haarr! Haarr!'

That was my chance to see if the rumours were true.

'S.O.E.,' I said, quietly.

Miss Winters's laughter abruptly stopped and she immediately stubbed out the still flaming cigarette.

'Special Operations Executive,' I went on. 'Am I allowed to say those words?'

'I'll give you this, Kid, you've got some chutzpah. But ask no more questions. If you try, I'll be obliged to kill you.'

And for a second I half-believed her too, but that impish smile and reckless laugh was never far away.

'Haarr! Haarr! Haarr! Haarr!'

'And no doubt, Miss Winters, you were taught at least seventy ways to do the deed...'

'Ha! At the very least! And I've thought of a hundred more of my own since! Haar! Haar! Haar!'

Miss Winters then grabbed that stubbed out cigarette butt and lit it again.

'Don't worry, Kid, I know people. You'll get a call from a lady who'll give her name as Dominique Doré. She'll tell you she only has one leg. Which is true. Domie lost her other *pied* in 1943, but she has a false one now and you can hardly tell the difference. Anyways, Domie will do the research. Create the right ghost. And more importantly forge an old book to give it life. My contribution – to pay the invoice. Haarr! Haarr! But we'll need more than one copy. Couple of dozen should do it. Your part will be to donate the doctored books to the local libraries and second-hand book shops. Oh, and those Oxfam places. Coffin Charlies ain't stupid. They do their research. Every town has a local rag, and I bet each time Miss Doris Stokes goes visiting she has eyes all over the columns of Deaths and Anniversaries. Especially the latter. Oh, but you're young, Kid, and a man to boot. The truth is you never forget the people you lose...'

For a moment Miss Winters seemed not to know where she was or even that I was there, but she soon recovered.

'Oh, but don't worry. Our Graveyard Grahams – those pathetic parasites who live off the dead, who are lower than a snake's arse – oh, they'll dig out your book and turn our lies into their truth. That's how we'll expose those bloodsuckers. Then it will be you living off them. Haarr! Haarr! You're gonna make a killing, Kid!'

The Sting

Overseas Operations. The Ministry for Ungentlemanly Warfare. The Baker Street Irregulars. Departments of wartime skulduggery had many names. From what I could ascertain, Aubrey had been a senior figure and had run agents in occupied France, which, I supposed, explained Dominique Doré. Exactly what Domie had done in the Resistance wasn't clear but I picked up rumours about a mysterious *femme fatale* with a limp and Nazi officers going missing. Weeks or months later a body would be discovered in the woods, unrecognisable after the wolves had got to it. 'Yet never was a bullet found,' folk said. I thought all this was a little fanciful, but as you'll discover, the truth was even more horrific.

I never did get that phone call from Domie, but one morning I found sitting on my desk at *THE CHRONICLE* two out-of-print Edwardian architectural books about seventeenth century houses in Suffolk. I opened the page where there was a bookmark and there among the illustrations was a photograph of an old rectory and next to it, on the same hard photographic paper so favoured in the early 1900s, was the image of a handwritten letter. I then discovered this letter to be forgery, for when I turned to the same page in the second book it wasn't there. Remarkable. Not only was the paper as aged and as worn as its companion illustrating the rectory, but also seamlessly spliced in by its side. To borrow a popular TV catchphrase of the day, *You really couldn't see the join*. Within the week, a dozen or so more guidebooks were delivered direct to my desk, each with that same flawless illustration and letter carefully added. Not surprisingly, when all this was over, those doctored books became a bit of a collector's item.

Anyway, here is what the letter said, followed by the editor's note on the back of that page.

Christmas Eve, 1822

My Dear Darling Bertie,

Oh, we are all in such excitement! The rectory fires glow warmer, the candles dance quicker and I can be in no doubt that even little Fuddle has barked more fondly in recent days knowing that you are to return to your childhood home. Yet, I fear I shall be in weeds until I see your face in the window of papa's carriage, and only in that instant will I know it all to be true. Home on Christmas Day!

Oh, my dearest brother, we shall have such a feast and so many surprises! It would be wicked beyond words for me to reveal too much but were not spiced pears a favourite of yours? Would Christmas be Christmas without them? I think not! Neither did cook. Oh, such a smile she had when Mamma told her of your homecoming. Indeed, the whole house smiles and even Dear Nanny Ghost, still who cries at night for the loss of her poor wards, will, we hope, grieve a little less this festive season. Papa has said often that these lamenting cries are but the howl of the wind in the chimneys but did we not see her once in the nursery? And on Christmas Eve! Oh, but if Dear Nanny Ghost appears tonight, I know it will be with joy for your return.

Oh, there will be such games and japes! We shall hunt the thimble and play Piggy Squeak, even though I will know from your first little yelp that it is you, my dearest darling brother. As I write, I smell the mince-pies baking, cook let me turn the mincer all by myself, and I even stirred in the currants and raisins. I must confess to you that I added more than cook's allowance, for I wanted the pies to be all the sweeter for you. Oh, how our tables shall groan! We have oranges and almonds and every delight that Christmas brings! And we must hide the port bottle where even Dear Nanny Ghost cannot find it. All Twelve Days will be, my dearest brother, as if you had never grown into a man and left us.

Christmas Day! I write it again! For I am still not able to believe it! Christmas Day! Oh, but it is true, it must be true, for Christmas wishes sake,

Hurry, hurry, your ever loving and devoted sister,

Kitty

Editor's note

This charming letter, dated 1822, makes reference to the legend of Dear Nanny Ghost. Parish records of 1712 have shown that a nursemaid lived at the rectory in the early part of the eighteenth century. The records further show that two infants were accidentally drowned on Christmas Eve in the year 1714 and that an unnamed woman who died that same night was later buried beyond the boundary wall of the churchyard. It has been surmised that she was the nursemaid to the two deceased young infants. Her place of burial in unconsecrated ground suggests, perhaps, that she took her own life following the tragic accident with her wards. The local story gathered by your Editor is that the nursemaid, no more than a girl herself, drinking port for the first time and not knowing its strength, fell unconscious as the infants were in their baths. However, this account could not be authenticated by any documentation. Locals say further that the legend of 'Dear Nanny Ghost' grew over the next hundred years and began to include in its narrative a bottle of port that

> went missing. This would explain the reference in Kitty's letter to the game of hiding the port bottle. This may appear to the modern reader a macabre sport for children to play, yet we should note that the tale has in it a moral lesson concerning the dangers of alcohol consumption. The parish records have a Rev Elijah Wilberforce residing at the rectory between 1809 and 1842 who was a well-known writer on abstinence, and so we may assume the 'port bottle' referred to by Kitty in her letter was merely called that for the purpose of the Hide-and-Seek game and did not contain alcohol.

So that was our bait. And a very clever creation it was too by Dominique Doré, whoever she was. Many hints and surmises that could so easily be embellished by our clairvoyants. Give them enough rope and all that. The next matter was where to cast the hook. But again Miss Aubrey Winters knew where to turn and the following week a short article appeared in *CONNECTION*, the magazine of British Fellowship for Psychical Research (originally The Oxford Phasmatological Society), stating that there was to be an investigation into recent 'activity' at The Old Rectory of Banfield St James, near Attleborough. Who among Aubrey's friends should take credit for this insertion I cannot say, but it worked a treat, for soon there were five days of scheduled appointments at The Old Rectory, where each medium had been allotted three hours. In fact, so many applications came in I had to extend the working day well into the evening and even include the Saturday.

My first day, the Sunday, was just me and the recordist setting up the equipment, and once I had learnt which buttons to press, he left me to my own devices. Psychics, I was to discover, were used to cameras and tape recorders, and not one batted an eyelid, though little did they know their ultimate purpose was not to catch a ghost but rather to snare them.

I was alone in that place for the rest of that day and I can honestly tell you I felt no vibes or strange sensations. No presence of life or death. It was nothing more than an empty house. The Old Rectory, Banfield St James, had stood vacant for many years, neglected more than derelict. Technically it was still on the market, but there'd been little interest of late due its water supply being dependent on an underground stream that had, according to the surveys, run dry. Ironically water had begun finding its way in through the roof, with the result that plaster was falling away and everywhere a pervading smell of dampness. Its decline would now be speedy and harsh. Sad but we all have our lifetime.

An unexpected arrival at The Old Rectory on the Monday morning was a large food hamper, courtesy of Miss Winters, with a note that read, 'Our ghost will be famished after all these years, so here's a few victuals to fill its tummy!'. Clearly a joke. On opening the hamper I noticed it contained, almost exclusively, a cold collation of various cooked meats. As I've said, I'm a vegetarian for taste and texture reasons rather than high moral principles. The jellied turkey, roast lamb, cured pork and assortments of other carcasses that for all I knew came from Mrs Lovett's Pie Shop, would no doubt be gorged on by our guests. But no. All our psychics turned out to be a faddy lot when in trancing mood and not one of the meats in the selection was touched.

When the clairvoyants did arrive, they immediately 'connected' with the place and all its eccentricities; the wide staircase that could easily take a coffin sideways; the library, now just rows of empty shelves, like some abandoned hive of learning, and the dining room, with its large mahogany table now faded to a misty grey due to the unhindered sunlight that came in from the east. You can read for yourself exactly what the crazies said about the house in the chapter entitled "The Ghost That Never Lived". Well you could, if it wasn't out of print. So to save you a rummage on eBay, here's an excerpt with some of my thoughts, overleaf, on that strange week at The Old Rectory, Banfield St James...

> 'Psychics come in unusual dimensions. Skinny, Plump, Stunted, Gigantean but never size Regular. One gentleman was so boney that as he spoke of those poor infants in the tub, I couldn't help thinking that if he took a hot bath he'd be more likely turn into stock than drown. I thought clairvoyants would wear funeral black, but most came dressed as a rainbow, with a plethora of astral jewellery hanging from ears and wrists. There were numerous purple perms, and not just among the women. Scarlet lipsticks too, and again this feature was spread across the genders. But what united them all was the nonsense they came up with.
>
> 'To be fair, I admired some of the more inventive embellishments. One psychic suggested that the girl who died was an Indian nursemaid, or *ayah*, not unlike the young lady in the famous painting by Sir Joshua Reynolds. Another insisted that the nursemaid hadn't killed herself at all but been pushed down the staircase by the Reverend, who'd lost control of his senses on discovering the dead infants. And she illustrated the moment by running up and down the wooden steps to Bedfordshire howling like a wounded yak.'

Well, that gives you a feel.

Most of the psychics had done their research as Miss Winters had predicted they would, but a few schoolboy errors had crept in here and there. 'I hear water overflowing... the tap has been left on... and the water brings with it death...' Oh dear. Never in its history did the house have a water supply to the upstairs. A quick visit to the estate agents would have revealed that. No, in 1822 all water to the bedrooms would have been carried in a pail.

I remember as well one of the psychics claimed very firmly there had never been an unworldly presence in the house, but then spoiled it by saying the spirits of the infants who had passed over were now very unsettled by the investigation and, through her, were saying it would be a good idea if I left. The majority of our clairvoyants, however, fell for our 'Dear Nanny Ghost' tale hook, line and sinker. Ate it all up. Every crumb. Here's a short transcript from one guy whose ever reddening face there was no forgetting:

> *'I feel her... she is here... great sadness. Oh! Oh! She's such a young girl. Angels of Heaven! I can smell something now... rich red wine... port, perhaps... I sense her mind is becoming lost! Her eyes are becoming a blur! She falls! Oh no! What is this I hear? Splashing and the cries of babes! Oh no, it cannot be. Why does no one else in the house hear? Music! Music! Christmas songs drown out their cries... drown... drown... Oh... Oh...'*

You get the picture. One lady psychic, I recall, turned the story on its head and came up with a mystery suitor as the real villain: '*The girl is telling me a man is making her drink the port. She's saying no, she must not, but he compels her.* [*NOW SPEAKING AS IF POSSESSED BY THE SPIRIT*] "*He's forcing the drink down my throat! I am done for! Done for!*"'

And so they went on. Looking at my notes as I write reminds me that I myself even began to feel pity for the careless nursemaid and her submerged infants, even though I knew all was fictitious. Anyway, testimonies were recorded, photographs taken and reputations were about to be destroyed.

I didn't think much about it then and there, but over the week the feast donated by Aubrey Winters most definitely dwindled. The meats laid out on that faded dining room table were gradually disappearing, despite the fact that there was only ever me plus one in the house. At first it was just a chicken leg or two, but then I noticed the shoulder of lamb was suddenly all bone. The house was hardly secure and so I put these losses down to a vagrant or perhaps a stray dog. It didn't trouble me. My main concern was the recordings, but by then I had enough material for an entire book, never mind a single chapter. Besides, I thought it better the meat was being eaten than going to waste.

It was now late on the final day and all the clairvoyants booked in had come and gone. As I was packing away the recording equipment I heard an untimely knocking in the entrance hall and so I left the dining room to investigate.

I've been somewhat derisive of the stagey showbiz appearance of some of our mediums but now, there standing in front of me, was an elderly lady who looked more like your friendly next door neighbour come round to borrow a cup of sugar than a communicator with the dead.

'I hope you don't mind, love, I let myself in. The knock you heard was on the table. I didn't mean to scare you. Oh, aren't I rude? Not introducing myself. I'm Winifred. Miss Winifred Evans. Sounds as if I should be Welsh, but I'm not. At least today. Ha! Ha!'

One of the 'means-well-but-bonkers' brigade, I thought. I've said many times that I believed I could read a woman by her smile, well, in Winifred's case her teeth didn't seem to be her own, for as she spoke, what appeared to be her dentures were troubling her. I couldn't help quietly laughing to myself as she put her fingers between her lips and made some sort of adjustment. Unlike the other visitors that week, the dress she wore was plain, I even spotted egg yolk stains down the front, and she carried a tattered canvas shopping bag in her hand. Her hair looked neat enough, thanks, I guessed, to home curlers. Wherever Winifred had come from, she'd certainly come as she was. So very normal. Only then she took from her shopping bag a copy of the book we had doctored. None of the others had done that.

I think she must have seen my look of surprise for she then said, 'Oh no, luv, I'm not here for Dear Nanny Ghost. Nor those poor kiddies. A sad tale, but that's all it is. A yarn you made up. No, I'm here for Kitty. Well, I say *for* Kitty, I mean more on *behalf* of Kitty. If you follow me? Don't worry, luv, all will become plain enough when he makes himself known.'

This wasn't making sense. Were the tables turned? Had Winifred rumbled our ruse and was she now here to make a fool of me?

'Nobody knows what he looks like,' Miss Evans then said. 'No paintings to my knowledge and he lived in a time before the black art of photography. But Kitty gave me a description of him, so, as sure as eggs is eggs, I'll recognise him when he does show. Which he will soon enough.'

Now I was completely lost. I had no idea what she was talking about. I tried to get her back on a more familiar subject.

'You're not here to communicate with Dear Nanny Ghost, then?'

'Oh dear, no. I've just said. That's an old wives' tale. Not that I'm the marrying kind,' she replied, firmly. Miss Evans then went over to an old chair, put down her shopping bag and took from it a plate of something covered with tin foil.

'I've baked some mince pies using Kitty's recipe. Well, if each has their own, it's the cook's recipe, I suppose, for being Georgian it has meat in it, which, of course, I quite like. Unnamed in the letter but Kitty tells me she was called Gladys. Not that it matters because, as I say, it's Kitty I'm here for. What with her being murdered.'

'Murdered?'

'How long ago was it now? Two hundred years? Oh my word, when you're as old as I am, you begin to lose track of time. Years come and go like hot days in summer. But, yes, Kitty was murdered. And gruesomely. I'd offer you a mince pie but it being an early nineteenth century recipe they have animal flesh in them. Being a vegetarian, you won't be wanting one, will you?'

'No,' I replied, not really thinking. It was a simple enough question, and her manner remained homely, yet everything she was saying and asking had taken on a menacing strangeness.

'I can't be a vegetarian, of course,' she went on, 'not in my line of work.'

That was my in. And my journalistic instinct came back with, 'And what is your line of work, Miss Evans?'

'Retribution. A very messy job sometimes.'

This elderly and rather frail lady then turned slightly away for a moment and began to cough and splutter. Denture trouble again? No, something else. More a clear of the throat, for she took an old handkerchief from a pocket in her dress, and, from what I could tell, spat something out. And I could have sworn that that something was moving.

Miss Evans then turned back to face me and said, 'Do excuse me, my love. They get rather enthusiastic when they sense the end. You see, for them it's feeding time.'

She again delved into her shopping bag, only this time took from it an ancient leather bound ledger, which she handed over to me.

'Read the Parish Records of 1823 for yourself. I've marked the places of relevance. They'll explain everything you need to know.'

'How did you manage to get hold of this?' I asked, opening it.

'Oh, I'm one of those women who'd rather ask forgiveness than permission. I'll return it from whence it came in due course.'

There was then a sudden clatter coming from the dining room.

'Oooh! That'll be him. Better if he didn't see me. For now. You take these mince pies, luv. We know he's hungry. Being dead for so long gives you an appetite. Ha! Ha! Oh yes, he's the one who's been eating all your meats. We were counting on it. That's why we provisioned them in the first place.'

Miss Evans kept saying 'we'. Was she somehow in cahoots with Miss Winters? No, that didn't make sense. But I was beginning to feel I had somehow been set up. Even so, I took the plate of mince-pies and walked back towards the dining room.

Before entering, I took a quick glance at the sections in the parish records that had a note by them. They stated that a Catherine Jane Wilberforce, seventeen, had married a William Seaforth Pemberton, twenty-two, in the May of 1823, but in another entry it was written that on Christmas Eve of that year Mrs Catherine Jane Pemberton had died in childbirth. I wasn't sure what any of this meant, but it made me feel very uneasy. And so when I pushed open the dining room door, I did so hesitantly, not sure what I would discover. Nothing could have prepared me for the sight of a very thin, stark naked middle-aged man, gorging himself on a joint of beef.

It must be a joke, I thought, but no one was laughing. You see, the most worrying side to this 'Miss Evans' was her unnerving veracity. And that man she said would be here now was.

The naked gentleman hadn't yet seen me and so just kept on making a pig of himself. I'd never seen a living man with such an appetite. Except this wasn't a living man, for when I looked closer I saw that his body was only partially complete. As he ferociously consumed the beef, more sinews, muscles and flesh began to form upon him, until at last, he became recognisably a robust man of being. And on seeing my plate of mince-pies, he immediately grabbed four and scoffed them down.

'Something sweet to finish,' he said, with a mouth still full. 'And one more won't harm, how can it? Hah!' he added, snatching number five from plate. 'At last, I'm myself again!'

I believe I wanted to ask '*Who are you*?' but the question that came out was, 'What are you?'

The gentleman laughed scornfully, then said, '*What* am I? Bloody *angry*, that's what I am! Who wouldn't be? I've been in this blasted house for two centuries, but has anyone ever noticed my presence? No! Then this week all these lunatics come along, who couldn't spot an elephant on stilts, nauseously proclaiming a lot of nonsense about infants drowning in a bath and some wretched girl who became worse for drink.'

'A-re... yo-ou... d-d-dead?' I asked, stumbling over the very weirdness of the question.

'My body did wither to a mere spectral presence, but as you can see young fella, I have it back now. Bone, flesh. Muscles, too. Oh, I've missed those.'

'So you're not a ghost?'

'Oh, preserve me from fools! I thought you scribblers were meant to know a thing or two. The dead come in all shapes and sizes, don't you know? I am one reconstituted. Thanks to your meats.'

'But the others never saw you.'

'I was in spirit. But those clowns! I waved, I shouted, but could they hear, sense or see me? No! So I had no choice but to become flesh once more. I will not be brushed aside. I deserve recognition.'

I then remembered what Miss Evans had just said to me.

'You're the killer. The murderer of Kitty.'

'Indeed. And I'm proud to say I got away with it, too. No impairment in saying so now. I was Catherine's – Kitty's – physician. Oh, but I was ignored even then. A doctor of fifty, disfigured by the pox. Kitty was one of the few who even dared look at me. Nobody knew how I longed for her. Wanted her. Oh, but she decided to marry some damn fool her brother brought to stay one Christmas. And he and Catherine were married by the spring. But I made sure he would not have her for long.'

'What do you mean?'

'I've told you, I was her physician. Even in the Age of Reason, there were those of us aware of the old ways. My travels had taken me to Mesopotamia and there I schooled myself in the Dark Arts. That's why I had to kill her where life begins. The morning of December the twenty-forth was when she began to bleed – and by midnight she was dead. *Harrrh*! Nothing like a corpse to spoil the merriment of Christmas!'

The door creaked open and Miss Winifred Evans entered, carrying, I noticed, a coarse hessian sheet.

'Oh, let the ancient gods defend me from yet another of your imposters!' the naked man shouted.

'What we see before us,' Miss Evans said, addressing me, 'is what we call a *revenant*, from an Old French word meaning "returning". As he's just said, our meats has now provided a corporal existence.'

Miss Evans again began to cough awkwardly, before walking over to the naked man.

'*Chuugh*! *Chuugh*!' she spluttered. 'But, having no desire to see a gentleman's undercarriage at my age, or at any age for that matter, I would ask you to kindly take this shroud – *chuugh*, *chuugh* – for modesty's sake.'

'Who is this decrepit old crone?' asked the man, throwing the hessian garment back at her.

'Oh, but his pernicious ways go beyond the iniquity of killing Kitty and her child. Is that not right, Doctor Edwards?'

On hearing his name, the naked man drew back, nervously.

'I say, what's going on here? W-w-who is this... this... hag?'

'Oh no, it's you who should be answering the questions. The big one being how you managed to avoid eternal punishment?'

The naked man stays silent.

'Cat got your tongue? Well, if you won't say, I will. It was an evil of sempiternal wickedness. He drank the sacred blood that comes from where life is born.'

As if a red hot poker, these words pierce through to my very soul and I'm not ashamed to say I lose control of myself. The Greeks have a word for it, *catharsis*, a 'purging', a 'spewing out'. Well that's what I did all over the floor. But my relief is physical only, for from that moment any spiritual cleansing has always eluded me.

'And that's how he circumvented,' Miss Evans goes on, 'the yawn of the churchyard when his time came. The two bloods – the purity of the unborn and the unconditional love of youth – became a shield to cheat divine justice. And we don't like swindlers, do we, kind sir?'

I shake my head, but say nothing. What words *are* there?

'And now our meats and pies have given him bone and flesh once more,' she goes on, 'we can turn to our purpose in coming here.'

'Our' and 'we'? My mind races. It seems Miss Evans and Miss Winters must have been working together.

The naked doctor suddenly becomes anxious and tense, for his bombastic arrogance has now deserted him.

'I wish to leave this house. Young man, you will take me with you. Yes. Take me from this place! Take me! I beg you!'

As he says this, he tries to move his legs but they will not oblige.

'Carry me out and bury me in the ground. Yes, as I am now, this flesh and blood, bury it to keep her from me!'

'Oh, I don't think so,' says Miss Evans. 'Besides, the very earth would spit you out for your crimes.'

'Then burn this house! With me in it. Dust! I am happy to be dust!'

I have said too often that I believed I could tell everything there was to know of a woman by her smile. Well, that of Miss Winifred Evans now reveals its terrible and monstrous nature. Where teeth should be, yellow maggots and purple worms writhe and twist like fiends. Her jaw drops to well below her breast and her mouth stretches to become impossibly wide. As it does so, it exhales a foul red breath that now surrounds and encases the naked man. All the time he shouts, 'No! No! No!' but it's hopeless, for the force of this grasping cloud is irresistible. *It has him*! And now it lifts him high and towards her heaving chest.

The cavernous mouth takes in the naked doctor feet first and the worms and maggots, now in their hundreds, fall upon him and eat his flesh, inch by inch, sinew by sinew. As they do, Time itself seems to become cruelly complicit in the agony, for every scream appears to go on forever.

When there is just the skeleton of his legs to see, two rows of sharp razor teeth like those of sharks grow from the monster's gums and then snap together as would a bear trap. The sound of cracking bones rattles round the room, as her jaws crunch and gnaw with ravenous appetite upon the splinters.

The cries of the naked man are shrieks of agony never heard on this earth before. And I hear them still at night in my dreams. And often in waking hours too.

I wanted to run. Break myself free, but I too was unable to move. Not even a finger. I tried to shut my eyes. But that was not possible either. Something held me. I cannot say for how long, for the passage of time could not be measured in minutes or hours. Or even days. The torture seemed eternal and lasted until every bone and sinew of the man had been consumed. Those parts of him that had fallen upon the floor were then devoured by devilish flies that came from the creature's ears and only returned when their needs were satisfied.

The ogre, or whatever this was, then closed its mouth and those lips became what once they had been. Well, not quite the same. For the face and body of the creature I saw before me had now become a woman of unrivalled splendour and beauty.

'I am the Witch of Endor,' she said. 'Necromancer. Enchantress. Read of me in the *Book of Samuel*. We are many. And you have encountered us ere this day. So now be reacquainted with ourselves!'

This unearthly being then raised its hands above its head and as it dropped them the witch became the matronly figure I recognised as my publisher, Eileen McGuffrey. She then transformed herself into another woman, who I assumed must be Dominique Doré, for she whispered with Gallic charm, '*Bonsoir, mon cheri*!' Her smile then became a row of growling wolf-teeth and as she spread her arms her lupine face became the woman I had known as Miss Aubrey Winters, only now her mouth was all fire and smoke. Finally this strangest of beasts morphed into the temptress who had set me one my way, the purring sex kitten, Elga Gumma. On our first meeting, her lips had coquettishly half-hidden her smile, but now it could be seen in its full glory, with each tooth as lustrous and as sharp as a butcher's knife. Hands again lifted into the air and as they dropped, Miss Winifred Evans stood once again before me.

'Oh, do you know, love, I used to do all that with incantations but my Aramaic isn't what it was. Besides, spells can be such a fuss and a bother, so now I stick to the sorcery of hands. Old fashioned elbow grease, you might say.'

'Where is he now? The naked doctor? Hell?'

'"Hell"? A place invented by the pious for people who have more fun in life than they do. No, the doctor's punishment is Absolute Emptiness.'

'What? Alone forever?'

'Oh, our doctor would give a thousand lives for that, for with "alone" you are at least aware that once there were others. No, Absolute Emptiness is a complete and infinite void. The most terrible retribution we know... Oh dear, listen to me wittering on. I'm not normally one for existential ponderings, but today I'll allow myself a bit of indulgence. Or should I say myselves. Ha! Ha! Ha! But we couldn't have done it without your contribution. We knew of his vanity and arrogance, but we needed to lull him into believing he was invulnerable, and the fake mediums did that.'

'But why me?'

'That chip on your shoulder. Not going to the right sort of school that gives you that leg up in life. Becoming so greedy for advancement you couldn't see past the end your own nose. And you thought yourself too clever to be tricked – but they're always the biggest fools.'

'As you... consumed him... I was unable to move. Why?'

'That roast beef sandwich was meat, but not from a cow. Oh I've eaten so many people I can't remember his name, but I saved a nice juicy slice just for you.' I would have retched again only my stomach had nothing left to give. 'Once you've partaken of human flesh with The Witch of Endor, you are hers for life.'

Miss Evans then reached into one of her pockets and brought out the red tie I had given Elga. 'This came in useful. For what purpose I will not say, but with it being red, you can't see the stains. Would you like it back? Or something else instead? As a thank you.'

The Witch then undid the top of her dress and took from between her breasts a silk lilac handkerchief braided with lace.

'Remember this? Belonged to Mr Stonehouse. Gave it to me when I visited him. He'll now change his ways. People will put it down to guilt but we both know the truth: pure Fear. It's a fancy hankie, but not a shade of purple I've ever liked, so you might as well have it.'

The Witch then placed the silk and lace in my hands.

'And as a further thank you, you have our permission to publish your book and make your money, but there must be no mention of what you have witnessed today.'

'Can I ever talk of this?'

'Well, do you know, it's a long time since I've been the leading lady in a story. Not since that first *Book of Samuel*. Elga, Eileen, Aubrey, Dominique, shall we let him? "*Yah.*" "*Yes.*" "*Yeah.*" "*Oui.*" Very well. When your own end comes you may write about the events of today and how they came about. Not that anyone will believe the ravings of a dying man. They'll think you've become the Final Fake!'

The Witch of Endor now picked up her shopping bag and looked around the decaying walls of the rectory.

'This house is at peace now and so will no longer be barren. For when those surveyors check it out again they'll find water flowing in that underground stream. A young family will move in and do it up with love and care. And within a year or so, a new life will be born where Kitty once slept. I am not, you see, the monster many people think.'

The Witch then paused and thought for a moment.

'Oh, that's right. We've run of out tea. Oh, Winifred, you'll have to stop off at the corner shop on your way home if you fancy that brew with your feet up.'

TOP SECRET

THE RETURN OF THE HANDBAG

As told by The Infamous Lady Herself

'I AM SPEAKING TO YOU FROM the Cabinet Room at 10 Downing Street. This morning the British Ambassador in Berlin handed the German government a final note stating that unless we heard from them by eleven o'clock that they were prepared at once to withdraw their troops from Poland, a state of war would exist between us. I have to tell you now that no such undertaking has been received, and that consequently this country is at war with Germany.'

My father could stand it no more and immediately switched off the wireless, saying to me, 'Margaret Hilda Roberts, we shall hear no more from him, for that is the voice of a lily-livered appeaser.'

It had belonged, of course, to the then Prime Minister, Mr Neville Chamberlain.

'My only regret,' my father continued, 'is not to have sent that coward a white feather, as General Kitchener would have done in the Great War. And now, for the want of a true and strong leader, we face another.'

As my pen puts the ink on the paper, a terrible storm is howling outside the walls of Downing Street. The winds are so blustery they are reaching the very bottom of the chimney in what was my office, but the secret diary just released has now allowed me to write my history, which, in a way, began that fateful Sunday morning in 1939, a few days before my fourteenth birthday. The weather then was rather subdued, but I do remember it being very cold and chilly, for my father never lit the fire on the Sabbath, or any other day for that matter. 'A vest may warm a man as well as coal,' he would say. Not a quotation from the Scriptures, but I always felt it deserved to be.

'Margaret Hilda,' my father went on, after the embarrassment of the awful broadcast, 'we will now kneel down and ask the Good Lord that one day this United Kingdom of ours will be blessed with a Prime Minister who is not afraid to stand up to dictators.'

Goodness me, little did I think as I was on my knees over those three hours that one day I would *be* that Prime Minister. And I like to believe that prayer of Mr Roberts, for that is what I always called my father, helped bring me to 10 Downing Street some forty years later in 1979. And it is in that very house where I write these words today. Yes, remarkable as it may seem, I'm still here. Of course I died, but when my critics were asked 'What sort of gravestone to give Mrs Thatcher?' and the answer came back: 'A very, very heavy one.' Well, I have to say it wasn't quite heavy enough.

You see, The Lady *is* for Returning!

Perhaps you could say that 10 Downing Street has become, as it were, my spiritual home. As you are probably aware, this house is the main residence of the Prime Minister of the United Kingdom, but Downing Street is also the central office of Government. One lives – how shall we put it – 'above the shop'. This always came naturally to me, for my father ran a corner store in Grantham in Lincolnshire which was also our family home. What a joy it was to share a bedroom with sacks of salt, knowing that each grain would be carefully weighed before being put into a brown paper packet and sold at a modest profit of four hundred and fifty-two per cent.

10 Downing Street is, it should be said, a much larger residence – in truth, it's several houses knocked together – and within it there

are over two hundred rooms spread across five floors. Unfortunately the building was constructed on a swamp, and with shallow foundations, and so for the last three hundred years has needed constant propping up. For some reason my husband Denis now comes to mind... oh yes, I remember – the original land, owned by the Abbot of Abingdon, was drained so they could build a brewery on it. And that's why perhaps the first thing Denis did when we arrived in May 1979 was have a dig around in the cellar.

Sadly, due to being constructed on shoddy foundations, the outside walls of Downing Street still bulge out considerably – most of my Chancellors had the same problem – and although the land was never paid for – it was confiscated by Henry the Eighth, though socialists, I suppose, would call that 'nationalisation'! – if one adds the maintenance costs over the years it works out to be, without doubt, the most expensive house in London. Yet it's a residence that offers no security of tenure. I was shown the door myself in 1990 or 'cut off at the stocking tops', as Denis so colourfully put it. Booted out by those I thought would be loyal to a Prime Minister who had won three elections and served her country for over eleven and a half years. I learnt that night that the most dangerous colour in politics wasn't red but grey.

Oh, but that was all long ago. Another century. But my many ghostly years in this house have allowed me a time of contemplation and reflection. And now as the rain hits hard against my window, I feel it is time to write my history and reveal the truth behind all my years in Downing Street.

Two or three centuries ago, who got the job was more by accident of birth than capability. Prime Ministers came from the era of aristocratic privilege where men – and it always was men – possessed a belief that they were born to rule. Even in 1902, Arthur Balfour essentially inherited his premiership from his uncle Robert, the 3rd Marquess of Salisbury – hence the expression 'Bob's your uncle'. And I had a few historical leftovers in my Cabinet, my 'Grandees' I called them. Do you know, they treated me as though I were the under house parlour maid. Oh, but I took great pleasure in reminding them who was boss. 'You're fired!', I would say.

Apparently, this has now become what entertainment persons call a catchphrase. But, like privatisation, the Poll Tax, the free market economy, cruise missiles, Clause 28, and all other good things, I thought of it first!

There are those who begin their premiership in the springtime of vitality, only for their world to turn in a breath to a dead winter. I witnessed that with Anthony Eden, the golden boy who became the broken man, and historians would point to the Earl of Rosebery, who by the end needed morphine to help him sleep. Never a problem for me because I always kept by my beside the collected speeches of my Foreign Secretary.

Historically, there are those Prime Ministers one might call tail-enders, those who simply run out of road. In my lifetime, I saw that with Alec Douglas-Home and my predecessor Jim Callaghan. Then there are those who 'break the eggs' but never have the chance 'to make their omelette'. George Canning, the last Prime Minister to fight a duel at dawn, was forced to step down after only a few months due to ill health. Incidentally, on the subject of eggs, any housewife will tell you hard-boiled is best. Far less washing up. If only Mr Canning had thought of that!

Yet, what matters most in a leader is how you take charge. Some preside rather than rule and prefer beneficence of heart over hardness of head. Well, it won't surprise you to learn I was not that sort of Prime Minister! No! No! No! Never seek the prize without the battle. Set the objective and put in place the strategy to achieve it. And I did it all in heated rollers before I made my husband's breakfast. Even the great Sir Robert Peel couldn't say that!

Some of my predecessors I admired tremendously, but most were a sorry lot. And I can say that with some certainty, for in my years in Downing Street I encountered most of them. But before I reveal too much of that, let me say a few more words about Downing Street itself.

As well as being one's office and home, Number Ten is a place for entertainment and receptions, though due to the unreliability of the floorboards, there's always a limit on numbers attending. What is less known is that Downing Street is also, in a manner of speaking, an art gallery, where the Prime Minister of the day – or in my case the entire decade! – selects paintings from the national collection to hang on the wall. This you could say is where my ghostly tale really begins, for it was something I did back in 1979, during my first days as PM, which ultimately allowed for my spiritual return.

The art a Prime Minister chooses reflects, I think, their personality and preferences. Edward Heath, the man I replaced as leader of the Conservative Party, insisted on Renoirs. Frivolous and, worse still, French. I can't stand their paintings or their cooking, for when the French say they could eat a horse, they actually mean it! No, when I entered Downing Street I insisted on portraits of British achievers. The whole point of art is the subject on the canvas and so I demanded scientists such as Michael Faraday, inventors like Humphrey Davy and engineers of the calibre of Isambard Kingdom Brunel. Yes, I brought back the Victorian Age to Britain. Soon the walls of Downing Street were chock-a-block with men of purpose and determination. Just like me.

However, one day, as I was walking down the long corridor that leads from the Entrance Hall to the Cabinet Room discussing arrangements for the visit of some President or other, I noticed two doors. I stopped to ask one of my civil servants where they led.

'Er, nowhere, Prime Minister,' Sir James replied.

'Poppycock!' said I. 'Doors must lead somewhere. That is the purpose of doors!'

'Well, this door, Prime Minister, takes you into the cleaner's cupboard.'

'The cleaner's cupboard!' I said, somewhat incredulously. 'And the second door?'

'Er, that I believe,' said Sir Edward, 'if Sir James would allow me to demonstrate, takes one into a telephone booth.'

Sir Edward then took out his keys and the door was unlocked and opened.

'Ah yes,' said Sir James. 'Sir Edward is right. That, as you can see, is a telephone.'

'I know what telephones looks like!' I told them. 'I have a portrait of the man who invented them hanging in my study. The point is, gentlemen, we must avoid the President of Wherever-it-is accidentally opening this door and finding a load of dustpans and brushes.'

'I understand, Prime Minister,' said Sir James. 'You don't want him thinking that's where you keep your broomstick.'

One of the junior civil servants started to giggle at this, though why a discussion about domestic cleaning appliances should have caused such mirth I cannot say. However, within days both cupboard and booth were gone and in their place was an alcove, where there was now room for a small sculpture of Sir Isaac Newton, and on the wall I suggested a looking-glass to give the area a greater sense of space. And that very mirror was where I found myself upon my earthly demise, which became, you might say, a passing *into* rather than a passing *over*.

Oh, but that mirror was cursed! For one thing I was unable to escape its frame and, secondly, although I could be stared at all day, I was never seen by anyone looking into the glass. Trapped and invisible! That would change, but before we reach that point in my history, I believe a brief tour of some of the main rooms in Downing Street would be appropriate. After all, if one haunts a house, the very least one can do is to show one's guests around.

As with most ghostly spirits I am unable to leave the building in which I reside, but I am able to take you as far as that famous front door. A bobby has stood on guard outside Number Ten ever since the First World War. In recent years it's a role that has become more for show, because nowadays they let in any old riff-raff. Even Liberals. The door itself, with that wonderful lion-head knocker, opens onto the Entrance Hall, with its distinct chequered black and white floor. My favourite feature, there in the corner, is a leather Chippendale hall-porter seat, with a pull-out drawer underneath. I did look inside once and immediately regretted it. A collection of scurrilous postcards. The type, shall we say, that are unlikely ever to see a stamp.

But let's now leave the lobby and take a walk down the long corridor which leads us into the Cabinet Ante Room. It's here that ministers gather before a Cabinet meeting. It was always such fun to listen at the door and hear them shaking in their boots. And now the Cabinet Room itself.

Strictly speaking, 10 Downing Street is the abode of The First Lord of the Treasury, but by custom this title is taken by whomsoever is the Prime Minister. Robert Walpole, as First Lord, was given the house by George II, but he gifted it to his successors and it is for that reason his portrait hangs on the wall. Eyebrows like hairy caterpillars and a gross double chin! I was always grateful I sat with my back to the man.

The Cabinet Room, so called after the secure retreat built into many an Elizabethan House, is much smaller than you might expect and is dominated by a table that Harold Macmillan described as shaped like a boat or coffin, depending on his mood. The Prime Minister's chair, the only one with arms, is traditionally left pulled away at an angle from the table in readiness. Quite right too. One is, as I have often said, always on the job. But let's now leave the Cabinet Room and go up the famous three-sided staircase, which has on its wall photographs or engraved-prints of every British Prime Minister, a tradition that began in 1907. And what a bunch of nincompoops most of them were.

From the landing at the top we enter the largest of the State Drawing Rooms, the Pillared Room, so named because of its ionic supporting columns. On the walls are several ornate mirrors, including a Chippendale with two illuminating candles. From here we can walk straight through to the room that is always referred to by the colour it is painted. Two of my successors had so many disagreeable young urchins running amok that for a while it was known as 'The Green Crayon and Red Pencil Room', with scribble all over the walls such as **UR DAD IS A WUSS** and **FIBS RULE OK**. It was here I would meet all the important world leaders, and occasionally President Mitterrand. You may even recognise, from television interviews, the marble face of the innocent young man at the centre of the mantel panel of the charming white marble fireplace.

And now, as we pass by these baroque gold leaf mirrors, we enter the third and smallest of the State Drawing Rooms known as the White Room. Here again is a marble fireplace, including a moulding of that same young man. This enchanting room, a favourite of mine, overlooks St James's Park, and several Prime Ministers insisted on using it as their bedroom. One such was Sir Henry Campbell-Bannerman, who passed away in this very spot. 'Doctor out, priest in,' as the saying went. His final words – strangely prophetic – were, 'You haven't seen the last of me!' Indeed we had not, as you shall discover.

Well, although the briefest of tours, perhaps now you can understand my frustration. All those rooms, all those mirrors, so much to see and hear, yet there was I, encased in a looking-glass in a tiny alcove in a corridor where people just walked by. Of course, I tried to make my presence known by waving my hands and even on occasion slightly raising my voice. But to no avail. Only one evening everything changed.

You see, it happened there was a reception for those in the theatre profession to celebrate the unique tradition of British pantomime. All rather silly. I won't reveal which Prime Minister came up with the idea, but I need only use the word 'clown'. Goodness me, what an array of bizarre costumes. Dick Whittington, Mother Goose, Aladdin, Abanazar, and, I overheard someone say, a character called Fleshcreep, though I later discovered they were actually referring to the Health Secretary. The last to arrive was a group of characters from *Snow White*, including several dwarfs and a woman in a very elaborate red headdress, who I assumed was the Wicked Stepmother. And I was right, for, noticing my little alcove, she couldn't resist coming over and saying, 'Mirror, mirror on the wall, who is the fairest of them all?' and I in turn replied, 'Not you, dear! I am always the fairest in this house – and my name is Lady Thatcher!' The poor dear fainted. Fell straight to the floor. Clearly she had both seen and heard me. And the dwarfs would have too, had they been taller, but I suppose if they were they wouldn't be dwarfs. Not that any of that matters, for the point is, I could now, if I wished, make myself known to every passerby, and, much more importantly, I discovered I had the ability to reside in any mirror in the house. From then on, when people read in the newspapers of ministers leaving Government due to stress or overwork, I can reveal it was nothing of the sort. Their mental breakdown came as a result of a telling off from me inside the glass. One poor chap, a rather dull man whose name I forget, even went on record as saying he found the image of me on the wall 'unsettling'. He pretended he meant my painted portrait, but we both know the truth. Anyway, being able to be in any mirror in the house opened up whole new worlds, but not always pleasurable ones.

I discovered, with no great surprise, that the male of the species tends to look at himself far more often and longer than the female. We ladies may occasionally check our lipstick or hair, but heavens above, the vanity of the male sex is quite extraordinary. Not that I wished to be privy to their narcissism, but one morning, I found myself in a mirror unknown to me. Although I resided in Downing Street for eleven and a half years, for obvious reasons I had never visited the gentlemen's lavatory near the Cabinet Room. One could hear it, of course, for its ancient plumbing had the loudest flush in Christendom. But really! I could just about cope with witnessing the Chancellor of the Exchequer picking spinach from his teeth – one's faith in sound money was not completely destroyed – but as for what the Justice Secretary got up to with that delegate from the Tasmanian Chamber of Commerce – well, I did not think such things were physically possible. However, I couldn't look away, for we spirits are unable to close our eyes and, as I have said, I was still confined within the glass of the mirror. But again, that was about to change.

One evening, while I was in that lovely Chippendale mirror in the Pillared Room, there was a large gathering – some sort of bilateral reception for German businessmen and politicians – and it happened that the Downing Street butlers had lit those two candles either side of the glass. In front stood two well-fed German bankers discussing the state of the British economy. Now when I was a young girl, there were many German refugees in Grantham and so my knowledge of the language has always been much better than I ever admitted, so I understood all that was being said. And there were some very derogatory comments. I did not wish to be the cause of a diplomatic incident, but as they mocked and sneered, I grew angrier and angrier – *Ich bin stinksauer*! – and with my huffing and puffing the candles blew out. Never before had any part of me managed to get beyond the glass. The German bankers, of course, only laughed louder and pointed to the candles and made more disparaging remarks about the uselessness of British technology. One of them then took out his gold lighter and started to flick it, but I continued to blow so hard he couldn't get the flame to stay. German efficiency is no match for British determination! Thankfully, a butler saw the situation and intervened saying, 'Allow me try a Swan Vesta, sir.' Of course, I then stopped my blowing and the candlewick acquiesced to his match. Oh, the red faces of those German bankers was a joy to behold!

After the reception, when everyone had left, I tried putting my hands through the glass and found to my pleasant surprise that they reached well beyond the candles. Oh, if only there were a full-length mirror, then I could escape my captivity by stepping out of it, however at that particular time there were none in Downing Street.

But then a stroke of good fortune. The large Soanes Dining Room, named after Sir John Soanes who refurbished it in 1825, had been undergoing a restoration that was now complete and so the two full-length mirrors were put back in place on the oak panelling. One day I found myself manifesting in one of them and, to my great satisfaction and relief, there was my trusty handbag at my side. I wasted no time in crossing over the threshold of the frame and onto the newly-polished floor and that meant I was now able to roam freely all over the house.

Just rejoice! Rejoice at that news!

Now you may think it odd, as I have been telling my story, that I showed no surprise in discovering myself to be a ghost. Well, the simple truth is, in my last years in office here in Downing Street, I encountered numerous apparitions of previous Prime Ministers. I even kept a secret diary, but before I reveal its pages, let me tell you when and how these strange visitations began.

It was 1988, a few nights before Christmas, and I had decided to spend the evening in the White Room, that State Drawing Room I mentioned overlooking St James's Park. My own study was a little too small for a Christmas tree and so Denis and I always put up our decorations in the White Room. That evening Denis said he was, in his own words, 'going AWOL with some golfing chums', and so I sat alone on the settee opening Christmas cards. One of my predecessors, Spencer Perceval, was assassinated by an angry voter because he didn't reply to his petition, so woe betide a PM who doesn't attend to her postbag! Unusually for me, I was having a glass of port instead of my regular whisky. More seasonal, I thought. One correspondent, who, from the postmark, lived in a far away place called Sunderland, had sent me a charming hand painted Christmas card of Ebenezer Scrooge with the inscription 'Thinking of you'. Such kind words, but I don't remember where in the story he had his head chopped off. But perhaps whoever had sent it, for some reason the note was unsigned, was aware that my own grandfather, who I admired tremendously, was in fact called Ebenezer.

As I was perusing my Christmas cards, the chimes of midnight struck. I then looked up and my eyes happened to rest upon the moulding in the fireplace. It was the face of that young man I spoke of earlier. Now, I must have seen that face day and night for much of my residency here at Downing Street and I'm sure you will agree that I have little of what once was called 'fancy' about me. Put plainly, I do not imagine things that aren't there. Let it also be borne in mind that, although I had seen all those portraits of previous Prime Ministers, I hadn't given any of them much thought over the last eight or nine years. And yet, as I stared at the mantel panel, I saw in the marble, without its undergoing any intermediate process of change, not a moulding of a young man but the face of William Pitt the Elder. Yet, as I looked fixedly at this phenomenon, it suddenly became a marble moulding again. To say that I was not startled would be untrue, so I went over and looked more closely. Goodness me, it once again became the face of William Pitt. And, to my astonishment, the phantom spoke.

'I say, are you the new cook? Bit of a scrawny creature, aren't you? Never trust a thin cook, what?'

I must admit I was quite taken aback by this and for a moment or two, unable to respond. Eventually I falteringly replied, 'No, sir, I am not the cook. Er, I am in fact, the, er...'

'Spit it out, woman!' he interrupted.

'Prime Minister!'

'Yes, I am. I am, indeed. That's why it's so damned impertinent you coming into the drawing room and helping yourself to my port, what?! But since you've opened a bottle, I wouldn't mind a glass myself. Go on over and pour it, woman! To the brim, to the brim.'

'Yes,' I replied, 'if that's what you want.'

'And my son next door, the other William Pitt, I'm sure he wouldn't say no to a glass. Ha! Ha! Not the sort of chap to leave a party before midnight, what?! What?!'

'William Pitt the Younger is next door?'

'Well, where else would he be? Better view of the Parade, he tells me. Always had an odd curiosity for tall guardsmen. I say, are you going to get those damn glasses of port or not, what?! What?!'

Even when in the strangest of situations, one has been brought up to maintain good manners, so I went over to the corner table and poured two glasses. As I did so, the double doors to the adjoining room swung open of their own accord, and yes, there in the moulding of the fireplace I saw the face of William Pitt the Younger.

'You can't be the Second Lieutenant?' he bellowed. 'Besides, I haven't finished with the first one yet! Oh! He knows how to stand to attention, if you get my drift! Haa!'

At that moment Denis came in and saw what was in my hands.

'I say, Old Girl, I know I've had a few, but am I really seeing double? Two glasses of port? Steady on.'

'They're not for me, they are for William Pitt the Elder and William Pitt the Younger.'

However, when I nodded towards to the faces in fireplaces both Pitts had become marble mouldings again.

'Corrupts the mind, does port,' said Denis, looking somewhat confused. 'Take it easy, eh? Mustn't work too hard, you know.'

I must admit, I did wake up next morning with a slight headache and so that's exactly what I put those silly visions down to: a bad bottle. For the rest of that Christmas, spent thankfully at Chequers, I kept to my regular whisky, saw no more ghosts and thought little more about the incident. But it was after one particularly difficult Cabinet meeting that the situation changed. And not for the better.

It was now 1989 and there were, shall we say, a growing number of political problems to be dealt with ranging from exceptionally high interest rates and worries about growing unemployment to the response of the Commonwealth to my vetoing sanctions on apartheid

South Africa. The Russians had once dubbed me *Zheleznaya Dama*, or Iron Maiden, the medieval instrument of torture enclosure with sharp spikes. Of course, I turned that intended insult to applause and acclaim when I called myself the Iron Lady. Oh, but my ferrous metal was certainly coming under pressure that year.

I had stayed in the Cabinet Room after the meeting to look over the latest trade figures, which were not at all encouraging, when I suddenly heard a voice. At first, I thought it was the Trade Secretary returning to discuss the numbers, but on glancing up I discovered standing over me none other than Herbert Asquith.

'My darling Venetia!' he said, taking my arm. 'Do I find you reading one of my passionate love letters?'

Now the private lives of politicians have never interested me in the slightest, but it was common knowledge that Asquith, who had been Prime Minister in the Edwardian era, kept a mistress called Venetia Stanley and clearly this ghostly Herbert thought I was she. I hoped that by closing my eyes the phantom would disappear, and it did, only when I opened them, in its place was a prostrate William Gladstone – those Victorian sideburns were unmistakable – flagellating himself in his underdrawers.

'*Ahh! Ahh! Ahh! Ahhh!* Tempt me not with your body! Cover your bosom, Madam! You are a lady of the night, lost to the devil. But I will save you! *Ahh! Ahh! Ahh!*'

It is a historical fact that Gladstone often brought prostitutes back to Downing Street in the hope of saving them from their shameful life. However, though the neckline of my dress was a little lower than usual, for the day was somewhat warm, one does not expect, when one is leader of Her Majesty's government, to be taken for a floozy. There are those who might think I should have been flattered, for Mr Gladstone, looking, I must say, every single one of his eighty-four years, continued to stare at my upper half, whipping his hind quarters as if he were some poor horse on Derby Day. I said to him, as firmly as I could, 'Would you kindly stop thrashing yourself into a frenzy while gawping at my bosoms!' So preoccupied was I by the apparition, I hadn't noticed as I said this that the Trade Secretary had indeed returned, and, by an unfortunate coincidence, had his hands deep inside his trouser pockets. I cannot say for certain exactly what he was doing – clearly Mr Gladstone was invisible to him – but the Minister immediately offered his profuse apologies and went on say that he had a secret devotion for me, and, if fortune were to smile, would consider leaving his wife. What a ridiculous notion! In the next reshuffle I had no choice but to put him on the naughty step by sending him to Northern Ireland.

It was after that distressing encounter with Asquith and Gladstone that I decided to keep a secret diary of all these ghostly visitations. Some were even written while the phantoms were present in the room. There were far too many manifestations to include every single one of them, but what follows offers you some indication of their odd and often appalling behaviour:

26th October, 1989

Extraordinary! I write this in my study. I have just this moment returned from a meeting with my Private Secretary. On leaving his office, I noticed the colour on the walls of the Cabinet Ante room had changed and so too the pattern on the carpet.

The bust of Winston Churchill has disappeared and in its place is one of Sir Robert Peel. But that is not the most miraculous occurrence, for over in the corner by a ticker tape machine, I see a bald man whom I immediately recognise as Clement Attlee. As it prints out its dispatch he says in that doleful voice I remember from his broadcasts after the war, 'Denis Compton. A century. Good man.' Not a Prime Minister whose words ever flew on wings. But then he moves towards the closed double doors that lead into the Cabinet Room and – my word! – simply floats through them as if they aren't there!

5th April, 1990

A note written in The White Room as the events occur.

I haven't encountered a Prime Ministerial phantom for several weeks now, but it's just struck midnight and suddenly a large bed has appeared in front of me. No ghostly corpus as yet, but I fear the worst for I smell pipe smoke in the air. Could it be Harold Wilson?

No! His pipe was for the public, in private he preferred cigars. Someone more historical! Oh my word! It's Stanley Baldwin under the sheets, puffing away and reading some cheap detective novel. 'The maid did it,' he is saying. 'Should have known. German. Never trust the Boche.' I nearly said, 'I agree with you!' but previous intercourse with ghosts did not go well, so I keep my powder dry.

Oh! The eiderdown is turning from turquoise to scarlet and as Stanley Baldwin disappears, Sir Henry Campbell-Bannerman takes his place. Yes! The same Sir Henry who died in this very room in 1908. 'I told them they hadn't seen the last of me!' he cries, as his head drops to the pillow. Good Heavens! It's now popped up again! 'I told you they hadn't seen the last of me!' Oh! And the head goes down once more... No it hasn't, it's up again... 'I told you they hadn't seen the last of me!' He's more like a yo-yo than a ghost!

Oh, but the eiderdown is changing colour. Royal blue... and under it is a man in a tin hat, wearing a golden dragon dressing gown. Oh! My hero! Winston Churchill! Oh and I can even hear doodlebugs flying overhead. The Great Man looks at me. 'Are you the new girl?' he says. 'Shorthand is all well and good but I like 'em pretty, too. And what do they call you, girl, eh?' I couldn't help myself, 'Roberts, sir,' I reply, offering to him my maiden name. 'Well, hand me that bottle of Pol Roger 1934. It's going to be that sort of night.' It was then that a furry black cat emerged from under the covers. 'Ah, Nelson,' said Mr Churchill. 'I wondered where you'd got to.' Next came the head of Stanley Baldwin, followed once again by Sir Henry Campbell-Bannerman. It's like that old song we sang at school: 'Four in the bed and the Little One said, "Roll over, roll over".'

But now they all fade away, except for Winston's pet feline, whose grin lingers like that of the Cheshire Cat.

Oh! Let me not be mad, sweet heaven, let me not be mad...

9th September, 1990

The Library.

What a very peculiar and very disconcerting experience! No ghost has ever appeared here before, but two just did! The Library is a place I've always avoided, for it overlooks Downing Street and one doesn't want to be caught out by the prying eyes of journalists and television cameras. However, as I was passing down the corridor that leads to Number 11, I heard crowds cheering. Not for me, I thought, as we were very down in the polls. The Library door was open and there, leaning out of the window onto the street, I see a man in tailcoats waving a piece of paper and saying, 'Peace in our time.' Neville Chamberlain! I immediately recall my father's words about that lily-livered appeaser and the sudden temptation to push him out of the window is simply too much. He's only a ghost, I think, he's already dead, so what harm could it do? And so over I go and push as hard as I can, only then I find my hands are on the posterior of a Downing Street footman, who turns to me and says, 'Oh, Mrs Thatcher! I'm very flattered but what would Denis say?'

I make some excuse about seeing some dirt on his tails. Odd, as I thought only Buckingham Palace footmen wore those. Oh, but I've been so preoccupied lately, maybe they changed the rules without me even realising. I ask the young man, whose face I must say is very familiar, what he is doing leaning out of the window and he tells me he has been wiping off what he calls the 'judgement of the pigeons'. I try to be polite, so ask him if he's worked here long. 'Oh yes, centuries,' he says. 'I'll outlive you!' And with that he flounces off.

Such brazen behaviour, but I have no time to argue, for I'm keen to know what's happening outside, as the crowd is still cheering. When I look out of the window, everyone is dressed in knee breeches and, good heavens above, there's the Duke of Wellington arriving on his horse, Copenhagen! A second later, I hear a horn and turn towards the street entrance and see Arthur Balfour arriving in a motor car, the first Prime Minister ever to do so. I very nearly say to myself out loud, 'I wonder who'll be next' only then, from a corner of my eye, I spot a BBC television camera crew – and suddenly the spell is broken, the cheering crowd disappears and the street is empty, except for those wretched pinkos, as Denis calls them.

Postscript – one week later. I've been keeping my eye out for that insubordinate young footman, but no sightings as yet.

Post Postscript – a month has passed. The footman must have left, as there hasn't been sight nor sound of him since. I do so hope he was fired. Outlive me, indeed!

Over my final eighteen months in Downing Street, the Prime Ministers immortalised in those photographs and engraved-prints on walls up the staircase all began to speak to me and I kept a note of each interaction and the date beside it.

9th July 1989
Passing the picture of Earl Grey, one might expect the odour of aromatic tea but, instead, one is greeted with the stink of dirty nappies. *Postscript* – No wonder! For I discover he had seventeen children! Thank heaven I had two at once and got it over with.

16th October 1989
Difficult to tell if the picture of Sir Alec Douglas-Home is a phantom or not, for his skull always made him look like a dead man even on one of his better days. But no doubt this morning, for as I walked passed, I saw two worms wriggle out of his nose and then promptly return inside through a hole where his ears used to be.

19th October 1989
A lesson learnt: when passing David Lloyd George, stick close to the banister; tonight he goosed me! Oh, that saucy hand was quick! Back in the frame before you could say '*Iechyd da*!' Welsh Wizard, indeed!

4th November 1989
Ramsay MacDonald has gone missing from his picture. He'll be lost in an empty corridor somewhere, like a lone man at a grave.

21st April 1990
Benjamin Disraeli is getting very tiresome. There is always a clever remark about the unsuitability of women for high office. 'Does your husband know you're here?' the portrait smirked just now. Well that was the last straw. I couldn't help myself. I said, 'General Elections.

I won three and lost none. You won one, but lost two. Very careless.' That wiped the supercilious smile off his face! However, what the President of Mexico, whom I was accompanying up the staircase at the time, thought of this I am unable to reveal, as he spoke no English. So, for once, I can honestly say, 'Thank God for foreigners!'

11th July 1990

It is a well-known fact that I have never liked men with beards, as to me it suggests they're hiding something and so not to be trusted. But that dislike has just grown to loathing, for as I passed the Marquis of Salisbury, the last Prime Minister to sport full facial hair, I saw hundreds of lice, dripping from his annoying beard onto a newly vacuumed carpet.

Postscript – At today's Cabinet Meeting there was a lot of fidgeting going on underneath the table that soon became endless scratching. It was then I realised those lice had found a new home around that intimate area of gentlemen where angels fear to tread. Luckily, my M&S stockings, being so smooth and silky, offered me immunity from their ascent. That's proper feminism for you!

IT MAY BE THAT YOU are wondering why, as I've been a-haunting myself, I haven't encountered any of the ghosts I met when I was alive. Well, it seems that's just the way things are with spirits. However, it does bring me to a confession I feel I must make.

As a democrat, one accepts the great British tradition of dissent and protest. Nevertheless, defacing public property is still a wrong-doing. However, what can easily be washed off with a damp cloth can hardly be regarded as a vindictive act of vandalism. And here I must hold my hand up, for when I became a ghost myself, I decided to get my own back on all those years of mockery. I went to that three-cornered staircase and drew Stalin moustaches on all the Socialists, using some mascara I found in my handbag. I then, with some lipstick, painted red noses on all those from my own party I considered namby-pambies. Disraeli got the biggest dollop and was made to look as if he belonged in the circus. I would have drawn a white feather on Chamberlain, only the afterlife hadn't provided me with anything suitable, so I had to settle on making him cross-eyed with the point of an old eye-liner pen. Of course, not all the Prime Ministers were subject to my facial daubs. Winston was exempt, obviously, the Duke of Wellington also, and since I'd read that Lord Palmerstone believed that 'cordite was the essential instrument of diplomacy,' he was excluded too.

But back to those notes written in my secret diary when I was alive. What would happen, I wondered, if the diary fell into the wrong hands? People would think that in my final years in office I had gone potty.

Although I kept the diary in a locked drawer in my study, all papers, notes and records in Downing Street, including those one puts in the waste paper basket, are carefully examined in case important papers might be accidentally thrown away. So, what to do with the diary? Inspiration came from an unexpected source.

In October 1990, I was working late one night in my study when all of a sudden the electric lights went out and the room became illuminated only by candles. Oh no, I thought, I'm going to be visited by Ted Heath, only remembered now for sending the country into darkness during the 1970s with all those endless power cuts. However, I then heard someone scrabbling about on the floor. I looked over my desk and there beneath was Lord North, the late eighteenth century prime minister.

'I've lost it!' he cried. 'I've lost it. He'll be very angry and upset.'

'Who will?' I asked.

'The King! King George!'

'Well, what exactly have you lost?'

'America, of course. Don't just sit there, woman, come round and help me find it. Look over there, by the fireplace.'

I had discovered by now that disagreeing with ghosts makes them very irksome, so to humour him I got on my hands and knees and crawled across the room to the fireplace, but whom should I find there, also on his knees, but Harold Macmillan, the prime minister who gave me my first job as frontbencher in the 1961. Mr Macmillan, always a rather charming man, today looked somewhat anxious. In his hands were some papers and he was using one of the candles to set light to them. 'Pages from the diary I wrote during the Suez Crisis when I was Foreign Secretary,' he said. 'The Suez Canal was ours, but the Egyptians, the blighters, nabbed it. Sent in troops, but Uncle Sam let us down and that led to an ignoble retreat and the last throw of the dice of the British Empire. And these diaries tell the sorry tale. Now I'm Prime Minister, I must burn them, for, my dear, one should never let history in on one's failures.'

Then I had it! I would burn my secret diary there and then. So I took it from the locked drawer in my desk, returned to the fireplace, and put the flame of one of the candles against its pages. As I did this, I felt what I thought to be a cold draught, for the candle blew out. But there were others on the mantelpiece, so I took one of those and put that to the diary. Only that flame blew out as well. This unexplainable draught was getting worse.

I then turned round and to my astonishment, there in the room were dozens of former Prime Ministers all puffing as hard as they could to prevent me from setting the paper alight, with Edward Heath at the front blowing the hardest! Worse, the combined power turned it into such an almighty gust that the diary flew out of my hands and went straight up the chimney. And there it has stayed until today and the arrival of that raging storm I spoke of earlier.

You see, that howling wind blew a blast so strong down the chimney that it somehow released the diary from its inner chamber. And that is why I have been able to include them in my history.

But if I don't want them to be known, why am I writing these words, you may ask? .

To fool you! Yes, you, Disraeli! And you, Lloyd George, you old Welsh goat! And you, Wilson and Callaghan and Attlee! And most of all you, Mr Edward 'Nancy Boy' Heath. I know you are all there watching me over my shoulder right now. I can't see you, but I feel your presence. You all believe this curious history of mine is going to be found and published. Well I've fooled you! I've only been writing it to make you think that. For I am now going to burn these papers and my secret diary. Oh look, there in the grate! I don't know where that came from, but someone has made a fire. That makes it all so much easier because now I'm going to...

And that is where Lady Thatcher's written testament from beyond the grave ends. What followed, after I snatched the pen from her hand, would simply be too distressing for mere mortals to read. Let me just say that the Lady was removed from this room and taken, kicking and screaming, to 'another place'.

Who then am I? On one point, Lady Thatcher was right: we were all standing over her at the end. You see, I embody all those whose lives were lessened or lost during her tenure in this house. I am the miner whose community was destroyed. I am the gay sixteen-year-old schoolboy when Clause 28 was made law. I am the woman who died waiting for a hospital bed. I am the Greenham Common peace protester, violently struck down to the ground for exercising my rights. I am the Argentinean conscript, barely eighteen, who forfeited my life on Las Islas Malvinas. I am all these and more. Not one person, but many. And I am also, if you haven't yet guessed, the footman in tails and the young man whose face became enshrined in marble. For I am The True Spirit of Downing Street.

Most Prime Ministers upon leaving office experience regret, remorse, doubt, and in death they become haunted by those things they ought to have done and by those things they should not. But Lady Thatcher, oh no, with her I have only witnessed self pity and silly spiteful tricks. And so she had to be removed from Downing Street against her will for the second time. I shall not go into detail as to the pain and anguish she experienced, but let me put it like this: the many breaths of everyone of her predecessors helped fanned the flames. One can hide one's mistakes from history, but not from the house that has seen it all.

Mrs Thatcher's Press Secretary would, each day, fill her in on the stories in that morning's newspaper. Overleaf is one from *The Chronicle* that she will never read, but perhaps you may find it of interest.

THE CHRONICLE

The Lady Is Not For Burning

■ **by OUR CORRESPONDENT**

"It's a funny old world" was the last thing Mrs Thatcher said to her Cabinet on the day of her resignation in 1990.

And if she were alive today she might want to say the same.

With perhaps the addition of the word 'inexplicable'.

On Tuesday night, a Downing Street security officer, as she was patrolling the garden at the north west of the building, is reported to have spotted a blazing fire on the first floor. This was identified as the Thatcher Room, which during her decade as PM, Mrs Thatcher used as her private study.

Yet here at *The Chronicle,* we have learned there was more than one witness to the mysterious blaze, for there were others both outside and in who claimed to have smelled burning.

One went so far as to say they could detect sulphur. Another witness we spoke to said she could clearly hear a woman screaming in agony inside the room, but this has not been corroborated by Downing Street sources.

However, when the Thatcher Room was quickly entered, with fire extinguishers at the ready, there were no flames, no smoke, nor any signs of burning. Nor was there a living soul inside the room.

Bizarrely, what was discovered was a handbag on the desk and early reports suggest it was the same design of handbag that Mrs Thatcher herself often carried.

Downing Street has refused to comment on whether they believe this was some sort of practical joke.

Yet however the handbag got there, it was swiftly removed.

One eyewitness claimed that handwritten notes and a black diary were found in the bag, but that 'men in grey suits' took them away. The phrase 'D-Notice', a Government edict requiring news editors not to publicise certain information for reasons of national security, was brought into force.

What exactly happened to the papers and diary found in the handbag, or indeed to the handbag itself, remains unclear.

One Downing Street source has since played down the incident and suggested it was a disgruntled employee 'having fun with flashing torches'. What a shame if it were.

Our hope at *The Chronicle* is that those handwritten papers and diary have been sent to the National Archive for examination and maybe in the future will be released and published. Though if they are what we think they are, that day may not come for another hundred years.

So let's instead hope for a ministerial leak in order that they can be read by the British public.

Or perhaps some other means.

As Lady Thatcher herself said, "It's a funny old world."

INEXPLICABLE:
10 Downing Street

'I Was Once a Haunted House'

The Unusual Memoir of a Victorian Institution

I

I HAVE ALWAYS BEEN VERY PROUD of my 'penny joints'. Victorian workmen took great care that the mortar between my red bricks was never more than the width of one of the bright copper pieces they had jangling in their pockets. And when minted that one penny coin would have had on its front, or obverse, to use the formal nomenclature, the face of a new Queen, the young Victoria, and beneath it the date 1844, for that was the year of my build.

My imperial bricks, red from the strengthening of iron in clay, have offered me a long and fascinating life, for, over the last two centuries or so, I have had several incarnations. I was originally conceived as a boarding school. This meant that as well as classrooms, an assembly hall and a chapel, I had a refectory, a laundry, and, at one time, my very own brewhouse. However that was destroyed in a fire in 1894. Later I became a sanatorium for those persons who, in the words of the clinician who ran the asylum, 'suffered from the delirium of brain fever.' I was also briefly, for a decade or thereabouts, a seminary for men of the cloth, but that period of my life has little bearing on the story I wish to tell.

As by birth I am Victorian, it will not surprise to you to learn, dear Reader, that my rooms are large and lofty, and, due to fine workmanship, much in them has survived to the present day. My oak floorboards, my sash windows, the plaster cornicing in my library, are all original, as is my ruby-coloured Bohemian glass in what once was the chapel and is now a dining area. My deep foundations, upon which lie blue Staffordshire bricks, made from Etruria marl, with a density that allows for little water absorption, are still robust, and my elaborate lead guttering has survived, as they say, in good nick, as have the bulk of my rose-red roof tiles. As one of the rustic Black Country builders who constructed me put it – somewhat poetically, I thought – 'all a house needs is a good hat and a strong pair of boots'. And with my roof and foundations I have been fortunate in both. That said, my drains are a little leaky, and on my outside walls, where once clematis and honeysuckle grew, there is now only clinging-ivy, which in places has penetrated into my upper stories, resulting in some dampness of minor import.

I would acknowledge that I am no ancient castle whereon a *chemin de ronde* once walked England's finest men of heraldic legend. Nor am I an ancestral hall, lichened and weathered by Time's shading brush. Most of my best Spode pottery has long gone, as have my four-poster beds. However, the portrait of my founder, the Duchess of Claverley, remains in place above the mantelpiece in the reading room, and lilac trees still grow along the tangled lanes that lead to my arched entrance. And I should add, because it is pertinent to our tale, that my four House of Atreus tapestries portraying Agamemnon's doomed return from the Trojan war, Electra and her libations, Clytemnestra's Eumenides and finally the madness of Orestes, have survived and now hang in what once was the Senior Masters' Smoking Room. Perhaps I am of limited interest to societies of antiquity, yet nevertheless, I am a house of substance and some worth. I am still as solid as a brick, for I *am* bricks. Not forgetting, of course, my green Minton tiles, my carved mahogany banisters, my terracotta chimney pots, my decorative stonework and my great and imposing fireplace that on my construction was taken from an abandoned abbey.

There's an old adage with houses, that the wider the fireplace, the more likely a ghost. But alas, dear Reader, here I must disappoint, for I am a haunt that has never been haunted. No severed head of a mythical king lies buried in my cellar, making itself manifest in the dreams of the restless. No floor is stained by the blood of innocents, whose mother still cries out in grief at their slaughter. My gables were not once the gibbets of gallows upon which the wicked were hung, and where their damned souls now return seeking vengeance. On All Saints' Eve, the glistering-red, bone-split countenance of the Lord of the Manor, whose musket accidentally blew his off face as he was taking pot-shots at rabbits, is not seen by guests meandering across my lawns. You will not feel the ice-cold hand of a crazed governess who drowned herself in the very bath that you now lie in. Nor see on my wainscoting, on the emergence of a new moon, scratches from the claws of dogs that once uncovered a priest hole that hid a shaking Jesuit in mortal fear. And the words *Mors Janua Vitae* – 'Death, the Gateway to Life' – will not write themselves in monkish Latin above the window, mysteriously left open in an attic bedroom.

For so old a house to be without a ghost is piteous indeed. But all that changed one nefarious night when a revenging phantom... oh, but I say too much, for I must not spoil the story. However, I will permit myself to tell you that the ghost was an uninvited guest and unknown to me. It was a spectre that brought with it both a friend and a foe. And one of those the phantom would destroy. But who is who, and which is which, well, that is the tale.

And you must forgive how it is told, for it is a yarn with herrings as red and as many as my bricks.

II

They say that windows have eyes and walls ears but my knowing of all that happens here is by sense and feel. Why I am so constituted, I cannot say, but it has forever been thus. There is much, therefore, I could reveal to you of my days as a boarding school, from the bizarre and blissful, to the wild and wretched, but I will refrain from that which is superfluous, and reference only those events in my years as an educational establishment which are pertinent to the tale I am to tell.

Now it is a guinea to a hot-cross-bun that boys of schooling age across the measure of Time are excited by the thought of ancient ghosts. It was our Greek master who, it must be said, looked as old as Geras himself, who knew, to borrow Achilles's phrase, that the idea of 'breathless dead' would be sure to enrapture his pupils. In their study of Homer, they relished Odysseus's visit to the underworld and his encounter with the spectres of Hades. And in their translations of Aeschylus, they revelled in Clytemnestra's ghost awaking the fury of the Eumenides. However, it was the class of the science master, who had a passion for theatre, both in and out of school, where young and impressionable minds were first exposed to a ghostly vision. However, here I speak of 'Pepper's Ghost', not a true phantom, but an illusion of the stage. Allow me to elaborate.

Our young science master, Mr Delves-Broughton, and his constant companion, a young Prussian aristocrat named Count Leopold, had on one of their frequent sojourns to London and the excitements of Drury Lane seen Pepper's Ghost in a dramatised presentation of Charles Dickens's *The Haunted Man*. And D.B., as the boys called Mr Delves-Broughton, had been so taken by what he and his dear friend Count Leopold had witnessed, that in the final science lesson of the Michaelmas term of 1864, the master offered a breathless description of the event.

'A ghost, boys! I saw a ghost! *Ego ipse credo*! Oh yes! I let myself believe it! Yet it was a ghost of pure mummery – a phantom phantasmagoria – oh, but it thrilled us both to the quick. So real, boys, so real! Count Leopold so trembled that when it first appeared, he grabbed me by the arm and held it tight until the ghost grew faint and disappeared into the ether.'

I could tell you that Count Leopold, when secrecy allowed, often held the science master's arm – and other limbs and a certain protuberance – even more tightly, resulting in a very different kind of tremble. However, to say anything more of these private indiscretions, fascinating though they maybe, would be to break my own rule of only relating those matters of relevance to our tale. And one such is the illusion that is Pepper's Ghost.

'But what is the science behind this phenomenon? An explanation is required,' exclaimed Mr Delves-Broughton to the bright faced boys. 'If a pane of clear glass is positioned on a stage at the edge of an open trapdoor, and at an angle capturing in its reflection an illuminated actor hidden beneath that stage, then what the audience will see is that actor seemingly floating in the air. A spectral apparition, indeed!'

D.B. did not have at his disposal the elaborate theatre machinery of Drury Lane to illustrate this remarkable occurrence. However, he did possess a Benjamin Pollock Toy Theatre, which, until that moment, had been concealed under a red velvet drape. Oh, such a charming plaything, much like a doll's house. The classroom shutters were pushed to and the room became deadly dark, excepting a small lantern that acted as footlights. The drama was now ready to begin.

Two toy figures, no bigger than the size of a thumb, enter stage left. These *dramatis personae*, being men of science, according to the plot devised by D.B., are discussing Charles Darwin's recently published work, *The Origin of the Species*. One of the toy figures speaks in a voice it will not surprise you to learn very similar to that of Mr Delves-Broughton.

'If a monkey were my great-great-great grandfather, must he then have had a soul? And if monkeys have souls, why not dogs and rats?'

The second toy figure laughs. A laugh, it should be said, that was the kindred echo of Count Leopold, secreted under the table.

'Ha! Ha! Ha! It is impossible for ze monkeys to have ze souls.'

'Why?'

'Becauze if ze monkeys had ze souls zer would be monkey ghosts. And moreovers ze ghosts of ze dogs and ze rats as well as.'

Right on cue as he says these words, there appears on that very toy stage the phantom of a giant rat, seemingly eating the head of the astonished disbeliever. Not a real apparition, of course, but a reflection, for, unnoticed by the boys, Mr Delves-Broughton had placed a pane of clear glass across the proscenium and had constructed under the toy stage a hidden compartment illuminated by tallow candles in which was hidden Count Leopold's white pet mouse. Oh, but how the boys cheered! And no doubt went home that Christmas and dreamt not of sprigs of holly and plum puddings, but of monstrous rodents bringing terror to crotchety aunts and their vile elder sisters.

At least then, by a trick of the theatre, I had witnessed the semblance of a ghost. And more were to come, for from that time onwards the young science master always ended term with a phantom conjured up by some principle of physics or chemistry, including a *laterna magica* and various other alchemies of illumination and shadow. And what wonderments they were.

But boys being boys a spate of japes soon followed, with ghostly apparitions, by means of white shrouds and floating heads, popping up everywhere about my corridors. And this tomfoolery came to be believed, so much so that even after the boys and masters had left, and I was a boarding school no more, my reputation as a haunted house had grown to be indubitable.

Ah, if only.

A ghost or two for company would have been a delight, but sadly I was uninhabited for many winters, except, of course, for my companions the rats. And unaware was I, until alone with these remarkable creatures, of the extraordinary resourcefulness of which they are capable. And my rats have remained under my floorboards ever since, even when human beings once more moved in above them. That was in the early part of the last century, when I became a seminary for the clergy and some years after a lunatic asylum for the insane, the only difference being that with the former one talks to someone who isn't there, and with the latter one hears from someone who isn't there.

It may not surprise you to learn that of these two incarnations, being an asylum was by far the more disturbing. Not, I should say, because of the behaviour of the patients, whose conduct may be excused due to their impairment of mind. No, I speak of the contemptible nature and actions of the clinician who ran the institution, where pitiless cruelty abounded. How such a man, who had two loving daughters on whom he doted, could commit such acts of atrocity on those put into his care, I really cannot say. And in my house! Shameful! But what could I do about it?

It was then I remembered those mischievous schoolboys and the ghosts they had conjured. I possessed more than winding-sheets and skulls on wires, for I had at my disposal creaking floorboards, cold draughts, whooping chimneys, and in my gloomy corridors there always lurked the uncertainty of shadows. Perhaps, then, I might send that callous doctor out of his wits as a punishment for the brutal tortures he inflicted on those poor simpletons. And I remember now how one of his young daughters would watch in fascination as I used the bulbous glass in my windows to transform the reflections of the moon into shroud-wearing phantoms and listen intently as I taught my chimneys to whistle tunes that were known to every sailor on shore leave. However, by the time I had perfected the craft of turning eddies of dust into fierce and fearful fiends, my life as an institution for the insane came to an end and I have remained unoccupied ever since. Excepting, of course, for my friends the rats.

So, patient Reader, you are now acquainted with the necessary knowledge of my history for me to begin the tale of my unusual and unexpected haunting. It was not long ago that there arrived on my doormat an envelope, upon which was typed in the top left hand corner the words: 'COUNTY PLANNING DEPARTMENT'.

It appeared I was no longer fated to be a whist old manor but, rather, I was to be unmantled and refurbished to become a Residential Conference Centre with all the inventions of the twenty-first century. And thrilled I was to the clay when I discovered the nature of the organisation that had booked me for what would be the inaugural assemblage.

III

'I wasn't at all surprised when I received the invitation to speak at this conference. I'm known, after all, for my regular appearances on television debunking all this ghost nonsense. You may have heard of me: Doctor Richard Dudley. My specialist field in psychiatry being delusional paranoia. I use the medicine of reason and logic to prove to the patient that dear cousin Ethel is in her grave and not standing at the end of their bedpost. No, no. In my view ghosts are nothing more than an Old Maid's Folly. And I'm sure, dear lady, you agree.'

'Nanti! Nanti! I love a nelly yada with the dead, for y'Auntie's a clairvoyant. And that's why today the glad rags you vada me in are *à la* Margaret Rutherford in *Blithe Spirit* as Madame Arcati. What a bona dona she was when she put on the slap.'

The psychiatrist, a slender soul, whose dull grey suit and thin tie declared themselves indifferent to any sense of sartorial style, did not respond to this surprise declaration. But the spirit medium stood his ground, not saying another word, with the result that these two silent immovables found themselves in the battle of the glare. Even an announcement for everyone to take their seats for the first session of the conference made not a jot of difference, and perhaps they would have stood there all day, but for the ringing of a bell, my old school hand bell to be precise, and its clang was so fierce and commanding, that, as if by magic, these staring statues, with unexpected synchronicity, broke away from each other and took their places.

The convenor of the gathering now began his introductory remarks from the lectern on the make-shift stage.

'Good morning and welcome. My name is Martin Ward and I am President of The Society of Paranormal and Psychic Investigation. We have called this conference "The Ghosts of Many Worlds" because we have here this week a real mixture of perspectives and opinions. Among you are historians, sociologists, clairvoyants, novelists, literary critics, scientists and mystics. And what that means is that some of you are believers in ghosts, others are not. However, we would ask you to show respect and courtesy to the views and beliefs expressed by all our speakers, whether you agree with them or not.'

Without, I think, intending to admonish anyone in particular, the conference convenor here caught the eye of both the spirit medium and the psychiatrist. Perhaps realising this indiscretion, Mr

Ward then cast his attentions all round Meeting Room One, which, though now carpeted and equipped with a projector and a screen, I still think of as my dormitory of the Upper Fourth. Exactly eighty-six people were present at the morning gathering, and I know this because during Mr Ward's opening remarks I counted them.

'My aunt Jane had her own expression for the ghost she claimed walked up and down her staircase every night, namely "blessed nuisance". But of course there are many words for ghost and spirits: bag-a-boos, bogies, banshees, kelpies, plus dialect terms such as "shim", a derivation of "shade", which comes from the Isle of Wight. It is said our venue, Claverley Manor, is haunted. I can't say for sure whether we'll have immured nuns popping out from behind the walls, but I can guarantee ghosts of a kind, because over the next three cold winter nights we are joined by several actors and actresses who will be giving us readings from classic ghost tales. And since there is a tradition that spooks don't like electricity, we'll hear these by candlelight. And speaking of tradition brings me to our first speaker this morning, Professor F.R. Curtis, Head of Cultural Studies at Pattingham College and his lecture entitled "The Templates of Nineteenth Century Supernatural Fiction", based on a paper published this year in *THE NEW VICTORIAN GAZETTE*.'

Dear Reader, I already know the ending of this tale, but I will tell it as if it is yet to happen, and I do this for the would-be detective, for there are clues to be discovered in what the next speaker says as to the nature of the ghost of our story. And to offer aid in this pursuit, I shall from time to time interject with a timely aside.

Ah! Professor Curtis is now standing at the lectern and ready to commence his address.

'Charles Dickens didn't invent Christmas, nor did the Victorians originate the ghost tale, but both gave us the narrative templates that still survive today. I want to first look at the methods writers of the period used as a pretext for getting the "hauntee", if I can call them that, into the house. In *The Red Bungalow* and *Number Ninety*, both by Bithia Mary Crocker, the properties were uninhabited for many years. Rents then are often "absurdly cheap", as Edith Nesbit says in one of her stories, and so the tenant believes they are getting a bargain. Only that bargain often comes at a costly price, which some Marxist academics have offered as a veiled critique in ghost stories of *laissez-faire* capitalism. But my talk is on tropes rather than politics.'

(*For which we all thank Heaven*!)

'Bad weather for the traveller, as in Edith Wharton's *The Triumph of the Night*, is another hauntee narrative device, as is what I call the "Dare Plot", where a character, usually a sceptic, is challenged to spend a night in a room or house said to be haunted. There's a clever twist on this template in W.W. Jacobs's *Jerry Bundler*, where travellers are staying overnight in a tavern rumoured to be haunted by a highwayman. An actor, Hirst, has a bet that he can frighten the sceptic who's gone off to bed early, by dressing up in an eighteenth century costume that he happens to have with him for a performance of *The Rivals*. Hirst goes to get ready but then returns claiming to have encountered the ghost for real on the stairs. Another traveller then says if *he* sees the phantom he'll shoot it on sight. And later that's exactly what he does, only it turns out to be Hirst, who is now in his disguise. Unusually there is ambiguity in the diegesis in that we never know for sure whether or not Hirst really did see the ghost. Maybe the claim was to scare everyone witless and so win his wager. If so, let his fate be a warning to our actors not to be too convincing in their performance, or it may put them in danger.'

(*And never, dear Reader, was a truer word said.*)

'Let's now move on to ghost conventions, or what Brander Matthews in *The Rival Ghost* calls "spirit lore". I would sum these up as the When, the Who, the Where and the Why of the ghost world. First, when exactly is the image of spectrality allowed to interact with the living? According to R.S. Hawker's *The Botathen Ghost*, it's laid down of old that "no angel or fiend, no spirit, good or evil, will ever speak until they have been first spoken to" and this folklore tradition is based on the "great law of prayer", for "God Himself will not yield until man hath made vocal entreaty". It's only half past ten in the morning, but I think I'll risk an entreaty: Is there anybody there? Is anybody there?'

(*If Doctor Russell expected a reply I have to disappoint and say answer came there none.*)

'Maybe the spirits in this house are hard of hearing or died of diphtheria. Anyway, let's up the volume: IS THERE ANYBODY THERE? IS THERE ANYBODY THERE?'

'*Woof! Woof! Woof! Woof! Woof!*'

(*The sudden barking of a dog that will not stop.*)

'*Woof! Woof! Woof! Woof! Woof! Woof! Woof! Woof! Woof!*'

(*Nervous laughter now follows from the audience, but the animal is soon quietened by a firm hand and an equally resolute voice.*)

'Calm down, Constable. Calm down!' instructs a lady on the back row. 'I'm so sorry, everyone. He's a spaniel, you see, and spaniels require constant stimulation. Oh dear, I'm afraid he must have become rather bored by all this talk.'

(*Oh! I fear from his tone that Doctor Russell has taken exception to this comment.*)

'Madam, I didn't realise domestic dogs were allowed at the conference venue.'

(*The lady seems not to hear this remark and simply goes on talking in a voice that would easily have brought down the walls of Jericho.*)

'I called him Constable because as soon as I saw him at the rescue centre, he reminded me of the spaniel in John Constable's *The Hay Wain*. So clever of the painter to have a dog guiding the eye of viewer as to where to look. So Constable it had to be–'

'*Woof! Woof!*'

'Oh, you do like to hear your name, don't you, Constable?'

'*Woof! Woof! Woof!*'

'And of course, it's not, as I discovered on a walk with my friend Winifred, a name one should try and shorten. Certainly not in a public park. Isn't that right, Constable?'

'*Woof! Woof! Woof!*'

(*Muffled giggles follow, but not from Professor F.R. Curtis, M.A. Phd. Phd., as spelt out in bold on his name badge.*)

'Oh, but my, I'm taking up far too much of your time, Professor.'

(*Says 'Mrs Jesop', for I have now read the name written in her own hand on her badge.*)

'Well, er, let's get on, shall we? Another "When" in ghost tales comes from the early Christian belief that souls in purgatory were most active the day before a holy feast day. Hence the importance in the spirit calendar of Halloween and Christmas Eve. There's also often in ghost stories some kind of limitation on how long a visitation can last – the arrival of the new moon being the ticking clock in *The Bridal Pair* by Robert W. Constable–'

'*Woof! Woof!*'

'I mean Robert W. Chambers, not Constable.'

'*Woof! Woof!*'

'I told you! He does so love his name, don't you, Constable?'

'*Woof! Woof!*'

'And for anyone who is interested, my paper in *THE NEW VICTORIAN GAZETTE* has a list of all the ghost stories of the nineteenth century with a Yuletide setting and they include *The Nurse's Tale*, *The Water Ghost of Harrowby House*, *Number Ninety* and *At Chrighton Abbey*. Given my own time is short–'

'*Woof! Woof!*'

'–and shortening with every second, I will now move on to my next "W": The "Who". What I'm talking about here are the ghost seers, who in Victorian fiction tend to be women, who are often thought of as giddy, unbalanced of mind and attention seeking.'

(*A noticeable glance here, I think, towards the excitable Mrs Jesop.*)

'However, if men see an image of spectrality they are likely to be told, as in Kipling's *At the End of the Passage*, that they are suffering from overwork or have "a touch of the sun". So we see here the perceived gender differences in nineteenth century fiction: for a woman, malady of the mind, for a man, physical affliction. In Victorian fiction the ghost seer also tended to be a socially liminal character, such as Sarah Chrighton in Mary Elizabeth Braddon's *At Chrighton Abbey*, who finds herself having to rely on the goodwill of her family connections. Sarah has the ancestral name, but has had to earn a living "in a position of dependence – a dreadful thing for a Chrighton to be obliged to do." And it's these in-betweeners to whom the ghost usually makes itself known. Outsider connects to outsider.'

(*And here I shall say, to help the Reader, that the ghost seer of our tale is one who, like Miss Crighton, has made a return to a grand old house.*)

'The next "W" is the "Where". Dickens's *The Lawyer and the Ghost* has a playful take on this, for the hauntee, somewhat puzzled, says to the phantom he finds it odd that "...when you have an opportunity of visiting the fairest spots of earth – for I suppose space is nothing to you – you should always return exactly to the very place where you have been most miserable." The ghost replies: "Never thought of that before" and so never comes back. Which makes it a very short short story. But most ghosts do have a purpose in being where they are, which leads us to the most important narrative "W", the "Why". As Shaugnassy, one of the men of science says in Jerome K. Jerome's *The Man of Science* puts it, "If one admits the possibility of spirits retaining any interest in the affairs of this world at all, it is certainly more reasonable to imagine them engaged upon a task."'

'Mine does!'

(*Oh dear! It's Mrs Jesop again. But here I would advise the would-be detective to listen most attentively to what she has to say.*)

'I am a writer of ghost stories and the tale I am currently plotting out certainly has a task. Except it doesn't belong to the ghost, but the woman who can see it. As you observed, the fairer sex has always been the more percipient. Only my ghost seer, as you would call her, does not consider this a mental affliction. Besides, the ghost she sees is in great need. Oh, but my! I'm interrupting you again, aren't I?'

'Yes, madam, you are. However, I can say with some confidence that I have been very thorough in the cataloguing of intentions, wants and needs, and so, as I now go through that list, I trust you will find the animus of your ghost.'

'Oh, I hope so. Do carry on!'

'Thank you. I will. Unfinished business was the task in one of the earliest literary supernatural tales. I refer, of course, to Daniel Defoe's *The Apparition of Mrs Veal*, where the ghost's purpose, since she left no will, is to tell her friend who should get what among her effects. Then there are ghostly foretellings and ghost abductions. A sub-category is the "Siren Ghost", for example F.G. Loring's *The Tomb of*

Sarah. But I'd also add here Sir Arthur Conan Doyle's 1883 tale *The Captain of the 'Polestar'*, where the name of the ship foreshadows the nature of the ghost's purpose. Then there are those stories where the ghost is Death, as in Julius Long's *The Pale Man*, Chambers's *Passeur*, and the gardener who clears away the fallen leaves in Burrage's classic tale *The Sweeper*. Now some of these tales are early twentieth century but you can trace their roots to the Victorian model.'

I was finding all this most fascinating, but I couldn't help noticing that one lady in the audience, a Miss Osborne according to her name badge, seemed not to take in one word of what Professor Curtis was saying. Her attention was elsewhere, though with so many people in her sight, it would be impossible to say exactly where she was looking.

'The avenger of his or her own murder,' continued the professor, 'is another popular trope.'

Ah! Now Miss Osborne does turn round to listen to what the professor has to say.

'Pre-post-modern narratives always had it that you can't escape justice and you'll find this axiom explored in W.W. Jacob's *The Well*, Edith Wharton's *Afterwards* and Vincent O'Sullivan's *An Enemy and Myself*. I see from the itinerary that tonight we have a reading of Ellen Glasgow's *The Shadowy Third*, written in 1916. A fascinating avenging ghost in that it's a child who died young and quite possibly as a result of the stepfather's actions.'

It would be remiss of me at this moment in the story if I failed to point out that Miss Osborne was holding in her hand a copy of that very book.

'Of course,' the professor went on, 'there is also reparation, as in the case of C. L. Ray's *The Corner Shop*, and guardianship, as in several stories by M.R. James. Plus there are those stories where ghosts are simply mischievous. As one character says in Bernard Capes's *An Eddy on the Floor*, "There may be disembodied spirits who seek to distress or annoy where they no longer can control." But, I think, in principle I have covered most motivations and tasks.'

'Not the one in my story,' shouted Mrs Jesop from the back row.

Before Professor F.R. Curtis had a chance to reply, the conference convenor, Martin Ward, who had spent the last few minutes looking at the clock with an increasing degree of concern, jumped up to thank the speaker for his excellent talk. A further lecture followed, entitled 'Now You See Me, Now You Don't', about the corporal nature, or otherwise, of ghosts. Polite applause ensued and our host, accompanied, I am proud to say, by a resounding ringing of my old school hand bell, announced it was time for coffee.

And you, courteous Reader, may well be thinking the very same thought. However, before joining the throng in the dining area allow me, if I may, to pass on an observation. There was a word used in Professor Curtis's address which caused much unease in one particular listener. I shall not say who, but I will reveal the word itself – *Murder*!

IV

If eavesdropping is a sin, cast me down into the deepest circle of Dante's Hell. However, I do not believe merely overhearing conversations can be a misdeed, unless it leads to false witness, and there my conscience is clear, for the exchanges I noted during coffee I now report verbatim. Among the clink and clack of the porcelain the most prominent opinions were those of the atheistic scoffer. Most ironic, as refreshments took place in what was my school chapel, where painted cherubim and seraphim looked down from on high with much bemusement at this unexpected congregation.

Here, a discussion between a historian and a sociologist:

'Ghosts of antiquity were in my view simply covers for poachers, highway men, smugglers and thieves. Haunted woods and caves with a bogie-man were clever ruses to keep prying eyes away.'

'In my paper on eighteenth century sightings for *THE SOCIAL REVIEW MONTHLY* I argue for the human agency of the cuckold as being the originator of many domestic ghosts. I quote numerous letters where wives when seen in flagrante delicto with a man not their husband, admit the indiscretion to friends, but tell their spouse it was a ghost. Sometimes even that of his dead brother or distant cousin.'

'And the husbands of the period bought these fairy tales?'

'Oh yes. Well it's a more acceptable deceit than infidelity. Saves face, certainly.'

'That's similar to when silver went missing from the pantries of the aristocracy and the servants blamed ghosts. Even though the lady of house almost certainly knew it was a light-fingered parlour maid, she went along with the pretence in order to avoid too much upset.'

'The rich bitch probably had more than enough teaspoons, anyway.'

'Ha! Ha! But I hardly think the white plastic ones they give you here are worth stealing.'

Oh, how the tongues on the faces of my stone gargoyles above them seem to me to grow longer and stick out further than they did before.

Next, a literary critic in conversation with a metaphysical scientist:

'On the train here I was re-reading E.F. Benson's *The Face* and there's a line about the past still being "alive in the mysterious sub-consciousness, which flows eternally, like some dark underground river, beneath the surface of human life." And what's that if it's not an image of spectrality?'

'Absolutely, but there is the potentiality of physical inheritance, too. My thesis at University of California proposes that the trauma of death leaves behind a residue of charged particles which then later registers as its "ghost" in the electrical brain activity of a living receiver.'

'Fascinating.'

'My colleagues call it "woo-woo science", but all pioneers were once thought to live with the goblins and fairies. Oh what a pity, they've run out of decaf.'

There are three stained glass windows in my old school chapel, with a saint in each, namely Andrew the Apostle, Jean-Baptiste de La Salle and Saint Alfred the Great, all closely associated with teaching and learning. Their countenances today seem somewhat surprised by the evangelical forcefulness of the arguments put forward by these modern deniers. Here a tetchy exchange between an ophthalmologist and a geologist.

'Whilst I acknowledge people do see what they *believe* to be ghosts, the explanation can be found in ocular trauma. Peripheral vision is notoriously unreliable, but the temporal lobe has to create something from the ill-defined information provided, so *ipso facto* it comes up with a ghost.'

'But your theory fails to explain why phantoms are only seen in certain areas. My own research is in geology. It is my contention that all ghosts are primarily the result of unusual geological formation in rocks causing hallucinatory visions. Literal castles in the air.'

'Really?'

'Oh yes. I did fieldwork on the very road Saint Paul took from Jerusalem to Damascus. Some of the magnetic readings were off the scale. I have no doubt when I say that whatever Saint Paul experienced on the road to Damascus was not theological but geological.'

The saint, we must assume, is now in the glory of Heaven, so his opinion on this matter cannot be solicited. However, a medieval portrait of Paul, hanging a few feet from the two gentlemen, appeared to me to be shaking its head in dismay at this heresy.

The most blistering remarks I heard during coffee were on the subject of ghost seers and came, not surprisingly, from Doctor Richard Dudley, the psychiatrist whom we met earlier in our tale. Perhaps it was the heat of the room or the mainly casual dress of those around him, but as he made his views known, Doctor Dudley carefully loosened and then removed his thin tie.

'I maintain that the charlatans who perpetrate rank deceit with their flummery should be on the receiving end of the full force of the law. And there's one such swindler here today. I'm a psychiatrist and I've seen how weak-minded people can be made to believe almost anything. But, if you are disciplined in reason, it is possible to make yourself immune to this sort of auto-suggestive mental trickery. And that's all a ghost is: an infection of the mind.'

A compelling theory to which many listened with great interest. However, the gentleman commanding the most attention in the room was the spirit medium, who I can now reveal, for he had recently attached his name badge, was called Billie Blooming. A most flamboyant way of speaking. Although I have a little Latin and Greek from my school days, his vernacular was unfamiliar to me, as it may well be to you. Yet with a little filling in of the gaps with imaginative supposition, one can at least gain some sense of his meaning.

'Heartfaces! We are all amongst the spirits, even though we can nanti varda them with our ogles. And y'Auntie believes that these fortuni omees and palones, omi-palones, palones-omees, who sadly have faked the fatcha and flung off their sling backs for the last time, still troll amongst us. And y'Auntie screeches this because she is herself a spirit, for aren't we all dwellers in latties of clay and a sparkle in feely embryo. One bona nochy, that lucoddy will be no more, but our dolly soul will live on.'

Oh! So tempted was I to shout out, 'Hear, hear!' for it is that reference to 'clay', which has led me to conclude, dear Reader, that in principle there isn't that much difference between us.

V

During refreshments, Mrs Jesop, it was noted by many, was wandering around by herself and occasionally adding to her tea a little something extra. This I can reveal came from a small gin bottle that she took at regular intervals from a side pocket in her voluminous loose-fitting skirt. Was it this, they wondered, that led the now very merry Mrs Jesop to sing on her way back into Meeting Room One that old ditty *Look for the Silver Lining*?

'"*A heart, full of joy and gladness, Will always banish sadness and strife, So always look for the silver lining, And try to find the sunny side of* – Oh!"'

Mrs Jesop's caterwauling stopped abruptly when she realised the conference convenor Mr Martin Ward was already at the lectern and the second session of the morning was underway.

'...my favourite author name has to be Ernest Theodor Amadeus Hoffman. When you're called that what else can you do but write ghost stories? Which brings us to next item on our itinerary, "Work in Progress", an opportunity for novelists who are here today to share with us ideas they are currently developing. I see from my notes that our first story up for discussion has the title *Ego Te Absolvo* but there's no name attached. The writer, is he here?'

'She!'

'What was that?'

'The writer is a she.'

'I'm sorry, I shouldn't have assumed.'

'No, you should not.'

'Well, who is this she?'

'Myself! Mrs Jesop. And *ego te absolvo* are the words a priest says in the Catholic sacrament of confession.'

'Er, is the ghost of your story a priest?'

'Oh no, no. A most unlikely thought. However, it is a mortal sin that leads to the presence of the ghost.'

'I'm not sure I understand, but, er, as you've booked this time – which I should say we must keep to a strict ten minutes – perhaps you'd now like to come up onto the platform and tell us all about *Ego Te Absolvo*."

'Oh yes, of course I will, oh but my, it isn't an easy plot to explain,' said Mrs Jesop, walking in variable directions towards the podium, with her dog Constable following close at heel. 'And I say that because, as yet, I've not written a word. But the idea has been with me a long time. I'm a prison visitor, you see. When you consider the number of sinners in a prison, you'd have thought it the perfect setting for a wronged ghost to make an appearance. Yet so few ghost stories feature such institutions.'

'Is your prison visitor the ghost?' asked the conference convenor, as Mrs Jesop took over his place at the lectern.

'Oh no, no, no. But she has the gift of seeing the ghosts of the murdered standing next to their murderer.'

'Murderer,' said the convenor, with surprise.

'Oh yes, in my story ghost and slayer are inseparable. And it's the role of my prison visitor to act as a go-between betwixt the living and the dead. Her task, one not mentioned Mr Russell, being deliverance.'

The Reader might well be correct in assuming that the frown that now appeared on Doctor Russell's face was his response to his full academic appellation being so wantonly ignored.

'You see,' Mrs Jesop went on, 'once a murderer repents, forgiveness can follow. Perhaps, if I explained my plot using the Four Ws of Mr Russell, whom I see there on the front row.'

Doctor Russell's frown turned to a scowl.

'First, *who* can see the ghost of Violet? Violet being the name I've given to the woman so brutally murdered. In my story, that's the prison visitor. As to the where and the when, well that's straightforward enough, because Violet is forever present at the side of her killer.'

'So Violet is a kind of projection of guilt?' asked a voice from the audience.

'Oh, no, no, no,' replied Mrs Jesop, 'how can she be that when the murderer can't see her? As I said, if you would listen, the only person who can see the ghost is the prison visitor. Only she can't.'

'I'm completely lost,' said Mr Ward.

'Oh dear. You see, when my prison visitor encounters the convicted murderer, a woman called Rose, there is no ghost standing at her side. Which means, of course, Rose did not commit the crime.'

'She's innocent.'

'Exactly so. But here's the complication: Rose confessed to the killing of Violet.'

'Why?' asked another voice.

'I don't know. That's why I've come here today to this conference. To find inspiration.'

'Does the true murderer get caught?'

'Well of course I want him to be.Who wouldn't? My prison visitor has discovered, you see, the identity of the real killer, for, as I said, the ghost of the one murdered is forever present at their side. In my story the prison visitor somehow encounters the true killer – perhaps even at a conference like this – and the murdered Violet at his side tells her how she was strangled, what perfume she wore and how the psychopathic killer changed the lyrics of her favourite song as he did the deed... "*A heart full of hate and anger, Will always carry with it a knife, So always look for the silver lining, And try to find the evil side of life.*" Oh but my, the police aren't likely to believe a giddy attention seeker with poor eyesight and a defective temporal lobe.'

'But couldn't your ghost seer turn detective?' suggested a voice from the audience.

'Yes. I think that's exactly what she intends to do. Build up evidence provided by the ghost of Violet in order to bring the wicked killer to justice.'

There was a moment of uncomfortable silence, but it was soon broken by another suggestion from the assemblage.

'Could it be that your innocent in jail, Rose, I think you said she was called, truly believes that she did kill Violet?'

'I'm beginning to think that's exactly what happened, for Rose was a very vulnerable woman. Oh, but my time is up. Thank you all so much for your help. The problem with my story isn't so much a plot hole, more the final missing piece. I know who did it and why, but how to prove such a thing? Oh, but doubtless I'll come up with the solution before the day is out.'

And on that note of optimism Mrs Jesop and her spaniel left the make-shift podium and sat down.

The writers' session continued with other presentations of stories with peculiar goings on. *Last Will and Testament* featured a vile gentleman, who on his death bed made two requests. The first that his entire fortune be spent on a portrait of himself to smile down on his son, whom he never much liked, and second that it be created with paint into which his ashes are mixed. However, the son, instead of commissioning the famous and expensive artist specified in the will, employs a lesser known and inferior portraitist, at a much lower fee, and so pockets the difference for himself. The artist, as requested, does stir the dead man's ashes into the paint on his palate, and slowly the figure on the easel comes, as it were, back to life. But therein lies the problem, for though the deceased is painted with a jovial expression, as requested in the will, when the artist returns next morning to his canvas, the father is found with a most bitter and angry countenance. No matter how many times the face is painted over, this diabolical grimace keeps on returning. After many days of this, the artist informs the son that his brushes can do no more and the portrait is delivered. As soon as it is unwrapped, the son sees how his father is present in the painting. Those eyes! So alive! And so powerful a stare that the son does not notice that the hands of his dear papa are slowly moving up the portrait towards his offspring's neck. And I'm sure, roused Reader, you are now in such a heated fancy that you will be able to guess for yourself what happens next.

The final story of the morning, which I thought had a certain poignancy, was set in the days of Burke and Hare, an era when those involved in medical research didn't ask too many questions as to the origin of corpses they sought to dissect. In the tale, a young boy, who is thought a weakling and a milksop, is goaded by the boys in his school to spend from dusk till dawn in the local cemetery. And after much bullying the boy declares he will do it. A moonless night. All is dark and still, but then the boy notices the figure of a woman by a newly dug grave. At first, he thinks it may indeed be a ghost, and he is inclined to run, for in truth he is a coward. But then he remembers his vow and instead approaches the woman, who proves to be very much alive. She tells the boy she is the mother of a son recently buried in the ground beneath her feet and that she spends her nights guarding his grave to prevent the body being stolen by the 'Resurrection Men'. It so happened the young schoolboy had recently lost his dear mother, and the two share their filial grief. With tears in his eyes, the young boy promises the lady that he will stand watch over the grave of her son, for after spending so many nights in the cemetery, she is almost lifeless from lack of sleep. The lady thanks the boy and makes her way towards the arch that is the entrance to the deserted graveyard. Every time she passes a stone under which lies a young man recently buried, there appears the ghost of his mother, who, though dead, watches over the body of her recently departed son. The young boy is no longer afraid and together he and the loving ghosts stand guard through the night. Eventually dawn breaks and with it comes birdsong. The spirits of the mothers now begin to fade, yet before the sun is high enough in the sky to cast its daylight beams across the boy's face, he feels a loving hand holding his. He knows that touch, for he has felt it since birth. And as the sun strikes his eyes, he sees, for a brief and blinding moment, the gentle face of his own mother, smiling and proud.

This melancholic yet tender tale ended the writers' session and my old hand bell announced lunch. All exited towards my chapel, with the exception of Mrs Jesop, who had dozed off. I noticed as well that something was left behind on an adjacent chair. That thin tie of the psychiatrist, Doctor Richard Dudley.

VI

When in the past dwellers of this house heard whispers outside their window it was merely the susurration of the leaves of my lilac trees and the soughing of the wind in their branches. When an unearthly chill was felt, it was but cold air drifting by from an unwelcome draught. When a rancid odour was detected, in truth it was just soporific mould from a piece of forgotten cheese. When the wick of the lamp gurgled and died, it was only ever the oil in its tarnished chamber reaching its end. And when in this house a cowled figure was seen among furtive shadows, it was but the morbid fancy of the mind, and with a dismissive shake of the head, the momentary vexation would soon be starved of the substance of thought.

But all that was about to change. For a true spectre would, by the height of the night's full moon, make itself known. And vent its anger.

VII

I do not wish to trouble you, forbearing Reader, with my ailments, but currently there's a raven caught in one of my chimneys. Such disorders give a house an uncomfortable feeling, akin to what you might refer to as indigestion. Which, by matter of coincidence, brings me to remarks made by a somewhat irritated, and, one has to say, none too steady on her feet, Mrs Jesop, who had belatedly made her way to the dining area, where she saw her beloved spaniel being fed various ends of steaks.

'Oh, I do wish people wouldn't give Constable their gristle and sausages. Much as he loves both, they are simply too rich for his tummy. People think a little bit won't harm, but if everyone does the same, Constable ends up with what amounts to a full bowl of fat – and that's not healthy for a dog.'

Constable was also the topic of a covert conversation between the conference organiser, Martin Ward, and Professor Curtis, the nature of which will become apparent as the afternoon session reveals itself.

In the prologue to our tale, I mentioned the science master and his *laterna magica*. Oh, dear Reader, those lights and shadows had no voice but now they spoke, and deafeningly so, from black boxes hanging on my walls! These living hallucinations, I know not what else to call them, were part of the talk given by Heather Freeman, a lecturer in Film Studies.

'...in that clip from *Nightmare on Elm Street* we saw Freddy Krueger. His motive for killing teens in Springwood, Ohio, is that they are the sons and daughters of the parents who burned him alive. And what I want to illustrate in my talk is that the revenge motif has its antecedence in Victorian supernatural fiction. It's there, for example, in Robert Chambers's *The Messenger*, where the wicked Black Priest not only curses the girl who caused his execution, but all her descendants. The truth is Hollywood has always been in hock to the Victorians and Edwardians for ghost characters and plotlines. William Hope Hodgson's detective Carnacki investigating ghost frauds that are covers for crime is pretty much every episode of *Scooby-Doo*. "If-it-wasn't-for-you-pesky-kids" and all that. In *The Horse of the Invisible* an enormous horse-head mask is even removed from the villain.

'But the nineteenth and early twentieth century ghost haunts cinema in more subtle ways, too. A man falls in love with a painting of a dead woman. That's Hoffmann's *The Deserted House* but it's also Hitchcock's *Vertigo*. And here I feel obliged to mention the concept in Film Studies we call "the male gaze", because there are strong voyeuristic and prurient elements in both tales. When talking about his "adoration of the mysterious being in the window" the narrator in *The Deserted House* states that he was "aroused and excited throughout all my nerve centres". Well, we don't need a close-up to tell us what's happening in his pants. And if you like your sex even more macabre, the love-struck corpse that won't die in the cult 1972 movie *Neither the Sea Nor the Sand* isn't a million miles from the dead bridegroom in Edith Nesbit's *John Charrington's Wedding*, of 1891. And for those foolish romantics out there, we have the 1947 movie *The Ghost and Mrs Muir*, which has certain parallels with Robert W. Chambers's *The Bridal Pair*, of 1902. Here's a taste of his style: "Give yourself to me, Rosamund; let me touch you – let me take you–" ... "Will you love me always?" ... "In life, in death, which cannot part us. Will you marry me, Rosamund?" She looked straight into his eyes. "Dear, do you not understand? Have you forgotten? I died three years ago today." Anyway, let's quickly have a look at this clip from *The Ghost and Mrs Muir*, starring Gene Tierney and Rex Harrison.'

How strange! The visions on the screen have lost their colour and become black and white. Oh but how everyone in the audience smiles at the close embrace of the ghostly lovers! All, I should say, except one.

'Personally folks,' the lecturer says as the images fade away, 'I prefer my spooks to be killers rather than kissers. Which brings us to John Carpenter. I won't be the first to point out the similarity of the ghostly mist of H. F. Arnold's *The Night Wire*, published in 1926, and that in Carpenter's 1980 classic *The Fog*. Though to be fair, the screenwriters, John Carpenter and Debra Hill, came up with a great back story of murdered fishermen who return to Antonio Bay to take their revenge. Take a look at this short clip when a boat and its crew out at sea are suddenly overtaken by a mysterious and luminous fog.'

Oh my word! Ghosts with swords! And hooks! Oh! Oooh! I never expected that! And in both eyes!

'Scary, isn't it? Carpenter: The King of Jumps. But his genius is that most of the time all you ever see is the outline of what appears to be there. The dread of what is coming we largely create for ourselves, because, ultimately, all great horror takes place in the mind.'

As Heather Freeman says this, she is momentarily distracted by muttering.

'I'd, er, like now, to, er, say a few words about the doppelgänger ghosts–'

The murmuring voice is coming from the elderly Miss Osborne sitting next to Doctor Richard Dudley in the second row. Only then it stops and the lecturer continues her talk.

'Yes, er, well you can find doppelganger ghosts in Charles Dickens's *The Haunted Man*, Henry James's *The Jolly Corner* and Edith Wharton's *The Triumph of the Night*. The duality in the tales of Wharton and James is primarily psychological and you can find a modern counterpoint in *The Double Life of Véronique* and even the Roger Moore movie *The Man Who Haunted Himself*. Let's take a look at Moore before he went on to become 007.'

Another vision appears, a rather handsome man, and doubly so since there are two of him. Yet my attention is taken from the screen, for Miss Osborne is once again wittering away, seemingly to herself. And even when the visions and music end she does not stop. Our lecturer, I think, has had enough.

'Is there something you'd like to say, madam?'

'Oh dear, I'm so sorry. Am I disturbing you? My name is Miss Osborne. And I'm here to do a reading this evening.'

The slender and somewhat spindly Miss Osborne then raises an open copy of a book she has been holding on her lap.

'*The Shadowy Third* by Ellen Glasgow.'

'An excellent choice. A tale with a feminist twist. But, er, Miss Osborne, would you mind keeping the reading aloud until tonight.'

'Oh dear! Yes. Yes, of course. But may I say, how very, very sorry I am. Very sorry, indeed.'

These words are said with such passion and sorrow that they take our speaker by surprise.

'Well, er, it's no matter, really. And anyway, I'm nearly at the end of my talk. Now I don't claim that the screenwriters of these movies have read or even heard of the ghost tales to which I've referred, but it is my contention that stories somehow become part of our collective DNA and so ideas, tropes, concepts and even plotlines get passed from one generation to the next. And to illustrate the point here's what Mrs Dorman says in a famous tale by Edith Nesbit: "They do say, as on All Saints' Eve them two bodies sits up on their slabs, and gets off of them, and then walks down the aisle, in their marble." Could her words in the tale *Man-Size in Marble* have been the inspiration for this scene in *Ghostbusters* where the statues come alive? I'll let you decide.'

Once again the screen lights up, this time with monstrous gargoyles, but it's Miss Osborne who once more commands my attention, for tears are streaming down her cheeks. And so many that she excuses herself and makes a discreet exit.

The visions on the screen fade away and the conference convenor thanks Heather for her fascinating insights. Her lecture was followed by one called 'Transgressional Queer Sex and the Victorian Spook', given by a person who referred to himself/herself/themselves as Pixie, throughout which the mouth of conference organiser remained so wide open I was worried someone might throw in a fish.

The next speaker, a delightful lady, offered a guide as to what one should have about one's person in order protect oneself from ungodly spirits, with a list including the Sacred Host, freshly cut flowers, silver and garlic, the *scutum Davidis*, plus pentacles and charms of various kinds and sizes. Billie, our 'zhooshy' spirit medium – to use his own vernacular – noted that Constable had a collar embedded with silver sixpences.

'Oooh! Duchess Gloria! What a bona Betty bracelet!'

Mrs Jesop couldn't help herself and explained very loudly that her spaniel's unusual lapel was made up of Maundy money once given to her aunt, who had lived to a great age. Hearing this, Professor F.R. Curtis then sprang up from his seat with the alacrity of one who believes the words he is about to impart will bring him glory.

'Our conference organiser has allowed me, in honour of Mrs Jesop's dog, an unscheduled addition to end this afternoon's proceedings, for I spent my lunchtime jotting down how in the Victorian ghost tale, our canine friends react when they encounter a spook. In Lord Edward Bulwer-Lytton's *The House and the Brain* man's best friend slinks back to the door, "scratching and whining to get out," Môme the dog in Chambers's *The Messenger* "suddenly whipped his tail between his legs, whimpered, and made off across the moor" and Constable's spaniel cousin in R.S. Hawker's *The Botathen Ghost* "ran backwards and away, like a thing dismayed and appalled".'

Constable, who had been somewhat sluggish since lunch, on hearing his name lifted up his head. Professor Curtis's list and tone, somewhat disparaging I would say, seemed to be raising suspicions in Mrs Jesop's spaniel, for Constable now rose to his feet and stared at the professor with a look of unease that I had not witnessed before.

'And then there's B.M. Croker's *"To Let"*, where the dog Pip is described as "bristling like a porcupine and trembling violently in every joint." The narrator then tells us that he "sprung off my lap and crawled abjectly under Aggie's chair, seemingly in a transport of fear".'

Was Constable too in a 'transport of fear'? I could not say for certain, but his four legs slowly made their way towards our Professor with mouth agape. Was he about to bark at or worse bite the learned man? No, indeed. For what Constable now dispatched from his throat was the entire contents of his stomach which landed all over the Professor's very expensive looking shoes and socks.

'Oh, but my, I did warn people not to feed him too much fat.'

The poor professor, like many of the dogs to which he had sneeringly referred, now made an ignominious retreat of his own, not exactly growling, but those nearest to him believed they heard a shortening of Constable's name, and one which could so easily be mistaken for that most unpleasant of Anglo-Saxon expletives.

'Well,' said Martin Ward, quickly jumping up to the podium, 'it's already getting dark, but the night is still young for after supper we have that reading from Miss Osborne of *The Shadowy Third*. There's blood to curdle, veins to chill, flesh to creep, hearts to hammer and spines to send shivers down...'

Proceedings then came to an end, except for the issue of the psychiatrist's tie which, according to its owner, had gone missing.

No longer was it hanging over the back of his chair where he had left it. It was a mystery, said, Doctor Dudley, as to who could have taken it.

Or indeed *what*, added Billie Blooming, the spirit medium.

VIII

After the welcome repast of supper, everyone gathered in Meeting Room Five or the Senior Masters' Smoking Room as was.

My darkened wood panelling, with four hanging tapestries displaying scenes from the cursed House of Atreus, had been deemed ideal for a candlelit ghost story. It pleased me no end that as they listened to the tale, a draught from my floorboards shook the hanging clothes, so much so that the sleeping Eumenides of Clytemnestra appeared almost to awaken and, with the flickering glow of the candles upon his face, the ill-fated Agamemnon seemed even to breathe.

The Shadowy Third by Ellen Glasgow was the tale of a nurse – a 'resolute woman' with 'infallible prescience' – employed by the master of the house, Doctor Maradick, to care for his wife, said to be suffering from hallucinations and ghostly fantasies. However, the nurse concludes Mrs Maradick isn't mad at all, for she too sees the spirit of the ghostly Dorothea, Mrs Maradick's young daughter from a previous marriage. Doctor Maradick, briefly the stepfather to Dorothea, is set on having his new wife committed to an asylum in order that he may take full possession of her assets. The doctor is a man of enviable confidence, but the ghost child, like our good nurse, sees through his illusory charm.

As she read the story, Miss Osborne, I noted, placed much emphasis on the line, 'I had quite vividly an impression that the old house was listening,'

(*and indeed, benevolent Reader, I was*!)

'– that there was a real, if invisible presence.'

The twist in the tale is that the husband trips and falls down a long flight of stairs to his death and does so on a child's skipping rope, which, 'as if dropped by a careless hand,' is later found on the staircase bend. The nurse concludes, in the last line of the story, that 'something had killed him at the very moment when he most wanted to live.'

Miss Osborne read with true passion, and much applause followed, but as it died down she turned her attention to the tapestry on the wall with Electra at the grave of Agamemnon.

'Electra, such a silly girl, I've always thought. Agamemnon deserts her mother, sanctions the blood sacrifice of her sister and then goes off to an unnecessary war. Yet Electra still blindly idolises her dear papa. Oh, but Dorothea, the heroine of our story, had no such illusions about her stepfather...'

The tale had seemed to tire Miss Osborne, who now bid *adieu* to the assemblage with these words:

May no ill dreams disturb my rest.
Or powers of darkness me molest.
Teach me to live, that I may dread
The grave as little as my bed.

Mrs Jesop, who for the evening's performance had sat herself next to Billie, the spirit medium, asked if he thought Claverley Manor was haunted.

'Pin back your danglers,' he whispered in her ear, 'and call y'Auntie a dizzy queen, but ever since I arrived in this gildy lattie I've felt the presence of a tristo anima. Pieno pianto.'

'So the house *does* have a ghost?'

'Nanti ghosts *of* this house... yet a fable dona spirit has come this yorno *to* Claverley Manor.'

'An angry spirit?'

'Moltissimo!'

IX

What is Fear?

Fear is the child of curiosity, for, when the curtain twitches, its hand is compelled to pull it back to see what lurks behind.

Fear lives and grows where darkness and shadows shape themselves into that which listens, watches and waits.

Fear is the contagion of deathly silence that in the night seeps deep into your very soul.

Fear is the remembrance of being seized by phantoms in troubled and ugly dreams.

Fear will not bear reason, for no words can expel a thought beyond denying.

Fear is that atavistic horror that comes from ancient lives, older than Man himself.

But above all, Fear reminds him that he is, in the end, an animal whose life at any moment can be stolen from him.

For one that night the darkness would never end and the fitfulness of every Fear that Mankind has ever known and felt would be lived until his dying breath.

X

The moon rising in the deep of the night sky. A dark panelled room where a lady sleeps in a chair with a spaniel dog at her side. A man approaching with hushed steps as silent as the grave.

Black leather gloves pull tight on a stretched out thin tie and with murderous intent the cord of death is lowered to the lady's throat...

'Murderer of Violet!'

The killer hears the voice and turns around to see from whence it came. The voice reveals itself to be Miss Osborne, who now emerges from behind the arras of Clytemnestra and her Furies.

As the man turns, the lady in the chair, Mrs Jesop, opens her eyes and kicks his legs with such forcefulness and surprise that he is brought crashing to the floor.

'Doctor Richard Dudley!' cries Mrs Jesop.

Miss Osborne looks to the killer's side and seems to hear words which I cannot.

'Violet,' Miss Osborne says, 'if you are able, make your ghostly self known to the living spirit of this house!'

A beautiful woman suddenly appears as if out of the air. I see she has a delicate face, but her eyes are ablaze with wrath. 'Let it be done,' says the ghost.

The spectre then casts her eyes around my room, at my floorboards, my mantelpiece, my sash windows, my wood panelling and then says to all as if they are one, 'House! I ask you to do what you must!'

My old school handbell shakes and from it comes the deafening noise of a dozen belfries. The dying cinders in my fireplace are transformed into an instant blaze. A squawk is heard from my chimney and the trapped raven now descends to the iron hearth dogs, bringing with it the dirt of generations. Dust fills the air, spread by the whirling wind of the raven's black feathers, and in the glow of the full moon this flight of soot becomes a thousand dancing demons.

The breeze in my chimney now whistles the tune Look for the Silver Lining *and as it does so my sash windows rise up and the invading night air brings with it the scent of lilac, the same sweet perfume Violet wore as Doctor Richard Dudley strangled her.*

The tapestries on my wall, with their worn-out graces, now twist and shake as their weaves become the face of the murdered woman. The doctor still lies on the floor, his body riveted by Fear, as my dark and menacing shadows wrap themselves around him.

And then they come. Just a scurry of scratches at first. But soon the floor is alive and moving closer to him.

MY RATS! MY RATS! MY RATS!

Hundreds of them. All hungry for human flesh. They are my creatures and they know the weaknesses of Man and where the softest tissues are. Soon the doctor's eyeballs are gnawed away by devouring teeth that would be the last image Richard Dudley ever saw.

The Man lets out a holler like a fox caught in a trap, but even this squeal of pain is denied him, for the rats now leap into his mouth and gorge out and eat his tongue.

'Rats and House! Enough, I say, enough!'

I hear the words of Miss Osborne and my scavengers scatter and return to the holes in the wainscoting from whence they came.

The Man is not dead, but his face – or what is left of it – is frozen like a statue in a rictus of bloody terror.

And through all this, Constable sleeps soundly by the feet of his mistress, dreaming, perhaps, of sausages.

XI

Dear Reader, in the course of this tale I have never lied to you, but I do now confess the crime of omission. In mitigation I offer this conversation that took place the next morning between Billie Blooming, the spirit medium, in a sombre black dress, styled, he claimed, on Joan Crawford in *Mildred Pierce*, and the elderly Miss Osborne, in a simple grey twinset and matching shoes and hat.

'Y'Auntie can sense a spirit ajax, but to varda the dona as you did. Oh! Such a bona gift.'

'Perhaps, though some might call it curse, to see crying eyes with tears that can never be wiped.'

'So Mrs Jesop's favola was nanti fiction.'

'Correct.'

'Hold my pearls! Tell all. My sentar lobes are yours.'

'I am the real prison visitor of her tale. The Rose I met in jail had indeed confessed to murdering Violet, who was, I can now reveal, her own sister. But I saw no ghost of Violet beside Rose, so knew Rose to be innocent. Therefore there were two mysteries to solve. First, why did Rose admit the crime, and, second, who was the true killer? And I discovered the answer to the latter question quite by chance.'

'Where?'

'On television. People say ghosts don't like electricity, well we both know that simply isn't true. Doctor Richard Dudley was appearing on a television programme and there, standing at his side, I saw the melancholy spirit of his victim Violet. Oh! I knew immediately it had been a most violent murder, for I saw all round her throat the dark purple bruises of strangulation.'

'Barbaro bestia!'

'Yes, indeed! A most savage attack.'

'As the Doctor was on the television, Violet couldn't parlay with you, so how did you conoscir it was Violet?'

'Because Violet and Rose were identical twins. Oh, how Doctor Dudley enjoyed the sound of his own voice. But his vanity and ego were his downfall, for had I not seen him on that television programme I would never have discovered the truth. He was talking about how he had been invited to Claverley Manor Conference Centre to debunk "all that ghost nonsense", as he kept calling it. As he espoused his theories on auto-suggestion, and how people can be made to believe anything, I began to understand how he might have made Rose think that she had indeed killed her sister. But to be sure I needed to be in the same room as the ghost of Violet.'

'So you had to schlep here to Claverley Manor with Mrs Jesop.'

'Exactly so. It is fortunate that The Society of Paranormal and Psychic Investigation had two spare places, one for a would-be writer and the other for an actress willing to read a story by candle-light. As soon as I arrived here, the ghost of Violet was able to tell me everything that happened. Oh, but there was sad news from the prison that I had to pass on to Violet. Yet how to do so without raising the suspicions of Doctor Dudley? Then came the perfect opportunity: those movie clips. The music was so loud that it gave me the opportunity to whisper to Violet without Doctor Richard Dudley realising what I was saying or doing.'

'All the omees and palones thought your parlay was you going through the fabbola you had to read last nochy.'

'Yes, and that is what they were meant to believe. But what I had to tell Violet... oh dear me, it was most distressing. It brought tears to my eyes. You see, until yesterday afternoon Violet didn't know that because of the psychiatrist's wickedness, her dear sister Rose had, while in prison, taken her own life.'

'Oh! That was the anger I sensed. Moltisimo rabia!'

'Of course I tried to persuade Violet to forgive, for that is my purpose, but I think it had all gone beyond that. There is much to be said for forgiveness, but so too of righteous anger. And I, like Violet, understood that anger. And personally, too.'

'Oh! Now I savvy! Mrs Jesop is your sister.'

'Well, that's not her real name, obviously. And it's she who is the actress, not me. "Mrs Jesop" was simply a role my sister played. And rather well, I thought. There was only ever water in that gin bottle. Her behaviour was very distracting, as was her dog and her "tipsy" presentation of the plot of *Ego Te Absolvo*. I could see how the story, especially the detail about the change of the lyrics to the song *Look for the Silver Lining*, was distressing our psychiatrist.'

'Oh, there's nishta gets past you!'

'He can't have known how it was possible, but Richard Dudley knew his secret was no longer his own. And that was why he had to kill again. This time my sister. Oh, but of course he wasn't to know I would be waiting for him.'

'Dropped the soap there, didn't he?'

'Indeed so.'

'But perque did Doctor Dudley kill Violet?'

'Oh dear. They had been lovers, you see, but it was the old story of the wedding dress that was never worn. All his promises were broken, but Violet wouldn't let him go. The psychiatrist then discovered that Violet had a twin sister, Rose, who had a history of mental disturbance. I don't know exactly how Doctor Dudley did it, but Rose became utterly convinced it was she who had murdered Violet.'

'Cativitá vellaco! A furba crudel omee.'

'There is a particular type of gentleman, who, as in Ellen Glasgow's *The Shadowy Third*, has the demeanour of effortless superiority. It is my experience of life that such men should never be trusted.'

'Oh! Nanti a more truer word was ever parlared. But such a punizzion.'

'I've always been very fond of Claverley Manor. I was a child here.

As you said, we have a soul even though we are made of clay. And I know this house is no different. I witnessed many years ago the uniqueness of Claverley Manor and its capabilities. Not just creaks in floorboards or bumps and bangs. Oh no, I saw with my own eyes how this house learnt to conjure monsters from the air.'

'Potento!'

'In those days it was a sanatorium, and it was my father who ran it. As a child, I idolised him, but in later life I discovered, from those who had been incarcerated here, the terrible things he had done. He died in torment and without forgiveness. And it was after his death that I began to see the spirits standing beside those who had done the wrong. And then I knew my purpose in life.'

'But was it Violet or this lattie which finally knocked the doctor's cheese off his cracker?'

'Now there I am not sure. I think somehow Violet connected with the soul of this house. When Clytemnestra sought vengeance for her murder, she summoned up the Furies – the Eumenides – in order to drive her killer mad. The house knew this legend, for there's a tapestry depicting the very event hanging in the room. That's why, I think, the house incited the rats to do what they did.'

'Attacca ravagiar!'

'Oh yes, most destructive. Doctor Richard Dudley will never speak, see or think a sane thought again. Forever imprisoned in the madness of his mind. And an asylum is not always a kind world.'

'Violet? Where is she now?'

'I don't know. She's gone, but to what place, I would not like to say.'

And neither, dear Reader, would I.

XII

I am no cadaver. I am a living spirit. And last night, my help was requested and it was given.

So there you are, my friend, our story is now at an end. You will not find in my home a thrice-locked door behind which lurks a dwarfish fiend, nor discover an ossuary containing the bleached bones of the dead who still cry out for their liberty. A child in the dark does not sing alone in the nursery, and the expiring breaths of its poor mother, who was tricked by her adulterous husband into drinking poison on Christmas Eve, are not heard when snow falls.

And yet, I have had my wish. For, one night, on the rise of the full moon, I am proud to say... I was once a haunted house.

The Strange Case of the Unaccountable Shadow

The Startling Diary of a Worried Mother.

Below are several diary entries, passed on to me ten days ago.

Monday 3rd

'Mummy, can we have a "dissecting room" in our house?'

What a question! And it was pretty much the first thing Nathan said as he walked through the door just now. Must have come up in his biology class, I thought. But no. It was that awful English teacher of his. Turns out they're studying *The Strange Case of Dr Jekyll and Mr Hyde* and Mr Morris had been explaining that Jekyll lived in a house where there was a set-aside space for cutting up dead bodies. Nathan put his hand up and said that chopping people up was naughty and those who did such things should be punished. All the boys in the class laughed at him and because of that Nathan now wants his own dissecting room.

Thirteen is such a difficult age.

I think I'd better cook Nathan his favourite for his tea: chips and fish fingers. And no peas!

Children blow hot and cold, so no surprise that after his fish fingers Nathan has decided he doesn't want a dissecting room after all. But before he finished his last chip he told me it wasn't just the other boys who laughed at him – his teacher did too.

I met that nasty Mr Morris once. Silly moustache and one of those smiles that just go up at one side. And I know from bitter experience such men can't be trusted.

😐 😐 😐

Four in the morning!!!!

Couldn't sleep and so got up to make a sandwich.

Oh, if only I was clever like his father. Cambridge University! And David has always been so ambitious for Nathan to go there too. But if his father finds out Nathan's grades have dropped to a seven and even a lowly five in maths I'll never hear the last of it. I read in magazines that you mustn't interfere with your child's education but what happens when you don't? That's right! They blame the mother. But what to do? Nathan can't change schools. Not in the middle of the academic year. Oh well, maybe my prawn in mayo will give me some inspiration...

Tuesday 4th

Thank you prawns! Or was it the mayo??? Who cares, for I woke up this morning with a brainwave – private tutoring!

My French from my years abroad has always helped out Nathan in his foreign language class, but I wouldn't have a clue with English literature. Never liked books. All those words! But I'm sure I can find someone who can help. I must do a little digging – *je vais faire quelques recherches*!

💡 💡 💡

Morning coffee time!

WhatsApp has proved a wonderful spade!

Found a local mother's group and a lady called Mrs Higgins who comes highly recommended. Just messaged her and she's coming round on Wednesday evening. Who's the best ever mother now?

Wednesday 5th

Well! Just met Mrs Higgins.

Very impressive. A lady who clearly knows how the system works. Mrs H told me a basic understanding of plot and characters would get you a pass, but for a grade 9 Nathan needs 'to write critically about the conceptual themes'. She then started talking about 'Petal'. I was confused and immediately thought of daisies and buttercups! But I've learnt in life not to let my face reveal what I'm thinking – all those years with David taught me that. As it turns out 'Petal' is one of those educational buzz words and stands for 'Point, Evidence, Technique, Analysis, Link.'

Would P.E.T.A.L. get Nathan into Cambridge University, I asked?

Mrs Higgins smiled – a nice smile that goes up on both sides – and said that if I was really aiming that high then Nathan needed to read 'around' Robert Louis Stevenson. Mrs H mentioned someone called Alison Cunningham who'd nursed Stevenson from the age of two. Apparently she kept a diary and extracts from when Robert was twelve had been published online. Well! Good omen! I've now started keeping a diary and Nathan is only just thirteen. And if Stevenson grew up to become a world famous author, why couldn't Nathan? That would be one in the eye for David!

Naturally, I gave Mrs Higgins the job on the spot.

Awkward moment as Mrs H left the house, though.

I felt almost back at school myself because Mrs H told me not to pronounce Jekyll as '*Jeck*yll' but as '*Jeek*yll'. Sounded wrong to me, but Mrs Higgins said that's because I'd been watching too many American films. 'Jeekyll' is meant to rhyme with 'seek', as in the game 'Hide and Seek'. As she said this, I accidentally knocked over one of David's many walking sticks which are still by the door. Mrs H asked if they were mine. I just said they belonged to someone who used to live here but doesn't anymore and left it at that.

I really should let David have them, I suppose.

He's always loved his long walks.

Friday 7th

Tonight was Mrs Higgins' first session.

Typical teacher! How they like to lay down the law. The tutorial hour must be done in a 'neutral space', front room or dining area. An adult must be present in the house at all times. I said that adult would always be me, but didn't explain why. Mrs H said all pets should be kept out of the way – she's allergic to cats, apparently – but the door of the teaching area (which we decided would be the dining room, because I still had David's old desk there), must be left open throughout the session. I was given the option of staying with them, but I told Mrs H I wasn't one of those 'helicopter' mothers, constantly hovering over their offspring. She laughed and said that would make her job a lot easier. I told Nathan to be a good boy and learn lots and then went upstairs, taking pussy cat Smokey with me.

I wouldn't say Mrs Higgins has a shouty voice but one couldn't help hearing her from my bedroom. I certainly wasn't listening in or anything, it's just one of those voices that carry, that's all. Not like Nathan. Such a quiet, sensitive soul. Difficult to tell what he's saying half the time. And certainly not when you're upstairs and he's down.

And a mother worries.

Well! I couldn't just sit all night in the bedroom, could I? Why not make yourself a nice a cup of tea, I thought. Of course I'd have to pass the dining room door to get to the kitchen and as I did I just happened to glance through the narrow gap where the hinges are.

Mrs Higgins had her back to the desk and Nathan was sitting opposite, but several feet away. He was asking a question about the dissecting room, so I decided to stay and listen.

I could see that Mrs Higgins had a book in her hand called *The Body Snatchers*, which, she was saying, Stevenson wrote just before *The Strange Case of Dr Jekyll and Mr Hyde*. Both stories featured the house of a doctor that had a dissecting room. Well! If Nathan ever mentioned this in class it would wipe the crooked smile of the face of that horrible Mr Morris.

Mrs Higgins then read out a section about grave robbers driving into the country to 'desecrate some lonely graveyard, and return before dawn with their booty to the door of the dissecting-room.' That's why, she said, Stevenson described the back door in Jekyll and Hyde as having 'neither bell nor knocker' and being 'blistered and distained' because what they took through it was secret and evil.

Nathan said the paintwork in our house was scratched too, because Smokey was always scraping to get in through the back door or pawing to go down into the cellar. Mrs H laughed and said as long as he didn't get in through their door she'd be fine, otherwise she'd be sneezing all night. Nathan then asked why evil had to be kept secret. Mrs H replied it was the nature of Victorian society to hide their wickedness. Could Nathan, she asked, think of what was shut away in Stevenson's story? Nathan mentioned Lanyon's letter revealing the truth about Jekyll that the lawyer kept in the private safe. She then told Nathan to write down the word 'concealment'.

Yet it was strange, because as she said this, the open door of the dining room began to close all by itself. Not completely, but I could no longer see or hear what was happening.

Just a draught, probably. But a mother worries.

Nearly bedtime!

After his cocoa I asked Nathan how the hour tutorial had gone, but all he did was put his finger to his lips. Well!

Secrets, I suppose, are a theme of *Jekyll and Hyde*, but I still thought it was an odd thing to do.

Tuesday 11th

Tonight Mrs Higgins' voice didn't seem quite as loud as it had before.

I'd put a book against the dining room door to stop it closing, but even if I stood just outside I was still unable to make out everything she was saying. And I really think it best if I do know everything.

From what I could tell, Mrs H was talking about what it meant to be a proper gentleman in Victorian times. Army officers were gentlemen, as were church minsters, and so too were lawyers and doctors such as Lanyon and Utterson in the story. She then asked

Nathan what his father did and he said, after a moment's thought, 'Banking'. Mrs H laughed and said that in the olden days bankers were thought of as tradesmen, not gentlemen. Nathan said it didn't matter if Daddy wasn't a real gentleman because he didn't live here anymore. The room went very quiet after that.

After his cocoa, I had a talk with Nathan about David. It wasn't his fault Mummy and Daddy were no longer Mummy and Daddy. Mummy was doing her best. And Mummy wanted Nathan to do his best at school. I asked what he'd learnt tonight and he said nothing that he didn't know already. I couldn't say anything because Nathan would then realise I'd been listening in. I just said that Daddy had to go away, but Mummy loved Nathan and would protect him from any harm and that was all that mattered now.

Wednesday 12th

This morning I made the effort to go and visit David.

I told him how well Nathan was doing. I explained about Mrs Higgins and even mentioned Cambridge. But as per usual, David wasn't very talkative. 'I suppose,' I said, 'you'd now like to go off on one of your walks. To get away from me, no doubt.'

He didn't reply but just stared like he always does.

It was then I remembered those silly walking sticks. Anyway, I told him I'd bring them all next time.

Thursday 13th

Today I got up bright and early and bought one of those Alexa cameras with an inbuilt microphone. Now I'll be able to make notes on what Mrs Higgins says.

Obviously I won't test Nathan, but at least I'll know for myself all about the 'thematic story concepts', as Mrs H calls them.

Which reminds me – I must pop up to the high street and buy a copy of the book!

Oh! It's truly horrific! Not the sort of story you should take to bed if you're on your own. What a very unpleasant man Mr Hyde is! Trampling all over a child. Very wicked. Any man who does that *deserves* to be taken to a dissecting room.

Friday 14th

Just linked Alexa up to my mobile. Very techy, but I got it to work.

Aren't I a clever mum?

Having Alexa in the dining room will mean I won't have to stand behind the door any more. Not that Mrs H ever saw or heard me. And she won't even know about the camera either because I've hidden it behind a cactus plant and put some tape over the green light that comes on when it's working. A mother always worries.

😐 😐 😐

Mrs Higgins just rang to cancel tonight's session and move it to Monday morning when there's a day off school.

She's been reliable so far, so I didn't ask why. Well! Why not use the time to do some research of my own? So that's what I did. And if Nathan asks why I'm so knowledgable all of a sudden about those 'thematic story concepts' I can honestly say 'Google'!

I looked up 'Alison Cunningham', the nurse Mrs Higgins had mentioned. 'Cummy', Stevenson called her. Rhymes with Mummy! I like that. Anyway, Cummy looked after the boy from the age of two and then stayed with the family for the next twenty years. She was a strict Calvinist and her strong religious beliefs had had a strong influence on the young Stevenson. Well! Good for her!

Maybe she went a bit too far saying playing cards were the Devil's Books, but to my mind all she was trying to do was warn the boy against gambling. And what's wrong with that?

Monday 17th

How peculiar! It's as if Mrs Higgins knew what I'd been reading because this morning she began her tutorial talking about Cummy.

Only her thoughts about Stevenson's nurse were very different to mine. Mrs Higgins called her a 'neurotic compulsive' and her 'ordinances' – I wrote down the exact words she used – were examples of 'religious mania' and that the Bible stories she told Stevenson gave him feverish nightmares which made him ill.

Mrs Higgins then asked Nathan if he ever read the Bible. What an odd question. I couldn't see Nathan's face to tell how he reacted to this because Mrs H had put both chairs in different positions, so on the screen on my phone I could only see the back of his head and the edge of her hair.

Anyway, Mrs H must have reached down into her bag because I suddenly saw in her hand a Bible. There were many religious references in *Jekyll and Hyde*, she said, and Nathan would get extra marks if he was able to quote a few examples. There's when Jekyll unexpectedly wakes up as Edward Hyde and in his confessional note it says: 'This inexplicable incident, this reversal of my previous experience, seemed, like the Babylonian finger on the wall, to be spelling out the letters of my judgement.'

Did Nathan know what 'the Babylonian finger' meant? Nathan didn't speak but I saw his hair shaking. Mrs H then opened the Bible and asked Nathan to read from where she'd put a Post-It note, which I could just about make out was from *The Book of Daniel*, which I have just looked it up in one of David's old Bibles.

'Fingers of a human hand suddenly appeared and began writing on the plaster wall of the royal palace, illuminated by a nearby candle. As the King watched the hand write, his countenance changed, his face grew pale, his legs limp and his knees knocked, for his mind had become troubled. The King called out for enchanters, soothsayers and astrologers to be brought and when they came the King said, "Whosoever can interpret the writing on the wall shall be clothed with scarlet and have a chain of gold put about their neck. That person shall then be made third in command in my kingdom".'

Nathan has never been brought up to believe in silly fairy tales and so I was very pleased when I heard him say a hand couldn't just appear out of nowhere. Mrs H agreed but then said the reference to the candle might suggest it was the *shadow* of a hand on a wall. She then got up, went to the window and drew the curtains. She came back, switched on the lamp and angled it so it lit up the wall. Then, putting fingers to the light, she cast a silhouette of a rabbit. This she turned into an elephant by sticking out two thumbs for the tusks and, upon moving her fingers, the elephant became a cat. Nathan laughed and said it couldn't be Smokey because he had only one ear. Mrs Higgins said they'd best get back to work, but at least he was now sure to remember about 'the Babylonian finger' if it came up in the exam.

Strangely though, even when Mrs Higgins lowered her hands, a dark shape remained on the wall where she had cast her shadows. Due to Mrs Higgins' allergy I was worried it was Smokey, who is as black as his name suggests. Only as I was staring at this shadow, I heard Smokey purring under my duvet, where he sometimes likes to sleep. But if not his, what was this unaccountable shadow?

A mother does worry.

Friday 21st

Mrs H began the next session by asking Nathan if 'anything was concerning or worrying him' (again, I wrote down her exact words).

Nathan didn't respond and then she added, 'I meant about the story.' Nathan said he didn't understand why Mr Hyde had to be so ugly and Mrs Higgins explained that there'd been a tradition that your inner spirit shaped your physical body. Plus there was the Darwinian theory that human beings were descended from apes.

Mrs H then asked Nathan for an example of where that ugly inner spirit of Mr Hyde had even managed to get inside the mind of Utterson, the lawyer. Nathan flicked to the page and then started reading aloud. '"To-night there was a shudder in his blood; the face of Hyde sat heavy on his memory; he felt (what was rare with him) a nausea and distaste of life; and in the gloom of his spirits, he seemed to read a menace in the flickering of the firelight on the polished cabinets and the uneasy starting of the shadow on the roof."'

As Nathan said the word 'shadow' that dark shape at the bottom of the wall appeared again, only now it was bigger and stumpy and lumpy, like an animal asleep. I jumped because at that moment the mobile rang. Michael. Friend of David. I didn't want to talk to him but he wouldn't stop asking me questions and by the time we'd finished our conversation Mrs Higgins's session had come to an end and the battery on my phone was at zero, so I couldn't tell if that dark shadow was still there.

Just rang Mrs Higgins at home to ask how she thought the tutoring was going. She said Nathan was a bright boy, but if I really was aiming for Cambridge he'd have to start thinking about the philosophical principles underpinning the story because how a writer sees the world is based on their cognitive reasoning.

She lost me there, but then said, 'What we see and what we think is dependent on what we believe to be true.' She'd begin the next session, she told me, with concepts of identity. Not so useful for the exam but essential if Nathan ever got an interview for Cambridge.

Wednesday 26th

Well! No idea what all this means but I made notes as best I could.

'Most modern philosophers,' said Mrs Higgins, 'doubt that there's such thing as one's "self".'

Nathan said, 'But I'm me and you're you.'

Mrs H replied, 'True, but we're like a cart that moves all by itself and what we call "I" or "me" is simply the horse we invent to pull it.'

Nathan said, 'I'm a boy, not a horse.'

Mrs H laughed and said, 'The point is, what we mean by "self" is disputed in philosophy. There's David Hume and the "bundle theory", where who we are keeps changing, depending on mood or who you're with. There's Sigmund Freud and the theory of the mind, where there's the Ego, our conscious self, the Id, where wants and desires lurk, and the Superego, which guards against the dark side of the Id. Stevenson thought the self could be split into two. And that's the central concept in *Jekyll and Hyde*, and other tales such as *Markheim*. Write this word down: 'duality'. And this quote from *Markheim*, "Evil and good run strong in me, haling me both ways." For Stevenson, we may believe ourselves to be principled moral thinkers, but just below that surface we're all primitive savages. And Mr Hyde is that "other self" or alter ego that lurks inside us all.'

As she was saying all this, the dark shape that was still there on the wall woke up. It was now alive and breathing. In and out and in and out. And even after the session came to an end, and Mrs Higgins and Nathan had left the room, the shadow remained, broodily moving about. I went downstairs to see it with my own eyes, only when I went into the dining room it wasn't there anymore. Must be hiding somewhere. Tomorrow, I'll buy an iPad and record the sessions.

And then I'll be able to see where The Shadow conceals itself.

Thursday 27th

I decided not to ask Nathan whether he'd seen what I'd seen. But I was curious how he'd react to the idea of a shadow existing all by itself, so I asked at breakfast this morning if he could remember in *Peter Pan* why Peter visited Wendy.

'To hear stories,' he said.

'Yes, but wasn't there another reason too.'

'To find his shadow. He'd lost it.' I then asked if a shadow could be alive all by itself and he said, 'Only in make believe.' I then asked about shadows in *Jekyll and Hyde*. He thought for a moment and said that Mr Hyde represented a darkness that lives in us all. He then said could we have chips and fish fingers for tea. And no peas.

Friday 28th

I recorded this evening's session on my new iPad and so I now have a transcript of exactly what was said.

Mrs Higgins: One of the themes that comes up in exams is Appearance and Reality. What we believe is true often isn't because people too often jump to the wrong conclusion. Can you think of anyone who does that?

Nathan: In the story or real life?

Mrs Higgins: In the story. First chapter.

Nathan: You mean when Mr Enfield sees Hyde going into the back door of Jekyll's house and comes back with gold and so he assumes Jekyll is being blackmailed?

Mrs Higgins: Yes.

Nathan: What Mr Enfield believes is logical, but that doesn't mean it's true.

Mrs Higgins: Exactly. Well done. And in the story, Enfield's assumption about blackmail is repeated so often it becomes accepted as a fact. Write these two words down: 'supposition' and 'conjecture'.

Nathan: What's the difference?

Mrs Higgins: I was afraid you were going to ask me that. Supposition is believing something without any real proof, whereas conjecture involves reaching an explanation by reasoning, even if doesn't turn out to be correct. Understand?

Nathan: I think so.

Mrs Higgins: But the important point with both, is that we allow ourselves to be deceived, not because of what we see, but what we believe we see or even make ourselves see. Can you think of a character who deceives herself in the story.

Nathan: The lawyer, Mr Utterson.

Mrs Higgins: I said '*her*self'.

Nathan: Oh yes, sorry... no, I can't... oh! The maid.

Mrs Higgins: Go on.

Nathan: She couldn't make out what was said just before Hyde murders the old man, yet she could hear Hyde breaking his bones with his cane. That doesn't make sense.

Mrs Higgins: Is she lying?

Nathan: No. I think when she sees what's happening she hears the noise in her head.

Mrs Higgins: Good. Now, do you know what I mean when I say the 'third person narrator'?

Nathan: The one telling the story.

Mrs Higgins: Yes. And this sort of storyteller is usually knowledgable and objective about what happens in the tale. But can you think where the third person narrator gets it wrong?

Nathan: Er, no. Unless you mean the rumours flying around about Hyde's past and his strange friends.

Mrs Higgins: Go on.

Nathan: Well, Hyde doesn't have any friends. And he can't have a past because he's only just been born. Not born... I mean Jekyll has only just... I don't know the right word.

Mrs Higgins: I don't think there is one! Perhaps you could say 'created him' or even 'released him'. But the point is, the storyteller isn't always accurate and this we call an 'unreliable narration'.

Well! Need I say more?

Mrs Higgins is clearly preparing Nathan for the day I tell him about The Shadow. He'll say it's an invention of my mind and isn't real. Oh, but it is. And it's there all the time now. During that last session, it climbed up the walls. And grew long hairy arms, like an ape. And it opened its eyes and showed me its teeth. I can see it right now. It's crawling along the ceiling.

Mrs Higgins knows all about The Shadow because Mrs Higgins created and released it. Mrs Higgins now wants me to tell Nathan what lurks and hides in this house. But I'm much cleverer than Mrs Higgins. I shan't tell Nathan about the evil Shadow Monster. Instead, I'll destroy it. I'll buy the most powerful light bulb in the world and I'll leave it on all day and all night. There'll *be* no Shadow then.

Tonight I'll take all the furniture out of the room and I'll put a sleeping pill in Nathan's cocoa, then he won't wake up and hear what I'm doing. Yes.

Everlasting perpetual light is how I'll kill The Shadow Monster.

Sunday 30th

It's early Sunday morning. I've come down to discover whether The Shadow is dead. Oh no! It's there at my feet. Alive.

No! No! No! It's attaching itself to me.

Oh! How it growls like a dog! And now it speaks.

'I am The Shadow inside... YOU!'

I try to move away, but it crawls with me. I lift my hand and The Shadow raises its fist. I move my fingers and The Shadow grasps at the air. I draw back the curtains to let in the light of dawn, but The Shadow only laughs.

'Hah! Hah! Hah! You cannot destroy me because I am you. We are each other.'

I turn around.

The Shadow laughs again.

'Hah! Hah! Hah! I'm still here. Je me cache ici. Je m'appelle l'ombre. Et toi, Je-kyll. Je kill. I kill.'

'"I kill"?'

'Hah! Hah! Hah Oui. Tu tues! And you must again. Kill!'

I now realise what it is that the Shadow wants me to do...

Monday 10th April – 14.33

As her designated psychiatrist, I would say that these diary entries give a very clear indication of the state of mind of the accused at the time of the death of Mrs Higgins.

As with Sir Danvers Carew in Robert Louis Stevenson's novella *The Strange Case of Dr Jekyll and Mr Hyde*, the victim's demise was the result of a frenzied attack with a walking stick. In short, she was bludgeoned to death.

For the record, it is noted that following a search of the patient's home by police, two other bodies were found. Her young son, Nathan, in his bed, and, alerted by the scratching of a cat at the door, the dismembered remains of my patient's husband, David, which were discovered buried in the cellar.

FOR THE HELL OF IT

By Steve Nallon

- Real bird nests or CGI?
– Would Keanu do a cameo as the severed head??
– Ring Paula at Paramount.
– Did Fox pass on this?

The sending of this MS does not constitute an offer.

FOR THE HELL OF IT

Screenplay Film Festival Awards

Best Unproduced Script in Feature
Nashville Independent Filmmakers Festival
July 2024

WINNER
BEST SCREENPLAY
ATHENS
Film & Art Festival
2024

Best Unproduced Script in Feature
Hollywood International Golden Age Festival
June 2024

WINNER
RIFF
RAMESHWARAM INTERNATIONAL FILM FESTIVAL
2024

WINNER
BEST ORIGINAL SCREENPLAY
Cleveland Arthouse Film Awards
2024

2 11 17
INTERNATIONAL FILM FESTIVAL
WINNER
2024

Best Screenwriting
Mei International Film Festival
2024

BEST HORROR
Kookai International Film Festival
2024

AMDG

EXT. SUNRISE - A DRY SANDY BEACH

The sound of waves gently lapping on a sandy beach - leaving behind them layers of cotton blossom foam.

A stronger wave comes in, bringing driftwood. From a boat or a tree? Can't tell.

Another wave and more driftwood, only this time it's curved and has white paint on it - definitely from a boat. Oh my, what's this? Looks like intestines, a kidney and a bit of spleen. And is that part of a human hand? Can't be sure, for a scavenging seagull swoops down, grabs it with its claws and flies off into the open sky.

The low morning sun transitions from blood red to syrup yellow in an almost ethereal way - but is that the strangeness of the light itself or how it's being perceived? Perhaps the answer can be found in the wide eyes of CALEB, who sits on a blanket some distance from the shoreline, staring out to sea.

CALEB's face becomes brightest white and his eyes are forced to squint - for the sun is now in its glory and a new day has begun.

CALEB stretches, yawns and then glances around and sees several people asleep on or under blankets on the sandy beach.

CALEB
(To himself in a whisper)
I usually wake up first... but not always.

CALEB involuntarily shakes his head.

CALEB (CONT'D)
Oh...

A weird thought just came into his mind, but then suddenly went. What was it? CALEB tries to remember but can't. Doesn't matter, if it's important, he'll recall it later.

CALEB sits and we see he has slept in his day clothes - loose cream linen trousers and vibrant purple shirt with suns and stars. Very 1960s. He reaches to the side of blanket for his suede vest with a cut fringe, which he then puts it on. We'll discover that clothes-wise CALEB is slightly out of time with the others on the beach, whose fashion style is more 1970s.

CALEB shifts along his blanket to pick up a thin scarf to tie round his neck, plus some sunglasses, which are round and made of blue glass. And once he puts these on CALEB's 60s hippie look is complete.

Glancing around CALEB now sees scattered across the beach flasks, cartons, a few Double Diamond beer bottles, one empty bottle of red wine, plastic glasses, plus paper cups and plates. Enough for a one-night sleepover, but no more. He's curious about the Double Diamond beer bottles, as if they are almost unknown to him. But again he shakes his head, ridding himself of the thought.

CALEB sigh and then lowers his head and sits in quiet stillness on the warm dry sand.

The people asleep on the beach (currently six in total, including CALEB) lie close enough together on their blankets to suggest 'good friends', yet far enough apart to tell us they're not what we now think of as 'friends with benefits'. But there's been a group like this in every generation since generations began. All at the right end of thirty-something, smart, argumentative, but sometimes a little too pleased with themselves. Not immature, but still young enough to learn a lesson or two.

One blanket bed, however, is presently unoccupied. It's further away than the others and has as a makeshift pillow a hand-knitted tank-top jumper. Just to its side is a white shirt and a copy of William Golding's novel LORD OF THE FLIES - and the price on the cover is 2/6 (two shillings and sixpence).

The vacated blanket certainly looks slept on, for there's a pair of men's shoes at the bottom of it, along with some woollen socks darned at the toes and heels... but where is the man who wears them?

The beach we now see is protected by a high rock cliff - and secured into it is a wooden stairway within a zigzag frame.

Dozens of seagulls who inhabit the crevices in the cliff fly to and from their nests. Inside one of the nests an adult gull has under its claws a struggling sanderling. The adult is tearing off its feathers and feeding the living flesh to its chicks. The second parent flies in with whatever it was that was scavenged from the shoreline. Oh yes... definitely a human hand, only there are two fingers missing. And the others won't be there for long, because the gull now tears off bits of skin and flesh to add to the chicks morning feed. Human meat for breakfast. Yum! Yum!

On the beach CALEB is still sitting with his hippie sunglasses covering his eyes and his head well down.

However, there are stirrings elsewhere, for PETER, lying next to DOCKEY, gives DOCKEY a mate's gentle punch.

PETER
Sleep well?

DOCKEY turns his head to PETER, only he keeps his eyes closed and puts on an *'I'm-still-asleep'* face.

DOCKEY
(With undisguised irony) Oh yes. I slept so, so well. All that sand up my arse. The crabs biting at my toes. The rain. You snoring. Oh, and did I mention those seagulls? Not animal whose throat has learnt the art of the whisper.

As if on cue, two seagulls fly overhead and squawk very loudly.

DOCKEY opens his eyes and looks up.

DOCKEY (CONT'D)
Exempli gratia.

JODIE, who is also awake, has been listening in to the conversation between PETER and DOCKEY.

JODIE
You might as well get it right, Dockey. *<u>Exemplorum</u> gratia.* Two seagulls, so use the plural.

This remark gets an *'eyes-to-heaven'* look from DOCKEY to PETER and mocking *'telling-off-finger'* from PETER to DOCKEY.

JODIE glances around the group and starts counting off the people on or under the blankets one by one, pointing to herself first.

JODIE (CONT'D)
One, two, three, four, five, six...

JODIE spots the unoccupied blanket.

JODIE (CONT'D)
Someone's not here.

DOCKEY looks to PETER and then nods over to CALEB, still sitting with his head low.

DOCKEY
(In a whisper to PETER)
And someone's not all there.

PETER and DOCKEY both enjoy a giggle at the expense of CALEB.

JODIE
Graham's missing. (To DOCKEY and PETER) Did you boys see where he went?

DOCKEY
(As if a child at school)
No, Miss Jodie.

JODIE notices what's at the bottom of the vacated blanket.

JODIE
Oh, Graham's not wearing his shoes and socks - so can't have gone far.

DOCKEY
That's right, Miss Jodie. Oh, you're so clever, Miss Jodie.

JODIE gives DOCKEY a look of annoyance and disapproval.

DOCKEY giggles at his own silliness.

JODIE points to the sky.

JODIE
What is it that's up there right now?

DOCKEY looks skywards.

DOCKEY
Heaven?

JODIE
A yellow ball we call the sun. And its gift of morning light is our cue to get up.

Both DOCKEY and PETER immediately hide their heads under their blankets and make loud snoring noises.

JODIE rises from her blanket and we now see that she wears tight black slacks and a man's loose fitting long blue shirt over them. She picks up her blanket from the sand and begins to fold it. As she does so, she looks around at the untidy mess the group seem to have made of the beach.

JODIE (CONT'D)
(Under her breath)
And who's gonna have to tidy up from the night before? Me, as per usual.

JODIE walks over to a large backpack next to CALEB, puts her folded blanket carefully on top of it, unzips one of the side pockets and removes a black bin bag.

JODIE (CONT'D)
(Loudly and to all)
Who wants a polythene rubbish bag? Don't all rush at once. Olga?

OLGA, still lying on her blanket, lifts her head with a look of annoyance.

JODIE goes to OLGA and puts her face right to OLGA's.

JODIE (CONT'D)
(Still very loudly)
Oh! That'll be me then, Princess. I'll be your tidy-upper. As always.

JODIE begins to tackle the strewn litter. Fingers are seen speedily picking up empty orange squash cartons, coke bottles, those brown beer bottles, the red wine bottle, plus colourful plastic cups and paper plates, which have a centre pattern of exotic birds of paradise.

OLGA
Oh, why do you have to spoil everything?

OLGA sits up and looks at the view. We see she is wearing an extremely beautiful orange and yellow 1970s Bohemian dress. Oh yes, it's very chic - and what the wafer-thin material lacks in substance it certainly makes up for in oodles of folds and layers.

OLGA (CONT'D)
Let your eyes feast on the majesty of the morning of the longest day. That's why we come here. For these special hours. Oh! Just look at the sun! The sky! The sea! What else does one need in life?

JODIE
(Under her breath)
Servants.

JODIE picks up a cheap plastic knife.

JODIE (CONT'D)
(Still under her breath)
And proper metal cutlery.

OLGA
We all agreed. 'We will share the wonder of this magical beach until the power of the tide brings the waves lapping at our very toes.'

JODIE finds an empty crisp packet and intentionally scrunches it up next to OLGA.

OLGA (CONT'D)
Oh Jodie! Do stop this unnecessary frenzy.

JODIE ignores OLGA's request and continues to put the bottles, plates and cups into the black polythene rubbish bag.

OLGA, now fully awake, tries to calm herself by taking in a large breath - and as she does so, she caresses the warm sand with her fingers...

OLGA (CONT'D)
Let the Time we live by be the rise of the sun, the advent of the moon, and the coming of the tide.

On the next blanket to OLGA lies AGNES who is now also awake.

OLGA (CONT'D)
Oh Agnes! Let us together greet the morning to the longest day! Take in the serenity of the sky, the allure of the sea and its allure waves.

A seagull flies over her and squawks as it passes by.

OLGA (CONT'D)
Oh and the beauty of the seagull's cry!

OLGA takes in her beloved view and hums what could well be a harmony line from *'All Things Bright and Beautiful'*. But whatever the tune is, OLGA suddenly stops, for she appears to spot something odd at the shore's edge.

A wave has washed up some knotted rope - boat rigging probably and possibly other nautical items to, only she can't quite make it out. OLGA is curious as to what it is, but now she's committed herself to the serenity of the view - and OLGA isn't one to lose face.

Even so, OLGA has a quick look around to see if anyone else has noticed this new arrival on the shoreline. Seems not: DOCKEY and PETER remain with their heads under their blankets, CALEB sits with his head lowered and JODIE is still busy knotting the black polythene bag full of rubbish.

OLGA now turns to AGNES, but AGNES is unlikely to have seen anything, for she wears over her face a thin white veil. Not only that, her eyes are closed. And now we see why, for AGNES is on her knees with her hands clasped together in prayer.

OLGA gives AGNES a *'Why-bother-the-Almighty-when-we-have-a-heavenly-view-right-there-in-front-of-us'* stare.

JODIE looks at AGNES intensely - and perhaps even longingly. AGNES may not have OLGA's exquisite style and beauty, but her porcelain skin is flawless. And as the wind gently blows, AGNES takes on the serenity of one of those marble sculptures by Antonio Corradini, where a diaphanous veil gently touches a female face in prayer.

JODIE takes this opportunity to get as close as she dare to AGNES.

AGNES seems to sense someone near her and her eyes open.

JODIE
(Trying to cover how close she is)
Oh, er. Put a word in for me. I'm a sinner, I suppose, in your eyes.

Hearing this, DOCKEY peeks out from under his blanket and looks over at AGNES.

DOCKEY taps PETER's shoulder and PETER's head comes out from under his blanket.

DOCKEY points to AGNES and makes a series of mocking and exaggerated signs of the cross.

DOCKEY leans in to PETER and whispers something - and together they laugh at whatever it was that DOCKEY said.

Irritated and distracted, AGNES now looks over to DOCKEY and PETER sniggering.

AGNES
Would you boys like to share the joke?

PETER

Dockey said life would be much more fun if, in the 'The Seven Deadlys', the angels had given the thumbs up to Lust but made Piety a sin.

Not funny, thinks AGNES, but she's no crushed violet and so isn't frightened of striking back.

AGNES

Well, please inform Mister Dockerty that if the angels replaced Wrath with Facetious Flippancy, the world would have no greater miscreant than himself.

PETER laughs, but DOCKEY offers only a half smile - and it ain't genuine.

PETER

(To DOCKEY)

Oh! Agnes has got you there!

AGNES

And Mister Dockerty, please inform your friend, young Peter, that no one likes a tell-tale-tit.

PETER stops laughing.

DOCKEY

(Now smiling for real)

Ha! Ha! You say it as it is, Agnes. We love you for it. I love you, you love me - we're all friends who love each other. Even Graham. Wherever he is.

PETER

Yes. Where is Graham?

DOCKEY

Perhaps he's been captured by pirates. Or lured out to sea by the siren voice of a mermaid. Or, like Jonah, he's been swallowed by a whale. Poor Graham. We will probably never see him again. At least not alive!

JODIE

Oh I suspect we will - look! Our wanderer returns.

JODIE points along the beach.

A distant bare chested figure walks towards the group, carrying something in his hands, though we can't yet tell what it is.

DOCKEY and PETER get up from their blankets. DOCKEY is wearing a 70s football strip and PETER has a flowery shirt and bellbottom denim trousers with a fashionable triangular cut of red at the hem.

PETER and DOCKEY both put their hands to their brows to shield their eyes from the sun in order to make out what it is that GRAHAM has found.

We see that the beach is extremely long and narrow, and seems to stretch for an eternity. Not a soul is in sight, other than GRAHAM.

GRAHAM is shirtless, but he is wearing grey cotton trousers which have a darker grey repair patch at the knee that doesn't quite match the rest of the material.

GRAHAM's slow walk is watched in silence by PETER, DOCKEY, JODIE, OLGA and even AGNES, who is still kneeling but has lifted her veil and has her eyes open.

When GRAHAM arrives we see what it is that he's been carrying: an enormous conch shell.

GRAHAM looks towards CALEB, who is still sitting with his head down. GRAHAM seems to be about to call him over, only he changes his mind and instead carefully places the prized conch on the sand and stands over it in reverential silence.

DOCKEY goes over to GRAHAM and lightly kicks the conch with the edge of his foot.

DOCKEY

Graham. Tut, tut, tut. (Looking down at the conch) You can't go about stealing someone's home.

GRAHAM

Or coffin.

GRAHAM's voice is deep and rougher than either DOCKEY or PETER - and of a lower social class too.

DOCKEY

(Mocking GRAHAM's deadly deep voice)

'Or coffin'. You would think of it like that, wouldn't you?

DOCKEY bends down and speaks into the conch.

DOCKEY (CONT'D)
(As if a spirit medium)
'Is there anybody there?'

GRAHAM
Or he could have been trapped inside the shell of his own making - and then eaten alive.

DOCKEY
(To the whole group)
Meet Graham, everyone. Our very own flat tyre. Bringing with him all the joys of apple pie and fish guts.

DOCKEY looks down at the conch - his slight kick has unearthed something under the sand.

DOCKEY (CONT'D)
Hello? What's this?

DOCKEY bends down and flicks away more sand to reveal an old Victorian copper penny.

DOCKEY (CONT'D)
"Find a penny, pick it up,
And all day long you'll have...
a penny!" No! You'll have "good luck!"

DOCKEY takes the penny and examines his find.

DOCKEY (CONT'D)
Who's this? (Seeing the face of the monarch) Ah, Queen Victoria! A relic of the past. Must have been lying in the sand for a hundred years.

DOCKEY spits on it.

DOCKEY (CONT'D)
"Spit on the head,
Give to a mate,
And double luck
Will be his fate."

DOCKEY passes the penny to GRAHAM, who looks at the gobbed on coin with disgust.

DOCKEY (CONT'D)
Your thoughts, Graham? I've paid my penny.

GRAHAM does not respond.

JODIE
Leave him alone.

PETER goes over to GRAHAM and puts his arm round his shoulders, only GRAHAM flinches away.

PETER
Oh come on, Graham. We're just having a laugh - (mockingly illustrating what laughter is) 'Ha! Ha! Ha! Ha! Ha!' Try it sometime - won't choke you.

GRAHAM
How do you know?

PETER
(To DOCKEY)
I wonder what Graham does for fun.

DOCKEY
(To GRAHAM)
What do you do for fun, Graham? Other than steal coffins.

GRAHAM
I make shoes for sparrows.

PETER
But sparrows don't wear sho-

DOCKEY gives PETER a mate's slap which stops PETER midflow.

PETER (CONT'D)
Oh... I get it.

AGNES rises from her knees and goes over to GRAHAM.

AGNES wears a plain, sensible dress, the sort you might imagine would be worn by a nun on holiday.

AGNES
Graham, I've been praying for your safe return. And my prayers have been answered. God has brought you back to us.

DOCKEY
No, his legs did that.

AGNES
Prayer is a wonderful gift. (To the group) If you would all like to-

JODIE interrupts AGNES by clapping her hands together.

JODIE
Blankets, everyone! Bedtime is over. We're all up and about now, so let's fold them neatly and then pack them away. The longest day will be all the better if it begins with a task completed. Blankets!

DOCKEY
(To JODIE)
If in 'The Seven Deadlys' Sloth was replaced by Overbearing Officiousness you, Jodie, would be our 'A-Star' sinner.

JODIE adjusts DOCKEY's fringe by brushing it away from his eyes with her fingers.

JODIE
And for that I'm putting you on blanket collection duty.

DOCKEY
Yes, Miss Jodie. No, Miss Jodie. Three bags full of imperious poo, Miss Jodie.

As JODIE walks away, DOCKEY roughs up his fringe.

PETER winks at DOCKEY and then nods towards JODIE - and then sticks his tongue out at her behind her back.

JODIE
(Without turning round)
And Peter, don't stick your tongue out at me.

PETER
(Surprised)
How did you know I'd done that?

JODIE
Because one of you always does. And today I guessed it would be you and I was right. (Clapping) Blankets!

GRAHAM goes over to his blanket and begins to fold it.

DOCKEY picks up his own blanket, but intentionally crumples it up.

PETER half folds his blanket and then tosses it to DOCKEY, only DOCKEY just lets it fall to the sand.

DOCKEY
(Laughing)
Ooops!

DOCKEY picks up PETER's blanket and adds it to his own.

PETER stares at OLGA in that odd way where you don't want the other person to know you're looking at them. OLGA is regal and has a standoffish vibe, yet there's no denying she's devastatingly attractive - and her full length dress blowing gently in the wind makes her even more so. Yet her eyes are fixed only on those alluring waves of which she's so fond.

DOCKEY now notices PETER looking at OLGA and his very clear interest in her.

DOCKEY smiles to himself and goes over to OLGA.

DOCKEY (CONT'D)
Your Highness, may I have the royal bedsheet?

OLGA gives him a look of disdain, but nevertheless hands over her blanket, but without folding it.

DOCKEY looks over to PETER and then sniffs the blanket.

DOCKEY (CONT'D)
Just yourself then last night.

OLGA gives him another look of disdain.

PETER blushes and starts aimlessly kicking the sand.

GRAHAM comes over to DOCKEY and ceremoniously hands over his neatly folded blanket. He then returns to where his blanket was and sits with his conch.

DOCKEY looks round to check on AGNES and CALEB.

AGNES is back kneeling in prayer on her blanket, so DOCKEY thinks better of disturbing her, and instead goes over to CALEB, who is still sitting in silent contemplation.

DOCKEY (CONT'D)
Cal-

But DOCKEY changes his mind, for he knows there's not much point in disturbing CALEB when he's in that mood. DOCKEY simply picks up CALEB's blanket and adds it to his pile.

DOCKEY goes over to CALEB's backpack and takes JODIE's neatly folded blanket from the top of it. He opens up the backpack and starts to press all the blankets down inside.

JODIE
Careful with mine, it's cashmere.

PETER hears this and looks over.

PETER
Jodie, you brought a cashmere blanket to a beach slumber party?

JODIE
Why not?

DOCKEY and PETER exchange glances.

PETER
(To DOCKEY)
I bet when Jodie was a little girl, she had to have the most expensive of everything. Always had the biggest doll just to make her friends feel small and insignificant.

JODIE
I never had any dolls.

DOCKEY
Or friends.

DOCKEY and PETER again share a snigger, but JODIE is not impressed.

JODIE
Mister Dockerty, if you learn something today let it be that no one (with a look to PETER), except an imbecile, finds any of your pathetic jokes remotely funny.

DOCKEY glances at GRAHAM, AGNES, CALEB and OLGA - GRAHAM is sitting contemplating his conch, AGNES is praying, CALEB has his head down and all OLGA can offer DOCKEY is another look of disdain.

DOCKEY
You're right. It's like playing to a morgue.

DOCKEY and PETER once more snigger away.

JODIE
Why do you come here, Dockey?

For a moment, as with CALEB earlier, DOCKEY is not sure of something. A thought that came and went.

DOCKEY
(Serious)
Why did I come here?

DOCKEY shakes his head.

DOCKEY (CONT'D)
(Suddenly changing mood and laughing)
Ha! Same as Caleb and the rest of you: for the hell of it!

DOCKEY picks up from near where his blanket was a pair of 70s 'Clackers' (two heavy plastic balls each suspended on eight inch lines of thin cord with a tab you can hold attached at the top.)

DOCKEY (CONT'D)
What else is there to do in this God forsaken world?

AGNES, still praying, opens her eyes and gives DOCKEY a scolding glance.

DOCKEY now plays with his 'Clackers'. Gripping the tab and by way of quick up-and-down hand motions, DOCKEY forces the two balls to swing high and then back, each time hitting each other, thus making the clacking noise that gives the toy its name.

PETER watches on, except every few seconds he glances over at the exotically beautiful OLGA.

DOCKEY is truly expert at this bizarre game of Newtonian physics - but the rhythm of the ever accelerating balls has to go out of sync at some stage... and when it does the heavy balls whack hard against DOCKEY's wrist.

DOCKEY does his best to show the harsh slaps haven't hurt him that much, but his supressed cry of discomfort and the sudden grimace on his face haven't gone unnoticed.

OLGA
Huh! The pain of the Clown.

PETER doesn't know who to look at now - his friend or the girl he'd like to know better. So he avoids both and again aimlessly kicks the sand.

JODIE comes over to the backpack to check on what DOCKEY has done with the blankets and sees how badly squashed down they all are.

JODIE
Huh! If you want a job doing properly, do it yourself.

DOCKEY
That's right, Miss.

DOCKEY and PETER again snigger away like schoolboys.

JODIE unpacks all the blankets and then starts to fold them up properly and neatly. As she does this, she looks over to CALEB with some concern.

A powerful wave arrives at the shoreline and it's brought with it something dark, round and hairy. But it's not yet clear to us what it is, as the water and foam still cover it over.

Back on the dry sand, JODIE is still studying CALEB and trying to figure him out.

JODIE
(To the others)
What do you think goes on in that head of his?

PETER
I look into Cal's eyes sometimes and it's like he's living on another planet.

DOCKEY
Wish he'd invite me there - I could do with a proper holiday. (To CALEB) Still dreaming, Cal? Where have you gone today - Narnia?

CALEB suddenly looks up and removes his sunglasses. Something or someone has disturbed him - for he stares intently towards the shoreline.

GRAHAM, still with his conch, instinctively raises his head, only his stare is to CALEB and not the shoreline.

DOCKEY, PETER and JODIE follow CALEB's gaze but can't see what CALEB can - or has imagined in his mind.

CALEB again shakes his head as if trying to rid himself of another unwanted thought.

PETER
What is it, Cal?

DOCKEY
The Loch Ness monster out for a swim?

CALEB ignores these comments, stands up and then dashes off towards the breaking waves.

JODIE
Come on, let's go have a look at what all the fuss is about.

JODIE follows CALEB, as does PETER.

DOCKEY
Graham! Agnes! We're off to parley with one of Cal's ghosts. You coming?

JODIE
(Insistent)
Yes they are. Come on, you lot. You never know, whatever it is might be real this time.

GRAHAM puts down his conch, stands up and begins a slow barefoot walk towards the shoreline.

AGNES makes the sign of the cross before standing up, wrapping her blanket around her shoulders and moving off to join the others.

DOCKEY
(To OLGA)
You must come too, Your Royal Highness. A chance to meet one of your subjects. Even if they are only make believe.

OLGA again gives DOCKEY one of her looks of disdain.

DOCKEY begins to skip backwards, and then forwards, waving his arms as he does so - all with the obvious intention of annoying the hell out of OLGA.

OLGA's perfect view has been ruined by this idiotic plebeian, so she too gets to her feet, puts on an Alice band that perfectly matches her Bohemian dress material, and makes her way towards those alluring waves she so loves.

OLGA
(A heavy sigh)
Huh!

Today the tide has definitely washed up something very real, for four pairs of feet (CALEB's, PETER's, JODIE's and AGNES's) are standing around a human head severed below the neck - with the scalp's long straggly hair spread across the wet sand.

Up close we see bits of sinews and torn away flesh, and there are even some vertebrae sticking out. Sure the skin is bloated, but the face has kept its features - including fearful bulging eyes with a stare of utter terror.

Oh, but those eyes! True they belong to a dead man, yet it's as if he is looking deep into your very soul.

DOCKEY
(Arriving and suddenly seeing the head)
Jesus!

AGNES
Don't blaspheme.

DOCKEY
Yes, but 'Jesus'!

OLGA joins the group, but on seeing the chopped off head she immediately turns around and begins to retch.

PETER
Don't look, Olga. It's horrible.

PETER seems to want to reach out to comfort OLGA, but the moment to do is lost.

GRAHAM slowly walks up to the head on the wet sand and looks down at it.

GRAHAM
I think he might be dead.

DOCKEY
'<u>Might</u> be dead'!?!

AGNES
We should all say a prayer (making the sign of the cross) for this lost soul.

DOCKEY
Well he's certainly lost something.

PETER
How do you think he died? Could he have been murdered? Might there be a killer out there?

CALEB stares ahead for a moment out to sea...

CALEB'S DREAM-SCAPE: EXT. NIGHT - AT SEA IN A STORM

What's now in CALEB's head is darkness, but with it a deafeningly sound scape of winds howling and waves crashing.

BACK AT THE BEACH (CONT.)

CALEB shakes his head to throw off the thought.

CALEB
Ahh...

The group round the head all look to CALEB.

CALEB (CONT'D)
No. No. No. He wasn't murdered.

GRAHAM tries to catch CALEB's eyes and attention - but he fails.

CALEB (CONT'D)
Something else... something else...

PETER
What then?

CALEB
Er... I don't know. But he wasn't murdered.

DOCKEY glances over to PETER. DOCKEY twirls his long fringe with one finger - maybe a habit but equally it could DOCKEY's way of saying to PETER *'Caleb-has-a-screw-loose.'*

Again GRAHAM's eyes tries to catch the attention of CALEB and this time they succeed. Their exchange of looks seems to have in them some sort of shared understanding.

JODIE
Does anyone know who he is?

PETER, DOCKEY and AGNES shake their heads. But not GRAHAM, though this isn't noticed by the others.

JODIE turns to OLGA who still has her back to them.

JODIE (CONT'D)
Olga?

OLGA is still making retching noises, but nothing is coming up. She turns around to take a quick look at the head.

OLGA
No...

PETER half offers his arm as a comfort to OLGA, but she turns back and away from him.

JODIE bends down to take a closer look.

PETER
Don't touch, it might be infected. Diseased.

JODIE
(Staring closely at it)
Hmm. Odd. There's flecks of white paint on the skin of the neck. Look.

CALEB bends down to see more closely.

JODIE (CONT'D)
The thing is: what we gonna do with it?

DOCKEY
Game of footy?

DOCKEY mimes a footballer kicking and then heading an imaginary ball.

JODIE
(Standing up again)
Dockey, please. Enough.

DOCKEY
Joke.

JODIE
We need to get in touch with the authorities. The police.
(MORE)

JODIE (CONT'D)
Only I don't remember ever passing
a telephone box.

OLGA turns to face the others, but tries to avoid catching sight of the head at her feet.

OLGA
Police! Telephone boxes! The
tranquillity of the bay was to be
our watchword! And our escape! The
vicissitudes of the life we-

JODIE
(Cutting off OLGA))
Look, we have to make a decision.
The way I see it is this: by the
time one of us walks to town,
informs the police, and then - if
even believed - the police agree to
drive here, the tide will have come
in and taken him away.

PETER
Good. Let it. (Looking to OLGA)
We can all stay. Together. And
whoever he is can float off to
another beach. Be somebody else's
problem.

JODIE
It's always 'somebody else's
problem' with you.

PETER
What's that supposed to mean?

CALEB
(Interjecting)
No. We can't leave him where he is.

CALEB looks up to the sky and sees several seagulls already circling overhead.

CALEB (CONT'D)
We have to deal with it ourselves.
And right now.

The group follow his gaze and seem to understand what he means when they see the seagulls.

DOCKEY now bends down to examine the bloated head more closely.

DOCKEY
And that means someone's going to
have to pick him up. Oh look!
There's a convenient hole where his
neck used to be.

JODIE
Please!

DOCKEY
Anyone got a stick? Wait! Cal,
don't you keep a knife in your
backpack?

CALEB
Yes.

JODIE
No need. We can use this.

From underneath her long blue shirt JODIE now produces from a belt a long sharp knife.

DOCKEY
Jodie! I didn't know you were a
psychopathic serial killer.

JODIE gives DOCKEY a dismissive look.

PETER
Don't trust men, do you Jodie?

DOCKEY
(Whispering to PETER)
I bet her knife is much longer and
sharper than Cal's.

JODIE tries putting her knife inside the head through the hole where the neck used to be but then pulls it out.

JODIE
We need something to put it on. So
we can take it with us.

DOCKEY
Oh, I've seen a lovely cashmere
blanket somewhere...

JODIE
No. I'll empty the polythene bag
and we can use that.

AGNES removes her blanket from around her shoulders.

AGNES
Here. (Handing over the blanket to JODIE) Have this. Let there be some dignity for this poor lost soul.

JODIE takes the blanket and puts her hand on AGNES's shoulder to thank her - only the hand stays a little longer than just a thank you.

PETER
What did you mean when you said 'Take it with us'?

CALEB
He's our responsibility now. Whoever he is.

OLGA
But did we not agree that the ascent of the moon would be the celestial signal for our departure. Let the flow of Time be our governed by-

JODIE
(Cutting off OLGA again)
So what do you suggest, Caleb?

CALEB stares ahead for a moment out to sea...

CALEB'S DREAM-SCAPE: EXT. NIGHT - AT SEA IN A STORM

What's still in CALEB's head is a tempest blowing, only now we see we're on the deck of a boat that is struggling to keep afloat in the raging waves of the storm.

BACK AT THE BEACH (CONT.)

JODIE (CONT'D)
Caleb?

CALEB has put his hands over his ears to rid himself of the images and noises in his mind.

JODIE (CONT'D)
(Concerned)
Caleb? CAL! Are you all right.

CALEB
Er, yes... Yes, yes, yes, yes, yes... but we must leave now and take it with us. We must take the head.

DOCKEY
What would you do with it, Graham?

GRAHAM looks to CALEB for a second before replying to DOCKEY.

GRAHAM
Keep it. Let its flesh rot and its skull become a *memento mori* - a reminder of our journey's end.

DOCKEY
Ah! Dearest Graham - as cheery as a dying dog without a tail.

OLGA
(Grandly)
You must each do what you will. But I intend to keep the promise I made and stay here.

OLGA puts her hand to her chest as if making a solemn vow.

OLGA (CONT'D)
I shall not depart these shores until the waves themselves are caressing my feet as I stand at the rocks of cliff.

DOCKEY
Obstinate Olga! As stubborn as the martyr at the scaffold.

OLGA
Not 'obstinate', but 'obdurate', for my decision has reason and purpose.

DOCKEY puts his hand on PETER's shoulders.

DOCKEY
(Laughing)
Don't ask Madam Thesaurus what they are, because I've a feeling she'll tell us.

PETER too laughs at OLGA - but reluctantly and without any conviction.

CALEB takes AGNES's blanket from JODIE and lays it down on some dry sand. With her knife, JODIE lifts the bloodied head from the wet shore and transfers it to the blanket.

DOCKEY (CONT'D)
Shall we give him a name? What about 'Eddie'? Or just 'Ed'?

EXT. MORNING - A SANDY PATH RUNNING ALONG AN INCLINE TO A PEBBLE BEACH

Waves crash against rocks. It's a pebble beach and one where the incline is a gently sloping embankment of rocks rather than a steep cliff.

At the top of the incline there's a wide sandy path, with marram grass growing all about it - and that's where we encounter the boots of two young POLICE SERGEANTS on patrol.

And now we see their faces. These POLICE SERGEANTS may not be twins, yet they have a strangely androgynous similarity.

POLICE SERGEANT TWO
Just another day for you.

POLICE SERGEANT ONE
Yes. Just another day.

As they walk away we see that they both have three chevron stripes on their epaulettes - but whereas POLICE SERGEANT ONE has a crown on top of his, POLICE SERGEANT TWO does not.

EXT. MORNING - THE CLIFF FACE AT THE SLUMBER PARTY BEACH

The sound of waves again, only more subdued for we are back at the slumber party beach, where OLGA sits alone on the sand, undaunted and unmoving.

Most of the others (CALEB, DOCKEY, PETER, AGNES and JODIE) are climbing up the solid wooden steps to the cliff top. Nearby, seagulls fly to their nests in the crags with scraps scavenged from inland or the sea.

GRAHAM is now wearing his shirt with his hand-knitted tank top over it, which we see, as it is a patchwork of squares, has clearly been made from left over wool from other knits. As GRAHAM stands at the shoreline with his precious conch, he reverently strokes its raised contours.

GRAHAM
Home. Coffin. And cage.

GRAHAM throws the conch into the sea and turns and walks towards where his shoes and socks are. He picks up his make-do-and-mend woollen socks, only he then looks to the group climbing up the zig-zag frame - and chucks the socks away.

GRAHAM puts his shoes on his bare feet and walks towards the cliff, picking up the bag full of rubbish on his way, but ignoring OLGA as he passes her by.

JODIE, who has just reached the top step, carries the knotted blanket which holds the severed head. DOCKEY, AGNES and PETER follow close behind her.

PETER stops for a moment as a seagull flies right by him. PETER then turns to look at OLGA alone on the beach.

PETER
(Calling)
Olga, are you sure you won't come with us?

OLGA ignores him.

PETER (CONT'D)
Olga...

DOCKEY
We came with seven. We're going back with six - and a half. Or should that be a quarter? One fifth? For who knows the measure of man...

JODIE
Olga will be fine. The moon is early this time of year, and so since it's the longest day it'll still be daylight at high tide. Only a seven mile walk back to town. Her Majesty will be gone from here well before dark.

GRAHAM arrives at the foot of the rockface with his black bin bag in his hand. He stops and looks at CALEB. GRAHAM again seems to want to say something to CALEB, only he again he makes the decision not to.

CALEB appears impervious to GRAHAM's attentions and simply indicates to GRAHAM to go up first - which he does.

CALEB, with the heavy backpack on his back packed with all those blankets, stops for a moment to take one last look to the beach and the sea.

CALEB'S DREAM-SCAPE: EXT. NIGHT - AT SEA IN A STORM

That tempest is blowing even stronger, for the sound scape of the wind and waves is even louder than before. However, this time we do see the hands and back of head of one of the crewmen of the boat tugging unsuccessfully at ropes in a vain attempt to control the sail on the boat's tall mast. Is that the same man whose severed head was discovered on the beach? Could be, but we can't quite tell yet...

BACK AGAIN AT CLIFF FACE (CONT.)

CALEB is taking in a deep breath. His face tells us he is disturbed by the images and noises that just came to him, only this time he seems more accepting of them.

JODIE (CONT'D)
(Calling down to the others on the steps below her)
There's a loose step near the top. Take care. (Shouting over to OLGA) Olga! Be careful when you leave. There's a dodgy step near the top.

OLGA hears this, for she turns her head, but doesn't reply to the call. Instead, OLGA sits and continues to take in the serenity of the sky, the calm of the sea and the allure of its waves...

EXT. MORNING - A SANDY PATH

Those boots of the two young POLICE SERGEANTS are still on patrol.

POLICE SERGEANT TWO
It's a lovely morning.

POLICE SERGEANT ONE
Yes.

POLICE SERGEANT TWO
The sea is very blue.

POLICE SERGEANT ONE
Yes.

POLICE SERGEANT TWO
And the sky is blue too.

POLICE SERGEANT ONE
Yes.

POLICE SERGEANT TWO
I suppose it's the sky which makes
the sea look blue.

POLICE SERGEANT ONE
Yes.

POLICE SERGEANT TWO
Do you like blue?

POLICE SERGEANT ONE
Yes.

POLICE SERGEANT TWO
I like blue too.

POLICE SERGEANT ONE
I thought you would.

POLICE SERGEANT TWO
It's a very beautiful blue.

POLICE SERGEANT ONE
Yes.

POLICE SERGEANT TWO
Thanks.

POLICE SERGEANT ONE
Well, it is your first day.

POLICE SERGEANT ONE smiles at POLICE SERGEANT TWO, but then suddenly his face changes to a more serious expression.

POLICE SERGEANT ONE (CONT'D)
Of course, it may rain tomorrow.
And then sky will be grey.

POLICE SERGEANT TWO
And will the sea be grey too?

POLICE SERGEANT ONE
Yes.

POLICE SERGEANT TWO nods and perhaps thinks of smiling, but decides against it.

EXT. MORNING - A ROCKY INLAND PATH, JUST WITHIN SIGHT OF THE DISTANT SEA

Our party of six, CALEB, DOCKEY, PETER, AGNES, JODIE and GRAHAM, are discovered strolling along a rocky pathway.

PETER
Who would you say among us are the fastest walkers?

JODIE
Why?

PETER
Well we don't all need to go to the authorities. Whoever is fastest should go ahead.

DOCKEY
Yes! Ahead with 'Ed the Head'!

DOCKEY's constant joking is now beginning to annoy even PETER.

JODIE
Okay, everyone. Let's stop for a moment and work this out.

The group come to a halt.

JODIE (CONT'D)
Cal's carrying the backpack, so he's excused.

AGNES
My duty is to that poor man we found. I must go to the church of Saint Francis and pray for his soul.

JODIE
Well, that leaves me, Dockey, Graham and (to PETER) you.

PETER
Jodie, you like to take charge. You have him, you keep him. Besides, I think I might have twisted my ankle on that loose step at the top.

JODIE
(To PETER))
Always passing the buck. 'Not me! Not me! Not me!'

PETER knows she's right, so decides not to argue the point.

DOCKEY
Look, why don't we toss for it?

PETER
We don't have any coins. Queen Olga again - 'No wallets! No purses!'

JODIE
Yes, well, royalty doesn't carry money.

DOCKEY
I found a coin and gave it to Graham. Graham?

GRAHAM takes the coin from his pocket.

DOCKEY (CONT'D)
So, how about this: 'Heads' you take the head. Seems right enough. But we must all play the game - even Cal and Agnes.

[*What follows is a jump-cut montage of coin tossing to decide who will take responsibility for taking the severed head in the blanket to the authorities: Hand throws up coin, the coin lands on palm, hand thrusts down coin on back of the other hand - followed by the reaction to each toss and result.*]

CALEB - it's 'Tails', but little emotion is shown. JODIE - it's 'Heads', a face of nonchalant acceptance. DOCKEY - it's 'Heads', a big grin, though whether this is real or for show who can tell? GRAHAM - it's 'Tails', but his face stays deadpan, and would probably have been the same had it come down 'Heads'. AGNES - it's 'Tails', as ever she makes the sign of the cross.

Now it's PETER's turn to toss the coin - and it comes down 'Heads'.

PETER
Best of three?

The others ignore his request.

JODIE
So it's me, Dockey and...

JODIE gives a look to AGNES that might suggest it was her name she wishes she were saying.

JODIE (CONT'D)
And... and Peter. Come on, let's hope we find a policeman on our way. Onward.

JODIE, still with that head wrapped in its blanket, marches off, with a final glance back at AGNES.

PETER is reluctant to follow, but DOCKEY grabs his arm and pulls him in JODIE's direction.

CALEB, GRAHAM and AGNES are now the only ones left of the group.

GRAHAM
(To AGNES)
You can pray anywhere, you know. Doesn't have to be in a church. And at any time. I could be praying for your soul right now for all you know.

AGNES ignores this observation and walks off on her own without even saying farewell.

GRAHAM (CONT'D)
I wasn't. But I could have been.

GRAHAM, with the awkwardness of a scholarship boy, attempts to embrace CALEB, but CALEB pulls back and so does GRAHAM.

GRAHAM (CONT'D)
Caleb. Be brave tonight.

Did GRAHAM just give CALEB a half-smile? Perhaps.

GRAHAM (CONT'D)
Till we meet again, my... my... till we meet again.

Still carrying that black bin bag, GRAHAM now hesitatingly moves away, offering a slow but purposeful wave to CALEB as he does so.

But CALEB doesn't move or even look in GRAHAM's direction - instead CALEB just stares out towards the distant sea.

CALEB'S DREAM-SCAPE: EXT. NIGHT - AT SEA IN A STORM

The tempest still rages, but now we see more clearly the face of that man trying to control the sail on the mast. And yes, it's the same as the severed head... And as he struggles we hear the soundscape of a rising chorus of a children's choir, attempting, as it were, to compete against the roar of the tempest.

BACK AT THE ROCKY PATHWAY (CONT.)

CALEB's eyes are wide open, as if mesmerised by what he has just seen and heard in his head. Yet the sudden juxtaposition of the tempest's roar with the quiet calmness all about, no longer unnerves him.

CALEB
The sea... The sea...

The water surface is like quicksilver, as it reflects the aura of the bright morning sun. Its shimmering power seems to draw CALEB to it - and as he walks toward the sea, the sound of the children's choir returns in all its strength and glory.

EXT. MORNING - A SANDY PATH

The TWO POLICE SERGRANTS are walking along.

POLICE SERGEANT TWO begins to sing.

POLICE SERGEANT TWO
'OH - '

POLICE SERGEANT ONE
Don't sing.

POLICE SERGEANT TWO stops mid note and offers POLICE SERGEANT ONE an embarrassed smile of apology.

POLICE SERGEANT ONE acknowledges the apology with a sharp nod.

EXT. MORNING - SLUMBER PARTY BEACH

Waves gently lap across the long length of the shore.

OLGA still sits alone in the middle of an otherwise empty beach. Well, not quite alone, for a seagull flies down and lands beside her.

OLGA begins to hum that harmony line, only this time it turns into something more recognisable - the melody of *'All Things Bright and Beautiful'*. And now the hum develops into notes that are sung in a ravishing soprano voice.

EXT. MORNING - ONE OF THE SEAGULL NESTS IN THE CLIFFS

The adult seagull leaves two chicks alone in the nest.

The chicks begin to squabble and fight - and then the bigger and the most aggressive of the two draws blood from his sibling's head.

The weaker chick retreats but that doesn't stop the attack.

Oh! The stronger chick seems to think his brother is food - isn't that adorable! And now he's broken past the thin skin and feathers and found the yummy flesh beneath. What a fat and big chick he's going to be when he eats up all of his little brother...

EXT. MORNING - THE SANDY PATH

JODIE, DOCKEY and PETER are walking along when PETER spots something - a red telephone box.

PETER

Damn it! You were wrong, Jodie.
Look: a telephone box.

DOCKEY though spots something even better - two figures approaching in blue uniforms.

DOCKEY
Forget about phone boxes. Our luck's really in. We've found ourselves a pair of P.C. Plods.

JODIE
They look very young.

PETER
I don't care if they're kids in fancy dress as long as we can get rid of this damn head.

JODIE, DOCKEY and PETER stop and wait for the police officers to be within speaking distance.

PETER (CONT'D)
(To the SERGEANTS)
First of all, I didn't kill him.

The TWO POLICE SERGEANTS stop outside the telephone box.

JODIE
None of us did. (Unwrapping the blanket to reveal the severed head) It's a head. It was washed up on the shore.

The TWO POLICE SERGEANTS look to each other, showing little surprise when what's inside the blanket is revealed.

POLICE SERGEANT TWO
Yes, that's definitely a head.

JODIE
If you look closely there are flecks of white paint around the neck.

The TWO POLICE SERGEANTS again look to each other, but not particularly at the head.

JODIE (CONT'D)
It might have been some sort of accident.

POLICE SERGEANT TWO holds out his hand.

POLICE SERGEANT TWO
Don't worry - we'll take it from here.

PETER nods to JODIE to hand the head over, but JODIE is unsure.

JODIE
Aren't you going to ask us any questions? Who we are? Exactly where we found it?

POLICE SERGEANT TWO pulls back his hand and looks to POLICE SERGEANT ONE. There is a moment's pause before POLICE SERGEANT ONE responds.

POLICE SERGEANT ONE
(Echoing JODIE's question)
'Who are you?'

JODIE
I'm Jodie, but really it's Joan. Joan Schofield.

DOCKEY
'Joan'? I never knew that. (To the TWO SERGEANTS) And I'm Dockey. Full name Simon Neville Dockerty.

JODIE
'Neville'! Ha! Someone was having a laugh there! Was it your mum, your dad or the vicar?

DOCKEY frowns at JODIE's remark.

The POLICE SERGEANTS turn their attentions to PETER and give him a questioning look.

PETER
My name? Well, er, yes, er, my name is, er, it's-

JODIE
(Butting in)
Peter. Peter Wailing.

POLICE SERGEANT ONE looks towards POLICE SERGEANT TWO as if to prompt him.

POLICE SERGEANT TWO
(Again echoing JODIE's question)
'And exactly where did you find it?'

JODIE
On the beach with the high cliff - where there are those wooden stairs.

POLICE SERGEANT ONE
Loose step at the top.

JODIE
Oh, you know it.

POLICE SERGEANT ONE
Yes.

Again POLICE SERGEANT ONE glances to POLICE SERGEANT TWO as if to prompt him.

POLICE SERGEANT TWO
Thank you for your co-operation in this matter. We'll look after the head from now on.

POLICE SERGEANT ONE
So, if we may, take the blanket?

Both POLICE SERGEANT ONE and POLICE SERGEANT TWO hold out their hands.

JODIE appears to be about to say something, only PETER tugs at her shirt and half shakes his head as if to say *'Don't-ask-anything-else-just-give-the-thing-to-them'*.

PETER
So, er, when we hand it over we're free to go?

DOCKEY
'Head off'? Ha!

Neither POLICE SERGEANTS laugh at DOCKEY's attempt at a joke and both JODIE and PETER give DOCKEY a dirty look.

POLICE SERGEANT ONE
Yes.

JODIE knots up the ends of blanket and hands it over to POLICE SERGEANT TWO.

POLICE SERGEANT TWO
Thank you.

POLICE SERGEANT ONE
Yes. Thank you.

POLICE SERGEANT TWO
On your way then.

JODIE, DOCKEY and PETER walk off, a little surprised about how well that went.

PETER
Not as difficult as I thought.

JODIE
(Puzzled)
Yes.

The TWO POLICE SERGEANTS watch as JODIE, DOCKEY and PETER disappear into the distance.

POLICE SERGEANT TWO
Not as difficult as I thought.

POLICE SERGEANT ONE
(With certainty and confidence)
Yes.

The POLICE SERGEANTS begin to walk away but as they do the telephone inside the red telephone box rings.

POLICE SERGEANT TWO stops.

POLICE SERGEANT TWO
Should we answer that?

POLICE SERGEANT ONE
(Still walking away)
No. It always rings at this time on a Thursday. That's why I know it's not for us.

POLICE SERGEANT TWO joins POLICE SERGEANT ONE and we now see their police uniforms in more detail. They definitely have sergeant strips, but they are perhaps more curvy and feathery than the standard issue.

CAPTION ON SCREEN: "AGNES, THE OVER-PIOUS ZEALOT"

EXT. LATE MORNING - THE CHURCH OF SAINT FRANCIS OF ASSISI

There's a church like this in every town. Nothing special, but those who go there know it as a friend.

Its high roof has now become a home for pigeons. One lands with bread in its beak, but so distracted by its meal, our feathered friend doesn't notice the swooping hawk, which, after it has pounced on its prey, immediately pecks out its eyes.

AGNES arrives at the steps of the church. There are pigeons here too, perched on the head and shoulders of a statue of this patron saint of animals - and as AGNES passes the smiling figure, she lowers her head in devotional reverence.

There are a dozen or so steps leading to the entrance - and AGNES is quick to ascend them, for now we see her knees - somewhat calloused - going up and down like a pair of well-oiled pistons.

INT. DAY - THE CHURCH OF SAINT FRANCIS (CONT.)

These wooden pews won't feature in a guide book, neither will the organ, the marble altar, or even the painted panel triptych of the crucifixion directly behind it in the chancel. And here today on the benches there's maybe six or seven people at most - each sitting or kneeling anonymously in the dark.

But AGNES is not of that breed, for now she walks noisily down the stone floored aisle, and the church's many echoes multiply her steps a hundred fold.

Those in prayer, furtively turn their heads as AGNES passes by. One figure, however, rises to speak to her.

FATHER PATRICK
Agnes.

AGNES stops and turns - it is a man she knows well.

AGNES
Father Patrick.

FATHER PATRICK, in black clerical garb, leaves his pew and joins AGNES in the aisle, only as he does so AGNES looks not at his face but his arm.

AGNES (CONT'D)
Oh dear, Father, has someone spilt something on you?

FATHER PATRICK looks down to his elbow where he spots a splattered white stain.

FATHER PATRICK
Oh dear Lord! Most churches have bats in the belfry, (looking up) but here at Saint Francis we are blessed with pigeons on the arches.

We now see about a dozen feathered friends up near the ceiling, all perching on one of the stone arches that supports the roof. Again there's nothing special here - except the arch is soaked to the core with water.

FATHER PATRICK (CONT'D)
They come in through the loose tiles in the roof. Oh, they may be God's creatures but I pray sometimes the good Lord had given them greater control over their bowel movements. Especially from great heights. Ha!

FATHER PATRICK smiles but AGNES does not. AGNES's face tells FATHER PARTICK that his 'joke', combining prayer and bird poo, is entirely inappropriate for a priest.

FATHER PATRICK needs to remedy his mistake - and sharpish.

FATHER PATRICK (CONT'D)
So, er, what brings you to our church today? I thought you were spending it with your friends at the beach. We agreed, Agnes, you needed more time away from here. There's more to life than this leaky old place.

AGNES
A lost soul, Father.

FATHER PATRICK
A lost soul, child?

AGNES
Washed up on the beach.

AGNES makes the sign of the cross.

FATHER PATRICK does the same - but more following her lead than an actual prayer.

AGNES (CONT'D)
(In a whisper)
A severed head, Father.

AGNES makes another sign of the cross.

Shocked by what AGNES has just said, FATHER PATRICK crosses himself again - this time for real.

AGNES (CONT'D)
Jodie, Peter and Dockey are taking it to the authorities, but that soul needs me here at that altar on my knees in prayer.

FATHER PATRICK
Yes... yes... I understand, child, but there's a novena later. And Jerome is coming in just before hand to play on the organ.

AGNES
I understand, Father.

FATHER PATRICK
(Thoughtfully)
A severed head... huh... some sort of terrible accident, I suppose. Yes, well, I'll say a prayer, too. God bless you, child.

AGNES begins to move off.

FATHER PATRICK (CONT'D)
Oh, Agnes, be careful as you walk. That dreadful storm we had last night loosened more tiles and dear Janet has only just finished mopping up the rain water that came down near the altar.

AGNES
(Walking away)
I will, Father.

FATHER PATRICK's eyes follow her with a look of benevolence which then turns to concern.

AGNES is opening the altar rail gate and is about to walk up the eight marble steps to the altar, when she spots a small puddle on the bottom stair that Janet must have missed. AGNES cautiously steps over it - and now those piston-knees do their business. Oh, but how sharp the edges of those marble steps look, for they have been cut at a surprisingly acute angle.

Once AGNES reaches the top, she kneels down in front of the altar. That marble floor is hard but AGNES's calloused knees relish any pain.

AGNES's prayers are now offered to Heaven - and they take us with them, up high to those pigeons on that stone arch. We see it has been repaired at some stage, for it's really several blocks cemented together. And rain water is still coming in. The arch is truly getting a good old soak.

A BLACK-VEILED WOMAN lights a candle in the Lady Chapel next to the main chancel and then surreptitiously glances over towards AGNES, mouths a short prayer, makes the sign of the cross and moves away.

The candle she lit slowly burns and we stay on it, with AGNES kneeling in the background. The shadow the candle casts changes in length and shape, for what we are witnessing is Time is passing...

JEROME, the organist, carrying some sheet music in his hand, walks in front of the altar rails, stopping half way to genuflect. When he reaches the other side, he makes his way up the wooden steps to the organ.

The flame of the candle in the Lady Chapel is dying - but AGNES is still on her knees, which have now turned purple in their pursuit of piety. But they've done enough, for when the organ music starts playing (Bach's 'Little Fugue' in G minor BWV 578), AGNES puts her hand on the altar and raises herself up from the marble floor.

The painted panel triptych in AGNES's eyeline is an iconic depiction of the crucifixion, including disciples, the Virgin Mary and a few onlooking Roman soldiers. AGNES never turns her back on the cross and what this means is she must walk backwards down the eight marble steps. She's done it many times before, only today, on that bottom step, her shoes aren't expecting to land in a puddle of rain.

Water and marble are a dangerous combination - and AGNES slips so badly that she lands face down across all eight steps. Without intending it, AGNES now looks like a prostrate medieval nun. And her jaw hit the sharp edge of the top step so hard that she cannot help but cry out in pain - but no bones are broken, so she is eventually able to manoeuvre herself onto her back.

AGNES's cry disturbs the pigeons, which fly from the stone arch in all directions. We can see that the constant drip-drip-drip of rain has created a crack between the stone pieces.

Suddenly the crack widens and a section of the stone arch - a block the length of yard or so - falls to the floor beneath. As it does, Bach's 'Little Fugue' builds towards its crescendo.

AGNES's knees, laying across the acute edge of the marble step, are struck by the heavy stone and the impact is so powerful that the lower part of her legs detach themselves from the rest of her body. AGNES now looks like the Wicked Witch of the East when Dorothy's house lands on her in Oz, except without the ruby slippers. Well, sort of. For blood drips down her legs to her ankle, turning her shoes a glistening trademarked Technicolor red. AGNES can do nothing about it except scream and scream and scream, all to the rising accompaniment of a Bach fugue.

But where did those pigeons go? Ah! They found safety on top of that wooden panel. Such iconography often has a dove hovering over the cross - and so now we see painted dove and live pigeon sharing a sacred moment together. Only the pigeon does a poo, which lands on the countenance of the mocking Roman soldier near the foot of the cross. It's now a face that isn't happy about having white do-do dripping down its cheek.

Up at the stone block there is now a wide gap - and through it we can make out the faces of two angels carved into the wood of the ceiling. But surely cherubim don't have cousins who are police sergeants? And what exactly are these familiar angels looking at? Oh! The large arch, for, without support, it now breaks away and plummets down to join its erstwhile companion.

AGNES must have seen it coming - for what we hear is her terrified cry of death. But only for a few seconds, because after it lands, all the screaming ends.

The Bach fugue has reached its climax and the last note fades.

The church is still and silent.

EXT. LATE MORNING - A CROSSROADS

JODIE, DOCKEY and PETER have come to a place where their sandy path splits in three.

DOCKEY is laughing away but JODIE and PETER are exchanging looks of annoyance. They're probably sick of each other's company by now - especially DOCKEY's silly puns and jokes.

JODIE
Well, it's going to be town for me.

PETER
North or south?

JODIE
South. You?

PETER
North.

JODIE and PETER look questioningly at DOCKEY.

DOCKEY
The moon... if there's a bus. There normally is on a Thursday. If it is a Thursday.

JODIE
Yes, it's a Thursday. And it's been a most memorable day.

PETER
I'd rather forget it.

DOCKEY
Forget what? Did something happen? Have I missed it?

JODIE stares at DOCKEY with a look of exasperation.

JODIE
(Ironically)
Who are you? And what are you doing here?

DOCKEY
(Suddenly serious)
There are times when I really wish I knew.

DOCKEY shakes his head.

DOCKEY (CONT'D)
(Changing the mood))
Goodbye, Joan. I'm sure I'll miss you as much as the step brother I never had. No, twice as much. What is twice as much as never?

JODIE gives up on DOCKEY and turns instead to PETER.

JODIE
Bye, then.

JODIE strides off.

PETER
Bye.

PETER gives JODIE a half-hearted wave, but JODIE doesn't see it.

DOCKEY and PETER stand for a moment in silence.

DOCKEY makes a big silly face and PETER replies with a smile.

PETER walks away, with a brief glance back at DOCKEY, who is still putting on that funny face.

PETER disappears where his path dips and DOCKEY is alone - and his face slowly becomes a sad one.

DOCKEY makes his move, and, perhaps to cheer himself up, he sings as he goes. Oh, and this is a surprise - DOCKEY has been blessed with a beautiful tenor voice.

DOCKEY
'SHOW ME THE WAY TO GO HOME,
I'M TIRED AND I WANT TO GO TO BED,
I HAD A LITTLE DRINK ABOUT AN HOUR AGO -
AND IT'S GONE STRAIGHT TO MY HEAD.'

'Head' Ha! Ha! Ha! Ha! 'Head' Ha! Ha! Ha! Ha! What skullduggery has been going on today? Ha! Ha! Ha! Ha! It was one hell of day! Ha! Ha! Ha!

DOCKEY walks off laughing and dancing.

CAPTION ON SCREEN: "GRAHAM, THE PARTY-POOPING MISERY GUTS"

EXT. MID-DAY - A DESERTED STREET

We join GRAHAM, still carrying that black bin bag, walking along an empty street. He stops, and, as best he can with his free hand, he shades his eyes to look up at the noon-day sun, giving it a contemptuous snarl before walking on.

GRAHAM comes across a large red-brick arch that is the entrance to an alleyway. Attached to the arch is a sign saying 'VICTORIAN ARCADE'.

It's midday, yet the walkway, with high walls either side, seems unnaturally dark. Almost as if it's dusk. GRAHAM glances up again at that maddening sun, then looks down the gloomy sequestered path. Oh yes, he knows which he prefers.

As GRAHAM walks along the cobbled alleyway, the walls become even higher, and now it's so shaded it feels like midnight. It's so dark he doesn't even see that old tin dustbin - and accidently knocks its lid off. But it's conveniently empty, so he disposes of that black bag he's been carrying for hours.

Further down the path there is some illumination, for lights are flashing blue, orange and green. The Victorian Arcade! GRAHAM opens the oak door and enters.

INT. MID-DAY - VICTORIAN ARCADE (CONT.)

The place is deserted, yet many creatures welcome him, for we are in a taxidermist's heaven, with numerous carcasses of birds of prey hanging on stiff iron rods from the ceiling.

There are human faces too. Well, in or on the amusement machines. We have 'Madam Zascha: The Gypsy Fortune Teller', whose alabaster head gazes out from under a silk Persian turban. 'What the Butler Saw' has a prurient bald man inviting us to peep through his keyhole, and in 'The Mysteries of the Pharaohs', there's a golden sarcophagus upon which lies the painted mask of a boy prince.

Next to these are the gambling games. There's 'The Silver Cascade', where old sixpences are piled up on platforms to form a kind of waterfall, and 'The Grand National', with a row of wooden handles which punters turn to make their horse gallop.

GRAHAM spots a sign reading 'OLD PENNIES ONLY'. His face betrays disappointment, but then he remembers the coin he carries with the head of Queen Victoria, which he takes out of his pocket.

GRAHAM walks further along this remarkable assortment of amusements and games, weighing up which machine is the most worthy of his offering.

A yard or two away is 'The Haunted House' - which GRAHAM likes the look of - and just ahead of it is 'The Laughing Policeman'.

As GRAHAM strides past the casement with the dummy, he trips over a banana skin and falls against the glass. As he does so, 'The Laughing Policeman' starts up of its own accord.

Was it the knock that caused the strange looking dummy to come to life? GRAHAM doesn't seem to care, but, as he didn't have to fork out for it, he stands and watches.

The Laughing Policeman dummy is dressed in a Victorian uniform and waves a long truncheon, but it's his weird grin that really spooks you out - and that weird mechanical laugh of his.

'Ha! Ha! Ha! Ha! Ha! Ha! Ha! Ha! Ha! Ha! Ha! Ha!'

But the supposedly contagious hysterics don't work on GRAHAM.

'Why is this funny? Why do people laugh at such nonsense?' Of course GRAHAM doesn't say these words, but from his deadpan expression you know that's exactly what he's thinking.

The Laughing Policeman now slows, as if the mechanism is somehow clogged up. And as a result this bizarre dummy becomes literally.... creepy. And his loud guffaws have turned sluggish and wheezing. No longer laughter, but something more strange and unearthly. Downright monstrous even...

'Harrrrhh... Harrrrrh... Harhhh... Harrrrrh... Harrrhhhhh! Harrrrrh...'

This deathlike rattle suddenly ceases and the Laughing Policeman becomes frozen in rictus stillness.

GRAHAM stares for a moment at the fixed grin. Oh, but he's had enough of this irritating man and so he moves on to 'The Haunted House' with his penny ready in his hand.

'The Haunted House' is on three levels, with living room, study and attic. The casement looks much like a doll's house, except there's no frontage and instead the rooms are boxed in by glass.

GRAHAM puts his penny in the slot. Yes, its movements may seem jerky, yet there's much to admire with this ingenious Victorian automaton and its ghostly effects.

As his penny falls down into the machine, the lights in the living room brighten, and the story begins...

A Victorian gentleman, dressed in a traditional opera cloak, enters the living room. All of a sudden, the chandelier flickers, a bust of Queen Victoria spins round and the gentleman's dog near the hearth sits up and barks. A panel in the wall flies open and out pops an old woman in a grey burial shroud. The gentleman raises his hands, revealing the deep red silk lining of his opera cloak.

He screams - well, the machine's scratchy mechanism makes the noise for him - and the room goes to blackout.

The study on the next level lights up. The same gentleman is in his armchair in a smoking jacket, enjoying his evening pipe. Books on shelves suddenly fall off (all clearly on wires), and as they do, his armchair is lifted high. Ah! What's this? The oil painting above the mantelpiece transforms itself - by way of a canvass on roller - from being a portrait of the gentleman into a red-faced demon. Then another blackout.

The attic bedroom lights up and the gentleman is discovered standing in his nightshirt, holding a candle. His bedsheets suddenly shake all by themselves and the large chimney breast opens up and through it comes the Grim Reaper holding aloft his scythe. The cloaked figure moves across the room on a track, and when it reaches our Victorian gentleman, it strikes the scythe down into his chest. A small bulb underneath the nightshirt glows scarlet and the gentleman floats up to the ceiling, and indeed into it, and, we must suppose, beyond that into the next life. The Grim Reaper turns to face GRAHAM - the hood falls back and under it is a skeleton with a large grin on its face.

GRAHAM then does something he hasn't done for years - he laughs! And laughs again, and then laughs some more. Oh but GRAHAM is not used to such a curious noise coming from his throat and suddenly the laughter becomes strained - worse, it turns into a gasping choke.

GRAHAM puts his hands to his neck in desperation, unable to control his panting hysteria. More breath is going out than is coming in and soon GRAHAM seizes up completely and falls to the floor.

As GRAHAM collapses, the automaton dummy comes to life with a full frenzy of chittering maniacal laughter.

'Ha! Ha! Ha! Ha! Ha! Ha! Ha! Ha! Ha! Ha! Ha! Ha!'

The Laughing Policeman continues hysterically for a few seconds more, and then, like GRAHAM, it gradually comes to a halt.

GRAHAM is dead, but his face is no longer 'deadpan', for Grim Reaper has given him a valedictory gift - a grin as wide and as rigid as that of the Laughing Policeman dummy.

EXT. LATE AFTERNOON - OUTDOORS, WITH THE SUN LOW IN THE SKY

The TWO POLICE SERGEANTS are digging with spades, but we can't yet see where or what.

POLICE SERGEANT TWO
I never thought part of our duty would be to bury a severed head.

POLICE SERGEANT ONE
There's worse. Much worse.

POLICE SERGEANT TWO
Really?

POLICE SERGEANT ONE
Oh yes. You drew the long straw today.

POLICE SERGEANT ONE stops digging for a moment and stares at POLICE SERGEANT TWO.

POLICE SERGEANT ONE (CONT'D)
Are those tears I see?

POLICE SERGEANT TWO
(Wiping his face with the back of his hand)
No, it's the sand - getting in my eyes.

POLICE SERGEANT ONE
Ah well, we're more or less done. You can drop the head in now. Unless you'd like me to?

POLICE SERGEANT TWO
No, I'll do it. Have to get used to this sort of thing, I suppose.

POLICE SERGEANT ONE
Yes.

POLICE SERGEANT TWO reaches down, picks up the severed head from the blanket lying on the ground and raises it to shoulder level.

He seems as if he's about to drop it, but then stops.

POLICE SERGEANT TWO
As this is going to be a grave, shouldn't there be a cross?

POLICE SERGEANT ONE
Hmm... but we've no wood or stone.

POLICE SERGEANT TWO
True - but I could at least make a mark with my foot.

POLICE SERGEANT ONE
Ha! I can tell you're going to go far.

Exactly what POLICE SERGEANT TWO does isn't seen, but from his body movements you might guess he's making the sign of the cross with his boot in the sand.

POLICE SERGEANT TWO again lifts the severed head into the air, only this time he holds it by its straggly long hair, in a way not that dissimilar to Caravaggio's 1610 painting 'Salome Receives the Head of John the Baptist'.

POLICE SERGEANT TWO turns the head round so he can see its face and he stares into the man's open eyes.

POLICE SERGEANT TWO
Blue eyes. Like the sea.

POLICE SERGEANT ONE
Yes.

POLICE SERGEANT TWO
(Still looking into the eyes of the man)
And the sky, of course.

POLICE SERGEANT ONE
Yes.

POLICE SERGEANT TWO
You like blue.

POLICE SERGEANT ONE
Yes.

POLICE SERGEANT TWO looks down.

POLICE SERGEANT TWO
Should I say anything? Any words?

POLICE SERGEANT ONE
No. Unless you'd like to.

POLICE SERGEANT TWO
I think I would. If that's acceptable to you?

POLICE SERGEANT ONE
Yes.

POLICE SERGEANT TWO thinks for a moment and then clears his throat.

POLICE SERGEANT TWO
Ahem. 'Together at last. United in sand.'

POLICE SERGEANT TWO drops the head into the hole they have dug.

Just before it lands, we see that near the top of the hole is a corpse severed at the neck. The headless dead body appears to have been buried in the sand standing upright and maggots, flies and other unmentionables crawl all over the wide open wound.

POLICE SERGEANT ONE looks down at where the head has landed - right on the shoulders where it should be.

POLICE SERGEANT ONE
Very good. Now pile the sand on top.

We see the top of POLICE SERGEANT TWO's shovel as it goes to work.

POLICE SERGEANT ONE and POLICE SERGEANT TWO step back - and we can see a bump in the sand with the outline of the indented cross next to it.

POLICE SERGEANT ONE (CONT'D)
I'll put in a commendation - job well done.

POLICE SERGEANT TWO
Thanks. Can we go now?

POLICE SERGEANT ONE
Yes. But don't forget the blanket.

POLICE SERGEANT TWO
Oh that's right. The blanket.

POLICE SERGEANT TWO picks up blanket in which the head has been carried and waits for POLICE SERGEANT ONE to make the first move.

POLICE SERGEANT ONE waits for a moment and then nods.

POLICE SERGEANT ONE and POLICE SERGEANT TWO then walk away.

As they leave we see exactly where they have buried the severed head: in a sand pit in a children's playground.

The head is covered over, but the flesh beneath won't be there for very long, for several large ravens swoop down, gather round the mound and begin to claw away at the sand.

CAPTION ON SCREEN: <u>"JODIE, THE SHOW-OFF"</u>

EXT. AFTERNOON - THE ENTRANCE TO A MAZE

We find JODIE standing just outside a boxwood maze.

Suddenly JODIE hears the cry of a LITTLE GIRL from somewhere inside the maze shouting, "Help me! Help! Help!"

JODIE runs into the maze and negotiates her way round the passageways of the vertical green hedges. Behind one of the corners JODIE finds the LITTLE GIRL, who stands waiting with both hands behind her back.

LITTLE GIRL
Ha! Ha! You fell for my trap.

JODIE is not impressed.

JODIE
That was a stupid thing to do. And it's not funny.

We see that the LITTLE GIRL wears a wide and baggy smock dress, patterned with blue canaries, and attached to a belt is a blue transistor radio exactly the same shade of blue as the canaries.

As JODIE approaches her, the LITTLE GIRL spreads her feet across the narrow passageway to the sides of the hedges so that JODIE's path is now obstructed.

LITTLE GIRL
This is a stick up.

JODIE sighs with annoyance.

JODIE
Huh... Really?

LITTLE GIRL
Yes. A stick up.

JODIE is having none of it and simply folds her arms.

LITTLE GIRL (CONT'D)
I said, 'This is a stick up.'

JODIE's getting impatient. She unfolds her arms and moves forward.

JODIE
Let me pass, please.

LITTLE GIRL
I've got a knife.

JODIE pulls back, for The LITTLE GIRL suddenly brings something out from behind her back - oh, it's only a plastic knife, the sort you might get with a playtime kitchen set.

JODIE
Oh you silly filly. I think mummy and daddy have let you stay up late and watch the wrong sort of movies.

LITTLE GIRL
This is a stick up. And this is my knife.

JODIE is beginning to lose her temper.

JODIE
No little girl, <u>this</u> is what a knife looks like.

JODIE produces the knife she used to lift up the severed head to put on the blanket at the beach.

JODIE (CONT'D)
I think you'll find mine is bigger and longer than yours - and sharper too.

But the LITTLE GIRL stands her ground and even begins to sway her body back and forth on the spot. In fact, her movement soon becomes like some sort of defiant dance.

JODIE puts her knife back in her belt and stands waiting for the LITTLE GIRL to get out of her way - only she doesn't.

LITTLE GIRL
This is a stick up. And this is my knife.

JODIE has completely lost it.

JODIE
LET ME PASS!

LITTLE GIRL
I do have other knives.

JODIE ignores this warning and pushes past the LITTLE GIRL, scraping herself against the hedge as she does so.

JODIE is about to walk on when she experiences a very strange sensation. She stops and puts her hand to her tummy and there she feels some hot slime. Well that's a surprise.

JODIE looks down and sees - oh no - it's her own blood - for a sword has cut through her from her back.

We now see the LITTLE GIRL peeping out from behind JODIE - and she's holding the handle of the sword that has just passed right through JODIE.

And what follows is another reveal, for what we see next is the LITTLE GIRL from behind - and hanging down her back, previously hidden by the width of the smock dress, is a strapped-on leather harness with numerous sheaves with blades sticking out of them.

LITTLE GIRL (CONT'D)
I said I had other knives.

JODIE collapses to the ground, with blood splattering everywhere.

LITTLE GIRL (CONT'D)
And they are all much bigger,
sharper and longer than yours.

The LITTLE GIRL switches on her transistor radio which is currently playing the 1971 Middle of the Road earworm hit *'Chirpy Chirpy Cheep Cheep'*.

The LITTLE GIRL then takes out all the blades from the harness and holds them between her fingers - giving her the appearance of Edward Scissorhands - and one by one, each knife finds a new home inside JODIE, who soon takes on the appearance of a macabre looking pin cushion.

After the LITTLE GIRL has used up all her blades, she casually jumps over JODIE's body, does her little dance and cheerfully skips off in her blue canary dress, whistling *'Chirpy Chirpy, Cheep Cheep'*.

EXT. LATE AFTERNOON - A STEEP HILL

Two sets of boots are climbing a steep hill. It's extremely breezy and sand and grass stems are flying everywhere.

POLICE SERGEANT TWO, who is carrying the blanket, is struggling with both the steepness of the hill and the winds and keeps having to shield his eyes. However, SERGERANT ONE seems much more used to the hill and the blustery weather.

POLICE SERGEANT TWO
It's quite a trek up.

POLICE SERGEANT ONE
Yes.

POLICE SERGEANT TWO
And very blustery.

POLICE SERGEANT ONE
Yes.

POLICE SERGEANT TWO
You could fly a kite.

POLICE SERGEANT ONE
Well, that's the idea in a way.

The POLICE SERGEANTS reach the top, though we don't yet see their view.

POLICE SERGEANT ONE takes hold of one end of the blanket and stretches it out so that it billows upwards between them.

POLICE SERGEANT ONE (CONT'D)
This is where the four winds meet,
but we must wait a moment until
they are at their strongest.

A huge blast of wind comes and nearly lifts the two POLICE SERGEANTS off their feet.

POLICE SERGEANT ONE (CONT'D)
Now! Let go!

POLICE SERGEANT TWO and POLICE SERGEANT ONE release the blanket.

The wind lifts the blanket high up in the air where it takes flight like a bird.

POLICE SERGEANT ONE (CONT'D)
The winds will help it find its way
home now.

POLICE SERGEANT TWO
Where to next? To the beach?

POLICE SERGEANT ONE
Yes. The beach.

CAPTION ON SCREEN: <u>"OLGA, THE STUBBORN PRINCESS"</u>

EXT. LATE AFTERNOON - THE CLIFF AT THE BEACH

Seagulls are squawking and flying about the wooden steps built into the rock cliff at the slumber party beach.

It's still light, but the moon has appeared in the sky and the tide is coming in at a pace.

Technically OLGA is still on the beach, for her bare toes are in the sand, but she has her sandals ready in her hands for the climb up the wooden steps. Oh, but not yet, for OLGA vowed she would wait until the sea water was lapping at her feet - and that's what she's waiting for now...

Waves are one of Nature's inconsistencies - some are slow and gentle, others surprise you with their speed, power and reach. And one does that right now, for suddenly a wave is splashing hard at her ankles. No matter. OLGA has now fulfilled her promise to herself.

OLGA puts on her sandals and begins the walk up the wooden steps, humming an indistinct tune as she goes. The stairs are secure, but OLGA is ultra cautious and so each step up is taken with great care. But she has plenty of time. As we can see from the green tidemark, the tide, even at its height, doesn't come up as far as the step she's already reached.

OLGA holds the rail tight and turns round to take a final look at the serenity of the sky - now a glorious red sunset - the calm of the sea - in truth not as calm as it was - and the allure of its waves - which, right at this moment, are crashing against the rocks of the cliff.

If she's careful, OLGA can lean over the rail and see into one of the nests of the seagulls. Oh, how lovely! Two excitable little chicks! Ahh! But where are Mr and Mrs Seagull? Out looking for a fish supper to bring home for the tinys, no doubt. How lovely it must be to have such a kind mummy and daddy!

OLGA safely pulls herself back and continues her ascent. Coming up is that loose step she was warned about, which she tests out with the sole of her sandal. Not even that loose - just a slight wobble. Even so, OLGA, ever cautious, misses it out and puts her foot on the step above it.

OLGA must be safe now - only few steps to go. In fact, she can already see the grass at the top. Oh but she must have one last glance at the serenity of the sky, the calmness of-

SQUAWK: "AWWW! AWWWW! AWWWW!"

Perhaps the mother seagull had seen OLGA peering into her nest - such birds are notoriously protective of their young - and so maybe it was that which made this particular mummy seagull so particularly maternally aggressive.

Whatever the reason, the attack on OLGA takes her so much by surprise that all her weight falls against the frame of the stairs, resulting in her feet and legs slipping under the gap between two steps, so that her body now falls backwards under the frame and OLGA finds herself hanging upside down from the wooden stairway.

Being attacked by seagulls - reinforcements have arrived - while perilously suspended from the top of a high cliff is not the best way of enjoying a late afternoon. And it's about to get worse, for the law of gravity will soon come into effect. Oh, it has! And down she goes.

The sea water is not deep enough to break her fall. Not that it matters much, because OLGA's perpendicular trajectory results in her neck snapping in two on impact.

The sand being wet means that at least some of her head disappears into it - and her voluminous orange and yellow dress blows like a blazing flame in the breeze.

OLGA wanted to stay on the beach - and now she has. Indeed, she has become part of it - at least until her beloved waves wash her away.

(OOV) POLICE SERGEANT TWO
It's a very pretty dress.

(OOV) POLICE SERGEANT ONE
Thank you.

The TWO POLICE SERGEANTS are revealed paddling in the shallow water nearby, only their outfits are more ethereal now - and we can see that they are really angels.

DUTY ANGEL (POLICE SERGEANT) TWO
I've heard there are other beaches.

DUTY ANGEL (POLICE SERGEANT) ONE
Yes.

DUTY ANGEL (POLICE SERGEANT) TWO
Happier ones than this?

DUTY ANGEL (POLICE SERGEANT) ONE
Yes.

DUTY ANGEL (POLICE SERGEANT) TWO
With swings and donkey rides?

DUTY ANGEL (POLICE SERGEANT) ONE
Yes.

DUTY ANGEL (POLICE SERGEANT) TWO
And candy floss and toffee apples?

DUTY ANGEL (POLICE SERGEANT) ONE
If you want there to be.

DUTY ANGEL (POLICE SERGEANT) TWO
Fancy a swim?

DUTY ANGEL (POLICE SERGEANT) ONE
Yes. But it will have to be brief.
We have one more call of duty.

As the two DUTY ANGELS/POLICE SERGEANTS walk into deeper waters, the sergeant 'stripes' on their arms - actually curving angel wings - suddenly flap with pleasure, just like the seagulls flying around and above them.

CAPTION: "DOCKEY, THE FACETIOUS JOKER"

EXT. EARLY EVENING (LIGHT FADING FAST) - A CUL-DE-SAC

We're on a dimly lit urban road, but any traffic noise is distant, for this particular street ends in a brick wall. Industrial buildings stand either side, with tall iron fences with long sharp spikes at a 45 degree angle to deter intrusion.

A group of eleven teenagers are in the middle of the street playing five aside football.

No goal posts or nets, but, as on many a cul-de-sac brick wall, someone has painted three white lines for a goal in want of the real thing.

The footballers wear the same strip, designed with an eagle emblem, but the two teams are playing a kind of tag football, where every thirty seconds players each swap sides. Well, except the goalie.

It's a strange game to watch because every time the ball 'goes in' there are cheers from both sides. Perhaps it's more a game of 'Beat-the-Goalie' - who frankly looks a bit put upon in that he has two sets of players against him.

DOCKEY now arrives and watches from a distance.

One of the lads miskicks the ball and it lands at DOCKEY's feet.

DOCKEY has a chance to impress these young whippersnappers with his skills at keepy-uppy.

POV - The camera becomes the football. We see smart, clever, quick kicks - high, low, angled, playful. It's all there in DOCKEY's foot work and ball control.

DOCKEY kicks for goal - oh my, how he bends it like Beckham and hits centre goal!

DOCKEY is very pleased with himself - but only for a moment - because the ball then ricochets off the wall and hits one of the long fence spikes. Oh no! Impaled, the ball now deflates with a whimper.

DOCKEY
(Trying to make light of this disaster)
Just like me: bursting with pride!

These teenagers don't like joke at all.

FOOTBALLER ONE
That was our ball.

FOOTBALLER TWO
Our <u>only</u> ball.

FOOTBALLER THREE
And now we've got nothing left to kick.

The group gather as one mass, only then the GOALIE pushes through them, comes forward and assesses DOCKEY.

GOALIE
That's true, lads, but I think
we've found an alternative.

The gang cotton on to what he means and begin to move in on DOCKEY.

DOCKEY tries to lighten the situation with nervous laughter - but it's a mistake. As is letting a gang of eleven teenagers get so close that it's now too late to run away.

The first kick was gentle enough - and FOOTBALLER ONE did it with a smile - as did FOOTBALLER TWO with his.

DOCKEY smiles back - as if he's in on the joke. But the next kick isn't funny, because it hurts and was meant to. Then comes kick four, kick five, kick six, kick seven, kick eight, knick nine, kick ten, kick eleven. But let's stop counting - besides there's too many now coming at once.

Ah well, DOCKEY is getting his game of football with a head - only it's his own. Of course, the gang's boots don't kick the head off, but one very accurate strike does result in one of DOCKEY's eyes popping out.

The gang laugh uproariously, for they find this extremely amusing - and several use the displaced eyeball to demonstrate their own skills at keepy-uppy.

POV - The camera becomes the eyeball, bouncing from foot to foot. One kick then sends the eyeball so high it can 'see' the whole scene below - the body it used to be part of and the socket it used to be in. And there's the mouth, gurgling with blood... still breathing, but only just...

Oh, but the footballing DOCKEY has now received Death's red card - for what we see, by way of his eyeball, is a slow fade to blackness. But at least he was 'sent off' accompanied by a laughing and cheering crowd.

CAPTION ON SCREEN: <u>"PETER, THE TELL-TALE-TIT"</u>

EXT. NIGHT (DARKENING) - AN UNLIT STREET

The urban soundscape is louder here than on DOCKEY's street, for we are near a busy road with heavy traffic going by.

The shops are closed, but neon lights flash in shop windows - "CLOSING DOWN", "ALL PRICES SLASHED", "EVERYTHING MUST GO". It's late, it's raining, and all that illuminates the street are those neon signs and the headlights of speeding cars.

PETER is found walking along the edge of the pavement nearest the road.

Two figures in hooded anoraks (ANORAK GUY ONE and ANORAK GUY TWO) approach and they too walk at the edge of the pavement, only the hoods prevent us from seeing their faces.

PETER moves aside to let them go by.

Suddenly a figure in a hooded tracksuit (TRACKSUIT GUY) comes running from round the corner and passes PETER so fast that PETER instinctively turns round to see what he does.

As the TRACKSUIT GUY speeds passed ANORAK GUY ONE and ANORAK GUY TWO, he hits them hard on their backs and each fall onto the road into on-coming traffic.

A car nearly hits them, but at the last moment swerves and then drives on without stopping.

The TRACKSUIT GUY carries on regardless and soon disappears into the darkness.

PETER sees all this but doesn't want to get involved and so walks away.

ANORAK GUY ONE and ANORAK GUY TWO, who are picking themselves up and struggling back to the pavement, clock PETER surreptitiously moving off.

ANORAK GUY ONE
(Calling to PETER)
Did you do that?

PETER turns and shakes his head,

PETER
(Pointing in the direction the TRACKSUIT GUY ran)
Oh no, it was <u>that</u> guy.

ANOKAK GUY ONE looks around but doesn't see anyone.

ANORAK GUY ONE
What guy?

PETER
(Pointing again)
<u>Him</u>!

ANORAK GUY TWO
What 'him'?

ANORAK GUY ONE and ANORAK GUY TWO, now on their feet, are puzzled because it's a long street and completely deserted.

ANORAK GUY TWO (CONT'D)
(Looking around)
There is no 'him'.

PETER
Oh. He ran off.

ANORAK GUY TWO
But there's nobody here. Or anywhere.

All traffic has now mysteriously disappeared and there is silence.

ANORAK GUY ONE
Well, nobody but you.

PETER
Oh... but... er... it... er... wasn't me. I've just said... it was the guy who ran off.

ANORAK GUY ONE
(To ANORAK TWO)
Do we believe him?

ANORAK GUY TWO
(To ANORAK ONE)
No.

Together ANORAK GUY ONE and ANORAK GUY TWO move towards PETER and then push him into what happens to be a huge juggernaut.

PETER's body is flattened and becomes like an enormous crushed up cherry tart, with red bits, black bits and light brown crumbly bits all mushed up together.

ANORAK GUY ONE
(To ANORAK TWO)
Did you do that?

ANORAK GUY TWO
(To ANORAK ONE)
No. Did you?

ANORAK GUY ONE
No. It wasn't me.

ANORAK GUY TWO
It must have been somebody else then.

ANORAK GUY ONE
Yes. And if anyone asks, that's what we'll tell them.

ANORAK GUY ONE pulls back his hood and reveals himself to be DUTY ANGEL ONE (that is POLICE SERGEANT ONE).

ANORAK GUY TWO
I agree.

ANORAK GUY TWO now reveals himself to be DUTY ANGEL TWO (that is POLICE SERGEANT TWO.

The two figures stare at the blood, guts and bones spread across the road.

ANORAK GUY ONE
Hungry? There's a late night café round the corner.

ANORAK GUY TWO
Do they do scones?

ANORAK GUY ONE
We can ask. I like my scones spread with lashings of strawberry jam.

ANORAK GUY TWO
I'm more of a blackcurrant jelly man, myself.

ANORAK GUY ONE
Well, we can ask.

The pair look down at their feet and see that some blood has been splattered onto their boots.

ANORAK GUY TWO
I got these boots new this morning. Now they have blood all over them. Bits of bones too, by the looks of it. Do you think the café will have a dishcloth?

ANORAK GUY ONE
We can ask.

The TWO DUTY ANGELS/ANORAK GUYS/POLICE SERGEANTS walk away into the night, leaving near perfect footprints of blood as they go.

Sewer rats emerge from the drains and begin to eat the flesh strewn all over the road. And crows too fly down from the night sky to enjoy an easy meal.

EXT. NIGHT - THE BEACH

The sky is velvet black, except for pin-pricks of diamond stars scattered across it.

CALEB has returned to the slumber party beach, where the tide is well on its way out. The sand is wet but a strange mist slowly rises from it, leaving it almost dry.

The beach is completely deserted. Well, except for a pair of darned woollen socks which have developed yet another hole.

CALEB puts down his backpack, picks up the socks, and takes from one of the pockets in the backpack a darning needle with grey wool already running through its eye.

CALEB begins to sit down as if about to darn the hole, only he hears something above his head and so looks up to the night sky.

CALEB sees an enormous dark winged shape floating down towards him, but he can't yet make out yet what it is.

Oh! It's that blanket - the same one the DUTY ANGELS threw into the wind.

The blanket lands flat on the sand, in a prefect fold as if ready perhaps for someone to sleep on.

CALEB laughs - something we've never seen him do before. He strokes the blanket and giggles and laughs some more.

CALEB

Hah! Hah! *Dies Marmotiensis*.

CALEB's face suddenly changes and becomes more serious, as he remembers exactly what happened on the boat.

CALEB'S DREAM-SCAPE: EXT. NIGHT - AT SEA IN A STORM

POV CALEB - The CREW MEMBER is shouting at YOUNG CALEB, "Caleb, I've told you before - get below with the others. You'll be safer there than on deck." The CREW MEMBER bends down to reassure YOUNG CALEB. "Please, Caleb. Go down!

Go now-" but just at that moment, the white painted mast swings across with such force that it swipes the CREW MEMBER's head and hand clean off - and we hear a boy's high pitched scream and cry.

The POV, now shaking with fear, turns to the roaring sea and catches sight of that severed head as it's tossed about by the ferocious storm.

That high pitched scream gradually changes into that divine top note from Gregorio Allegri's 'Miserere'. And in a faded superimposed image we see that the choir boy is the YOUNG CALEB.

BACK AT THE SLUMBER PARTY BEACH (CONT.)

The older CALEB standing on the beach can still hear his own glorious note from his past. It's a sound of great beauty - and as he listens and remembers, CALEB finds a moment of grace and joy.

But the music soon disappears and the noise of the waves takes its place.

CALEB throws down the socks he was holding and puts away that darning needle - at least for the time being. He opens the backpack and takes out the blankets that were packed away earlier.

CALEB bends down to feel the sand with his fingers. Yes, it's still very slightly damp. Not that it matters, for it always dries out completely overnight.

Next he walks round the beach and lays each blanket neatly on the sand ready for the arrival of his friends, taking a moment to think about the empty blanket-beds now all around him.

CALEB returns to the backpack and unzips one of the side pockets, removes something (but we don't see what), leaving the flap open and hanging down. He next goes over to his blanket, removes his Hippie neck tie, lays it carefully next to his blanket, and sits and waits.

Suddenly we hear the heavy beating of a bird's wings. A seagull? No, for what lands close by CALEB is an owl.

The owl holds in its beak a live rat, desperately struggling to escape. The owl could so easily swallow or kill its prey, yet it chooses to drop the rat and lets it go free.

The rat scampers up CALEB's leg and disappears under his shirt - yet, even with those sharp claws running all over him, CALEB doesn't bat an eyelid.

CALEB reaches out to the owl and strokes its feathers. The owl hoots - and as it does so its eyes turn from deepest black to iridescent orange. Then the owl flies off into the darkness.

CALEB lifts his hand and reveals what he took from his backpack - it's his knife.

CALEB (CONT'D)
'Aegroto, dum anima est, spes esse dicitur.'

SUBTITLES: 'It is said that, for a sick man, while there is life, there is hope'. Cicero

CALEB, now smiling again, raises up the blade and slits his own throat. His neck gurgles out blood - but there is little or no fear in his eyes.

The sky is sprinkled with sapphire stars. The heavens might be looking down on CALEB kindly tonight, for a shooting star soars across the breadth of the firmament.

The bloodied body of CALEB begins to fade and even disappears. Has CALEB made it off the beach? No. The body of CALEB now rematerializes, but without the open wound on his neck or the blood - and that shooting star is no more. Oh, perhaps he will escape tomorrow.

CALEB looks up to the now black and empty sky with disappointment, but he accepts his fate. He lays his head on his blanket ready for sleep in preparation for yet another new day.

EXT. JUST BEFORE DAWN - CLIFF TOP OVERLOOKING THE BEACH

The soundscape is exactly the same as the opening scene - waves gently lapping on a beach - and we again see, in the breaking light of dawn, how they leave behind layers of white cotton blossom foam.

The TWO DUTY ANGELS, our POLICE SERGEANTS and also our ANORAK GUYS, watch over the beach from the cliff top where the same seven thirty-somethings we saw in the first scene are back where they started, spread out on their blankets, alive but but sleeping.

DUTY ANGEL (POLICE SERGEANT) TWO
How long have you been in charge of this beach?

DUTY ANGEL (POLICE SERGEANT) ONE
Since they died.

DUTY ANGEL (POLICE SERGEANT) TWO
Really?

DUTY ANGEL (POLICE SERGEANT) ONE
Yes. I was here on their first day.
Would you like to see?

DUTY ANGEL (POLICE SERGEANT) TWO
I would.

DUTY ANGEL (POLICE SERGEANT) ONE
Close your eyes. Tight.

DUTY ANGEL TWO firmly shuts his eyes.

DUTY ANGEL ONE raises his hand to his face and swipes it across his eyes.

DUTY ANGEL ONE next stands behind DUTY ANGEL TWO and places his hand on DUTY ANGEL TWO's forehead and presses down hard. DUTY ANGEL ONE next removes his hand to reveal on DUTY ANGEL TWO's forehead the eyeballs of DUTY ANGEL ONE - for now we see that DUTY ANGEL ONE's eye sockets are empty.

WHAT WE NOW WITNESS IS DUTY ANGEL ONE'S MIND MEMORY AS SEEN BY DUTY ANGEL TWO:

EXT. NIGHT - AT SEA IN A STORM

Six children, all in choir outfits, huddle together in a cabin on a boat with water flooding in from under the door. The children are aged about eight or nine years old, but they are still recognisable as JODIE, DOCKEY, GRAHAM, AGNES, PETER and OLGA. They are scared and fearful, for they know they are about to die.

DUTY ANGEL TWO
Oh! They were children!

DUTY ANGEL ONE
Yes. Children.

The one who is missing is CALEB, who we now see in his choir boy outfit struggling along one of the boat's corridor. CALEB then opens a door which leads onto the deck of the boat - and there is that CREW MEMBER who will soon lose his head.

DUTY ANGEL ONE (CONT'D)
And they've remained who they were
in some ways.

DUTY ANGEL TWO
And all from the same choir?

DUTY ANGEL ONE
Yes. They sang beautifully. And still do when chance allows. They drowned on their way to a concert in the Channel Isles. I'll show the day they first woke up on my beach, if you'd like to see.

DUTY ANGEL TWO
Yes, I would. Thank you.

EXT. DAY - THE BEACH SLUMBER PARTY (STILL THE MIND MEMORY OF DUTY ANGEL ONE)

The same SEVEN YOUNG CHILDREN we saw on the boat wake up on the beach in ordinary dry clothes. It's their first ever day there, but of course they don't know they're dead. And as we watch these images we hear, as voice-over, the ongoing exchanges between the two DUTY ANGELS.

(OOV) DUTY ANGEL TWO
They grew up here?

(OOV) DUTY ANGEL ONE
Yes. That's what makes this beach special. Everyday their bodies awake slightly older. But they don't know that. I'll show you more, if you like.

(OOV) DUTY ANGEL TWO
Yes please.

EXT. DAY - THE BEACH SLUMBER PARTY (STILL THE MIND MEMORY OF DUTY ANGEL ONE).

Those same seven children are now SEVEN TEENAGERS, then they morph into SEVEN YOUNG ADULTS, then SEVEN TWENTY-SOMETHING GROWN-UPS. Finally we see them aged thirty-something - in fact, the CALEB, JODIE, DOCKEY, GRAHAM, AGNES, PETER and OLGA with whom we've become familiar.

(OOV) DUTY ANGEL TWO
What about Father Patrick, the maze, the arcade, the little girl?

(OOV) DUTY ANGEL ONE
All modelled on the books they read, or people they knew.
(MORE)

(OOV) DUTY ANGEL ONE (CONT'D)
I just throw in a bit of something of my own. Like Caleb's darning needle or the dress with the blue canaries.

(OOV) DUTY ANGEL TWO
Canaries are usually yellow.

(OOV) DUTY ANGEL ONE
Yes.

(OOV) DUTY ANGEL TWO
Or green.

(OOV) DUTY ANGEL ONE
Yes.

(OOV) DUTY ANGEL TWO
But yours were blue.

(OOV) DUTY ANGEL ONE
Yes.

(OOV) DUTY ANGEL TWO
You like blue.

(OOV) DUTY ANGEL ONE
Yes. You can have whatever colour you wish when it's your beach. I'm sure you'll be given your own one day. Then you can have all the candy floss you want. And blue if you like blue.

(OOV) DUTY ANGEL TWO
But what about their clothes?

(OOV) DUTY ANGEL ONE
Two decades dead, but since time and fashion have moved on I thought that should be acknowledged. And that's why I throw in an empty bottle of red wine - and those bottles of Double Diamond. Of course they don't drink any of it, because there never is a night before.

(OOV) DUTY ANGEL TWO
But why all this?

(OOV) DUTY ANGEL ONE
Lessons must be learnt. No one dies in a state of perfect grace. Except guide dogs.

(OOV) DUTY ANGEL TWO
Yet they were all such little sins. Showing off a bit. Being miserable. Or stubborn. Or silly. Hardly grievous crimes. Seems so unfair, cruel and... (hesitating to say this) ... unjust.

(OOV) DUTY ANGEL ONE
Theirs was an unfair, cruel and unjust world of tooth and claw - why should this one be so different?

(OOV) DUTY ANGEL TWO
Will they ever leave this beach?

(OOV) DUTY ANGEL ONE
Oh yes. When they learn what they need to learn. It nearly happened to Caleb last night, but the stars changed their mind.

(OOV) DUTY ANGEL TWO
And if they don't learn?

(OOV) DUTY ANGEL ONE
In that case they will simply age and die. Except it will be a different kind of death.

(OOV) DUTY ANGEL TWO
And then?

(OOV) DUTY ANGEL ONE
They move onto another beach. You hope one of the happier ones. Though not always. But that's not my decision. I'll have my eyes back now, if you don't mind.

EXT. SUNRISE - SLUMBER PARTY BEACH (CONT.)

DUTY ANGEL ONE takes his right hand and swipes it across the face of DUTY ANGEL TWO so that the eyes on the forehead are taken away. DUTY ANGEL ONE next presses that same hand on his own face, with the result that his eyes are now seen back in their sockets.

DUTY ANGEL TWO spots a severed head at the shore.

DUTY ANGEL TWO
The head. It's washed up earlier today. And not in the same place.

DUTY ANGEL ONE
Yes. Every day is different. Slightly. Including how they die.

DUTY ANGEL TWO
But they don't remember.

DUTY ANGEL ONE
Graham does, sometimes. He did today, I think. Caleb definitely. It comes back to him in flashes as the day goes on.

DUTY ANGEL TWO
But Caleb doesn't tell them.

DUTY ANGEL ONE
He's tried to many times, but they never believe him. Caleb was the lonely boy who lived in a world of his own fancy. Always making up stories. And that part of himself is still very strong.

DUTY ANGEL TWO
So now only the dreamer knows he's in a dream.

DUTY ANGEL ONE
The beach is not a dream. And the pain they feel when they die is very real.

DUTY ANGEL TWO
I suppose we better go now?

DUTY ANGEL ONE
Yes. They'll be waking up soon. And we mustn't be seen here when they do. (Looking up to the Heavens) We'd be in trouble with The Keeper if we were.

DUTY ANGEL TWO
And so another day begins.

DUTY ANGEL ONE
Yes. Just another day.

DUTY ANGEL ONE and DUTY ANGEL TWO fade away likes ghosts in the night...

EXT. EARLY MORNING - BEACH SHORE

Waves gently lap on a beach, bringing with them white cotton blossom foam that now lays lightly on the sand.

PETER wakes, sits up and looks to the shoreline. Something he notices disturbs him.

PETER leans over to where DOCKEY is sleeping and PETER shakes DOCKEY awake.

PETER

Dockey! I think I see something -

A lone white dove glides overhead and then flies high up into the sky - taking us with it.

What we now see is a bird's eye view of this peculiar world, which, it is revealed, is made up of hundreds and thousands of individual beaches spread across an infinite shoreline.

What we hear as the dove soars higher and higher is YOUNG CALEB singing *The Song of Simeon* (Luke, Chapter 2, verses 29-32, which comes from *The Book of Common Prayer*, 1662) also known as 'Nunc Dimittis'. The melody and accompanying music is by Geoffrey Burgon.

THE VOICE OF CALEB AS A BOY.

'Lord, now lettest thou thy servant depart in peace according to thy word.
For mine eyes have seen thy salvation,
Which thou hast prepared before the face of all people;
To be a light to lighten the Gentiles and to be the glory of thy people Israel.
Glory be to the Father and to the Son and to the Holy Ghost,
As it was in the beginning is now and ever shall be world without end.
Amen.'

THE END

THE GHOST LIGHT

A Theatre Ghost Story of Malevolent Murder and Dramatic Vengeance

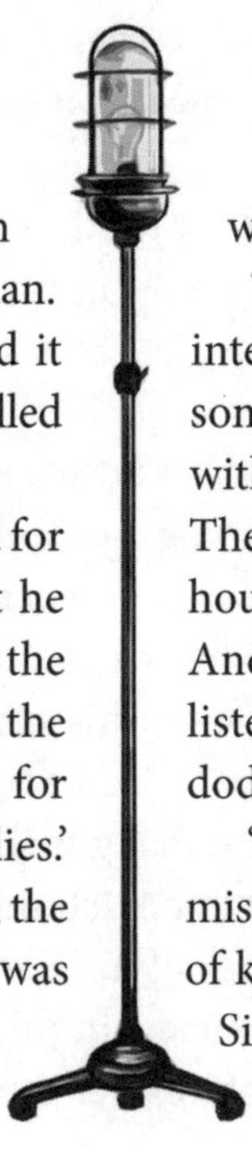

AS I REMEMBER IT, AND MY memory has always been my most blessed of gifts, the woman spoke first, and then the man.

‘Murder! You disguised it with lies, but I know you killed him.’

‘It was suicide. Very sad for all of us that he did what he did, but you cannot ignore the doctor’s evidence at the inquest. The prescriptions for painkillers. Those weren’t lies.’

‘Just like the rest of us in the village, Doctor Jefferies was fooled by your wicked dissembling, but then he began to grow suspicious. And that’s why, Sir Arnold, you had to kill him, along with the vicar’s wife.’

‘My dear madam, a most interesting theory, but somewhat difficult to prove without a murder weapon. The police searched the entire house, yet never found one. And besides, who is going to listen to the ramblings of a doddery village postmistress?’

‘Perhaps. But a village post-mistress knows the importance of keeping records. Your past, Sir Arnold, casts a long shadow. You have always prided yourself on servicing your own car – and said so often in your campaign leaflets for Parliament.'

'I was in the Royal Engineers. It's common knowledge. I learnt to regard anything mechanical as a challenge. The voters agreed. I always had unassailable majority.'

'Indeed. But your interest in wheels and cogs began early, for I have discovered, as your wages were paid out in postal orders, that you were once a boy apprentice at a watchmaker's.'

'What of it?'

'Dismantling the workings of an old grandfather clock would not have been too difficult. And reassembling those pieces, after you had used them to kill Doctor Jefferies, would, I believe, have been the kind of challenge you rather enjoyed.'

'What nonsense, dear lady.'

'Your mistake was that you did the job too well. Mrs Jefferies told me how the clock seemed to strike so much on the note after the death of her husband. But it wasn't her ears or grieving mind playing tricks, as you suggested. Oh no, the clock strike was different, for your expertise had enhanced its tone. I was always very fond of that grandfather clock. Less so now that it hides a secret.'

'You'll never prove it.'

'Oh, but, Sir Arnold, I don't need to. My evening gown is hardly elegant, but its "frumpery", as I overheard you call it, hides a mystery of its own.'

'What do you mean?'

'That day I visited Dr Jeffries I discovered that my own clock was running down. Time is now against me. Even if you were arrested and tried, I would not live to see you hang. Oh, doubtless you think of me as a sad and lonely spinster, but in my youth, I loved him. True passion never leaves you. So, for his sake, I will deliver retribution with my own hands.'

'What are you doing with that gun?'

'The hands of the clock approach midnight. Count the seconds down, Sir Arnold, for you shall not live to see another day. At the stroke of twelve, you will hear again the chimes of murder. But this time, your own! Seven. Eight. Nine. Ten. Eleven...'

And at that moment, the lady pulled the trigger. But alas, no bang.

'Oh bugger. This bloody gun! It's jammed again. Props! Darling, Tom, if it happens on the night I may have to resort to stabbing you to death with my hat pin!'

'Ha, ha! Well at least now, my angel, I get to live a little longer.'

The actor on the stage then looked out into theatre auditorium and shouted, 'Derek, is that tea? For me and Julia, at least.'

A faceless voice from the dimly lit stalls echoed back.

'Tea? Well, er, I suppose it is. Perhaps. Yes? No?'

There are two types of directors in the theatre: those who bend to accommodate everyone and those who insist on having their own way. Derek Marr was definitely in the 'try-and-please-everyone' camp, so much so that any capacity to make even the simplest of decisions had long been bred out of him.

'Tea for you Tom and Julia. I think maybe... yes. Or not? No? I only wanted to run that scene for the new blocking. I think it's important, don't you, that the audience can see the grandfather clock? I think so. Yes, no? I do. Yes, I do. Much better. Yes? I realise it's awkward for you, Tom, being so much more upstage, I do, but, but it helps visually. I'm sure you agree. Yes, no? Hmm? I'm so sorry, but wires must have got crossed somewhere. You see, they've not put in the two front rows we wanted. They thought *The Chimes of Murder* was a musical! That's why the pit's been left open. I understand you want to play it more downstage to be closer to the audience, and all that, but the sight-lines to that damned clock are so awkward if we do. They'll sort it out for tomorrow night? Yes? No? And we must get that bloody gun fixed. Someone? Anyone there in the wings? I don't know who's here today. I'm sure someone is. Yes? No? Oh dear, guns that go off in act three. That Chekhov has a lot to answer for. I say, Tom, Julia, ha-ha, I say, ha-ha, Chekhov has a lot to answer for... ha... ha... yes... After tea, then, we'll have a full understudy run for the covers of the two principals. Hello... hello? Anyone in the wings? Yes? No?'

A figure dressed in black peered out from behind the curtain and said, 'In costume?'

'Yes, I think so. Yes, no? In costume, yes, most definitely. Is that all right with you, er, er, Ron?'

'Full run?'

'Oh yes. Act one, then two, then three.'

'Re-set for one then.'

'Re-set? I think so. Yes?'

'But tea first?'

'Oh yes. No?'

'TEA! OFFICIAL!'

And with the sort of bellowing voice that distinguishes all stage managers from lesser mortals, the disembodied head of Ron disappeared behind the curtain.

'Darling,' said Tom to Julia, 'for us that sounds more than just tea. An early lunch, I think. How lovely. See you all at the half!'

And with that Tom and Julia left the stage and sauntered off hand in hand to their dressing rooms.

Whenever actors bring visitors backstage I have often observed how utterly confused such guests become by our theatre talk. 'Kill the workers!' yells a stage manager and outsiders think they're in the presence of slaughtering fascists. However, once it is explained that the phrase means 'switch off the working lights located above the stage' their fears are abated. As with every profession, we in the theatre have our own somewhat idiosyncratic language, which, for the uninitiated, might as well be a local dialect of Mandarin.

I will now take this opportunity, therefore, to clarify those theatrical expressions pertinent to our story.

Derek, our fussy and rather hesitant director, spoke of 'blocking', a word that simply means the precise positioning and movement of actors on the stage. The 'pit', well that's simple enough, for that is the orchestra pit, which it seems, due to wires crossed – or more likely utter incompetence – has been left open. 'Principals', I think that's self-explanatory, but just in case, the term refers to the leading actors, as opposed to those with only the odd line, who spend most of production moving furniture. The two principals in *The Chimes of Murder* are, for the record, Julia Fontaine and Tom Garrick. Two people who may not share a name, but they do a bed, and something not always required by actors on tour, namely a marriage certificate. As for Chekhov, well, I assume you know he is a Russian playwright, but his 'gun' refers to his dramatic rule that if a pistol is mentioned in act one, it should go off in act three. In other words, every element introduced to a story must be relevant to the final outcome. A belief, incidentally, you should hold in mind as I tell this tale. Though of course why incidents are introduced may not at first be apparent.

There was mention too by Tom of 'the half'. This is the thirty minutes before the play begins, when all actors are required to be present in the theatre building. Strictly speaking it's the half-hour before 'beginners', the five-minute call given for those actors who appear in the opening scene. I tell you this because what happens in the half is key to our tale. Which is, in its own way, a murder mystery. And very real, not like that silly plot in the play.

And now I think it is time I introduced myself. I am the theatre's Ghost Light. Again, there will be those of you unfamiliar with this term, so I shall explain. Whenever a theatre is temporarily unoccupied, 'goes dark', as we call it, a symbolic light is placed centre stage in the hope that one day the thespian art will return. All theatres have a Ghost Light, though it is fair to say I am different to most. I am, if you will, the spirit of The Ghost Light. I embody – if you would allow an expression somewhat incongruous to my nature – the voices of this theatre's past, for I am the spirit of those who spent their days treading the very boards on which I stand. My theatre was built in the Victorian era, and so there have been many voices, but now they have all become one and I am he.

I am only able to observe and hear what happens within my realm, which, to be clear, incorporates the stage, the auditorium, the dressing rooms, front of house and the corridor that leads to the stage door. I am not, however, privy to what occurs beyond that. The theatre is my only world. But it is enough for me.

I have heard Ghost Lights in other theatres are locked away in cupboards, abandoned among common lamps, follow spots and reflectors, but here at The Chertswood I reside proudly in the wings. My lamp has no gel or shade, except a protective steel mesh, and so I offer, when required, an illumination that can spread far and wide.

But I am proud that the popularity of The Chertswood has rarely necessitated my services. I did hear that The Albany in Drillington was dark for almost two years before it became – oh, unmerciful Heaven, I hardly dare say the words – a carpet warehouse. It all begins with a leak in the roof, damp sets in, the building is left to rot, and, as night follows day, it is then gutted to leave only its four walls. But of course, The Albany was never, as I am, a Number One touring venue. Oh yes, we get them all here, even silly little potboilers such as *Let Justice Stand Blind*, *Death at the Brass Rubbings* and *The Chimes of Murder*, a scene from which you have just witnessed. Hardly Marlowe or even Beaumont and Fletcher, but it's all about bums on seats these days, and such melodramatic nonsense helps fill the coffers.

So, there you have it. That's my world and my theatre. And now my story. All I have told you so far has a bearing on the terrible tale of revenge I shall reveal. Think of it as The Prelude. And so now, to continue with the theatrical parlance, let us proceed with Act One.

The sleuth in *The Chimes of Murder*, as you have heard, is a village postmistress, an interfering gossip called Miss Eaves. I will leave the wit and merit of this nomenclature for you alone to judge. I must say, I'd imagined Miss Eaves as rather rumpled and dowdy. However, Julia Fontaine, once upon a time quite a name in the world of British film, clung onto the belief that she was still a star and so insisted upon being provided with four costume changes and outfits that emphasised her youth. Or what was left of it. Miss Fontaine also had it in her contract that she should wear her own jewellery, from her halcyon days on the silver screen, which on no account was to be shared with her understudy. And it is to the understudy dress run, that is in full costume, to which our attention now turns.

Daphne, now in the role of Miss Eaves, had been supplied with only one outfit. The company producing *The Chimes of Murder* – I will not reveal their name, let's just call them 'Tacky Tours', as that's what everybody else did – was notorious for casting less on the basis of talent and more on waist measurements and what they had in stock. Daphne, therefore, had been given a tweed skirt, which needed neither taking in nor letting out, and a couple of blouses. However, for the late night confrontation with Sir Arnold, which was meant to be taking place after a dinner party, Daphne thought that she should at least be allowed some adornment. And to that end she went in search of the theatre's Bric-a-Brac Box, wherein are kept all sorts of oddities from previous productions. And here dearest Daphne found a rather wonderful emerald opal necklace.

'Oh perfection!' she said.

Now in truth, I rarely if ever take much notice of understudy runs. Frankly, they are uninspiring affairs, and the standard of acting hardly raises itself above adequate, at best. Yet, that final scene between the dowdy postmistress and the pompous former colonel was electrifying. Dearest Daphne had little more than said her lines during the previous two acts, but suddenly in that confrontation there on display was an extraordinary passion. Even Ron, the jaded stage manager, lifted his head to witness the drama. But the true strangeness for me came at the curtain call. Yes, it may come as a surprise to you but curtain calls – referred to as 'Who's best?' by the more cynical members in our profession – are indeed rehearsed. An empty and silent auditorium bestows on the bows a sense of the surreal. However, when Daphne took hers, from on high, somewhere in the Upper Gallery, which we call 'the Gods', there was sustained applause. You will wish to know from whom it came, for I have both ears and eyes. Yet, I must tell you though I heard clapping, hands I saw not. Most mysterious.

Dearest Daphne was what we might call a dizzy actress. Limited in talent but their endless bonhomie can be quite an asset on tour when not everyone's mood is so wonderful. Believe me, Hitler in his bunker is nothing compared to an intemperate actor in his dressing room, festering over some imagined slight or other. But that day, following the dress run, a feeling of elation permeated the company. Daphne, everyone said, had been quite magnificent in the scene with the grandfather clock. What had she been drinking? And could they have some of it? Quite mesmeric, they said. I wouldn't go quite that far personally, but when the gun went off (someone had thankfully fixed it by then), and Sir Arnold dropped down to the ground for his confessional death speech, I took in not a word he said. He could have been reciting pages from *Exchange and Mart* for all I knew, for my attention stayed on the magnetic actress who'd shot him. The way Daphne stared at him. Penetrating, as if her very soul had lived only for that moment.

Daphne herself seemed only half aware of the power of her performance. She was not even distracted in the scene by the arrival of a flickering moth, not a good omen in the theatre, and she was completely oblivious to the mysterious applause that came from the darkness in the Upper Gallery. However, having lived in California, and known, she said, a woman who healed with the power of crystals, Daphne put the energy of her performance down to the emerald opal necklace she wore around her neck. She had felt something, she said, as soon as she had put it on. The 'apple aura', as she called it, was the colour of Rebirth, and opals were able to heal painful memories and bring the spirit and body back into balance. Some of the cast exchanged dubious glances at this – not all actors live with the fairies – but there was no denying the vitality that had inhabited her on stage. And when Daphne left the theatre for her late lunch, she did so still wearing the opal necklace, though whether this was forgetfulness or by intent I cannot say, but there was no doubt her cheeks were redder and her eyes brighter than they had been since her arrival.

About those emerald opals. I recognised them from somewhere, but as we have welcomed so many productions over the years, it was difficult to place them. It was only after the unfortunate accident that I realised where I'd seen them before. Oh, but I get ahead of myself, for we haven't reached that part of the tale yet.

Tom Garrick and his wife Julia Fontaine had left early for their long lunch and so missed the excitement of Daphne's performance. Principals rarely enjoy watching their understudies. The prosaic explanation is vanity, the fear of someone being better than you, but the more metaphysical reason is the sense of mortality it brings, to know that life, and especially the show, will always go on without you. Of course, even if you choose not to be present at the understudy performance, your fellow actors will no doubt oblige you with a detailed review of how good your rival was.

Tom, a popular actor at The Cherstwood, was rare among his breed in that he seemed immune to praise or criticism, either of himself or anyone else. Tom, I would say, was a solid, resourceful man, if somewhat lacking in emotion, but leading a company requires a steady hand on the tiller and he certainly had that. 'I'm a pit pony actor,' I once heard him joke, 'a pat on the head and a lump of sugar and I'm happy as a pig chiffon.'

Julia on the other hand was more needy. She was Tom's second wife, after the tragic death of Evelyn, and lived somewhat in the former's shadow, as the subsequent often does. Julia and Evelyn were cousins, and both had known Tom when they were bright young things, but the insecurity of being second choice never quite goes away. Add onto that the constant reassurances a leading actress on tour requires, plus today your understudy's luminosity being the talk of back stage corridors, and you have a potentially volatile combination. But this is where Derek Marr came into his own, for he was what one may call a woman's director, and when he entered Julia's dressing room, he knew exactly what to say.

'Oh, I do hope you and Tom had a lovely lunch. Oh my angel, how you deserve it. Julia, you've worked so hard. So hard! Oh, but it all shines through, it really does. You've found a side of Miss Eaves that even I didn't know was there. You've discovered nuances that I can assure you the writer didn't even know were there! Ha-Ha! Yes you have. It's quite wonderful. Quite wonderful!'

'I heard Daphne did a very good job this afternoon.'

'Who? Daphne? Oh. Oh no. Oh well... yes. Of course she's very competent is Daphne. Yes, yes, very competent. You have to hand her that. And she wasn't at all disturbed by the moth.'

'The moth?'

'In my day the old thesps were terribly superstitious about moths on stage. A sign of death, they said. But no, no, no, Daphne doesn't have what you have. It's what Ellen Terry said, you know. A star has that little something extra. Except with you it's not little, not little at all, my angel, no, no. Yes, you see, you've found in that final scene a way of bringing to life a heart that had not truly lived for many, many years. Do you see what I mean?'

'Go on.'

'Well, my angel, you have discovered in Miss Eaves a life force of desire and passion. And conviction. Stanislavski himself couldn't have done it better. Or Mrs Stanislavski, I should say. If there was one! I don't know. Ha-Ha!'

'*Heart*, you say.'

'Oh yes. Pumping on all cylinders. But we have discovered one thing from the understudy run – and that is the gun now works. Oh, I know tonight you're going to be quite, quite wonderful. Don't you think so? Oh, I do. I do. I do. Only you could possibly bring everything off. Only you, dear. An old spinster... Well, not old, really. No. More bereft. That's the right word. Bereft. But you've found the blood in her and it's on the stage for all to see. And I must say as well how stunning you look in that final scene. They've come to see a star and you gift them your glitter and glamour. Those emerald opals. How splendid.'

'What emerald opals?'

'Oh dear, what am I thinking of. I don't know. What do they call it now... a senior moment? No, I mean your diamonds. Yes, your wonderful diamonds. How they sparkle! Sparkle! Sparkle! Sparkle!'

'What do you think Evelyn would have done with her? Miss Eaves.'

Derek as you will have gathered had a torrent of words for any occasion, yet I suspected from his momentary pause that this question was not one he had anticipated. But he recovered quickly and soon knew exactly what to say.

'Oh, dearest Evelyn. Oh, yes. Such a sad loss when she died. A bitter sad loss for Tom. And all of us in the profession. I knew her well. But Evelyn, you see, was always herself. She had many qualities but she couldn't be anyone else. Do you know what I mean? Yes? No? She was a remarkable woman in many ways but not an inhabiter. But you, my dear, like all the great actresses, are a true chameleon. Do you know what I mean? Julia, you can become anybody. Evelyn could never ever do that.'

'Tom hardly talks about her, but today her name came up at lunch. The waiter remembered her and Tom, you see. Said he didn't know about the fall.'

'Tragic. Tragic. Tragic how it happened. How Tom came home and found her lying there at the bottom of those stairs. Frayed carpet, they thought. Oh, I'm sorry. I'm so sorry. We shouldn't talk about it. It's too upsetting. I loved her very much but I can honestly say Evelyn could not have achieved in this play what you, my angel, have achieved. Really. Oh no, no, no, no. This is *your* play. They will talk about this production for years to come. I know it! And Mother's always right!'

I only observe. I cannot go inside someone's mind and see what they are thinking. However, I will go as far as to say that I sensed a certain unease between Julia and Tom when they signed themselves in at the stage door following their lunch. It would be wrong to speculate, but one can't help but think that Evelyn was the subject of much of the conversation as they ate their fish pie.

Now dearest Daphne was one of those actresses who seem to survive on fresh air, and when she did eat, it was always something with soya beans or lentils. 'I bet she even knits her own muesli,' I heard one of the other actors say under his breath. I shouldn't say who, but I will. Peter Sinclair. The Joker of the Pack. One of his favourite lines being, 'Never heard of me? Truth is, neither have I! Ha-ha-ah!' Oh yes, Peter was always coming out with silly little gags and quips. All companies have them. Most irritating, they are. 'I said to my agent, what I lack in talent, I make up for in availability. Did I tell you I have representation in New York which has opened up an entire continent of unemployment. Ha-ha-ha!'

Yes, well I did tell you he was annoying.

Thankfully, however, Peter has little relevance to our story, except that it was he whom Daphne sat next to in the Green Room when she returned from her late lunch at the next door tea shop.

'The lovely lady who runs it, Mavis, I think her name is. Or is it Maureen? Well, she said, "Hello, m'ducks," the way she does. At first, I thought the tea shop was empty, and I always like to share a table with someone interesting, but then I spied in the corner this lovely lady who had just finished her tea. Anyway, she smiled and asked me if I was one of the actresses in the play – people always think I'm an actress, I can't think why – so I said, well, I was and I wasn't. She then said I couldn't be both, surely, and then I had to explain that I was the understudy. Then I think she understood why I both was and I wasn't. Ha! Ha! Anyway, this lady then said that she was coming to the play tonight and could I go on just for her. And I laughed and said, no, they wouldn't allow that. She told me to put in a request but I said if I did the Company Manager's reply would be given the blue pencil. Which is how they censored naughty words in a play in the old days. And then she laughed at that and then asked me to join her at her table. I could smell the tea was Earl Grey and she had just finished a slice of cherry pie. Oh, I used to love cherry pie, but now it sends my tummy into a commotion, so I avoid it. Tomatoes, too. And onions. And mushrooms. That's why I ordered the egg flan. Plain and simple. Like me! Ha! Ha! Anyway, the lady who'd just finished her cherry pie told me how much she loved The Cherstwood. I asked if she was local and she said, no, but she'd made a special trip because tonight it would be a murder mystery. I asked if she liked other types of shows too and she said liked musicals best. *Salad Days* was her favourite. Was it? I said. Mine too! And then we sang together "*We Said We'd Never Look Back*". Well, as I said, the teashop was empty, except for us. And I didn't think the counter lady would mind. And of course she didn't. She just kept smiling at me. The way people do, sometimes. The lady then asked what *The Chimes of Murder* was about and I said that like all good whodunits it was about something real. Something truly felt. And then she asked who did do it, but I said I couldn't tell her because that would spoil the ending. And she said she hoped it wasn't me who was the murderer, and then we both laughed again. Then the lady said what good skin I had and I told her I used a cream a bought in California. And she then held my hand. Oh, it can be so lonely on tour and then suddenly you meet someone, and you chat away as if you've somehow known them forever. I'm out front watching the show tonight, so perhaps I'll see her again. A drink or something before I go back to my digs. Did I tell you the toilet doesn't flush? My landlady says you've got to surprise it.'

Peter Sinclair took this as his cue to moan about his digs and before long he was going into the lurid details of an amorous adventure from the previous night, the details of which, keeping to Chekhov's rule, I will spare you. In fact, nothing of any note occurred until just before the half. And what happened then led to our act one curtain: Julia lying unconscious at the bottom of a flight of stairs.

How did she fall? Did someone push her? If so, who? Or should that be what?

The theatre profession proclaims itself to be egalitarian, and does so with a passion, but the truth is it has a strict pecking order with its own caste system. The smaller your name on the bill, the higher up the building you're put. Daphne, on the very top floor, had to go down to the one below to use the Ladies. And it was after leaving the lavatory, she said, that she found Julia at the bottom of the stairs, unconscious. That's when Daphne screamed. Peter Sinclair, whose dressing room was nearby, was first to arrive, as he was already in the corridor. Daphne's cry then brought Tom, Derek, and Ron, all of whom quickly made their way to the upper staircase, but by that time Julia had already begun to come round.

Julia seemed more in shock than anything. She'd gone upstairs, she explained, as she couldn't find her diamond necklace for the third act, which she always set out at the beginning of the half, and had wondered if her understudy had borrowed it, only Daphne wasn't in her dressing room so she went back down the stairs. At first Julia couldn't say how she fell but then thought she remembered a hand against her back. This led Ron to ask Peter if he had seen who had pushed Julia and Peter said he hadn't as he was at the other end. Tom asked Peter what he was doing hanging around in the corridor, to which Peter replied that he had learnt from bitter experience not to fart in a dressing room without windows. Julia said it might not have been a hand she felt at all, merely a muscle spasm in her back. She tried to stand up, but it was clear she had suffered a bad sprain, for she could hardly move her leg. Derek dithered as to what should be done and so it was left to Ron the stage manager to say that they had no alternative and Daphne must go on in Julia's place. He would ring for an ambulance for Julia and in the meantime find some ice to put round that swollen ankle. Daphne said it was nearly beginners and she wouldn't be ready for at least twenty minutes and would they make an announcement delaying curtain up. The stage manager went off muttering under his breath, 'Oh, why does everything always happen to me.'

So far in this tale I have only related those incidents and conversations that could have been observed, or were later shared, by a member of the company. However, I have not yet revealed why these events are connected and how they will inexorably lead to a death. But perhaps you have, for all the clues are there. Of course, I see everything. The very reason I am able to tell you this story is because I have a privileged sight line. A house seat, as we say in the theatre. Yet, to say too much at this point would be to give away how it ends. And that would be the cardinal sin of the whodunit.

Waiting in the wings is a theatre expression that has now become common parlance. No matter how important, grand, or seemingly indispensable you believe you are, there is always, always, someone in those wings ready to take your place. And that night it was Daphne.

Derek was wrong about nearly everything, but he was right in saying Julia had star quality. What it is, where it comes from, and how it manifests itself, is why thespians still talk of the gifts bestowed by the theatre god, Dionysus. To Julia he was generous, but to Daphne less so. Sadly the Greeks had no god of adequacy, for if they did, no doubt Daphne would have been his leading disciple. However, there was one member of the audience that night who was very curious to see Daphne on stage. I refer to the lady who ran the tea shop, who was always given complimentary tickets for the opening night in the hope that she would recommend the show to her customers. But here I jump ahead, for we must save her review until after the drama is over. To my mind the actual performance of the play was somewhat pedestrian. Again, it was only in the grandfather clock scene that it truly came to life. And I use that phrase advisably.

I have told you that I am not witness to what goes on in someone's mind. Yet having witnessed Tom Garrick's performances of the past, including those with his first wife Evelyn, it would be fair to say that whether playing priest, politician or pastry chef, Tom's role-playing was essentially the same. It was odd therefore to see how disconcerted he was by the appearance of Miss Eaves. And here I refer to the way Daphne was dressed. Tom was one of those actors who never looked their fellow performers in the eye, preferring instead a distraction free mid-distance. Yet that night Tom Garrick's stare at Daphne was intense and unremitting. But perhaps not so much at her as that emerald opal necklace she wore. And then came the confrontation between Miss Eaves and Sir Arnold.

'Murder! You disguised it with lies, but I know you killed her.'

Oh dear. That wasn't right. The victim in the play was a woman not a man. But Tom was a seasoned professional and covered it well.

'It was suicide. *His* suicide. Very sad for all of us that he did what he did, but you cannot ignore the doctor's evidence at the inquest. The prescriptions for painkillers. Those weren't lies.'

'Like the rest of them, the doctor was fooled by your duplicity and wickedness. I say once more, you killed her!'

Why had Daphne as Miss Eaves got it wrong again? But once more Tom was able to think on his feet.

'My dear madam, I believe you are becoming somewhat confused. Say what you like – and as often – but it will be difficult to prove without a murder weapon. The police searched the entire house, yet never found one. And besides, who is going to listen to the ramblings of a doddery village postmistress.'

'The murder weapon was your own hands. Tom you pushed me down those stairs. You altered the time on the clock that fell from the table in order to give yourself an alibi.'

Hearing these words, Tom's face turned as white as a winter's frost. But more was yet to be said.

'True passion never dies. It lives beyond the grave. And so now I will deliver retribution for your treachery with my own hands.'

Perhaps Tom recognised the cue, perhaps he didn't. Either way no more words came forth from the leading man until Miss Eaves took out the gun from under her blouse.

'What are you doing with that gun?'

'Your midnight approaches. Count the seconds down, Tom, for you shall not live to see another day. At the stoke of twelve, you will hear again the chimes of murder. But this time, your own! Seven. Eight. Nine. Ten. Eleven...'

Miss Eaves, or Daphne, or should we really say Evelyn, lifted the revolver and pointed it at Tom – and the shot was fired. Tom in that moment sighed the sigh of man who truly believed he was about to meet his end. But of course it was a blank. Yet the twist is that that sigh *would* be his last breath.

As I have told you, I am the spirit of all those who have tread these boards – alive and dead – and so I am privileged in what I see. Oh, but what explanation can I offer as to what happened next? For there is none in your world.

When Daphne dropped the gun to the ground, the hand that had held it glowed green. That ghostly emerald hand then freed itself from its mortal casement and flew through the air with murderous intent. The green hand, with its phosphorus luminance, knew where its destiny lay and its fingers placed themselves on the man's breast. The spectre's hand could not be resisted, for mere flesh and blood were no match for its unearthly power. The man staggered under its force. Did Tom know where he was being taken? I cannot say, but it was seconds only before his foot had reached the edge of stage. And then he stumbled, tottering for just a moment before falling into the open pit.

Musicians are notoriously untidy and an old wooden music stand had been left in the place where Tom's head and neck would meet it. Death, they said, was instantaneous.

And now what they call the denouement, the 'unknotting'.

To say what hand pushed Julia down the stairs, would not be the same as to say whose. I could not truly tell you it belonged to Daphne, for, after the deed was done, she simply walked along the corridor to the Ladies, oblivious to the prostrate body beneath her feet. You see, our director Derek Marr was wrong when he said Evelyn could not inhabit someone else, for in those moments she became Daphne. As for the missing diamond, yes, I believe Daphne, possessed by Evelyn, took those without even knowing what she was doing. And for those with an eye for detail and plot holes, I can now reveal they were later found in the Ladies.

What of that ghostly hand? Well, it seems only I saw that green spectre. Perhaps Tom did too, but we can never be sure. His ghost, as yet, has not returned to haunt my theatre. At least he died on, or near the stage, unlike the indignity of that poor actor who met his demise as he came down in the lift at the Frinton-on-Sea TravelBour.

The audience I should here add left the theatre believing what they had witnessed was an accident, for all they saw was a man stumbling across the stage and falling into the orchestra pit. It was mainly an older crowd and, though shocked, they left calmly enough. The only observance worth passing on came from the lady who ran the tea shop, who said to her companion as they went passed the Grand Circle Bar, 'That actress who fired the gun was in my shop earlier. Ordered my egg flan. But she was very odd. The place was completely empty, yet she chose to sit at a table where I hadn't yet cleared away the dirty plate and tea cup. And then she spent her entire time talking to herself. Actresses do that sometimes, it's how they learn their lines. But then she started to sing that lovely song from *Salad Days*, "*We Said We'd Never Look Back*." They did that show a year or so ago. In the cast was that actress who accidentally fell down the stairs. Come to think of it, she was once married to the poor chap who fell off the stage tonight. Strange how things happen in twos.'

Ah, so that was where I'd seen that emerald opals before. Oh, and green is such an unlucky colour in the theatre.

I stand now centre stage and my ghost light shines bright in the deserted theatre. So, so alone, I am. Well, except for an irritating moth, who is inescapably drawn to my glow.

No one would agree as to who should take the blame for the 'accident'. The insurance company said management were negligent, refused any payout and declined any further financial indemnities. So we are now dark. There's already a leak in the roof and I can feel the damp creeping in. I had a glimmer of hope a few days ago. Two men came in via the stage door. Only then I noticed they were each wearing protective yellow helmets, carrying clipboards and they went on to spend most of their time making measurements.

Who Fed the Cat?

A Sensual Feline Tale of Sound, Touch, Smell, Taste and Sight.

I HAVE A FRIEND CALLED VODKA. We fell out once when I discovered I'd been betrayed, but vodka can be as persuasive as a Colt .38 in your ribs and so we are back together now.

You may have even noticed a glass in my hand when you came in. And you looked as if you needed one too, for it takes some chutzpah for a detective on a murder case to show up at the wake of the victim when the killer is still on the loose.

What were you thinking, Lieutenant Drayton, when the Bay City boys stopped you at that five barred-gate? Would they let you pass? Did you have to show them your badge when they pointed to the brass sign that reads: BRUFORD ESTATE: NO ADMITTANCE? And as you were driving your worn-down Packard along the road, where the pepper trees hang like fountains of cascading green, were you asking yourself, 'Should I make the arrest to-day?' But did you have enough on the murderer whom we have both suspected from the word go? When you turned right at the bridge, where the churning gravel turns yellow and the trees become long lines of shading oaks, did you imagine what you would say when you took the killer into custody? And when you stopped at the house, stepped out of your Packard and saw those box-squares of Japanese Holly, with sharper edges than the controlling blade that cut them, did you know for certain the killer would even be inside?

At the porch entrance no doubt you were greeted by a man in a dark blue suit, bulked out by a shape all too familiar to you. The man would then have walked you here, to the rear reception room, the largest room in the house, with its faultless black marble fireplace, tall bookcases and carpet as thick and lush as an English meadow in July. I watched as you nervously looked around at the chesterfields and davenports, where on late nights nefarious deals had been done while drinking rare Rebello Valente vintage port; at the carved oak desk, where the stroke of a pen had destroyed so many lives; at the card table, where a famous fortune had been lost and won, and at those half dozen easy chairs that have never offered any sitter any ease at all.

You then turned your head and studied the photographs that hung in identical slate-grey frames on walls painted in flat army green. Men on horses. Men in uniform. Men behind podiums. Men shaking hands on the steps of Congress. And even men with Eskimos and their recent kill. Each photograph reeking money and yelling power. You know these guys don't count their greens in the folding kind but in the noughts on letters sent weekly with the embossed heading: Chase National Bank. But one photograph in particular draws you to it. President Coolidge with a young girl on his lap. Coolidge was a man with the face of a New Jersey accountant, overshadowed by a forehead the size of Texas. Elected twice, so people must have thought there was a big brain behind it. That's my theory anyhoo. The photograph must be twenty years old and though it's in black and white you must have recognised the unmistakable curls of her hair.

By now mourners were looking at you, but your eyes evaded theirs and focused instead on the large stained glass window above the folded-back French doors that lead you to the garden. The colored glass tells a story if you know how to look. With this one it's Aesop's fable of the tongue-dry crow who dropped five heavy pebbles into the half-filled pitcher so that the water would rise and he'd be able to quench his thirst. The moral is patience rewarded, the theme of the day, but the message to visitors of this house is 'Welcome to a world of ostentatious wealth', for that water pitcher among the leaded glass is made of twenty-four carat gold. And as you stared at the window, I asked myself, 'Does Lieutenant Drayton of the Los Angeles Homicide Police Department know the significance of the crow?' *Krähe*. The German word for 'crow' and the maiden name of the late wife of Henry Bruford. Turns out you did. *Sehr gut gemacht*. And you knew too that the Bruford fortune came from Fräulein Krähe, daughter of a count in Bavaria whose bloodline of dungeons and bats can be traced all the way back to Mrs Beelzebub.

Your long study of that clever crow was interrupted by two maids. The first gave you a plate and a napkin, the second offered up her silver tray. I saw how you raised your eyebrows. Only in Pasadena, you thought, would you be served spumoni at a wake. For to-day, and only to-day, the centerpiece in the largest room in the house is an open casket in which lies Miss Velma Bruford, 1917-1946. No flowers, of course. Even rich men have weaknesses and Velma's old man has extreme allergic rhinitis, or plain hay fever to simple folk like you and me.

While standing awkwardly eating your spumoni you take a furtive glance at her sleeping face and those extraordinary curls of auburn hair. The last time you saw that face was at the crime scene at her apartment in West Adams. The neck had been shot through with a Webley .45 revolver. What did your sergeant say? 'A gun so common the Duke a' Windsor could of done it.' The face has changed since then. The best mortician's magic that Hollywood can buy.

Did I know who the killer was? Yes. And why wouldn't I? I'm a shamus. A private dick. Twenty-five dollars a day plus expenses. I knew you knew, but knew too you couldn't prove it, so I decided to stay my side of the street. Why did he kill her? Well, we both know that in this town we would all kill if cornered. And corners in L.A. take many shapes.

And what of you, Lieutenant Drayton? Is it true down at the

station they call you 'Smiler', on account of lips that have never been seen to curl. The perverse humor of the city cop. They think you're a bit of a lug, but I've heard your captain gives you a wide berth because you get results. Slum-bred but not one of the hard-boiled kind. Not your way to work a guy over with a blackstrap. You made your name on the Lampard case where you found a mascara-ed eyelash among the pages of Shakespeare's *Merchant of Venice*. Oh how the chemistry boys loved that and their clever work put the dame at the murder scene. Serves her right, the guys at the precinct joked, for being literate.

But mocking isn't your style. You don't wise crack. You don't rattle cages. No. You're mulish. You watch. And wait. Because there's always The Mistake. In the Velma Bruford case it was 'Who fed the cat?' No prints on the tin in the trash, but, knowing her body wouldn't be found for days, someone had cared enough to feed Gyb. That someone knew Velma. And the cat. A strange looking creature, with mustard eyes as ancient as spells and witches.

The reveal of the murderer will unravel a scandal. But I'll skim that part. Except to say that when the trial comes the exhibits will include a pin seal wallet, a smut book, a promissory note, a trust deed for property in San Marino and a Kraut cigarette case with a hidden compartment. There'll be testimony from that window-peeper near Velma's apartment and the material witnesses will be a peanut grifter called Joe, not forgetting that queer B-movie screenwriter with many names. Yeah, and Peachy Malone, that is if the Chicago mob don't get to him first. And one you don't know yet, a former big shot banker who had the bite put on him by the Brufords. The trial will be a mix-up of maybes and pretty thin circumstantials, but the D.A. knows that it isn't what can be proved but what can be made to look like a crime that gets the verdict. This is Los Angeles, so it's always the story that wins the case. And what a story it will be. Some young hungry newshawk from a Democrat supporting rag in Boston will piece it all together in a maze of words that should win him the Pulitzer and on that day his friends shall toast his celebrity with gimlets in his favorite downtown bar. 'Here's to crime,' they'll say. But will that be before or after the killer fries?

That was the thought in my head when the prowl car arrived with an unexpected passenger on the back seat. Gyb. Velma's cat. When I saw you carry her in I poured myself another vodka. I needed to hear the weight of the liquor landing in the bottom of the tumbler. The heavy gurgle that sounds like gutters overflowing when there's a rain storm. That's why I never drink champagne, for it only ever falls into the glass like whisper-steps at a fairy dance.

But Gyb's presence doesn't just surprise me, for the whole room stands as still and silent as soundless shadows. The sharp diamond pupils in Gyb's mustard eyes suddenly become pure black and then it happens and the first pebble drops.

Gyb lets out a cry. But it's not the sound of a cat. It's the rippling sound of a human throat gasping its last breath. Everyone hears it as if it were inside their own head. Then the second pebble drops. The spumoni, made of pistachio, cherry and vanilla, had left a sweet taste in the mouths of the mourners but all they can taste now is iron. Heavy and thick. Like blood. Because it is blood. The third pebble drops. This time not everyone recognises what it is, but you and I do. We've smelled it many times. Cordite. To be precise cordite from a Webley .45. Then the fourth pebble drops and the prize of the crow is almost within reach. All those present feel the touch of a woman's soft hand on our necks.

At this moment the killer closes his eyes and remembers Velma and the first time they met. How she wrapped herself round him like velvet. How his carnal needs turned them both into beasts. Clinging. Gripping. Wanting never to let go. And right now, he felt all that again for real, for her hand *was* on his neck. Only this time her fingers had turned into claws...

He opened his eyes and saw Gyb's sharp digging nails drawing blood from his neck in the same place he had shot Velma. She had returned but could not speak and so had used Gyb to resurrect the murder scene in sound, taste, smell, touch and now sight. Krähe had dropped her five pebbles into the pitcher and gained her prize.

That's when you came over to the killer and made your arrest. How could he deny it? He had killed Velma and now his crazed mind was ready to admit it. But he wanted to tell it his way. And so, he said, yes, he'd go with you but on condition that he will write his own confession. Or rather that I'll write it for him. That's when I began to speak as myself.

'Lieutenant Drayton, he's just a hack. Those dime novels he pens about bug-eyed monsters from space or drunken cowboys in dusty saloons. They'll all be forgotten. No, *I'll* be the one who'll be remembered. His best creation. Me. Sam Reagan. The twenty-five dollar a day private dick. But before we go, and I'll go peacefully, I don't want to upset all these mourners, I do have a request of my own. When they have my statement read out in court, I want one of the Barrymores to do it. I'm sure the Screen Actors' Guild will give permission. At the union rate, of course.

'Did I tell you, Lieutenant Drayton, that once a year I like to have a whisky sour? Well, you have to mark Christmas somehow. But you known the hooch I'll miss most when I'm in San Quentin. And I think that's how I'll begin his affidavit. Yeah, I'll start with the words "I have a friend called vodka..."'

An Angelic Tale of Wonderment and Weirdness.

ANGELS. SUCH MISUNDERSTOOD CHAPS. NO PARTICULAR talent for choral singing, nor are they especially adept at the harp. In fact I've known some angels take years, if not centuries, to reach what musicians on Earth would call Grade Four. The etymology of 'angel', as some of you may be aware, comes from the Persian word *ángaros*, meaning 'mounted courier', which over Time gave way to the more familiar Latin term *angelus* or 'messenger'. Add to that the philosophical belief that angels are disseminators of the Divine Will and you have a function that combines, as it were, both the theophanic and telephonic. To be fair there is some truth in this, but, on the whole, angels are more night-watchmen than the disembodied thoughts of the Almighty.

So what is the purpose of an angel? Here we encounter a paradox. Angels are immortal and of spirit, yet their main aim is to give human beings, of flesh and blood and limited by Time – the opportunity to become fully alive. For there is nothing more beautiful in creation. I know this because I was once an angel myself, retired now, and as it happens my name is mentioned in passing in the story I am to tell. A word or two first, though, about feathers.

Angels appear to come out of nowhere, and at speed, so the fanciful notion they have been gifted some sort of aeronautical attachment does have a certain logic to it. However, wings, along with rosy cheeks and golden hair, are for the painters and the poets. In practice you're more likely to encounter a Scotsman in a bowler hat than an angel with feathers down their back.

That said, there is an element of truth in the idea of angels 'earning their wings', but I should stress that what we have here is life imitating art. You see, so loved were all your folktales where 'every time a bell rings an angel gets its wings' that 'Management', as we called the Almighty, added to the angelic status certifications and proficiencies. Only certain angels, for example, are qualified to enter human dreams. I mention this because it is pertinent to our tale.

However, before we progress, a warning about mistletoe, which happens to be the catalyst in our story. The Greeks called it 'oak sperm' and the Celts thought it was the semen of Taranis, their god of thunder. Mistletoe over the years has been seen as a cure for the bites of snakes and mad dogs, a remedy for dandruff, warts, ringworm, syphilis, and even useful for the regeneration of fingernails. In the Roman Saturnalia festival, held in late December, and which Christmas replaced, mistletoe was hung over doorways to safeguard homes, and Aeneas took some with him on his visit to Hades as an armament against the forces of the Underworld. And it's this concept of the protection that mistletoe affords that is perhaps most relevant to our story – which I will now begin.

It was Christmas Eve in Heaven and for angels the busiest night of the year. It was therefore with some trepidation that one Supervisor, Jeremiah, arrived at the Office of Archangels with a serious problem that needed immediate attention.

'Raphaella,' said Jeremiah, 'a word, if I may.'

(I began by saying that angels were such misunderstood 'chaps'. That was wrong of me, for angels are 'gender fluid' and Archangel Raphael transitioned to her identity as 'Archangel Raphaella' in the year of The First Council of Jerusalem).

'Whatever the problem, Jeremiah, it will have to wait. Every angel is booked out or en route for the myriad of tasks that always arise on this night. Extra smiles for babes, warm greetings for neighbours and that extra touch we add to rum punch that brings joyous laughter. I will not have my evening spoilt with bad news.'

'Mistletoe,' was Jeremiah's only word of response, but he needn't have said more.

'Oh,' sighed Raphaella, 'that infernal weed. What has it done now? Unlock thy tongue, Jeremiah, unlock thy tongue.'

'As you will be aware, ma'am, the ancients used mistletoe as a cure for melancholia, what the moderns now call depression. Held over the head of the sufferer, it has the power temporarily to remove unpleasant memories that dwell on the mind. Well, ma'am, it seem one of the Old Spirits–'

'–I might have known. I was against allowing them back on Earth, but the traditionalists overruled me, even though I reminded them of the destination to which the road of good intentions lead.'

'Indeed, ma'am. But it seems, in this particular instance, a Russian mistletoe was used, rather than the indigenous varieties known in Britain. I should have explained that the gentleman in question is British. It appears the removal of his distressing memories isn't quite as temporary as one might have hoped.'

Jeremiah then became silent for a moment.

'I can see from your greying hair that *that* isn't the worst of it. Unburden yourself, Jeremiah, unburden yourself.'

'As ever, ma'am, you are most astute. It seems the Old Spirit, Norse, I believe, held this unusually potent mistletoe over the head of the gentleman for far too long, with the result that, er, all his memories have been permanently erased. Good and bad. Old and new.'

'Armpits!'

'Ma'am?'

'It's at moments such as these that I long for the human ability to curse. But "Armpits!" is about as far as I ever dare go.'

'It's "armpits", indeed, ma'am, but the problem is fixable. As you know, all human memory is stored in The Celestial Locale of the Utility Database System. Or C.L.O.U.D.S. for short.

'But that's only meant to be accessed at end of life. I take it this gentleman has many more years ahead of him?'

'Indeed, ma'am. He's a mere thirty-two. Many more Christmases to come.'

'But Jeremiah, even if special access were allowed, there are still no angels available to install the memories. Armpits, Jeremiah, it's still armpits!'

'Ah, but this time, Raphaella, I will not join you in your exclamatory incantation of hirsute crevices, for I have taken the liberty of looking through some personnel files and technically two angels are available.'

'Go on.'

'Well, ma'am, there's Burt.'

'No! I won't allow it. Just hearing his name is enough to make one shout out "Hairy Bottoms!" Oh dear... I just did.'

'I agree, but all ethereal spirits must learn some of the nature of mortal life and although Burt's time on Earth left him cynical and mocking–'

'–Burt is an angel in name only. And I won't have another word said about him.'

'Very well, ma'am. The only other alternative is Benny.'

'Benny? Remind me?'

'According to the files, Benny's last visit to earth was 1843. He did no real harm but it was thought that his child-like mind would not be appropriate for further assignments.'

'Oh yes, I remember that case. Oh, Benny. *Blessed be the innocent*. But if these are all there is, Jeremiah, all hope is lost. Even though it be Christmas Eve.'

'If I may venture a suggestion, ma'am.'

'Anything to get us out of this hole.'

'We send both of them. As a team.'

'I'm not sure that would be–'

'–If I may be allowed to go on, ma'am. Benny may live on the other side of the rainbow, but his sense of goodness cannot be faulted. As for Burt, not quite a fallen angel, but certainly one who made his way to the edge of the precipice. But together they may work. *Ab stultis saepe sapientissima*.'

'"From fools comes wisdom".'

'*Experientia docet*.'

'"Experience, the best teacher". Hmm, I suppose life on Earth must have taught Burt a few tricks and Benny's simple ways...'

'Together, Raphaella...'

'*Manus manum lavat.*'

'Exactly. "One hand washes the other".'

'Oh yes, I'm glad you've kept up with your Latin, Jeremiah, for we angels should never forsake that sacred language. Yes, ours is a good plan. I believe we've cracked it.'

Jeremiah smiled at the words 'ours' and 'we', but let them pass.

'Remind me,' Raphaella asked, 'where were Burt's lost years spent?'

'Yorkshire.'

'Ah, explains a lot.'

'Burt's vocabulary may not always be felicitous, that's what comes of being a navvy and a brick layer, but it has its own rustic charm. As for Benny, yes he may be a cherub short of a full choir, but his artlessness brings with it a slice of Heaven. This, I think, is how we should proceed...'

Here I must intervene for fear of redaction. The secrets of C.L.O.U.D.S. are not in my gift to reveal. However, I am at liberty to say that it was decided the best method of restoring the lost memories would be via dreaming (even human science is aware that the formation of dreams and memory storage share the same part of the brain) and as luck would have it, both Burt and Benny had been certificated with Dream Entrance, which was a great relief, as much paperwork was thus avoided.

There was, it should be said, some dispute as to the access of the angles to the human senses of taste and smell. Jeremiah argued that these were important in understanding memory, but Raphaella said that they were too closely associated with the pleasures of the flesh and may lead an angel astray. As it happened, all the human characteristics were allocated to Burt and Benny due to an overworked junior angel not reading the Exemption Licence properly. Burt, however, was issued with a Non-Intervention Notice, which he studied in great detail. In brief, he was under strict instructions not to alter or change the memories of the gentleman in any way. Benny was able to avoid the imposition of a N.I.N for the simple reason he couldn't read.

Once on Earth, the passing of Time would become key, for every memory had to be restored before the gentleman woke up at dawn. And so, in a poetic touch, Raphaella set the first chirp of the robin as the deadline.

When Burt arrived on the street, with a misty fog gathering all about, the first thing he did was look down at his boots. Yes, it felt good to stand once more on firm ground. The terraced houses along the road were much alike, for each had decorative lights or a Christmas tree in the window. Well, except for one. And that was where Burt now headed.

The garden in front of the house had been paved over, but one brave weed had dared to creep through the cracks. The red bricks he recognised were of Victorian workmanship, and Burt, as he tapped them, nodded his approval. He wasn't one of those angels who enjoyed walking through walls, particularly brickwork he admired, so to gain entry to the house he used the skills he had acquired on his last visit and circumvented the handicraft of the locksmith with a quick sharp snick with an old nail he found in the yard.

From a hasty look through his memories, Burt had gathered that the gentleman who lived here was a bachelor in his early thirties. There were few recollections at all before the age of seven, but when he was ten it seemed his mother and father, both in the armed services, were posted abroad and it was thought best he should stay in England with his uncle. Burt had been warned that emotional traumas could be tricky, for memories that disturb the mind often result in the subject waking up and that would jeopardise the entire mission. But that particular problem was something to worry about later.

For now what concerned even the hard-nosed Burt was the lack of any joyful childhood memories. Where were those treasured pictures in the mind's eye of ice-creams on the beaches, of pink balloons and clowns, of tadpoles and ponds? But most of all, where were his friends?

'Oh Lawd. A lonely boy wanting to play Hide-and-Seek, only no one came to find him.'

Burt, it should be said, often talked to himself, a habit developed during his lost years living in the Yorkshire Dales.

From what was there in the database it was clear that the gentleman certainly knew how many beans make five. What Burt had seen in his memories were equations and algebra and geometry and all sorts of human hocus-pocus that he could never fathom. Not surprisingly the gentleman had done well at school, and university followed, and after that a good job in a local science laboratory. But where were the memories of his nights out? Of his mates? Of his lovers? Of these there were none.

'Poor fellow. Half his life over and all he's got to show for it is a pile of empty yesterdays.'

It was true that Burt had a reputation as a cynic, yet his lost years had given him an understanding of loneliness and sadness unmatched by any other angel. Burt soon shook off these thoughts, for he had a job to do. He wasn't here to fix the gentleman or solve his problems.

The uncle with whom he had lived did feature in his memories, but not as someone who was loved or was loving. He had died some years ago and left the property in which Burt now stood to his nephew, so at least there were no financial worries. But looking round the hall and the kitchen, Burt noticed very little difference between the house as it was now and when the boy had first moved in. The uncle had been a smoker and his bizarre collection of pipes, ranging from huge to minuscule, still hung on the wall. There were no paintings or photographs or indeed anything that makes a home a home. But most worryingly of all, not one single Christmas card.

Burt entered the living room and found the gentleman slumped unconscious in an armchair, with the offending mistletoe lying on the floor where the Old Spirit must have dropped it as she fled. As memories rarely include one's own face, Burt was now able to examine the countenance of the gentleman for the first time.

'Not a mush to break your heart, nor one to put you off your breakfast. You're not fat, you're not thin, just a guy who dutifully cleans his plate.'

Burt's eyes were then drawn to the half-full tumbler on the side table and the empty bottle of whisky on the floor.

'Oh Lawd. White lightning can bring cheer to many, but only makes the sad sadder. Ah, but at least your shoes are well polished. Brigade standard. There's hope for you yet, young man.'

Burt began to reach into his pocket to take out the crystals that contained the gentleman's memories, but suddenly froze on hearing a strange fluttering noise. From behind the Minton-tiled Victorian mantelpiece, it seemed. At first, Burt thought it was a pigeon caught in the chimney, but after a yelp and a clatter, two black shoes with ornate silver buckles, bringing with them years of unswept dust and soot, dropped down and hung in mid-air just above the empty grate.

'Saints and sinners! What the merry heck have we got here? Hello? Hello? Is there someone up there? I'm counting two feet, so I'm assuming yes.'

A plaintive voice then answered, 'It is I.'

'Well "I", show thyself!'

'I would so do, but the top half of I is stuck.'

'Well, let's give the bottom half of "I" a tug and see what happens.'

Burt grabbed the buckled shoes and pulled. The chimney released its captive and a tall figure, as thin as a flute, fell onto the stone hearth, covering Burt in a century of muck and grime. The figure wore a patched-up green double-breasted jacket, red waistcoat and a white (or rather now dirty grey) voluminous neck-tie. The figure rose to his feet and then promptly sneezed. 'Hells bells and jumping frogs, *cughh*, *cughh*, *cughh*, what have they sent me? You look like something Monday threw away and Tuesday didn't want.'

'I be Benny. And who be thou?'

'What?'

'"Watt!" 'Tis a name of renown. He that be James.'

'No, I'm Burt.'

'What, not Watt?'

'I'm not a Watt or even a whatnot. And who's this James?'

'James Watt.'

'Don't you start with all that "what-ing" again, or I've a feeling we'll be here all night.'

'James Watt. Inventor of the marvel that is the steam engine.'

'The steam engine? When were you last time on Earth?'

'*Anno Domini* 1843.'

'Lawd, help us. And why come down the bleedin' chimney?'

'Christmas Eve. Is it not traditional?'

'Yes, for St Nicholas, you daft pancake. And look at the mess you've made, but we'll sort that out later. Dust yourself down as best you can, we've got work to do.'

Burt now raised his hand to his pocket and took from it one of the crystals he had been given. 'Our job is to put what's stored in here back into that gentleman who's resting there. He will then dream these memories, so that when he awakes, he won't ever know he even lost them.'

''Tis a wonder of a plan.'

'Yeah, well, young fella, m'lad, they needed an angel with a bit of nous to come up with a good idea.'

'And 'tis twice a wonderment, for 'tis exactly the same plan was told by the Seraphim who sent I here.'

'Oh, er, was it, now... What a coincidence, eh? Ha! Ha! Better make a start. Time, as the old farmer would say, to put the bucket under the cow.'

Benny looked around for a moment, but, seeing neither bucket nor cow, appeared a little puzzled.

'"Bucket under the cow" is a figure of speech, m'lad.'

'Oh, I see. 'Twas one such that led me to trouble last I was here and had I sent back.'

Benny went over to where the man was slouched and picked up the whisky glass from the table. 'A libation alone on Christmas Eve?'

'His way of life is none of our business,' replied Burt, firmly. 'We're here to put back his memories and that's where it begins and ends. And best if he sleeps soundly, so let's carry him upstairs to his own bed. I'll take his shoulders, that's where the weight is, and you can take his legs. Oh, and put that mistletoe on the floor in your back pocket, we may just need it.'

'Never had I met a Seraphim before this night.'

'Oh, I've come across a few of those. *Keep his legs together, if you can.*'

'Has thou ever met an Archangel?'

'Yes. *Steady as we go round the door.*'

'Which Archangel hath thou encountered?'

'Michael. Not much of a talker. *Careful! The man's heavy. Need to rest him on the stairs a minute.* I did once meet the Archangel Gabriel. Much happier, they say, since he came out.'

'From where?'

'Sorry?'

'Thou said he "came out". Out from where?'

'Ah, well. Benny, er, perhaps I should explain that a lot has changed since 1843. Let's just say that Angel Gabriel enjoys a bit of dancing like everyone else, but does it to a different tune. *Let me get a proper grip of his shoulders, huh, huh, then we can be on our way again.* What you been doing for the last two centuries?'

'Looking at the stars. They are very beautiful.'

'Well, I don't think you've missed much down here. The 1960s were best. "Make Love, Not War". Didn't quite work out, but folk had a damn good time trying. *Keep him steady! Now let's get him round this top stair. Legs to the right... no, no, no, I mean* your *right. That's it. Now to me, now to you, now to me.* His bedroom door don't look locked so my backside can be the turnkey.'

Benny pushed against the pine door and the two angels entered the room. They put the gentleman on his bed and stood a step back to admire their handiwork.

'Is he a believer, do you think?'

'I don't know,' answered Burt, 'and I don't want to. But if you want my thoughts on such matters, I say when you take a pig to market what matters isn't how it got there, but how good's the pig.'

'Thou art a wise man.'

'Yes. And with it being Christmas there will be three more like me turning up later on.'

'Ha! Ha! Thou's funny!'

Burt was in no way vain, yet he was of the opinion that anyone who laughed at jokes could do not wrong. And so in that instant Burt and Benny became firm friends.

'The poets say that memory,' said a still smiling Benny, 'is what allows mankind to smell the roses in December.'

'Oh well, the poet would. But when it comes to roses, it's folks like us who have to put on the manure. So to speak.'

Burt now placed in the palm of his hands one of the silver-like crystals and began to rub it with his fingers. He threw the crystal into the air and it broke into a hundred pieces, floating above the sleeping man.

'Every one of these is a memory.'

'They be like snowflakes.'

'Yes and we're gonna have to work like stink to put all these, and a few more, back in his head by morning.'

'I wish to touch one first. See inside. A memory with love and happiness in its heart.'

'Love and happiness, I'm sorry to say, are in short supply.'

'But I sense this one has joy,' said Benny, reaching towards a sapphire-like crystal that shone brighter than the others. 'Yes! The gentleman loved someone called Sam...'

'Sam? Short for Samantha?'

'No, Sam be a he. The gentleman loved him very much. Treasured their long walks together, and even let Sam share his bed.'

'Let me see that,' said Burt, taking hold of the blue crystal. 'Oh dear Lawd, Sam was his *dog*. Oh well, at least he had someone. Anyway, we better start putting all these back in his head...'

And here we must break away from the narrative as the precise method used to place these memories in the gentleman's mind as dreams cannot be revealed to mortals. Except to say, that the speed of angels is as fast, as Burt so expertly put it, 'as a pickpocket's fingers'.

The work went well. The gentleman's memories were mostly mundane and matter of fact, and this allowed for excellent progress. It was likely they would complete their task well before dawn, for only one crystal now remained.

'All Christmas memories are kept together,' said Burt, 'in this one crystal.'

'"I am sure I have always thought of Christmas Time, when it has come round – apart from the veneration due to its sacred name and origin, if anything belonging to it can be apart from that – as a good Time: a kind, forgiving, charitable, pleasant time: the only time I know of, in the long calendar of the year, when men and women seem, by one consent, to open their shut-up hearts freely, and to think of people below them as if they really were fellow-travellers to the grave, and not another race of creatures bound on other journeys".'

'Good Lawd, Benny! Where did you learn such a way with words?'

'Oh, those not be mine,' Benny replied. 'Those be coming from a man by the name of Charles Dickens. I don't suppose the gentleman came to anything. I told him that the Eve of Christmas has an uncommon power, where past, present and future hopes all come together as one. He said that idea would make a very good tale.'

'Did he now?'

'Oh, I always loved Christmas. Pink ribbons. The building of snowmen. Warm fires. Pine cones. Bringing the outside in and wanting everything to be of wonder. And longing for it to be upon you.'

Burt stood for a moment in silence and then said, 'Well, er, Benny, it will be a disappointment, I know, but I'm afraid our gentleman has no such memories. This Christmas crystal should be of bright shining reds and greens and golds. But look at it. A dark grey. But we have a duty to put them back, unhappy though they may be.'

'Could we not observe these memories before they are returned to him?'

'It won't make any difference. We can't make them better than they are.'

''Tis true, but perhaps...'

'Don't you do any suggesting! No. We can't change him or his memories. We must let the world be the world it must.'

Benny lowered his head and sighed.

'We are here to do our job,' said Burt, 'nothing more nothing less. It's not our place to question or interfere. And you'll thank me for saying this. I mean, we don't want the Higher-Ups putting us on guard duty till the end of days.'

Burt then threw the grey crystal into the air. The shapes it made were jagged and sharp and they hung as heavy as a thunder cloud. Even so, the two angels went about their work, putting each memory into the gentleman's dreams, but as they did so he began to stir anxiously.

'I was worried this might happen,' said Burt. 'I'm no Daniel but these night fancies are causing him trouble. All our efforts will be wasted if he wakes up.'

'Is there naught we can do?'

'Well, there is that mistletoe. Putting it over our heads will allow us to see into his dreams. Then we can at least offer him a warm hand of comfort to settle him during the worst of it.'

So Benny took the mistletoe from his back pocket and passed it to Burt, who raised it high above them.

'Burt, the sun comes through the window, yet I feel a chill as cold as the eternal winter.'

'That's the way with joyless memory. Here, something's happening... I think it's his mum and dad coming in...'

We see the boy's bedroom has Christmas decorations hanging on the wall, and toys, including a model Santa Claus, are scattered about the floor.

'Your uncle is going to look after you for a few months...'

'You'll still have Sam. Your uncle has been persuaded... well, er, he's kindly agreed you can keep him...'

'We've had a good Christmas...'

'And when we see you next year, we'll bring you some candy. That's what they call sweets in America...'

'And some doggy chews for Sam...'

The sky beyond the window has turned black, for it is night, and the boy is heard crying in the dark.

'Burt, is that the boy I hear?'

'Think so.'

'And I can smell smoke.'

'Me too. Tobacco. Must be his uncle...'

The uncle enters the bedroom, switches on the electric light and we see that all the Christmas decorations have gone. In his hand the uncle carries a copy of THE CHRONICLE *and the headline reads 'Husband and Wife Killed on Active Service'.*

'Your father and mother were very brave and now you must be too. They did their duty and so will I, for you have now become my obligation to them...'

'Did they not come back?'

'No. Both lost in one of the too many recent wars. The goodbye that Christmas was his last memory of his mum and dad.'

The scene changes to another Yuletide.

The boy is older now and his tears are more subdued. On his bedside table is that Santa Claus toy we saw lying on the floor. In anger the boy grabs it and smashes it on the ground.

'Oh, Burt, don't your heart go out to him.'

Another Christmas.

The sun outside is shining, yet the room stays dark and gloomy. The uncle enters.

'Canines often leave their habitat when they know their hour of death is near.'

'Sam isn't a canine. He's my dog and he wouldn't leave me alone on Christmas Day.'

'Animals have no understanding of such festivities and as you are aware, neither do I. This is a humanist house. I do not celebrate Christmas because it is a falsehood. A lesson you must learn is to accept life as it is, not as you would want it to be. The day will come

when you will thank me for it. Now get dressed and come down for your breakfast. You have three minutes.'

Burt can't help but think how close these words are to those he himself had spoken. Benny notices this too, but when he glances over to his fellow angel, he sees that Burt has lowered his head to avoid his gaze.

We are still in the bedroom of that same Christmas Day, only now it is night and it is black outside. Yet the boy lies under the sheets with only a candle on his bedside table for illumination.

'The boy,' whispers Benny, 'I can hear him praying for Sam to come home.'

'Oh Lawd. Unanswered prayers and hopes that died on the pillow.'

'The boy is much distraught. Let us hold his hand to bring him solace.'

Benny and Burt move to take the boy's fingers, but suddenly the scene changes.

The boy, a teenager now, is no longer lying on the bed but staring out of the window onto the snowy street. The world beyond the casement is bright and sunny.

A big breath from the boy steams up the glass on the window and on it he draws the outline of a snowman. The boy finishes it off by giving his new friend a big smile.

But the snowman on the pane of glass now becomes overlaid by the reflection of the stern face of his uncle, who has just entered the room carrying a heavy book.

'The snow outside would ruin your shoes. And shoes cost money. However, I do have this to make your day productive and help with your learning. It explains the origin of our universe and solar system. Most instructive. You may read it after lunch, which will be in fourteen minutes. Today is Thursday, so pilchards on toast and later two hard-boiled eggs for tea. I have some of the German rye bread left over from yesterday. No point in letting it go to waste.'

'This cannot be Christmas Day,' says Benny.

'If people don't want to celebrate Christmas even angels can't make them.'

'German rye bread?'

'I tried it once. About as edible as Stonehenge. But since we've been given the gift of taste, I think, before we leave, you should partake of some pilchards.'

'Are they pleasant to the tongue?'

'No, but after eating them anything else will seem a blessing.'

Suddenly the bedroom becomes an eerie void. A frozen world of empty oblivion.

'Hell's bells and frogs!'

'Burt, where are we?'

'I don't think we're anywhere.'

'That cannot be so.'

'I think we're in a deep place in his mind where Christmas has been completely blocked out.'

'I can taste a hot burning in my mouth.'

'That's the whisky. We better get out of here.'

Burt drops the mistletoe he held in his hands and we now see the gentleman asleep on the bed.

'Burt, such sadness should not be without hope.'

'I know. But the future is written in its past, as every acorn knows. We've done our duty. We could not have done more.'

To witness someone's life as they see it is a rare gift, even for angels. But tonight it became an unwelcome endowment, for in the gentleman's memories they had felt so much pain. And even the cynical Burt now reflected on what he had seen.

'What was it you said about Christmas?'

'Ribbons. Games. Bringing the outside in.'

'Nah, something else.'

'Wanting everything to be of wonder? The longing for it to come.'

'That's it! Oh Benny, you're as rare as the phoenix. It's *wanting*, and *longing* that's missing in his life.'

'But thou said our task was at an end. Soon it will be the hour of our return.'

'Never whistle 'til you are out of the forest.'

'But thou sayest we cannot change his memories.'

'And we're not going to. Nor can we make up memories for him.'

'Then what, pray, is thou suggesting?'

'Rule Four. Subsection B of the Non-Intervention Notice. "An angel may, with discretion and in consultation with a secondary angel, offer guidance on that which is possible within the capability of the subject." Now, would you agree that our gentleman has strong enough arms to build a snowman?'

''Tis certain,' replied Benny, a little puzzled.

'And would you further agree that cats in gloves catch no mice?'

'That be true also,' said Benny, now even more confused. 'But why does thou speak of "cats in gloves"?'

'Because that's what we are. And we need to take them off, for rules must sometimes bend to sweetest grace.'

'What art thou suggesting?'

'We are gonna learn him how to build a snowman. I was a brickie and navvy once upon a time. I know how things are made and put together. And you Benny, like no angel I've ever met, can think as a child. So what should the perfect snowman look like?'

'Tall. With a lovely big hat and even bigger smile. The widest smile in the longest history of smiles!'

'Ha! Ha! What a combination! We are going to show this gentleman how he can make a snowman of true wonderment. But we better get a move on before Mister Redbreast starts his cheery chirp.'

'Oh, Burt!'

'Half the joy of Christmas is thinking what you're gonna do on the day. The fun and laughter to come. But he's never had that. So we're going to give it to him. With the help of a snowman...'

By daylight the misty fog had cleared, but what took its place was a blast of cold air from the Arctic. The weather forecast had said there might be sleet, but as predicting anything in life is difficult, especially the future, it should come as no surprise that our row of neat and friendly homes woke up on Christmas Morning to a road covered in several feet of snow. And their street had an unexpected new resident: the largest snowman anyone had ever seen. Wearing a tall hat (in truth a cracked garden terracotta plant pot), a tartan scarf (really a frayed travel rug double-folded) and with eyes as blacks as coals (for the simple reason they *were* coals), this snowman stood proudly in front of the house of Our Man. He had a large carrot for a nose and two rows of hard-boiled eggs to give him indeed the widest smile in the longest history of smiles, but what was extraordinary, and one might even use the word magical, was that from his mouth came a large pipe that was most definitely smoking. Snowmen we know can smile, but puffing on a pipe was something else entirely. How was all this possible? And that was a question that drew several neighbours, some still in their STAR WARS pyjamas, out onto their street. That and the fact that the snowman was nearly twenty feet tall.

A little explanation at this point in the narrative is perhaps required. On waking up to the cheery chirp of the robin, Our Man, with a bit of a rough head, looked out of his window and saw the deep and flawless snow. Exactly why he had a sudden urge to build a snowman, he could never quite explain, but the wanting and longing to do so was simply overpowering. Most snowmen end up looking like a pile of mashed potatoes, but Our Man's was perfectly constructed, as if it had been designed by expert builders, for his body was tall, solid and muscular, while his head was as perfectly round and as white as the glorious full moon, which, as it was still only half past five in the morning, still hung in the sky.

Where all his inventive ideas had come from, well, he couldn't explain that either, as he was not in any way artistic. But Our Man's final touch to his creation was his own. He had added the biggest pipe in his uncle's bizarre collection for the snowman to have in his mouth. But then a thought struck him. 'I wonder...?' he said to himself and quickly grabbed hold of the keys to the science laboratory where he worked and set off at a brisk pace. Why, you may now be pondering? Well, as Burt would say, 'there is reason even in the roasting of eggs'. You see, Our Man soon returned with some dry ice. 'I'll put some in the bowl at the end of the pips,' he laughed to himself, 'and it will look like he's truly smoking.'

And so it did. With our happily fuming giant now complete Our Man went back inside his house to cook himself breakfast, which would have been scrambled eggs had he not used them all up on the smile of the snowman. However, he had bought some smoked salmon and cheese intended for lunch, but he was hungry after all his exertions and so decided to have it there and then as a treat. No time like the present, he thought. And when he finished it all off – and very yummy it was too – he sat in his chair and for the first time in many years smiled the smile of a contented man.

As he was sipping his coffee, there was a knock at the door. Odd, he thought, there's never any post on Christmas Day. He glanced out of the window and saw two small children standing under his porch. Must be carol singers, he concluded, and dug into his pocket to get ready to offer some change. But when he answered the door, the two youngsters, who were called Connie and Eddie, did not burst into '*Away in a Manger*' as expected. Instead they simply said as one, 'Mister, can you help us build a snowman?'

The girl and boy would never know why the man's eyes filled with tears, but fill with tears they did. Old memories are never forgotten but maybe they can be vanquished by the birth of new ones.

The street Our Man lived on was a cul-de-sac, so he suggested the three of them build their snowman at the end of the road. But they would need, he explained, a pair of Wellington boots, two walking sticks, two brooms, and, oh yes, some yellow kitchen gloves. The children were a little puzzled by this, for Our Man's own magnificent creation had none of these. However, the girl and boy, who, after a short while, grew to a party of seven girls and boys, went cheerily about their task under his careful instructions. As the figure formed, the children kept their smiles, but couldn't help noticing that their snowman wasn't quite the shape it should be.

Notwithstanding this, they brought out their brooms and Our Man carefully dug out some of the snow on the large top ball and placed the ends with the bristles securely in holes so as to make a 'V' shape. And it was on the tops of these points that he now placed the Wellington boots. The walking sticks were skewered either side of the same large ball and the yellow kitchen gloves put on their ends. Then the girls and boys burst out laughing for, without realising it, they had built a snowman standing on his head with his legs in the air. And they laughed even more when Our Man threw snowballs at the Wellington boots and they began to spin as fast as wooden tops.

Winifred, one of the elderly neighbours in the street, had watched all this from her upstairs bedroom window and made the decision to do something she hadn't done for many Christmases: bake some mince pies purely for pleasure. She was sure she had some jars of mincemeat leftover from her last job, and besides, preserved fruits doesn't go off. The pastry was easy to make, for she had flour and some lard, and the glory of mince pies is they don't take long to cook. Winifred's timing was just right, for, as the potato buttons were being fixed to the snowman's portly middle, she took out her plates of hot pies and gave them to two boys, Erik and Teddy Ray, to offer around the group who now had gathered next to our upside-down snowman.

Among them were Adam and Calvin, a couple who lived two down from the nice mince pie lady. They too had seen what was going on and had brought out some homemade (and quite lethal) parsnip wine. Adam and Calvin said they had some of that winter vegetable left over and so the children's snowman was given a parsnip nose. Their friend, Billie, wearing an exact match to the startling red gown and crystal shawl worn by Judy Garland in *Meet Me In St. Louis*, joined the crowd and carolled them with that seasonal favourite '*Have Yourself a Merry Little Christmas*' made famous by the singer in the film. This ditty was followed by a pair of gentlemen, unknown to any of the neighbours, who gave the most beautiful rendition of '*Hark! The Herald Angels Sing*' that anyone had ever heard. Afterwards, when asked if they were professional in any way, the older of the two men said, 'Well, you could say that.' They too were offered mince pies on a tray taken round by another two boys called Joshua and Oliver. However, the youngsters were a little surprised when the thinnest of the men replied that he hoped they tasted better than pilchards, which, he explained, he'd just had on German rye bread toast for breakfast. Grown ups can be very odd, they thought, but pilchards at Christmas were worse even than sprouts. Still, the man loved the mince pie and so did his friend. 'They're champion!' he observed, in his strong Yorkshire accent.

Later that morning, Our Man had another knock at his door. This time it was the mothers of Connie and Eddie who had come to thank him for keeping their two mischievous urchins out of their way as they cooked Christmas lunch. Bea and Debs, wives to each other, as they stood in the doorway, couldn't help but notice that above his head was some mistletoe. Our Man followed their eyes up, but claimed he had no idea how it got there. They laughed, for they certainly didn't believe him, even though it was perfectly true.

Our two angels stood by unobserved.

'We had to put that mistletoe somewhere,' said Benny.

'Yes,' replied Burt, 'can't do any harm now its spell is broken.'

'In my day folk did say it is bad fortune not to use the mistletoe. Does thou think he'll get a kiss?' asked Benny.

'Two, I hope. He deserves them. And maybe an invitation to lunch now he's used up his eggs.'

And so it came to pass that Our Man spent the entire day with his new family and was being called 'Uncle' well before it was even bedtime.

Night fell and the street was very quiet. The two angels, with beaming faces, stood in front of the large smiling snowman they had inspired.

'Does thou believe he will find his own love?'

'Oh that's all in the wind, but from now on I don't think he'll be the cat that wanted the trout but was too frightened to get his feet wet. For he'll go to bed tonight with hopes once again on his pillow. But time now for us, like the morning mist in May, to quietly disappear. We do, though, have these to take back for storage.'

Burt produced from his pocket a small crystal that sparkled red, green and gold.

'These are the Christmas memories he's made today. And they'll shine bright all his life.'

Burt threw the crystals into the air and, oh, how they sparkled .

'I hath set my eyes upon every star in the universe... but this is the most beautiful sight I have ever seen.'

'Now, Benny, I never asked earlier, but what was it thou did – you did – oh whatever – all those years ago that got you sent back to the stars?'

'When I spoke with that Mister Dickens of the singular power of the Eve of Christmas I confided in him that I was an angel. He said I could have knocked him down with a feather. I happened to be holding a chicken at the time and so I did. Words, they do confuse me sometimes. Poor Mister Dickens. That bump on his head put him to sleep for three days. Those that be became so worried that it was decreed it would be best if I returned to the Heavens.'

'Oh.'

'But the dream Mister Dickens had as he slept became his Christmas tale of Ebenezer Scrooge.'

'Well, I don't think those that be will be too worried about what you did this time.'

And indeed they were not. The two supervising angels were more than happy with the results of the night, even though rules had been bended slightly.

'*Fin coronet opus*,' observed Jeremiah.

'Yes,' replied Raphaella. 'And in the words of Milton, "the sable cloud turn silver on the morn".'

Such is the power and wonder of Christmas. And I say this unto you as Daniel, The Diviner of Dreams.

That Christmas was too late for Our Man to put up decorations, but the following year he went in search of a Christmas tree for the first time in his life. The shopkeeper offered him a fine specimen, the perfect shape in fact, but Our Man's eye was drawn to an odd-looking tree, with two branches sticking out at the top. That, he said, was the one he wanted. The shopkeeper was a little mystified by Our Man's choice, but smiled away when the wallet was opened.

Our Man bought fairy lights in red and green and gold and on the two branches at the top he placed a pair of angels. He had many visitors over Christmas, for he always celebrated it now and would become known for making the best rum punch going – easy on the cloves and generous with the cinnamon was the secret, he said. But his friends asked him why two angels. Our Man said he didn't really know. Except that just one looked at bit lonely, so he was always going to have two. You see, he didn't want anyone to be by themselves at Christmas.

Not even angels.

Appendices

Appendix I

Thoughts on the Ghost Tale

> 'Then what can you want to do now?' said the old lady, gaining courage.
> 'I wants to make your flesh creep,' replied the boy.
> *From* The Pickwick Papers *by Charles Dickens*

EVERY SUNDAY WHEN I WAS A BOY I would visit my great aunt Marjorie and her husband Robert at their two-up-two-down in Clifton Avenue, Harehills, Leeds. It was a house Uncle Bob had lived in all his life; he'd even been born there. Auntie Marjorie was elderly and rarely left the place, except once a week to get her hair done, so I thought it odd when I overheard her saying to Uncle Bob that the previous night she'd seen his sister, Ethel. Then I twigged – she meant her ghost. Yet it was all very matter of fact. 'She was on'turn up t' landing. And I saw your Mavis on Friday.' Years later, when I was sixteen, Auntie Marjorie asked if I would do some wall-papering for her. I asked where. 'Oh, the staircase,' she replied.

The house was old and the walls uneven, but the intricate pattern of red roses would help hide the bumps. Over the two days it took me to complete the job I had a constant sense of being watched by people I couldn't see. No ill intention towards me, more curiosity. And, gentle Reader, that was the nearest I ever came to encountering a real ghost. I say real, because on those Sunday visits Auntie Marjorie and I would watch old movies together. She especially liked those with ghosts.

One movie I remember in particular was *Between Two Worlds*, a 1944 American fantasy featuring passengers on a ship who don't understand why they're there. Well, *we* do – it's because they're dead but don't know it. Yet there are two on board who in the real world haven't quite died and this leads to the twist in the story. The Ealing film *The Halfway House*, also from 1944, featured travellers with shady pasts who take refuge from a storm in an inn run by a father and daughter, who, we discover, were killed in an air bombing raid. Except here, time has gone backwards and they're not dead yet, although both know they will be as their bodies cast no shadow. During their stay at the inn the guests re-assess their lives and, because of the switch in time, are able on leaving to make a new start with different choices. What I was learning, sitting on the settee with my Auntie, was that ghost stories aren't really about ghosts. They're tales that can make you think – and sometimes sneak in a moral message too.

Other ghost films I remember are *The Ghost and Mrs Muir*, *The Ghosts of Berkeley Square*, *Dead of Night*, *The House of Mystery* and *The Ghost Train*. I loved haunted house movies too and a particular favourite was *The Cat and the Canary* with Bob Hope – 'Don't big empty houses scare you?' 'Not me, I used to be in vaudeville.'

Oh yes, I discovered ghost stories could make you laugh too.

> What if you slept
> And what if
> In your sleep
> You dreamed
> And what if
> In your dream
> You went to heaven
> And there plucked a strange and beautiful flower
> And what if
> When you awoke
> You had that flower in your hand
> Ah, what then?
>
> *Samuel Taylor Coleridge's poem* What If You Slept?

The World of Story

Over the years I've come to think of stories as part and parcel of our human survival kit. And it all begins when we're children with that unquenchable thirst for a good yarn. Through stories we experience what it's like to walk in someone else's shoes, and so develop the ability to understand the feelings of those not like ourselves. As we mature, the story world becomes a place where we can encounter and grapple with real life conflicts in a relatively safe way. Stories are often morality tales and we like the idea of natural justice where bad people get their comeuppance. But fortune is a fickle friend and pure chance can sometimes lead to dire consequences, and such tales reflect a bleaker, more nihilistic view of the world. Then there are those never fully explained, where truths are relative and ever changing. The point is, all philosophies of life can be found in the tales we tell.

Story then is a playground of exploration for the mind, but it can also be a gym for emotions and feelings. At its most basic level what we're talking about here is sheer physical sensation, but stories can also purge the mind by pity and fear, a concept Aristotle calls *catharsis*. Some story theorists even suggest that we carry our psychological responses into the real world. We process the story, mull it over, question it, argue it, and in doing so, the tale stays with us sometimes throughout our lives. Ah, but you may be thinking, 'That's all well and good, but what about the joy of the rollercoaster ride that story has to offer? The twists, the turns, the suspense, the thrill, the jokes, the fun and colourful characters. We go to the story funfair for entertainment, after all.' Yes, that's true as well, but there's something else we've missed out.

I said that I visited my Auntie Marjorie every Sunday, but not why. Frankly, it was to escape problems at home. When I was nine, my mother came back from work, laid down on the couch and died. After that, my father, a diagnosed schizophrenic, found life an impossible challenge. I never saw the men in white coats but I knew they'd been because my father wouldn't be there when I woke up. But his time in hospital was never permanent and so he'd come home and we'd be back to where we started. My Auntie Marjorie's settee and the films we watched together offered me a world where I could feel safe and forget for a few hours the one I had to return to. When I taught story theory as an undergraduate course at the University of Birmingham I would always say to my drama students, 'Never mock escapism if you've never lived a life where you needed to escape.' Of course, I've since learnt that I wasn't alone. John Gardner in his fascinating book *On Becoming a Novelist* points out that writers are often people who learnt in childhood to turn, in times of distress, to fiction and make-believe. And that's certainly what I did.

So where do ghost tales fit in to all this rambling story theory? Well, let's start with that most basic and primeval of all human sensations: fear. With fear comes distinct physical changes in our body. Hairs stand on end, flesh tingles, limbs become rigid, faces are blanched white, mouths stay open, blood runs cold, and shivers go in search of a spine to run down. Okay, some of those are more fanciful than physiological, but that's what being afraid feels like, especially in the catalepsy of a nightmare. As E.F. Benson puts it in *A Tale of an Empty House*, 'as that limping step moved down the passage I felt fear, the hand of the nightmare that, as it clutches, paralyses and inhibits not action only, but thought.'

But why would we want to experience and even pay for such a thing in our waking life? Well, let's not forget we are animals and hearing the tread of something that does not wish to be seen is still there in our atavistic memory of oncoming darkness and its lurking shadows. And that fear is all the greater if you believe those footsteps belong to the dead who've come to take you with them. Sitting in our electrically-lit homes, it perhaps does no harm occasionally to be reminded that we are still vulnerable flesh and blood.

When we're reading about someone who is afraid or watching them on the screen, we walk empathetically with them and share that fear, yet we always keep a level of control. Choosing to be frightened is very different from involuntarily being frightened. Even so, if we allow ourselves the blood poison of a scary story, well, that results in sensations which shut out all else. As one of E.F Benson's characters observes in *The Bus-Conductor*, 'I want to be made to creep and creep and creep. Fear is the most absorbing and luxurious of emotions. One forgets all else if one is afraid.' A bizarre sort of escapism perhaps, but at least when in rictus fear you're not worrying about the gas bill. And when we experience that sudden adrenalin rush of terror it reminds us we're alive. Let's be honest here, when it's the other guy that gets it, we say, 'Rather him than me. They're dead. I'm not. Let's eat.' Oh, and one more thing, a ghost tale is the perfect date movie, for scary scenes offer an excuse for sudden embrace. That nervous hand that grabbed your knee as you watched *A Nightmare on Elm Street*. Who'd have thought all these years later you'd now be celebrating your Ruby wedding.

But the shiver factor isn't the only response to a ghost story. In fact many writers would prefer their tales to be unsettling rather than scary. E.F. Benson in his brief preface to *The Room in the Tower, and Other Stories* (1912) wrote that his stories were written 'in the hopes of giving some pleasant qualms to their reader.' M.R. James had something similar in mind when, in his preface to *Ghost Stories of an Antiquary* (1904), he wrote, 'If any of them succeed in causing their readers to feel pleasantly uncomfortable when walking along a solitary road at nightfall, or sitting over a dying fire in the small hours, my purpose in writing them will have been attained.' Notice the reference to that solitary road. M.R. James wanted his stories to stay with you long after you'd read them. Not just a physical thrill for the moment, but a psychological agitation that remains with you as you walk among the darkening shadows of the night.

It should be said that in recent years writers, especially screenwriters, have used the ghost story not to frighten an audience but as means of exploring social issues, political injustice and sexual acceptance. Think here of *All of Us Strangers*, *His House*, *Under the Shadow*, even Disney's *Coco*. On personal note, after watching *Coco* I went in the attic to find a photograph of my maternal grandfather to put it in a frame, as he was the only grandparent whose picture was not on display in my house. The general point here is that the otherness of the ghost has become an avatar which has allowed the storyteller to shape a complex message to a wide audience who probably would not have sought out an overtly polemic tale.

> 'No man who doesn't believe in ghosts ever sees one.'
>
> *George Bernard Shaw, writing to Henry James*

Calling All Spooks

One character in Jerome K. Jerome's *The Man of Science* (1892) says, 'I think it illogical to disbelieve anything that we are not able to disprove.' Equally you could argue it is illogical to believe in a something whose existence is unprovable, yet that doesn't stop people having faith in some sort of ongoing life after death. But if there is such a thing, what are the right words to describe what we become?

The English language has the benefit of having a varied linguistic ancestry and so has several different ways of referring to those who have departed this life. The word 'spirit' originates from the Latin *spiritus*, meaning 'breath', and so spirit even when referring to those no longer with us, still has a real sense of life about it. In another linguistic tradition there's the word 'ghost', which comes from the German *Geist*, which has its derivation in the Old Icelandic *geiski*, meaning 'fear', which gives it a linguistic history evoking unease and trepidation. Etymologies aren't always that useful, but perhaps partly because of their different derivations, ghost and spirit have developed particular meanings and usage. Clairvoyants, for instance, are far more likely to say 'spirit' than 'ghost', because for them the *spiritus* is a soul that has simply moved on to a higher realm of existence. Equally, if a headless ancestor turned up at your bedpost waving chains, it's more than likely you'd refer to such a fearful apparition as a ghost. That said, many people use ghost and spirit interchangeably, including most of the characters in this collection. The exception though is Billie Blooming, who, not surprisingly is a psychic medium.

A follow on from all this is, what if the supernatural entity or presence or whatever is neither ghost nor spirit? If you wish to get pedantic you could argue that several 'ghost tales' by M.R. James don't actually have a ghost at all – in the sense of someone who died and has now returned to haunt you – for his tales instead often feature a supernaturally empowered artefact or document. Think here of the peculiar binoculars in *A View from a Hill* and the cabalistic testaments found in *The Tractate Middoth* and *The Uncommon Prayer-Book*. And then there are all those weird spiders in *The Ash Tree*, the demon in *Canon Alberic's Scrapbook* and whatever it is in *Casting the Runes*. M.R. James, incidentally, never considered Charles Dickens's *A Christmas Carol* to be a 'ghost story'. Marley, as a former living human being, is a ghost, but the others, call them phantoms, spectres, shades or shadows, are essentially spiritual incarnations of concepts of Christmas and Time.

And what of the word 'sprite', that supernatural entity of European folklore? Or 'ghoul', which comes from the Arabic *ghūl*, a demon-like creature that robs graves and eats corpses? Then there are banshees, boggarts, lemures, kelpies, bag-a-boos, imps, poltergeists and the rest. And should we really include in a 'ghost story' anthology the vampires found in Théophile Gautier's *Clarinonde* and E.F. Benson's *Mrs Amworth*? What about all those Gothic demons in the tales of Sheridan Le Fanu or the mummy in Arthur Conan Doyle's *Lot No. 249*? And we haven't even mentioned yet the gastropod aberrations in the stories of H.P. Lovecraft. Then there are those stories where the natural world turns unnatural, such as the strange behaviour of birds in Philip MacDonald's *Our Feathered Friends* or that Christmas fir tree taken, with deadly consequences, from its rightful home in H.R. Wakefield's *Lucky's Grove*. All these tales can be found in popular 'ghost story' anthologies, yet none has an actual ghost.

In the Victorian era, tales of the supernatural and the marvellous were collected under the general title *Weird Tales*, as in Charlotte Riddell's collection of 1882, as the word weird in those days had connotations of the supernatural or the alien. Sheridan Le Fanu used the term 'romantic horror', Robert Louis Stevenson referred to 'crawlers' and Robert Aickman spoke of 'strange stories'. Stephen King talks about his 'fearsomes' and the 'shudder pulps' of the 1930s, but in more recent years 'ghost stories' has become the umbrella term under which all weirdness shelters. In this collection there are tales which clearly involve actual ghosts, but there are also Christmas angels and a phantom shadow that's perhaps more monster than spook. Yet in all the stories there is a supernatural element, or at least that which is perceived to be supernatural, and that I would say is the prerequisite of the 'ghost tale'.

> 'In the first act get your principal character up
> a tree; in the second act, throw stones at him;
> in the third, get him down gracefully.'
>
> *Anonymous,* Bridgeport Herald *in 1897;*
> *subsequently attributed to numerous writers,*
> *including George Abbot, George F. Kaufman*
> *and Vladimir Nobokov among others*

Weaving a Ghost Tale Plot

Most stories begin with some kind of change that alters the status quo, creating a problem, or exacerbating one that's already there. And this story theorists call the 'catalyst event'. In Shakespeare's *Hamlet* it's the arrival of a ghost that upsets the apple cart, but the trigger for action, or 'inciting incident' in theorist language, comes specifically when the ghost says to Hamlet, 'If thou didst ever thy dear father love... revenge his foul and most unnatural murder.' Now Hamlet has an action: vengeance.

In Noël Coward's *Blithe Spirit* it's a séance that puts the cat among the pigeons, for it results in the return of Elvira, Charles's first wife, who died seven years previously. The ghost of Elvira, unsurprisingly, takes an instant dislike to Charles's new wife and does all she can to mock Ruth's dowdiness and lack of sexual allure. Two competing actions result from all this: for the newly-married Charles it's to get rid of Elvira and for Elvira it's to keep Charles all to herself; the only way she can do this is by bringing about his death. In other words, she's intent on becoming an abducting ghost. And spiriting you away is an action that can found in many a spooky tale.

Tales of ghostly abduction allow a writer to explore the theme of obsessive passion and jealousy, and how that can turn malignant and deadly, which is certainly the case in Mary Elizabeth Braddon's *The Cold Embrace* (1860). The abduction in Rosemary Timperley's *Harry* (1955) is particularly disturbing because it involves a child, but the brilliance of that tale is how the writer creates sympathy for all the characters, including the ghost abductor. A curious take on the 'I'm-coming-to get-you' scenario, and a particular favourite of Roald Dahl, is L.P. Hartley's *W.S.* (1954), in which a novelist, Walter Streeter, receives a bizarre series of postcards from someone who claims to be a character from one of his own stories and with each delivery the postmark gets closer and closer...

The idea of a siren ghost, one with mesmeric powers of attraction, features in Robert W. Chambers' *Passeur* (1897), Grant Allen's *Wolverden Tower* (1896), F.G. Loring's *The Tomb of Sarah* (1990) and Sir Thomas Graham Jackson's *The Lady of Rosemount* (1919) – 'On his ears fell the words, "You are mine, you are mine," and he was helpless to resist the spell that drew him on and on farther into the gloom of the ruined nave.' Perhaps you might also include here Sir Arthur Conan Doyle's 1883 tale *The Captain of the 'Polestar'*, where the name of the ship foreshadows the nature of the ghost's purpose. Other notable abduction ghost tales include E.F Benson's *The Face* (1924) and, in it's own way, Mary Wilkins Freeman's *The Lost Ghost* (1903).

As said, the motivation of the ghost in *Hamlet* is revenge and this too is a popular action of the ghost tale. Vengeance is central to Edith Wharton's *Afterward* (1910), Vincent O'Sullivan's *My Enemy and Myself* (1896), W.W. Jacobs' *The Well* (1902) and Ellen Glasgow's *The Shadowy Third* (1916), a reading of which occurs in '*I Was Once a Haunted House*'. In these tales it pleases fate that events conspire to put the guilty in a place where their wrongdoing can be uncovered and thus punished. Ghost stories featuring supernatural redress are popular perhaps because they offer a sense of justice that's not always there in the real world, where far too many people, often the rich and powerful, get away with their crimes.

More in the tormenting mode of the Gothic ghost we have

Eveline's Visitant by Mary Elizabeth Braddon, first published in 1867, where a dying man warns his killer, 'My ghostly hand shall drop a poison in your cup of joy.' The killer, the narrator of the tale, doesn't take the threat too seriously, for 'if men had power thus to avenge themselves, the earth would be peopled with phantoms.' Oh dear, that's a foolish thing to say in a ghost story and of course he will live to regret it. Vengeance's sibling is retribution, but the distinction is that retribution comes from a higher authority and is exacted as a recompense for the crime. In this sense *The Ghost Light*, within these pages, is a tale of vengeance, whereas *The Final Fake* is most definitely one of divine retribution.

There are many reasons why a ghost goes a-haunting, but the key point from a narrative perspective is that a plot needs an action, and indeed counter-action, as with Elvira and Charles and the internal struggles within Hamlet. And action requires a plan. As MacShaugnassy says in Jerome K. Jerome's *The Man of Science*, 'If one admits the possibility of spirits retaining any interest in the affairs of this world at all, it is certainly more reasonable to imagine them engaged upon a task such as you suggest, than to believe that they occupy themselves with the performance of mere drawing room tricks.'

An obvious task for a spook is to deal with unfinished business and you'll find this in one of Britain's oldest ghost stories, *The Apparition of Mrs Veal*, published as a pamphlet in 1706 and usually attributed to Daniel Defoe. Another ghost task is to make some sort of reparation and this features in Lady Cynthia Asquith's *The Corner Shop* (1926), sometimes published under the pen name C.L. Ray, which tells the story of an antique dealer who comes to realise his wealth was based on theft and in death wants to make amends. Then there's the protective territorial ghost, as in E.F. Benson's *Naboth's Vineyard*, and, related to this some sort of guardianship. The duty of the spectre, for example, in M.R. James's *A Warning to the Curious* is to protect the last of the holy crowns and whatever creature it is that's in his tale *The Treasure of Abbot Thomas* it exists to frighten away those who come near whatever treasure it is.

Of course there is that spook who by its nature is malevolent and just goes about killing people, as in H.R. Wakefield's *A Black Solitude* (1951), where the destruction of man is its 'delight' and 'orgasm'. Plus there are those ghosts who haunt more from a sense of duty and habit, as in Oscar Wilde's comic tale *The Canterville Ghost* (1887). And the situation of the haunter at Canterville Chase brings us to the idea of the ghost's 'inner need'.

Need and want come from a sense that something within oneself is lacking or missing. Sir Simon de Canterville is a restlessness ghost, but through Virginia, the wise daughter of the Otis family, he is given release. What we have with Sir Simon is needful deliverance. And it's a popular theme in ghost stories. It's prominent in Margaret Oliphant's *The Open Door* (1882), where the soul in pain cries out, 'Oh, mother let me in! Oh, mother, mother, let me in! Oh, let me in!' Only when its plight is acknowledged and pitied, and the spirit of the boy is shown mercy by Reverend Moncrieff, can its soul be persuaded to go to its mother who's now 'with the Lord'. And in such stories the task is with the ghost seer rather than the ghost itself.

It's worth bringing in here what story theorists call the 'decision of surrender'. This is where a character gives up on something they once held dear, be it a belief, an object, a person or whatever was the initial desire and goal. What then follows is the character coming to an understanding and embracing of that which is truly needed in themselves – and it's this self-revelation which leads to their inner transformation. A classic ghost story example of this is Scrooge at a gravestone just before he sees his own name carved into the stone, when he says, 'I will honour Christmas in my heart, and try to keep it all the year. I will live in the Past, the Present, and the Future. The Spirits of all Three shall strive within me. I will not shut out the lessons that they teach.' It's this relinquishing of his old ways at his moment of crisis that leads to his waking-up in his own bed and his rebirth and reclamation – 'I don't know how long I've been among the Spirits. I don't know anything. I'm quite a baby. Never mind. I don't care. I'd rather be a baby. Hallo! Whoop! Hallo here!'

And the casting off of a belief that was once held true leading to a spiritual transformation brings us back to *The Open Door*.

The action of deliverance in Oliphant's tale is by no means easy, for there is much resistance from the spirit of the boy, but, after a prayer to the Lord he departs (the surrender that leads to his own transformation). It's a long scene and has within it what theorists call the 'battle' and the 'climax', where ultimately there can only be one winner. The climax in a story is the final turning point and the change that comes with it is absolute and irreversible. In the battle in *Blithe Spirit* between Charles and Elvira it looks as if Elvira will triumph, for she tampers with Charles's car with the intention of causing a fatal accident to bring him to the spirit world, only the faulty car is unexpectedly taken by Ruth, his new wife, and so it's she who is killed and returns as a ghost.

In *Poetics*, Aristotle divided plots into what he called 'simple' and 'complex'. In simple plots there is a gradual change of fortune across the whole drama, whereas in complex plots there's what he called *peripeteia* – a sudden reversal of the expected outcome – which is often accompanied by *anagnorisis* – recognition or discovery of a truth – and it's these together which bring about the change of fortune. In layman's terms what we're talking about here is 'The Big Twist', which is often a key element of any ghost tale. And the unexpected outcome of Elvira not killing Charles but instead turning Ruth into a ghost is a very clever one.

A good twist can also make you re-assess all you've previously read or seen. Think here of movies such as *The Others* and *Sixth Sense*, which are so brilliantly constructed that viewers are eager to watch them a second time just to see what was always there in plain sight. And without intending to sound too highfalutin about all this, re-assessing that which you thought was one thing but turns out to be the opposite is something we experience in life. Nothing is ever quite what it seems and the ghost story provides us with a lesson in that.

Many a ghost tale concludes with a letter or document offered to the reader as an explanation or as background to the supernatural manifestation. You'll find examples of this in Bernard Capes's *An Eddy on the Floor* (1899), Lord Edward Bulwer-Lytton's *The House and the Brain* (1859) and Amelia B. Edwards's *Was it an Illusion?* (1881). In E.F. Benson's *The House with the Brick-Kiln*

(1908) the dark deed that happened at the house is discovered in a local guide-book and in his hotel room tale *The Other Bed* (1912) a previous occupant's suicide is read about in an American newspaper. What the letter (or whatever expositional device it is) often sets out is the history of the ghost, or what theorists call the back story. In its widest sense back story is all that happened before we first joined the tale, but in practice it usually refers to the traumatic incident from the character's past that still troubles them. One story expert, John Truby, even refers to this aspect of story as 'The Ghost'. Anyway, whatever you want to call it, the 'back story' is essentially the emotional open wound of hurt that comes from somewhere in the character's history. In *The Canterville Ghost*, it's the tragic tale of Sir Simon's wife, Lady Eleanor de Canterville, and in Margaret Oliphant's *The Open Door* it's the history of the prodigal son Willie, who returned only to discover his beloved mother was dead.

A letter at the end of a tale can also act as the surprise twist, as in Mary Wilkins Freeman's *The Wind in the Rose-Bush* (1903). Another type of twist is the sudden introduction of a second narrator, who takes over the storytelling from the original narrator and it's that which brings about the reveal. You'll find this literary device in Wilkie Collins's *The Woman in White* and I use it in *The Return of the Handbag* and to some degree also in '*The Strange Case of the Unaccountable Shadow*'. A further literary technique is to keep the twist or reveal until the very last line, and you'll find this in Richard Middleton's *On the Road to Brighton* (1912), E.F. Benson's *The Step* (1926), Lady Cynthia Asquith's *The Corner Shop* (1926), Henry James's *The Romance of Certain Old Clothes* (1868), Robert Louis Stevenson's *The Body-Snatcher* (1884), and more recently in Jeanette Winterton's *The Spare Room* (2023).

Abrupt endings are popular in ghost tales, but a narrative sometimes requires a proper resolution or dénouement after the story's climax (dénouement comes from the French word *dénouer* meaning 'unknot'). What we're talking about here is the wind-up, where all the strands of the plot are drawn together and loose ends explained. '*I Was Once a Haunted House*' is essentially a whodunit and so inevitably requires a scene where the one who unmasked the killer reveals how the ruse was achieved.

So there you have it. Catalyst event. Problem arising or exacerbated. Trigger for action. Inner need and want. Task. Counter action. Back story. Reveal. Battle. Surrender and transformation. Climax. Resolution. But is there a word for how all these elements are put and held together?

Theorists talk about scaffolding, the frame and even the skeleton, but here the etymology of the word 'text' is useful, for it comes from the Latin *texere* meaning 'to weave'. And that's what storytellers do. They weave all the material of their tale together in such a way that we can enjoy the pattern without noticing how it was made. My own experience is that story structure in the actual writing is a largely unconscious act. Yes, you're aware that you're selecting and composing events – the task, the battle, the reveal and so on – and all with the intention of creating a response from those who will read your tale, but the story itself as you write it so often takes on its own life. Where exactly that life comes from is a bit of a mystery.

It should be said that not all ghost tales are an array of plot points and story beats and they're none the worse for that. With the ghost tale there are those 'simple' plots, to use Aristotle's term, where a presence slowly becomes a manifesting entity, as in several E.F. Benson stories such as *And No Birds Sing*, *The Corner House* and *A Tale of an Empty House*. But 'simple' doesn't mean lesser, for these types of tale are often just as effective as those with big plot twists. Then there are those that wish to explore a curious situation, such as becoming a ghost, as in G.W. Stonier's *The Memoirs of a Ghost* (1947), or a theme like memory, as in Louis de Bernières's *This Beautiful House* (2004). Such tales are not driven by action or need, but rather by anticipation and suspense and the pleasure in reading them can be found in the writer's skill in creating tension and foreboding. *The Whisper in the Woods*, published anonymously in 1880 in *ALL THE YEAR ROUND*, the magazine founded and edited by Charles Dickens, is a tale that is pretty much pure atmosphere – and a very fine piece of writing it is too.

> 'With her head tucked underneath her arm
> She walks the bloody tower
> With her head tucked underneath her arm
> At the midnight hour.'
>
> 'With Her Head Tucked Underneath Her Arm', *written in 1934 by Robert Patrick Weston (1878–1936) and William Herbert Lee (1880–1946) for Stanley Holloway (1890–1982). The 'she' in the song refers to Anne Boleyn.*

Ghosts: A Biographical Guide

No two ghosts are quite the same. However, without, I hope, turning into one of those zealous lepidopterists with a sharp pin and sticky label, it might be useful to consider some general types. With this biographical guide I hope to show the range of ghosts open to the writer, but it should be said from the off that the category of ghost doesn't necessarily set the tone, be it comic or tragic, of the story itself.

'He had passed on without pausing; without looking at me; I could almost have believed, without seeing me!' says a character in Amelia B. Edwards's *Was it an Illusion?* (1881). Let's call this the 'oblivious ghost', who has little or no awareness of your presence. Another example can be found in George MacDonald's *Uncle Cornelius His Story* (1869), where there is an encounter with a woman who 'looked as if she had walked straight out of an ancient drawing-room in her evening attire.' The word 'ancient' leads us on to the 'time-slip ghost', who appears to be living in a different time dimension rather than a parallel spiritual realm. Think here of the characters in old fashioned dress in the coach in *The Ghosts of the Mail* (from *The Pickwick Papers*, 1836) by Charles Dickens.

Then there is the 'stranded ghost', who may have escaped the punishment of the ungodly, but is not yet able to receive the reward of the righteous. Sir Simon de Canterville, for example. And here you might add the maritime legend of *The Flying Dutchman*, the phantom ship condemned to sail forever. A variation on the trapped ghost is what you could call the re-enactment or 'echo ghost', who is confined in our earthly plane and for some reason is forced to relive a terrible trauma or offence. This metaphysical concept is explored in detail in E.F. Benson's 1922 tale *In the Tube* – 'For it seems certain that the spirit of a man, after the death of his body, is obliged to re-enact such a crime, with a view, I suppose we may guess, to his remorse and his eventual redemption.' In such stories it's the spiritual nature of the suffering that tends to be the focus and theme.

A cousin of the echo ghost could be said to be the 'imprint ghost', the idea being that the walls of a room or the bricks of a house have somehow soaked up the psychic energy of an event, often traumatic, which a living person close by then senses. A curious 1972 British television horror drama called *The Stone Tape*, written by Nigel Kneale (writer of the BBC series *The Quatermass Experiment*), explores this idea. The story features a team of experts who move into a Victorian mansion that has a reputation for being haunted. After a ghostly sighting the scientists try to determine if the stones of the building really are able to record past events. The drama had a great impact and following the broadcast there developed the hypothesis that became known as the 'Stone Tape Theory'. However, the concept of a ghost being the result of an event somehow imprinted in time or absorbed by its surroundings isn't new, for it's there in Margaret Oliphant's *The Open Door,* written in 1882, where it's postulated that a trauma event of the past 'might impress itself somehow upon the hidden heart of nature.'

An entertaining take on the imprint ghost is A.M. Burrage's *The Fourth Wall* (1915), where friends rent a cottage once lived in by an actor who toured for years in a play. The cottage in the mind's eye of the visitors is transformed into a stage with one of the walls disappearing to reveal a watching audience (the title of the story refers to the conceptual barrier in a theatre between the stage and the people in the auditorium). The explanation for all this is that the actor who lived there imbued the cottage with such strong memories of his performances that the guests became able to see them.

However, this is perhaps more a form of ESP or Extra-Sensory Perception than an actual haunting.

Let's move on to the 'incognito ghost', where a person encounters a character who seems alive enough, only is later discovered to be dead or to have recently departed this world. Examples of this type of ghost can be found in Charles Dickens's *The Portrait Painter's Story* (1861), Edith Wharton's *Afterward* (1910) and A.M. Burrage's *Smee* (1929). Over the years, the incognito ghost has become probably the most overused of all ghost scenarios and a regular reader of supernatural tales can usually spot this twist coming like the fleet at D-Day. That said, it can be useful as a decoy. Frankly it's as clear as sunshine that in Nancy Spain's 1952 tale *The Bewilderment of Snake McKoy*, Mrs Bellwood, the writer in the attic, is a ghost and that the tale is leading to that revelation, except the big twist comes in the final line. And a real killer it is.

Another popular ghost scenario is where a character dresses up as a supposed ghost, only for the real one to turn up. You might think of this phantom as the 'usurping ghost' and you'll find an entertaining example in *The Ghost* (1928) by Catherine Wells, wife of H.G. Wells. In such tales the pretender or hoaxer often meets an unpleasant demise, as in Louisa Baldwin's *The Real and the Counterfeit* (1895), where 'the Cistercian monk passed them like a white mist that sank into the wall, and Musgrave and Lawley were alone with the dead body of their friend, whose masquerading dress had become his shroud.' Fans of *Alfred Hitchcock Presents* might recognise the phoney-ghost-turns-out-to-be-real scenario from a 1959 story called *Banquo's Chair*, where a retired detective plans to employ an actress to make a murder suspect believe he's seeing the ghost of the woman he killed and so confess the crime. And the ruse works – 'Get out whoever you are or I'll kill you again!' – only the actress who was meant to play the murdered lady turns up after the event, saying she'd been delayed. Who then (or what) was the ghostly figure the killer saw?

There is as well the 'doppelganger ghost', who has a physical similarity or spiritual affinity with the main character of the story, as in Charles Dickens's *The Haunted Man and the Ghost's Bargain*

(1848) and *The Signal-Man* (1866). Another example is the protagonist in Henry James's *The Jolly Corner* (1908), where Spencer Brydon encounters a version of the man he might have been, and even offers a horticultural metaphor to explain the situation: 'It comes over me that I had then a strange alter ego deep down somewhere within me, as the full-blown flower is in the small tight bud, and that I just took the course, I just transferred him to the climate, that blighted him for once and for ever.' Desmond MacCarthy's *Pargiton and Harby* (1926) offers a more psychological approach in that it's a portrait of a guilty man who appears to be haunting himself.

A different kind of duality can be found in Robert Louis Stevenson's *Markheim* (1885), but here the supernatural figure, who arrives after a murder has been committed, is more an angel or incarnation of conscience, though there are hints of a physical resemblance: 'At times he thought he knew him; and at times he thought he bore a likeness to himself.' And we mustn't forget in the modern era Muriel Spark's *The Leaf-Sweeper* (1952), where one version of Johnnie is flesh and blood and the other is a ghost and each have a very different attitude to Christmas. But leave it to Sheridan Le Fanu to outdo all these doppelgangers in his 1872 tale *The Haunted House in Westminster* (also known as *Mr. Justice Harbottle*), where there are three troubling lookalikes that unnerve the wicked Judge Harbottle, including a caricature of himself who acts as judge in his own murder trial. When it came to doubles, Sheridan Le Fanu was not one, as it were, to do things by halves.

One of the most regular phantoms in supernatural fiction is the 'omen ghost', or what Edith Nesbit in *Man-size in Marble* (1887) calls 'a presentiment of evil'. In these stories the sighting of a historical spook, or sometimes its appearance in a dream, is thought to be a precursor of death. Think here of the ghostly old squire and his hunting party in *At Chrighton Abbey*, where the housekeeper observes, 'You've seen that which always brings misfortune and sorrow to this house, Miss Sarah. You've seen the dead.' Yes, it's impending doom for the unmarried son, but the actual focus of the tale is on the cold and unfeeling nature of his fiancée and the change that bereavement brings in her attitude to those less fortunate than herself. Another example of the omen ghost can be found in Charles Whibley's *Twelve O'Clock* (1926), the supposed story of Thomas Lyttelton (1744-1779), known as 'the wicked Lord Lyttelton', who in Whibley's tale is visited by a spirit who tells him he will die in three days time. And indeed he does, for the twelve o'clock of the title becomes the hour of his death.

In Rudyard Kipling's *At the End of the Passage* (1890), encountering the apparition becomes the means of the demise: 'He was scared to death. Look at those eyes. For pity's sake don't let him be buried with them open!' and in Julius Long's *The Pale Man* (1934) the spook turns out to be the Grim Reaper. *The Sweeper* (1931) by A.M. Burrage features a tramp who comes begging, but the unkind lady of the house makes him sweep her garden in payment for food, only as he does the job he dies, saying that one day he will come for her and she'd better be ready. From then on the lady makes amends for her behaviour and insists to her servants that anyone coming to her door asking for food is given some. As with *At Chrighton Abbey*, a brush with what we may call 'the ghost of death' turns a character's haughty nature into kindness.

Another reoccurring spectre is the 'possessing ghost', where a spirit takes over the physical body of the living, often with ill intent, as in Lennox Robinson's *A Pair of Muddy Shoes* (1919) and Lady Cynthia Asquith's '*God Grante That She Lye Stille*' (1947). A tale which proved a popular take on the possessing spirit was D.H. Lawrence's *The Rocking Horse Winner* (1926), which was twice made into a movie. The story features a boy in a luckless family who when riding his rocking horse discovers the name of the winning horse in a race yet to be run, but the price to be paid for this knowledge gained on the rocking horse is the boy's life.

A different type of possession is where a spirit inhabits an inanimate object, as in Algeron Blackwood's *The Kit-Bag* (1908), 'where the canvas fell into a fold like a nose and forehead, and the brass rings for the padlock just filled the position of the eyes. A shadow – or was it a travel stain? for he could not tell exactly – looked like hair. It gave him rather a turn, for it was so absurdly, so outrageously, like the face of John Turk, the murderer.' You might also include here the glove in Elizabeth Bowen's *Hand in Glove* (1952) and the strange book in Margaret Irwin's *The Book* (1930). Plus there's the supernatural portrait in Hume Nisbet's *The Old Portrait* (1890) and whatever it is that's in the porcelain ornament in C.H.B. Kitchin's *The Chelsea Cat* (1952). Saki's *Laura* (1914) takes a different possession tack and explores the idea of a spirit returning as an animal or a young boy.

The 'child ghost' is usually harmless enough, as in Hugh Walpole's *The Little Ghost* (1933) and A.M. Burrage's *Playmates* (1927), although the nature of the child ghost in Mary Wilkins Freeman's *The Lost Ghost* (1903) is far more ambiguous. The young twins in E.F. Benson's *How Fear Departed From the Long Gallery* (1911) become unthreatening when shown pity and sympathy, which brings about 'a wonderful sense of peace.' However, we have the Edwardian master of the ghost tale to thank for making ghost children truly frightening. I was thirteen when I first saw the TV adaptation of M.R. James's *Lost Hearts* and frankly it freaked me out. The story features a predatory old man, a boy called Stephen (with the same name and of a similar age to me), but it was those corpse-like child ghosts with their lifeless green faces and long finger nails that stayed in my head for years to come. Even to this day I find the music made by a hurdy-gurdy a shiver giver. Ultimately the child ghosts are Stephen's protectors, but the reveal of the boy's chest, showing where his lost heart had been, is a terror I will never forget.

The 'suicide ghost' is often revealed in the back story to be the reason why a place is haunted, as in O. Henry's *The Furnished Room* (1904), E.F. Benson's *The Other Bed* (1912) and *The Story of Clifford House*, by an anonymous author (the story first appeared in *The Mistletoe Bough* in 1878, edited by Mary Elizabeth Braddon). Elizabeth Bowen has an unusual take on the suicide ghost, for in *The Apple Tree* (1931) it's the tree on which a girl hanged herself that is the manifestation.

The Bells, the 1871 play by Leopold David Lewis, has it that one Christmas Eve, Mathias robbed and killed a man and now he hears the bells of his sledge and sees the dead man before him and in

William Shakespeare's *Macbeth* the cry is 'Avaunt! and quit my sight! Let the earth hide thee!' when the murderer sees Banquo's ghost at the evening feast. Key to both plays is that it's only the killers (and of course audience) who see the manifestation. It's a moot question, but are the ghosts here real or phantoms of a disturbed mind?

Demons in Sheridan Le Fanu's tales are presented as primarily supernatural, reflecting a world view where, as Barton says in *The Watcher*, 'There is a God – a dreadful God – and that retribution follows guilt. In ways, the most mysterious and stupendous; by agencies, the most inexplicable and terrific; there is a spiritual system – great Heavens, how frightfully I have been convinced! – a system malignant, and inexorable, and omnipotent, under whose persecutions I am, and have been, suffering the torments of the damned!' The sins of the past haunting the agitated mind of the living is a key theme in many of Le Fanu's tales. Curiously Le Fanu's *The Haunted House in Westminster* and Lewis's *The Bells* have a similar basic plot in that both Mathias, the burgomaster, and Judge Harbottle are haunted by the ghost of a man whose death they brought about, leading to a dream where they are tried for murder and presented with rope with which in real life they then hang themselves. Freud not doubt would have explained the dreams as projections of guilt and so lets call what we have here the 'guilt ghost'.

Following on from all this we have what you might refer to as 'the psychological ghost', where an explanation involving the mind is probably more feasible than the one relying on a supernatural agency. The ghost in Edith Wharton's *The Triumph of the Mind* (1916) can easily be construed as an unconscious instinct warning the traveller who has taken shelter in a house of the dangers that lurk within it. In Desmond MacCarthy's *Pargiton and Harby* (1926), where a guilty man essentially haunts himself to death, the term 'incipient persecution mania' is used to explain what may or may not be spooky events. The key point is that the exclusivity and certainty of the supernatural, so essential to Gothic ghost tales of Victorian fiction, had by the Edwardian era faded to doubt and ambiguity.

A different kind of ghost is the 'shadow ghost', as in Tom Hood's *The Shadow of a Shade* where there is an awareness 'that the light of her single candle flung what seemed to be two shadows of the sick man on the wall.' Another strange shadow on the wall can be found, not unsurprisingly, in Mary Wilkins Freeman's *The Shadow on the Wall* (1902), where a shadow appears after the death in a family and no light from any lamp can affect it. Creepy. Likewise the shadow in Edith Nesbit's *The Shadow* (1905), which isn't a ghost as such, but something perhaps more like a shadow of past deeds haunting the present. However, the writer who used the power of the shadow most effectively in the ghost tale was H.R. Wakefield. *The Cairn* features a peculiar shadow that could move and change its shape and in *Into Outer Darkness* the shadows at Whitling Manor which stain the wall lead to death. Perhaps though Wakefield's most menacing shadow can be found in *He Cometh and He Passeth By,* where a dabbler in the occult sends a man a cut out paper outline of a beast, with a figure painted on it. Soon an unaccountable shadow begins to haunt the man and it's revealed that it's the six words of the title which brought the monster into being. Here I should acknowledge that the phrase 'unaccountable shadow' in that story became the inspiration for the phenomenon in *The Strange Case of the Unaccountable Shadow*.

Of course there are other types of spook, including the 'unknowing ghost' who doesn't realise they are dead, as in Algernon Blackwood's *Transition* (1916) and Louis de Bernières's *This Beautiful House* (2004). And the unknowing ghost can be found, albeit briefly, in the early scenes of such films such as *Ghost* and *Always* and, if you've seen them, is the big twist at the end of two classic ghost movies. Then there's the 'erotic ghost' or femme fatal ghost, as in Algernon Blackwood's *A Threefold Cord...* (1931) – '"I wish so long to find you," she said in a low, husky tone that was almost a whisper; "for so vairy long I watch you – here in this same place"' – and Ernest Theodor Amadeus Hoffmann's *The Deserted House* (1817), where the ghost seer becomes 'aroused and excited through all my nerve centres.' Plus, of course, Coward's enticing Elvira. Famous people, or rather the ghosts of the famous, occasionally make an appearance in fictional tales, including the legendary cricketer W.C. Grace in *Lord Dunsay's Autumn Cricket* (1949), William Shakespeare, plus sidekick Ben Jenson, in Denis

Mackail's *The Lost Tragedy* (1926) and the Emperor Tiberius in Rose Macaulay's *Whitewash* (1952).

There are those tales as well where a place is the ghostly apparition, as in Bernard Capes's *The Vanishing House* (1898) and Ralph Adams Cram's *The Dead Valley* (1893), which H.P. Lovecraft singled out for achieving 'a memorably potent degree of vague regional horror through subtleties of atmosphere and description.' Plus there's the ghostly mist in H.F. Arnold's *The Night Wire* (1926) and even that spooky Christmas tree in H.R. Wakefield's *Lucky's Grove* (1940).

There are as well a number of spook stories which seem to involve a haunting or supernatural event, only in the end it's all explained away as human agency. You might call this the 'false-alarm ghost' and several feature in the Carnacki tales of William Hope Hodgson. In Richard Harris Barham's *The Spectre of Tappington* (1840), there appears to be a spook who steals the breeches of Lieutenant Seaforth, only it turns out Seaforth is a somnambulist who has been spending his nights digging a grave for his trousers, breeches, pantaloons, silk-net tights and patent cords. An equally bizarre explanation for what is taken to be a supernatural happening can be found in Wilkie Collins's *The Traveller's Story of a Terribly Strange Bed* (1852). The story is presented as if it's some monstrous bed that has the power to encroach on the person lying in it. However, it's revealed the guest has been drugged and the bed is a contraption operated from the upper floor in order to kill those who sleep in it and steal their money. It's still a four-poster grave, but one of human rather than supernatural agency. Then there's Mary Webb's *Mr Tallent's Ghost* (1926), the curious tale of a man who, as a psychological experiment, fakes his own death in order to observe the reaction of his family and friends to his 'ghost'. A thought, I suspect, which has been the fancy of many minds over the years.

Stephen King says in *Danse Macabre* that 'without the sacred, there is no profane.' Similarly there can be no ghost without a ghost seer and, from a creative perspective, there is always a symbiotic relationship between the two. The ghost and ghost seer complement each other in the same way a protagonist and antagonist do, because that is how stories are constructed and designed.

> 'The little girl – she was the sweetest child I ever saw – died just two months ago of pneumonia.'
>
> 'But she couldn't have died.' I was a fool to let this out, but the shock had completely unnerved me. 'I tell you I saw her yesterday.'
>
> *From* The Shadowy Third
> *by Ellen Glasgow, written in 1916*

The Ghost Seers

Who can see the ghost and what makes that possible, then, are often significant elements in a ghost plot. Historically those thought most attuned to ghosts have been women, dogs, sexually ambiguous men, the bereaved, horses, simpletons, children, people of colour, the blind, the lonely and those known to make a monopoly of their troubles. Phrases such as 'brain fever', 'agitated mind', 'cerebral excitement' and 'hysterical temperament' often crop up when describing second sighters or the twice-born, or, as E.F. Benson calls them, 'sensitives'.

Sheridan Le Fanu in *The Haunted House in Westminster* writes of Judge Harbottle being 'feverish', 'in the vapours' and falling 'among his blue devils', all terms of the period linked with depression. Some past trauma may also come into play. As the narrator observes in Edith Nesbit's *In the Dark*, 'It may – though I don't pretend to understand how – have been the development through intense suffering, of a sixth sense, in a very nervous highly-strung nature.'

Rustics and servants usually know there are ghosts, but on the whole choose to avoid them or pretend they're not there. At the other end of the social scale it's said in Brander Matthew's *The Rival Ghosts* (1884) that the ghost never appears to the master of the house, which is not untypical of Victorian tales. What all this means is that the ghost seer is often a socially liminal character or a guest, or a traveller, or rootless wanderer or some other outsider. Miss

Sarah Chrighton in *At Chrighton Abbey* has the family name but not the status, and so is faced with having to earn her living 'in a position of dependence – a dreadful thing for a Chrighton to be obliged to do.' Unsurprisingly Sarah turns out to be the ideal ghost seer and as an intermediate is perfectly positioned to observe the social hierarchy of the Victorian world she finds herself in.

The idea that it's only those recently bereaved who can see ghosts is central to Rudyard Kipling's very moving tale *They* (1904), written five years after the death of his young daughter Josephine from pneumonia. In the same story, there's a blind woman who can sense the ghosts who says 'we blindies have only one skin, I think. Everything outside hits straight at our souls. It's different for you. You've such defences with your eyes.'

Another type of ghost seer is the professional medium, who really should be called a clairaudient, as mediums tend to hear ghosts rather than actually perceive them with their eyes. Madame Arcati is the eccentric medium in Coward's *Blithe Spirit*, but the twist is that it's the housemaid, Edith, with her unconscious psychic abilities, who has summoned Elvira and so it is only Edith who has the power to get rid of the ghost, which she does by singing the song *Always* by Irving Berlin.

> *Hamlet*: My father – methinks I see my father.
> *Horatio*: Where, my lord?
> *Hamlet*: In my mind's eye, Horatio.
>
> Hamlet, *Act 1, scene 2*

To Reveal – or Not to Reveal – The Ghost

Stephen King in *Danse Macabre* makes a useful distinction between terror and horror, suggesting that terror is what the mind imagines – the fear of the half-know, what may or may not be lurking behind the door – whereas horror is what the eye sees in plain sight – 'Oh look! It's a bog-eyed monster!' In some stories there is what King calls 'gross-out' and that leads to neither horror nor terror, but revulsion. King argues that, artistically, horror is best, next is terror and then revulsion.

Interestingly Roald Dahl says in his introduction to his collection of his favourite ghost tales, *Roald Dahl's Book of Ghost Stories* (1983), that the best ghost stories don't actually have ghosts in them, or at least you don't see the ghost as such but only the results of their actions. That's not actually the case in several of the tales in Dahl's collection – it's horses for courses after all – but his general point is a fair one because it's what you're imagining in your head that's often key to any spook tale. It's essentially the same point made by Stephen King, who also argues that in the movies the power of the mind to imagine is always more commanding than special effects.

It's worth mentioning in this context M.R. James and 'flash or stab' at the crescendo of the tale, where, for the briefest of moments, you see the phantom and sometimes the terrible deed it has done – 'His mouth was full of sand and stones, and his teeth and jaws were broken to bits. I only glanced once at his face'. And one look was enough for that narrator of *A Warning to the Curious*. Modern screenwriters, incidentally, refer to this element of a story as 'the kick', but it's a dramatic moment you could argue going way back to ancient Greek theatre. Violence, murder and sex were not permitted on the Athenian stage. However, the consequences of murder, the dead bodies of those killed in the play, were allowed to be seen, if briefly, via the *ekkyklêma*, which was a platform rolled out from the *skene*, the building behind the playing area where masks were changed. M.R. James would probably have been aware of this tradition, yet perhaps it's more the reticent nature of his narrators which keeps the description of the supernatural encounters within a certain limit. That said, *The Diary of Mr. Poynter* does have an extended crescendo, as does my homage to M.R. James, *The Portrait of a Looking-Glass*.

Miles Morecroft, a lecturer at Claverley Manor's conference symposium *The Ghosts of Many Worlds*, offers a talk on the corporeal nature or otherwise of ghosts, entitled 'Now You See Me, Now You Don't'. His lecture covers among other things whether or not ghosts can make noises with their footsteps or leave behind imprints. This you can read in Appendix III. The conclusion Morecroft comes to is that Victorian supernatural fiction required the ghost to have some degree of physical form or at least be capable of some kind of physical act.

Is it possible to have a ghost story with a haunting but no actual ghost and no outside human agency? Well, Ruth Rendell's *A Bad Heart* published in 1994 gets close. What's curious about this tale is that it mirrors to some degree the early part of the plot of *Macbeth*, where Duncan is murdered at the residence of the Macbeths. Story theorists, incidentally, call this technique 'textual or mythical infra-narrative'. In *A Bad Heart* the visitor is called Duncan, obliged to stay at the home of a husband and wife who, for complicated back story reasons, would be better off if he were no longer around. References to *Macbeth* abound, with quotes and names, and it's established early on that it's the only play the three of them ever saw together. Anyway, as Duncan tries to sleep he becomes fixated on the play and develops an obsession that the couple are out to kill him. I won't say what happens in the end, but let's just say Rendell's tale is one that very literally is not for the faint hearted.

> For the ghost story a slight haze of distance is desirable. 'Thirty years ago,' 'Not long before the war,' are very proper openings.
> *M.R. James, from the Introduction to the V.H. Collins edition* Ghosts and Marvels *(1924)*

Setting – Time

The Gothic tradition of the ghost story was that it should be set in the past. 'Thirty years ago' is the phrase which begins the tale told in Sheridan Le Fanu's *The Haunted House in Westminster* (1872) and perhaps this is what M.R. James was thinking of with his 'thirty years ago' observation in his introduction to *Ghosts and Marvels*. James goes on the say that 'on the whole (though not a few instances might be quoted against me) I think that a setting so modern that the ordinary reader can judge of its naturalness for himself is preferable to anything antique.' James's point is 'to allow the reader to identify himself with the patient' and that the reader of a tale set too far in the past falls 'into the positions of the mere spectator.'

But even in his own work there's no hard and fast rule. Some of his tales are set in the past, often with the date stated in the first paragraph – 1883 in the case of *Canon Alberic's Scrapbook* (written between 1892 and 1893), 1811 in *Lost Hearts* (also written between 1892 and 1893) and as far back as 1730 in *The Residence at Whitminster* (first published in 1919). Others such as *'Oh, Whistle, and I'll Come to You, My Lad'*, *Casting the Runes* and *A View from a Hill* have what appear to be contemporary settings. My M.R. James homage, *The Portrait of a Looking-Glass*, follows the 'thirty years ago' advice, for those are the first words of the story. That said, the actual writing of the tale, which is a tale in itself, is happening right in the here and now of the narrator.

Charles Dickens understood the need to identify 'with the patient', as M.R. James has it, and that's perhaps why he set his 1843 *A Christmas Carol* in the contemporary world, aka 'The Hungry Forties', reflecting the dire economic situation of the period. And as one of the charity collectors says, Christmas time is chosen 'because it is a time, of all others, when Want is keenly felt, and Abundance rejoices.' Christmas Eve is also the night before a religious festival, when ghosts were thought to be most active, and since it's the anniversary of Marley's death seven years previously it's the perfect night for a ghostly visitation. Dickens didn't invent the ghost story at Christmas but *A Christmas Carol* certainly set a trend. Outside the snow is falling, but within all sit gathered around a blazing fire waiting for the tale to commence... *Marley was dead: to begin with...* Oh, and what a great opening line, because you know from the start that this Marley guy won't be staying dead for long...

You could fill a book with the titles of Christmas ghost stories alone, but a few I would recommend, some funny and charming, others menacing and deadly, are John Kendrick Bang's *The Water*

Ghost of Harrowby Hall (1920), Rosemary Timperley's *A Christmas Meeting* (1951), Bithia Mary Crocker's *Number Ninety* (1895), H.R. Wakefield's *Lucky's Grove* (1940), Charlotte Riddell's *A Strange Christmas Game* (1868) and Frank R. Stockton's tender tale *Old Applejoy's Ghost* (1900).

Aside from Christmas Eve there is another evening in the year when ghosts are thought to enjoy a good night out and that is the eve of All Saints, or Halloween, and you'll find examples in Mrs Henry Wood's *Reality or Delusion* (1868) and Edith Nesbit's *Man-size in Marble* (1887), though it's the eve of All Souls in George MacDonald's *Uncle Cornelius His Story* (1869).

New Year's Eve is the night when life and its transitional nature are thrown into sharp focus. In storytelling, it often functions either as a deadline or a marker of psychological change.

Movies especially use New Year celebrations as a backdrop because of the contrast it offers between those who are enjoying the party and those who are miserable. There are fewer ghost tales set at New Year than Christmas, but two of note are E.F. Benson's redemptive tale *How Fear Departed From the Long Gallery* (1911) and H.R. Wakefield's *'Look Up There!'*, which features Gauntry, a house where no-one is supposed to have spent the night of New Year's Eve for three hundred years. It's also perhaps worth mentioning a movie called *Repeat Performance* (1947), in which Sheila Page kills her husband on New Year's Eve, but then wishes she could relive 1946 and so avoid the mistakes that led to his death. Not exactly a ghost story in the traditional sense, but it does have a supernatural element of sorts.

As well as Halloween, Christmas and New Year, there are of course those tales where people just happen to turn up on the night when the dead return, as in Robert Aickman's *Ringing the Changes*, where a young couple arrive in Holihaven on the night when the ringing of bells summons the dead to dance with the living. And real spook fest it is!

> 'We are the stones of a living fabric.'
> *The High Priest of the Assembly of Dead Builder and Dead Victims in Grant Allen's* Wolverden Tower

Setting – Place

Currently without a tenant. An absurdly low rent. Servants who refuse to stay the night. A previous occupant who came to sticky end. These aren't exactly the requirements of a haunted house, but ghost story writers repeatedly make use them in their tales. And appropriate names helps. If there were prizes for such things I'd give them to 'Chillingsworth', the inherited property in Gertrude Atherton's *The Bell in the Fog*, 'Pit End', the hamlet in Amelia B. Edwards's *Was it an Illusion?* and 'Brickett Bottom', the narrow glen in Amyas Northcote's tale of the same name.

In the Gothic tradition hauntings went on mainly in abbeys with overgrown graveyards and castles with tall towers, but over years there's been a bit of downsizing. The castle of Sir Walter Scott's *The Tapestried Chamber* (1828) and the manor house of Mary Elizabeth Braddon's *At Chrighton Abbey* (1871) have given way to Ralph Adams Cram's *No. 252 Rue M. le Prince* (1895) and O. Henry's *The Furnished Room* (1904). By the Edwardian era the typical setting of a ghost tale was a rented property. You could even say that the haunted holiday-let is to E.F. Benson what the supernatural ancient artefact was to M.R. James. Think here of *Home, Sweet Home*, *The Corner House*, *The Temple*, *The Gardener*, *The House with the Brick-Kiln* and *Roderick's Story*.

An important development in the ghost tale has been to make the haunted place not just background setting, but an active player in the tale, as in Shirley Jackson's *The Haunting of Hill House* (1959) and Stephen King's *The Shining* (1977). Early examples of a house having some sort of human-like capability can be found in Edith Wharton's 1910 tale *Afterward*, where the narrator says 'the house knew' and the library 'could have borne witness'. Ellen Glasgow's *The*

Shadowy Third is narrated by a very down to earth nurse, who has the vivid impression that 'the old house was listening,' a line picked up by Miss Osborne when she does a candle lit reading of that tale in '*I Was Once a Haunted House*'.

But the haunted place needn't always be made of brick and mortar. There's the ghost-on-the-road, as in Ambrose Bierce's *The Moonlit Road* (1907), Richard Middleton's *On the Brighton Road* (1912) and more recently Nicole D. Sconiers's *A Bird Sings By the Etching Tree* (2023), which is one of the tales in *Out There Screaming*, Jordan Peele's anthology of new horror stories by black writers. There's also the Ann Bridge ghost tale *The Buick Saloon* (1931), where it's the car that's haunted. Nowadays your ghost can pretty much haunt anywhere they like and in *Visiting Hattie* it's Adam and Calvin's downstairs toilet. However, I have yet to find a ghost tale set in a nudist colony or a fish and chip shop in Scarborough or a ghost that haunts an air conditioning unit or condom. As to why this is the case, well, I'll let others draw their own conclusions.

> 'He was dressed in the costume of a bygone period; his hair was powdered, and round his wrists there were ruffles of lace.'
>
> *From Charlotte Riddell's* A Strange Christmas Game, *first published in* THE BROADWAY *in 1868.*

How Shall I Go A-Haunting?

'What shall I wear?' Well, a ghost has to decide. Logic might suggest that a soul, if that's what a ghost is, would have no need of clothes and therefore any apparition should go naked. Yet most ghosts seem somewhat bashful and so present themselves either wearing a shroud or winding-sheet, or in the clothes they died in or were known for in life. And we mustn't forget all those chains.

It should be said the long chains worn by Marley's ghost weren't an invention of Dickens. Dickens noted in *A Christmas Tree* (1850) that the ghosts in haunted houses were 'reducible to a very few general types and classes; for, ghosts have little originality, and "walk" in a beaten track,' adding that when a ghost is about you may hear the 'haunted sound of a spinning-wheel, or a hammer, or a footstep, or a cry, or a sigh, or a horse's ramp, or the rattling of a chain.' However, Francis Grose in *A Provincial Glossary* (1787) wrote that chains were 'the accoutrements of foreign spectres,' and stipulated 'English Spirits are free.' So where does this chain thing come from?

Pliny the Younger, 61AD-c.113AD, wrote hundreds of letters to his friend Lucius Licinius Sura, 247 of which survive. Letter 27 of *Book 7* features the story of the philosopher Athenodorus Cananites, who, haunted by a ghost rattling chains, followed the apparition to the courtyard where it disappeared. Next day, Athenodorus went to the magistrates who ordered that particular spot to be dug up – and underneath were found bones intertwined with chains. Had a living man been bound to prevent escape? Or were the chains put around the corpse of a wrong 'un in order to keep its spirit from roaming? Whatever the reason, the bones were buried at public expense and the ghost was never seen again. It seems likely Dickens knew of this tale and developed chains into a kind of afterlife punishment. Rattling chains also feature in Oscar Wilde's *The Canterville Ghost*, but since have rarely featured in ghost stories, except in parody.

Apart from what to wear, there's also the question of how a ghost ought to move. In R.S. Hawker's 1867 tale *The Botathen Ghost* the spectre 'floated along the field like a sail upon a stream, and glided past the spot where we stood, pausing'. The apparition is even compared to what ancient writers describe as lemures, who 'swoon along the ground, neither marking the sand nor bending the herbage.' But all options are open. In Charlotte Riddell's 1882 story *The Open Door* (not to be confused with Margaret Oliphant's tale of the same title) there is a ghost that fights like a wildcat, 'shifting her body as though she had not a bone in it.' Mary Louisa Molesworth's *The Story of the Rippling Train* (1887) has a phantom 'which came always rippling in, till at last it began to rise as it still came on, and I saw that the figure, a tall graceful woman's figure, was slowly advancing, backwards of course, into the room... it was not like ordinary walking.' Later a living person enters, passing through the ghost 'as you may walk through a wreath of mist or smoke.'

> 'The guest' always sleeps in the haunted chamber on Christmas Eve; it is his perquisite.
> *Jerome K. Jerome's* Told After Supper *(1891)*

Tropes of the Trade

By the late nineteenth century the tradition of the ghost story at Christmas had so many accepted conventions that Jerome K. Jerome was able to take a playful aim at them in his 1891 comic tale *Told After Supper*. In addition to those spooks who like to walk the earthy plane on Christmas Eve, Jerome lists several other categories of ghosts, including those who celebrate 'the anniversary of the hanging of someone's grandfather', those 'who never give the parish a single night's quiet until someone has paid for a first-class funeral for him', not forgetting the omen ghost – 'He does love prophesying a misfortune, does the average British ghost.' In *Told After Supper* Jerome also mocks the convention of the story-within-the-story: 'Do not ask me how it is I recollect his own exact words – whether I took them down in shorthand at the time, or whether he had the story written out, and handed me the MS afterwards for publication in this book, because I should not tell you if you did. It is a trade secret.'

Sometimes story tropes and literary conventions become so well-known, formulaic and commonplace that they become clichéd and open to parody. Yet tropes get used in stories because they work and are popular. As Samuel Goldwyn famously told his movie writers when looking for the next hit, 'Let's have some new clichés.' Sounds oxymoronic, but when putting a story together there is some truth in what he says, for a genre plot requires certain story beats because that's simply how it needs to be constructed.

An obvious story beat at the beginning of a ghost tale is some sort of warning or interdiction. If it's a haunted house tale this will often come from a servant, as in the case of the housekeeper in *The*

House and the Brain ('Few ever stayed a second night') and *Mrs Marjorum At Chrighton Abbey* ('Do you know, Miss Sarah, that the gates of the north quadrangle have been locked and barred for the last forty years, and that no one ever goes in there except through the house.') Cautioning establishes the jeopardy and the risks that will follow if warnings are ignored. However, there would be no story if it weren't for inquiring minds that lead people astray. As the narrator of *An Eddy on the Floor* writes, 'It was as if, swelling in the silent hours, the tumour of curiosity had come to a head, and in a moment it was necessary to operate upon it.' And the cost is usually a close encounter, sometimes deadly, with the spook.

Another popular trope in the ghost tale is the claim that the story is factual. 'The circumstances I am about to relate to you have truth to recommend them.' So begins Amelia Edwards's 1864 tale *The Phantom Coach* (also known as *The North Mail*). Starting with an assertion of a ghost tale's veracity goes way back to Daniel Defoe's *The Apparition of Mrs Veal* (1706), which begins with a preface saying that the story 'was sent by a gentleman, a justice of the peace, at Maidstone, in Kent, and very intelligent person.' Defoe, a journalist by trade, understood that if any news item is to be believed it needs to be vouched for. And the fascinating background behind this supposedly true tale can be found in Roger Clarke's excellent book *A Natural History of Ghosts* (2012).

There's an assertion of truth in the opening lines of Edith Nesbit's 1887 tale *Man-size in Marble*, yet here there is the caveat that it will probably not be accepted as such: 'Although every word of this story is as true as despair, I do not expect people to believe it'. But Mary Louisa Molesworth's *The Story of the Rippling Train*, published in the same year, might suggest this technique was becoming overused because there's an opening exchange where one character notes, somewhat dismissively, 'They're all "authentic", really vouched for, only you never see the person who saw or heard or felt the ghost. It is always somebody's cousin or friend's friend.'

Apart from simply saying so, a neat way of making a ghost tale appear factual is to pack it with detail, a technique used extensively by Sheridan Le Fanu. The title *The Authentic Narrative of the Ghost of a Hand* is itself a claim to truth, but when Sheridan Le Fanu writes about the Tiled House also being spelt Tyled House he's saying to the reader, 'Look at the careful research I've done into this place.' Only he hasn't; he's making it up. But it's often the historical niceties and minutia which are so important in making tales appear credible that makes them so disturbing. Just ask M.R. James.

Writers have also found it a useful ploy, especially with first time ghost seers, to put at the top of their tale a reference to an illness or the need for a quiet convalescence. You'll find this in Eileen Bigland's *The Lass with the Delicate Air* (1952) and Ann Bridge's *The Buick Saloon* (1931). In Robert W. Chambers's *The Bridal Pair* (1902) it's there in the opening line where an advisor says, 'If I were you, I should take three months' solid rest.' What illness often suggests is some sort of recent breakdown, thus setting up the hauntee as someone of a nervous disposition. And it's such people, of course, who traditionally have been perceived and cited as ghost seers. In E.F. Benson's *The Face* (1924) it is, ironically, the doctor's suggestion of a quiet time away for a woman troubled by seemingly veridical dreams that results in her going to the very place where the ghost she dreams of will find her.

One challenge for any ghost story writer is to come up with original ways of describing those crepuscular shapes of twilight. Finding new modifiers for darkness and shadows ain't that easy when past writers have already used up 'grasping', 'furtive', 'wavering', 'uncertain', 'pulsating', 'encroaching', 'germinating', 'creeping', 'flaunting', 'distorting' and 'enveloping'. So hats off to Lord Edward Bulwer-Lytton in *The House and the Brain* (1859) for 'It was a Darkness shaping itself forth from the air in very undefined outline' and George MacDonald in *Uncle Cornelius His Story* (1869) for 'I thought, in the first interval of unreason, that it was a shadow from my own horse, but reminded myself the next moment that there could be no shadow where there was no light.'

One way of bringing newness into a ghost tale is to introduce contemporary technology. For example, the murdered Ethel in H.R. Wakefield's *That Dieth Not* (1928) manifests herself first in a telephone call, next via a wireless broadcast, and after that while the murderer is at the cinema watching a Charlie Chaplin film. Here Ethel takes over the movie, putting herself quite literally in the frame. Another tale which makes a clever ghostly use of the telephone is E.F. Benson's *The Dance* – 'There came a little goat-like laugh, just audible, and then a voice. "Settled in comfortably, dear boy?" it asked. "I'll look in on you before long".'

> I suppose I must have fallen asleep; I hope so, but I fear, for all that followed was startlingly real – so real that now sitting here in the broad, full sunlight of the morning, I cannot in the least believe that it was all sleep.
>
> *16 May diary entry by Jonathan Harker in Bram Stocker's* Dracula *(1897)*

The Twilight Chamber

On the night of 7 March 1890, Bram Stoker had a bad dream and jotted down on some notepaper '*Young man goes out – sees girls – one tries to kiss him not on lips but throat – Old Count interferes – rage & fury diabolical – This man belongs to me – I want him*.' Later, Stocker apparently told his son Noel that such nightmares had been the source of *Dracula* and one found itself relived in fictional form in the diary entry of Jonathan Harker.

In *The Step*, E.F. Benson writes about that 'twilight chamber' of the brain that is 'half-way between waking and sleeping.' It's a place writers know well, for they are often dependant on it for their stories. Stephen King in his foreword to his short story collection *Night Shift* says that the horror writer is at his best when not quite asleep and not quite awake, when dreams seems real and reality is more like a dream. He talks as well about that world between the conscious and sub-conscious, where allegory and images most naturally occur. And for Stephen King, horror stories, what he calls his 'fearsomes', are packed, like dreams, with fantasy visions that connect and resonate with our deep anxieties and perplexing paranoias.

It's in dreams that ghosts so often make themselves known and a classic example is the E.F. Benson story *The Face.* Dreaming is a motif that runs through many E.F. Benson tales, where they often become real or act as a warning. Think here of *The Room in the Tower, The Other Bed, The Bus-Conductor* (one of the stories in the classic Ealing film *Dead of Night*) and *Pirates* – 'I have dreamed this before, and then I woke and found myself elderly and alone again, but this time it is real!'

The idea of dreams becoming reality is also in *The Mysterious Sketch* by Emile Erckmann (1822-1899) and Alexandre Chatrian (1826-1890). A painter awakes at one o'clock in the morning and immediately starts drawing a courtyard, only it turns out to be a place where a real murder took place and when the sketch is seen by the authorities the artist is arrested. He tries to explain that the image came from a dream, but it is only when he draws the murderer he saw at the scene on his cell wall that the real killer is identified and the psychic sketcher is saved.

Then there's that oft told tale of a person who dreams of a close relative, only to receive a message the next day informing them that the loved one has died. Such a scenario features in Perceval Landon's *Thurnley Abbey* and Henry James's *The Way It Came*, published in 1896 but which he renamed *The Friends of the Friends* in 1909 as he thought the original title a little colourless.

Yakumo Koizumi (1850–1904), born Patrick Lafcadio Hearn, suggested that the fear of ghosts, as well as our belief in them, had its origins in dreams. He says in *Nightmare-Touch*, 'It is a peculiar fear. No other fear is so intense; yet none is so vague.' And perhaps it's the vagueness of dreams which allows them to be the catch-all explanation when someone claims to see a ghost, as when Mrs Marjorum says to Sarah in *At Chrighton Abbey*, 'You've dropped off in your chair before the fire, and had a dream, that's it.'

But why shouldn't a ghost in a dream be real? Shakespeare's ghosts came in dreams, but that wouldn't have stopped his audience from believing that they were true. Julius Caesar haunted Brutus in a dream and so did all those ghosts who disturb the sleep, but not the conscience, of the murderous Richard the Third.

> In his leisure hours Dr. Teesdale was a considerable student of the occult, for like most advanced and proficient physicians, he clearly recognised how narrow was the boundary of separation between soul and body.
>
> *From E.F. Benson's* The Confession of Charles Linkworth *(1912)*

Who's Who in the Ghost Tale

Spook tales don't just need ghosts and ghost seers, but also people who will deny them, conjure them, refuse to stay in the same house as them and ultimately send them back to where they belong.

Let's start with the occultist, who uses spells or some sort of paraphernalia to conjure up spirits. Dabblers sometimes get away with it, but if they are driven by desire to usurp the natural order, the occultist usually comes a cropper. One of the most remarkable is Apuleius Charlton in H.R. Wakefield's *A Black Solitude,* who is described as a 'psychological freak' and the last survivor of the Mauve decade. The idea that it's the homosexual male who sees ghosts goes way back to Reginald Scot's *The Discovery of Witchcraft*, which is discussed in the lecture 'Transgressional Queer Sex and the Victorian Spook' given at Claverley Manor. Black magic, séances and occultism notably feature in several E.F. Benson stories, including *Spinach*, *At Abdul Ali's Grave*, '*And the Dead Spake–*', *Outside the Door* and *The Thing in the Hall*. Had his father lived long enough to read them, such subject matter may well have led to interesting exchanges over Sunday lunch as Edward White Benson was for many years Archbishop of Canterbury.

At the opposite end of the spectrum there are the sceptics, who uses terms such as 'bosh', 'bunkum' and 'humbug'. Often sceptics are from the medical profession and the one in Margaret Oliphant's *The Open Door* is very pleased with himself when the ghost doesn't appear. 'It is just the same with tables and all other kinds of ghost apparatus; a sceptic's presence stops everything,' says Doctor

Simpson. Yet when the ghost does manifest itself 'the scoffer could scoff no more. Light touched his own face, and showed a very perplexed countenance.' Simpson clings to the explanation of 'phonetic disturbances' and 'ventriloquism' but he's convincing no one. Not even himself.

There are many cases where the sceptic is challenged to spend a night in a room or house said to be haunted. Think here of William Hope Hodgson's *The Whistling Room* and Ralph Adam Cram's *No. 252 Rue M. le Prince*. H.G. Wells's *The Red Room* features a room with a reputation for it. Candles are mysteriously blown out and 'the shadows seemed to take another step towards me.' But our sceptic isn't convinced and argues that what really haunts the room is man's inner fear – 'Fear that will not have light nor sound, that will not bear with reason, that deafens and darkens and overwhelms.' A score draw, you might say, between haunted room and doubting Thomas.

Sceptics in spook tales offer an array of explanations for the ghost, ranging from the scientific to the sociological. Scrooge puts the ghostly vision of Marley down to something he'd eaten, 'undigested bit of beef, a blot of mustard, a crumb of cheese, a fragment of an underdone potato', as does Warder Draycott in *The Confession of Charles Linkworth* and the narrator of Sheridan Le Fanu's *An Old House in Aungier Street*, who says, 'What of that? Was this singular apparition – as full of character as of terror – therefore the creature of my fancy, or the invention of my poor stomach? Was it, in short, subjective (to borrow the technical slang of the day) and not the palpable aggression and intrusion of an external agent?' A trick of the light and the mist is a popular explanation for 'the White Lady' phenomenon and then there are shadows, drugs, hallucinations and that old stand-by 'a skinful of port' alluded to in Vincent O'Sullivan's *When I Was Dead* (1905).

In Sceptics' Corner in '*I Was Once a Haunted House*' some rather fantastical explanations are offered by scientists, among them ocular trauma, magnetism in rocks and electrically-charged particles that are emitted at the moment of someone's death. Then there are all those legends of ghosts discussed in Roger Clarke's book *A Natural History of Ghosts* that were probably covers for poachers in woods and smugglers in caves invented in part to scare people away. On the other hand, there's *Fisher's Ghost* (1859) by John Lang, based on a real case where interest in a supposed ghost sighting led to the uncovering of an actual killer. The story originated with the disappearance on 17 June 1826 of an English-born Australian farmer from Campbelltown named Frederick Fisher whose murdered body was discovered where his ghost was said to have pointed.

E.F. Benson offers many speculative metaphysical explanations for the supernatural in his stories: 'In reality there is no "me", no "you", no "it". Everything is part of the one and only thing which is life' (*The Man Who Went Too Far*); 'How inextricable is the interweaving between mind, soul, life – call it what you will – and the purely material part of the created world' (*Outside the Door*); 'There's eternity outside Time: Time is a sort of mist lying around us. Now and then the mist clears, and then – how shall I express anything so simple? – then we look down on Time, like a little speck of an island below us, quite clear, future and past and present, and awfully small' (*The Bed by the Window*).

On a more prosaic note, the Irish Terrier in E.F. Benson's *The Room in the Tower* is described as one of those dogs who is bristling with rage 'as if he was ready to spring at something.' Dogs are known for their sudden and inexplicable barking, and while this probably comes from heightened senses – feeling changes in atmospheric pressure and hearing high-pitched sounds – it does often seem as if they have spotted some sort of supernatural phenomenon. Much is made in '*I Was Once a Haunted House*' of Mrs Jesop's barking dog and the somewhat patronising Professor F.R. Curtis puts together a list of supposedly ghost sensitive dogs, however a few were missed off, including the keeper's dog in R.H. Benson's *Father Macclesfield's Tale* (R.H. Benson being the younger brother of E.F. Benson and who became a Catholic priest) and Margaret's beloved dog Sheen, which in Lady Cynthia Asquith's '*God Grante That She Lye Still*' turns against her as she begins to be possessed by the 'she' who should have lay still in her grave. Cats, incidentally, feature as ghost seers in fewer stories than dogs, but the cat Spooner is a key player in Eleanor Farjeon's 1952 tale of the same name.

Dogs sensing the as yet unseen supernatural visitor functions as a way of setting up strangeness and danger before the ghost or phantom is actually encountered. Horses too seem to have an instinct for danger and a popular scene in a vampire story is when a horse balks and refuses to go further. A variation on this trope is when Sir Laurence Olivier's Van Helsing, in the film *Dracula* (1979), investigates the grave of his daughter, who he suspects is a vampire, and the horse starts stomping the ground with its hoof and then runs away in terror.

Oh, and a special mention here for moths. In E.F. Benson's *The Dust-Cloud*, *Expiation* and *The Outside Door*, the hovering and flicking moths are merely disconcerting, but in Robert W. Chambers's *The Messenger*, where they are described as 'Death's Messenger', they act as harbingers of death, as they do as well in Tom Hood's *The Shadow of a Shade* where 'these little fellows emit little drops of a red-looking fluid at certain seasons, and sometimes so plentiful that the superstitious think it is a shower of blood.' I have heard anecdotally that certain actors are superstitious about moths in theatres and perhaps that's not surprising as moths, like actors, know how to find a spotlight and fluttering wings can distract. With this and the harbinger superstition in mind, it seemed therefore appropriate to include a moth in my theatre tale, *The Ghost Light*.

> Being an extract from the singular journal of
> JOHN M'ALISTER RAY, student of medicine
> *The words that introduce* The Captain of the 'Polestar' *by Arthur Conan Doyle*

Narrative Design

E.M. Forster made the famous observation in *Aspects of the Novel* that the king died and then the queen died may be called a story, but when the king dies and then the queen dies of grief, well, now you have a plot because a causal connection has been made between the two events. However, what Forster didn't say was how that tale should be told – from the perspective of the prince, a rival king in another land, or for that matter the court jester. And should the tale be told with the benefit of hindsight or as if it's happening right now? Are the events to be presented as a first person narration, in the third person (what theorists call the assumed author), or even second person, where you the reader are directly addressed as an involved character?

Then there's the question of whether the tale is imparted exclusively through narrative description with occasional dialogue, or might the whole thing be told through letters or emails or even exclusively direct speech? All these are important questions, not least because the writer must come up with answers well ahead of any actual narrative composition and together these choices make up what is narrative design.

In *The Captain of the 'Polestar'*, the journals of John M'Alister Ray are introduced at the top of the narrative by a person unnamed, and this is a technique I've used in *The Strange Case of the Unaccountable Shadow*, though their identity is revealed at the end. Diaries and journals that are found have the advantage from the very start that any outcome is possible. The fate of the 'Polestar' is always in doubt, because it may be that the journal of the ship's young doctor was discovered years after that frozen ship became its crew's grave. Another point is that handwritten or official documents add a degree of authenticity to a tale.

Strictly speaking the epistolary form refers to those narratives written as letters ('epistolary' comes from the Latin *epistula* meaning 'a written communication'). Nowadays, however, epistolary has come to mean a story presented through any form of first person record or communication, including letters, journals, diaries, emails or even WhatsApp messages. It's letters that tell the tale, for example, in Rhoda Broughton's *The Truth, the Whole Truth, and Nothing but the Truth* (1886) and William Fryer Harvey's *The Clock*, though with the latter it's as a single letter to a friend. F.G Loring's *The Tomb of Sarah* (1900) is presented in diary form with a short paragraph of introduction.

As said, letters do sometimes play a narrative role in more

standard ghost tales in that at the end of the tale they are often used as a way of revealing the back story of the ghost. For example, Amelia B. Edwards's *Was it an Illusion?* (1881) and Bernard Capes's *An Eddy on the Floor* (1899). It's a structural device that works well in written fiction, but is less successful in movies, where audiences tend not to like too many explanations following the climax encounter.

Of course writers have many narrative design options open to them. Elizabeth Gaskell's *The Old Nurse's Story* (1852) is presented as a direct address to her young wards and is technically more a dramatic monologue than a literary first person narrative, though it is very long and the children listening would need to keep still for quite a while to hear it all. H.R. Wakefield's *The Nurse's Tale* is similar, except there are exchanges between the nurse and the children, but the important point is that both tales are presented exclusively in direct speech, without any outsider narrator description.

It's worth noting before moving on that a relatively recent development in the ghost story is where the ghost is the first person narrator. This is the case with G.W. Stonier's *The Memoirs of a Ghost* (1947), Jenn Ashworth's *Dinner for One* (2014) and Louis de Bernières's *This Beautiful House* (2009).

A popular narrative structure for a ghost story is the framing device of the story-within-a-story. The classic example of this is the armchair ghost tale told in front of a roaring fire after an evening meal, and you'll find variations of this format in Francis Marion Crawford's *The Upper Berth* (1894), Thomas Street Millington's *No Living Voice* (1872), Mary Louisa Molesworth *The Story of the Rippling Train* (1887) and Perceval Landon's *Thurnley Abbey* (1908). You might also add here Sheridan Le Fanu's *The Account of Some Strange Disturbances in Aungier Street* (1851), which talks of 'a circle of intelligent and eager faces, lighted up by a good after-dinner fire on a winter's evening, with a cold wind rising and wailing outside, and all snug and cosy within.' The advantage of a story-within-a-story is that it offers an opportunity for those listening to comment on the tale, including whether or not it's even true.

The veracity of a ghost story, and by association the storyteller, brings into play the idea of the 'unreliable narrator'. The unreliable narrator is a concept much talked about in the literary world, but it has its problems, for it's become a bit of a catch-all term that doesn't distinguish between the narrator whose deliberate intention is to mislead and the narrator who is imperfectly informed or naïvely misinterprets what they see. The latter might more reasonably be called a 'fallible narrator', where fallibility can include naivety, reticence, insanity, overt moral censorship, and obtuseness.

The key point is that the reader's evaluation and interpretation of events is usually at odds with the storyteller. And it's this which makes the unreliable/fallible narrator so popular in the literary world, for it's this discrepancy between the way the narrator sees things and the likely perspective and perceptions of the reader, who suspects that something else is going on, that creates irony in the narrative. The classic example in a ghost tale is Henry James's *The Turn Of The Screw* (1898), where a doctor presents the journal of a governess who believes she see ghosts, yet whose tone of writing suggests paranoia is an equally likely explanation. As is often said, with Henry James you are always one remove from certainty. But isn't that so often the case in life?

On the whole, ghost stories keep to what you may call traditional narrative designs, be they epistolary, first person, third person or direct speech. A rare example of a multiple perspective narrative, with presentations of three different points of view (with the ghost communicating, as it were, through a medium), can be found in Ambrose Bierce's *The Moonlit Road* (1907). It is also worth mentioning Oliver Onions' 1928 tale *John Gladwin Says...*, which is told from the point of view of one man, John Gladwin. What makes this tale so unusual is that it's a non-linear series of scenes and what you realise at the end is that what is being described are the images inside the mind of a dying man whose life is passing before him.

> 'Nothing is ever seen, nothing is heard. As far as I can find out, people just have the horrors there, and have them so bad they have to go to hospital afterwards.'
>
> *From* No. 252 Rue M. Le Prince
> *by Ralph Adams Cram*

Yes, But What is it About?

A common criticism I have heard of ghost stories is that they're not about anything. There's a haunted house, a suspenseful build-up, and eventually a ghostly encounter the hauntee either survives or doesn't. That's it. Such tales are spooky and diverting, but that's about all there is to them. Well, that may be true in some cases, but I'd say most writers, no matter what genre, would rarely write a story if they had nothing to say. And one of the best champions of the writer, and their intentions and purposes, is the masterful Stephen King.

Danse Macabre is King's fascinating treatise on the horror tale, which includes a section on the ghost story. He talks about what he calls 'phobic pressure points', and these, he says, apply to both the psychology of the individual and the broader anxieties of society. His theory is that when they are pushed and probed in horror fiction, they operate at a symbolic level that helps us understand and deal with our real and very deepest fears. King explores the fear of our own mortality, of the outsider, of the machine, of what's under the bed, of disfigurement, of the night, of secrets uncovered, of disease, of madness, of a bad death, of sex, of otherness, of isolation, of technology, of the animal within us, plus the fear of whatever it is that we individually fear, be it spiders, snakes, rats or whatever. As King puts it, 'You try to catch the madness in the bell-jar so you can cope with it a little better.' And it's easy to see how many of these fears tie in with the ghost story genre.

King acknowledges how there is a paradox in paying to feel uncomfortable, but for him horror tales are ultimately life enhancing because by showing the miseries of the damned they help rediscover the small joys of living. He also argues that those who refuse to engage with fantasy tales because they're not factual simply lack the 'muscles of the imagination'. Yet, says King, the idea of story must always be paramount over theme, symbol and message, or, as he puts it in typical Stephen King parlance: 'I like my stories without billboards.'

King's references are extraordinarily broad. He argues, for example, that *The Book of Job* is a 'classic horror' because its existential theme is that bad things happen to good people, highlighting the fact that like life, horror tales are often unfair and unjust and that we live in a tooth-and-claw world. Bringing us more up to date, King considers how the ghosts in the stories of Henry James and M.R. James so often reflect in some way the soul of those who behold them and in this context he sees Shirley Jackson's *The Haunting of Hill House* as a tale about how the sexual anxieties of Eleanor manifest themselves through the strange house she finds herself in. But surely these are the exception rather than the rule. I mean, you couldn't claim the same about Noël Coward's *Blithe Spirit*. Or could you? Is *Blithe Spirit* simply a silly supernatural comedy-of-manners or is something more complicated going on? *Blithe Spirit* creates a situation where a man encounters a former spouse whose sexual magnetism is clearly greater than that of the new wife. Sounds familiar? Well it should because that's exactly the same plot as Noël Coward's *Private Lives*. Sexual jealousy, fears of inadequacy when compared to a former lover are at the heart of both plays and it's a theme that's there too in other plays, notably *Design For Living*. Yes, *Blithe Spirit* may be a ghost tale, but it's very much about living people and their relationships.

Theme, suggests John Gardner in *On Becoming a Novelist* (1983), is simply another way of saying what the character's main problem is. And an example of this in the ghost tale is loneliness and grief. In Marie Belloc Lowndes's *The Unbolted Door* (1929), the ghost of a son lost in the Great War returns in order to reconcile his unhappy parents, in what is a tender tale of loss and acceptance. In fact there are many supernatural stories that don't aim to scare the living daylights out of you, but rather offer an insight and understanding into loneliness. And Marjorie Bowen's *The Crown Derby Plate*, A.M. Burrage's *Playmates* and Rudyard Kipling's *They* are fine examples.

All stories need disorder but the nature of the 'What if...' at the heart of many ghost tale allows the writer to explore ideas and situations which reality fiction couldn't allow. Take the ghost tales of Sheridan Le Fanu. It's true they are macabre, sensational, and occasionally voyeuristic, and, yes, they appeal to those of a prurient nature, but there's something else going on too. Often in a Sheridan Le Fanu tale the central character is an abuser of power who uses his social position for evil pleasure and personal gain. Such people were recognisable in Le Fanu's time and although it would be pushing it to say that his stories are polemic or political, they do use the dark secrets of the past as a way of exploring contemporary injustice. In such tales, the ghost is the literal past disturbing the present so that historic crimes and hidden sins can be exposed.

On a lighter note, ghost stories offer a way of looking at social and cultural changes as past and present collide with each other. Oscar Wilde's *The Canterville Ghost* is a comic example of this, where the clash is between the ancient and modern and the very contrasting cultures of Britain and America. Ghost tales can also be fables and most fables have a moral. W.W. Jacobs's *The Monkey's Paw* is a careful-what-you-wish-for morality tale. As the sergeant-major who carries it says the holy man who put a spell on it 'wanted to show that fate ruled people's lives, and that those who interfered with it did so to their sorrow.'

Arthur Miller used to say that as soon as he discovered what a play was about he would type it out in one sentence and then pin it to his typewriter to make sure that everything in the story was about that. And it's fair to say that most ghosts tales are about something other than ghosts. *The Story of Clifford House* explores sibling rivalry, Arthur Conan Doyle's *The Story of the Brown Hand* looks at colonialism and reparation, and Edith Nesbit's *In The Dark* digs deep into human psychosis ('He said I shouldn't be able to get rid of the body. And I can't get rid of it. I can't I can't.') And V.S. Pritchett's *A Story of Don Juan* (1941) is simply about hot sex. Read it to discover why it gives an entirely new meaning to the phrase 'laying the ghost'.

Writers often have overarching themes in their work. With Henry James it's identity, with Robert Louis Stevenson it's our dual nature, with Algernon Blackwood it's the natural world's capacity to unsettle us, with Margaret Oliphant it's the nature of spiritual redemption and with Robert Aickman it's simply the ever puzzling strangeness of life. E.F. Benson's tales I would say are harder to pin down but I would offer this observation from a character in *The Horror-Horn* as the Benson guiding principle – 'In us all I suppose looks some inherited germ of that ineffable bestiality, and who knows whether, sterile as it has apparently become in the course of centuries, it might not fructify again.' Benson was the archetypical Edwardian gentleman of impeccable good taste and manners, but read his stories and you'll find he knows the beast within.

> 'They who are most happy are they who have no story to tell.'
>
> *Anthony Trollope, Victorian novelist*

The Ghost Story Teller

When I was around seven years old and lived in a terraced house in Leeds, we had a damp cellar that had within it a brick enclosure, probably once used to store coal, blocking out any chance of light. It was, as they say, as dark as death. Perhaps I was a strange child but I would go down into that world of blackness and challenge myself with fear. Whatever lurked in the darkness would eventually come alive in my mind and I would then do a runner, often tripping myself up on the sharp edge of the steps and scraping my knee. Those scabs were the price I paid for my experiments with fright.

Was I crazy? I don't think so. Stephen King points out in his book *Danse Macabre* that human beings have a tendency to return to what frightens them and I think what I was doing was testing myself and in the process strengthening my resolve. But perhaps something else was going on too. My father's schizophrenia manifested itself as religious mania, for he truly believed that the voices he heard in his head were demons. And sometimes he saw these monsters too. One night he told me that the world was going to end and he could prove it by turning the grass blue. Of course the world didn't come to an end and the grass stayed green and I slowly came to realise he was mentally ill. I mention my father's situation in the context of the cellar story because a playwright once said to me, 'Has it ever occurred to you that what lurked in the darkness was your father's madness – and that's what you were frightened of and so wanted to control?' Hmm. Not sure. But I do think that in that dark damp cellar lay the genesis of my fascination with stories weird and wonderful.

My father, on his saner days, was a charming and funny man. And very bright. When I gave him an old computer he went inside its workings and, without any training, started analysing the coding. People say a writer needs a compost mind from which stories can sprout and grow. Perhaps that odd childhood of mine was ultimately his gift to me. A few hours on the psychiatrist's couch might lead to some answers but I've never sought that kind of analysis. I still think my fascination with ghost tales comes mainly from the movies I saw, plus television series like *Randall and Hopkirk (Deceased)* and *The Ghosts of Motley Hall*. And I doubt I would ever have written '*I Was Once a Haunted House*' had it not been for how, every Tuesday, I would run home from school to catch *Scooby Doo, Where Are You!*.

> He turned over the pages till his eye was caught by a marginal note: 'A Parable of this Unhappy Condition', and he thought he would see what aptitudes the author might have for imaginative composition.
>
> *From* Mr Humphreys and His Inheritance *by M.R. James*

Montague Rhodes James, Litt.D., Fellow of King's College, Cambridge

H.R. Wakefield directly references the ghost stories of M.R. James in *The Nurse's Tale*, where the nurse accuses her ward Gilbert of reading too many ghost books, adding that those of James gives her the creeps, and in *The Triumph of Death*, where the wicked Miss Pendleham insists her paid companion read her some stories by James. But why are the ghost tales of Montague Rhodes James – 'Monty' to his friends – so admired and respected by fellow ghost story writers? There are many ways of answering that question, but for me it's that his stories have the strange power to linger and stay with you, haunting, as it were, your mind long after you've finished reading. Yet exactly how he achieves this feat is annoyingly elusive.

So who was Monty?

M.R. James, Litt.D., Fellow of King's College, Cambridge, like many of his protagonists, was a crusty bachelor who lived in the enclosed world of academic life. He was a traditionalist, a devout Anglican, conservative by nature and resistant to change, and known for his dislike of radicalism and ideas. There's the oft reported incident, originally told by his colleague Nathaniel Wedd, of James catching two students discussing some philosophical point and saying, 'No thinking gentlemen, please.' What dominated his scholastic life was instead a fascination with ancient manuscripts and artefacts. Yet therein lies a paradox, for so often in his stories it's such objects from the past impinging upon the present that leads to the misfortune or even death for the over-curious antiquary.

Montague Rhodes James was born in 1862, went to Eton College in 1876, and then to King's College, Cambridge in 1882, where he graduated with Firsts. James's working life was spent exclusively in academia, whether working at the Fitzwilliam museum, or as Dean of King's or as Provost of Eton. James was known to be a very convivial companion, was friends with the Benson brothers, and was a member of the Chit-Chat Club founded in 1893, which was known for its witty and erudite conversation. It was at the Chit-Chat Club that James would read his ghost stories aloud by the light of a single candle. When James died the *Nunc Dimittus*, the night prayer, was sung in chapel.

As a child, Monty read and admired the tales of Sheridan Le Fanu and in later life edited an edition of his work. At Eton he read Walter Map's *De Nugis Curialium*, which featured stories of vampires and ghosts. James was known to enjoy bicycle rides and horseplay and ragging, plus church architecture and the lives of martyred saints. He was as well a good actor and mimic.

It is said that James had a fear of spiders, clammy touch and hair, yet all feature prominently in his tales. People have read into his stories a fear of the female sex, especially regarding the vagina dentata monster in *Casting the Runes* – 'He put his hand into the well-known nook under the pillow: only, it did not get so far. What he touched was, according to his account, a mouth, with teeth, and with hair about it, and, he declares, not the mouth of a human being.' Critics have found symbolic manifestations of homosexual anxiety in *'Oh, Whistle, and I'll Come to You, My Lad'*, where the sheet in the next bed comes alive and moves towards the bachelor, who, in the opening scene of the tale 'quivered' at the idea of sharing a room with a male colleague. Much has been speculated about James's sexuality, particularly his close friendship with his illustrator James McBryde, who died in 1904, aged thirty. Letters to McBryde used terms such as 'My dear boy' and 'Ever yours affectionately'.

But what about the ghost stories themselves? James knew well the Suffolk landscape (his family moved to Great Livermere soon after he was born) and several tales are set in the bleak landscape of the Suffolk coast. James knew its people, and would have been aware of their superstitious nature and esoteric interest in the supernatural. His servants, doorkeepers and innkeepers, such as Mr Collins, Mr Brown and John Hill, are particularly characterful, and their ways of speech, together with their malapropisms, are written phonetically into their dialogue. James always had a keen sense of place and atmosphere and was especially fond of Queen Ann houses and old churches.

M.R. James's prose is simple, direct, and often understated ('The night he passed is not one on which he looks back with any satisfaction'), yet there is as well a subtle dry humour ('Had not the landlord at this moment knocked at the door, it is probable that quite a long poem might have been laid before the reader'). His narrators, often first person but distanced in some way from the actual events of the tale, are selective in what they say ('It is not, however, relevant to my purpose to record his conversation') and sometimes inexact

('After taking some exercise – I forget exactly how or where – Anderson went back to the Golden Lion'). His story tellers are usually reticent and unwilling to say too much, and therefore there are often gaps left unexplained that the reader must fill in. It's rare, but occasionally his narrators drop into the use of the present tense.

Many narratives make use of various sources, for example *Count Magnus* and *The Stalls of Barchester Cathedral*, and James must have put in a lot of planning for them to work as well as they do. James tends to bring in an element of strangeness early in the tale, for example Mr Abney in *Lost Hearts* repeatedly asking Stephen how old he is on their first meeting or the early reference to keeping 'ghosts off' in *'Oh, Whistle, and I'll Come to You, My Lad'*. The introduction of strangeness, be it casual or otherwise, is an essential technique of the ghost tale in that it sets up and to some degree narratively justifies the supernatural manifestation that comes later in the tale. And James is particularly brilliant at pacing, building of menace and creating psychological unease that climaxes in that 'infinitesimal flash' which structurally he referred to as 'the stab'.

Recurring motifs include a believable setting; a solitary, sexless protagonist with scholastic expertise; nostalgia for a world long gone; obsessive curiosity; unsettling dreams; enclosed or claustrophobic spaces; the disturbance of something from the past impinging upon the present; supernatural guardians; the ignoring of warnings; a reckoning or punishment; the manifestation of a powerful force of demonic evil; a monster with claws and hair that grasps or grips, plus black magic, paganism and folklore.

Here are a few of Monty's own words of advice taken from various introductions and prefaces from editions of his ghost tales:

'The truth is, I suspect, that the genre is too small and special to bear the imposition of far-reaching principles... In fact, it is absurd to talk of them as rules; they are qualities which have been observed to accompany success.'

'I think that, as a rule, the setting should be fairly familiar and the majority of the characters and their talk such as you may meet or hear any day... Another requisite, in my opinion, is that the ghost should be malevolent or odious: amiable and helpful apparitions are all very well in fairy tales or in local legends, but I have no use for them in a fictitious ghost story.'

'Sex is tiresome enough in the novels; in a ghost story, or as the backbone of a ghost story, I have no patience with it.'

'Two ingredients most valuable in the concocting of a ghost story are, to me, the atmosphere and the nicely managed crescendo.'

'Here [referring to a ghost tale in *Wild Wales* by Norfolk novelist George Borrow (1803-81)] you have a story written with the sole object of inspiring a pleasing terror in the reader; and as I think, that is the true aim of a ghost story.'

'The reading of many ghost stories has shown me that the greatest successes have been scored by the authors who can make us envisage a definite time and place, and give us plenty of clear-cut and matter-of-fact detail, but who, when the climax is reached, allow us to be just a little in the dark as to the working of their machinery. We do not want to see the bones of their theory about the supernatural.'

When asked if he believed in ghosts, James said, 'I am prepared to consider evidence and accept it if it satisfies me.'

In the preparation of this summary I acknowledge indebtedness to Darryl Jones's book *M.R. James: Collected Ghost Stories*, Oxford University Press. His introduction and explanatory notes have proved indispensable and I would commend it highly.

> They seemed to belong to another age, an older age, an age when things spiritual were different from this of ours, less certain; an age when omens and witches were credible, and ghosts beyond denying.
>
> *From* The Red Room *by H.G. Wells*

Where Have all the Ghost Stories Gone?

Freud they say killed the ghost when he persuaded us that phantoms come not from without but from within. For Sigmund, all mental aberrations originate in the unconscious mind, and even the ultimate spook, God Himself, is really just a manifestation of the fear of an angry father on a grand scale. To put it simply, psychology and not the light of the dawn laid the ghost.

But there's also a social and political aspect to the decline of the ghost tale. After the Great War people had had enough of death, and although the likes of E.F. Benson and Lady Cynthia Asquith's editions of *The Ghost Book* certainly kept the ghost story going for a while, interest in it was in decline and after the Second World War it faded even more. Then there's the argument that every genre has its day. The ghost story had its glory hour in the Victorian and Edwardian era, so best leave it at that and enjoy the exceptional tales they passed on to us. I mean, it's not as though there'd be a stampede to buy *The Best Ghost Stories of the 1950s.* Well, perhaps, but why did the ghost tale flourish in the nineteenth century anyway?

The argument for the historical rise and fall of the ghost story goes like this. The ghost tale came into its own in the short story form and so was perfectly suited to the plethora of magazines and periodicals that were published in the Victorian era. And because educational standards were rising there were more child, and later adult, readers. As M.R. James said, 'The proper habitat of our game is the magazine, the annual, the periodical publication destined to amuse the family circle.' The short story form is impactful and arguably short is the most practical size for a ghost story which, if it were to go on for longer, might raise questions of credibility and believability. Of course the ghost story needs a fine writer and in the nineteenth century there were the undeniably talented pens of Charles Dickens, Elizabeth Gaskell, Robert Louis Stevenson, Rudyard Kipling, Edith Nesbit, Charlotte Riddell and Sir Arthur Conan Doyle, all of whom turned their hand to the ghost tale, and in so doing gave it a literary status that to be frank it has not held since.

Then there's the Victorian interest in all things weird and marvellous. It was a world where séances flourished, mesmerists prospered and phantasmagoria abounded. It's true that many people had moved from the countryside into a modern urban environment, but many clung on to the old beliefs and superstitions. And in this sense you could argue that Gothic tales of castles and abbeys acted as a kind of psychological and spiritual counterbalance to the Age of Reason and widespread industrialisation. Interestingly, the emerging urban middle classes became fascinated by all things supernatural and in 1882 this was legitimised by the forming of The Society for Psychical Research. Add to this the Victorian obsession with death – think of all that Dickensian funeral porn – and it's easy to see why the literary world took to the ghost. Only then came the twentieth century and the rise of the rationalist and scientific materialist, with views of the world where, after Darwin, Einstein and Freud, pretty much everything was explainable. Ghosts included.

You could say then that for the last hundred years or so what we've had is the ghost story without the ghost. As Elizabeth Bowen said in the introduction of *The Second Ghost Book* (1952), edited by Lady Cynthia Asquith, 'Ghosts have grown up.' Her point was that the modern age exploited the horror of what was latent in real life rather than the winding sheets and bones you may come across in castles and graveyards. You might add that modernist ghosts stories tend to be existentially disturbing rather than outright frighteners. And what they're about, or what even goes on in them, isn't always clear and so you have to look between the lines for meanings and understanding. An early example is Edith Nesbit's *The Shadow* (1905), a tale of implications rather than actualities, where what the shadow is, or what represents or projects, can't easily be put in words. A previous generation might have simply said 'sin', but that's a word modern readers eschew. Yet it's that very struggle to find meaning in its ambiguities which makes *The Shadow* such a brilliant tale – and one that lurks in your mind and stays with you long after you've put it down.

All that said, the one thing a straightforward supernatural story doesn't require is a rational explanation. There's no need for psychological angst or neurosis complexes. A ghost is a ghost – it's that simple. And that has certainly been my own attitude putting together this collection.

> 'The horror thriller offers the serious actor unique opportunities to test his ability to make the unbelievable believable.'
>
> *Vincent Price*

The Ghosts of the *Lanterna Magica*

The writing style of E.F. Benson's tales is far more cinematic than say that of M.R. James. For one thing Benson's dialogue reads like a screenplay, conversational and relaxed, but perhaps the main influence of the moving pictures are those scenes in Benson's stories that turn on the exchange of looks and glances that a movie director would call 'reaction shots'. In fact ghost stories written today tend to owe a debt more to the cinematic form than the wordy and sometimes overheated style of Sheridan Le Fanu. I'm thinking here of Jeanette Winterson's 2023 collection *Night Side of the River* and Jordan Peele's anthology of new writing from black authors in *Out There Screaming*.

It's certainly true that reading a creepy book by yourself can be scary, but fear is contagious and so the horror tale certainly suits the cinema. Yet literalness can be the enemy of horror in that the cinematic 'gross-out', to borrow Stephen King's phrase, can become laughable. And ghosts don't like being laughed at. But it's also true that, with honourable exceptions, the ghost tale now lives more in the cinema and television than in print. And in recent years the ghost story has been reinvented by screenwriters by adding aspects of another genre, for example, time travel in the movies *Last Night in Soho* and *Lost Christmas*, the sporting back story in *Field of Dreams*, riotous slapstick in *Ghostbusters*, the romantic drama in *Truly, Madly, Deeply* and the zany Vaudeville comedy of *Beetlejuice*. Ghosts have featured in classic television series such as *Twilight Zone* ('Night Call', 'The Hitch-Hiker', 'The Grave'), *Boris Karloff Presents* ('What Beckoning Ghost') and *Thriller* ('One Deadly Owner'). *The Avengers* also played with the haunted house concept in 'The House That Jack Built'. Ghosts, or what are thought of as ghosts, have been a regular feature of *Doctor Who*. In the classic *Doctor Who*, 'Day of the Daleks' begins with an investigation of what is believed to be a spectre, though it turns out to be time travel, and 'Ghost Light' has the setting of a Victorian haunted house. In *Doctor Who*'s modern era, 'The Unquiet Dead' is a Christmas ghost tale featuring Charles Dickens, where the supposed ghost is revealed to be an alien. There's also the television series *The Living and the Dead.*

A word here about the BBC supernatural anthology series *A Ghost Story for Christmas*, which aired from 1971-1978 and featured five stories by M.R. James, including *Lost Hearts,* which freaked me out as a child and still does. The majority of the episodes were directed by Lawrence Gordon Clark who had been inspired by Jonathan Miller's *'Whistle and I'll Come to You'* which had been made as part of the *Omnibus* arts and documentary series. Interestingly Miller's adaptation was filmed in black and white and owed much to expressionistic techniques. In recent years, the mantel of Lawrence Gordon Clark and Miller has been taken up by Mark Gatiss, whose adaptations of classic ghost stories are always a highlight of the BBC's Christmas schedule.

Television, Film Directing and Writing Credits

Several movies and television shows are mentioned in this essay and also in the lectures and the ghost stories, but without the details of their directors and screenwriters. Here then is a full listing of the films discussed and their directing and writing credits.

All of Us Strangers (2023) Director – Andrew Haigh. Screenplay – Andrew Haigh and Taichi Yamada.

Banquo's Chair (1959) An episode in Alfred Hitchcock Presents. Director – Alfred Hitchcock. Teleplay – Francis M. Cockrell and Rupert Croft-Cooke.

Beetlejuice (1988) Directed by Tim Burton. Screenplay by Michael McDowell and Warren Skaaren. Story by Michael McDowell and Larry Wilson.

Berberian Sound Studio (2012) Directed by Peter Strickland. Screenplay – Peter Strickland and Kephas Leroc.

Between Two Worlds (1944) Director – Edward A. Blatt. Screenplay – Daniel Fuchs and Sutton Vane.

The Birds (1963) Directed by Alfred Hitchcock. Screenplay – Evan Hunter. Based on the short story *The Birds* (1952) by Daphne du Maurier.

The Bishop's Wife (1947) Director Henry Koster. Writing Credits: Screenplay – Robert E. Sherwood and Leonardo Bercovici, based on the 1928 novel of the same name by Robert Nathan.
Bride of Frankenstein (1935) Directed by James Whale. Screenplay – William Hurlbut. Story by William Hurlbut and John L. Balderston. Based on the novel *Frankenstein* (1818) by Mary Wollstonecraft Shelley.
The Cat and the Canary (1939) Director – Elliott Nugent. Writing Credits: Screenplay – Walter de Leon and Lynn Starling. Based on the 1922 play of the same name by John Willard.
Cocaine Bear (2023) Directed by Elizabeth Banks. Screenplay – Jimmy Warden.
Coco (2017) Directors – Lee Unkrich and Adrian Molina. Writing Credits: Original Story – Lee Unkrich, Jason Katz, Matthew Aldrich and Adrian Molina. Screenplay – Adrian Molina and Matthew Aldrich.
Day of the Daleks (1972) An episode in the *Doctor Who* television series. Director – Paul Bernard. Writer – Louis Marka. Producer – Barry Letts.
Dead of Night (1945) Directors – Alberto Cavalcanti, Charles Crichton, Basil Dearden and Robert Hamer. Writing Credits: Screenplay – John Baines and Angus MacPhail with T.E.B. Clarke (additional dialogue). Original stories by H.G. Wells, E.F. Benson, John Baines and Angus MacPhail.
The Double Life of Veronique (1991) French title: *La double vie de Véronique*, Polish title: *Podwójne życie Weroniki*. Written and directed by Krzysztof Kieślowski.
Dr. Terror's House of Horrors (1965) Director – Freddie Francis. Screenplay – Milton Subotsky (founder of Amicus Productions).
Dracula (1979) Director – John Badham. Writing Credits: Screenplay W.D. Richter, from play by Hamilton Deane and John L. Balderston and based on the 1897 novel by Bram Stoker.
Enys Men (2022) Written and directed by Mark Jenkin.
Field of Dreams (1989) Director – Phil Alden Robinson. Writing Credits: Screenplay – Phil Alden Robinson, based on the 1982 novel *Shoeless Joe* by W.P. Kinsella.
The Fog (1980) Directed by John Carpenter. Screenplay – John Carpenter and Debra Hill.
Frankenstein (1931) Directed by James Whale. Screenplay by Garrett Fort and Francis Edward Faragoh, (also Robert Florey and John Russell, both uncredited) Story by Richard Schayer (scenario editor). Based on the 1818 novel *Frankenstein* by Mary Wollstonecraft Shelley and the 1927 play of the same name by Peggy Webling and John L. Balderston.
Get Out (2017) Written, directed and produced by Jordan Peele.
The Ghost and Mrs Muir (1947) Director – Joseph L. Mankiewicz. Screenplay – Philip Dunne. Based on the novel *The Ghost of Captain Gregg and Mrs. Muir* (1945) by R.A. Dick.
Ghost Light (1989) An episode in the *Doctor Who* series. Director – Alan Wareing. Writer – Marc Platt. Producer – John Nathan-Turner.

The Ghost Train (1941) Director – Walter Forde. Screenplay – J.O.C. Orton, Val Guest and Marriott Edgar. Based on the 1923 play of the same name by Arnold Ridley.
Ghostbusters (1984) Directed by Ivan Reitman. Screenplay – Dan Aykroyd and Harold Ramis.
The Ghosts of Berkeley Square (1947) Director – Vernon Sewell. Screenwriters – Caryl Brahms, S.J. Simon and James Seymour.
The Ghosts of Motley Hall (1976-1978) Creator – Richard Carpenter.
The Grave (1961) An episode in *The Twilight Zone* series. Written and directed by Montgomery Pittman.
The House That Jack Built (1966) An episode in *The Avengers* television series. Director – Don Leaver. Writer and series creator – Brian Clemens.
The Halfway House (1944) Directors – Basil Dearden and Alberto Cavalcanti. Screenplay – Denis Ogden, Angus MacPhail and Diana Morgan.
His House (2020) Director – Remi Weekes. Screenplay – Remi Weekes, Felicity Evans and Toby Venables.
The Hitch-Hiker (1960) An episode in *The Twilight Zone* television series. Director Alvin Ganzer. Teleplay – Rod Serling. Based on the 1941 radio play *The Hitch-Hiker* by Lucille Fletcher.
House of Mystery (1961) Written and directed by Vernon Sewell.
It's a Wonderful Life (1946) Director – Frank Capra. Writing Credits : Screenplay – Frances Goodrich, Albert Hackett and Frank Capra, with additional scenes by Jo Swerling, based on the 1943 short story *The Greatest Gift* by Philip Van Doren Stern.
Last Night in Soho (2021) Director – Edgar Wright. Writing Credits: Screenplay – Edgar Wright and Krysty Wilson-Cairns, story – Edgar Wright.
The Living and the Dead (2016) Created by Ashley Pharoah. Directors – Alice Troughton and Sam Donovan. Writers – Ashley Pharoah, Simon Tyrrell, Robert Murphy and Peter McKenna.
Lost Christmas (2011) Director – John Hay. Screenplay – John Hay and David Logan.
Lost Hearts (1973) part of the series *A Ghost Story for Christmas*. Written by Robin Chapman, produced by Rosemary Hill, and directed by the series' creator, Lawrence Gordon Clark. Based on the 1895 ghost story of the same name by M.R. James.
The Man Who Haunted Himself (1970) Directed by Basil Dearden. Screenplay – Basil Dearden, Michael Relph and Bryan Forbes. Based on novel *The Strange Case of Mr Pelham* (1940) by Anthony Armstrong.
Neither the Sea Nor the Sand (1972) also known as *The Exorcism of Hugh*. Directed by Fred Burnley. Written by Gordon Honeycombe (screenplay) and Rosemary Davies (additional dialogue). Based on the novel *Neither the Sea Nor the Sand* (1971) by Gordon Honeycombe.
Night Call (1964) An episode in *The Twilight Zone* television series. Director – Jacques Tourneur. Written by Richard Matheson, based on his own 1953 short story *Long Distance Call*, also known as *Sorry, Right Number*.

A Nightmare on Elm Street (1984) Written and directed by Wes Craven.
The Old Dark House (1932) Directed by James Whale. Screenplay – Benn W. Levy and R.C. Sherriff (uncredited). Based on the novel *Benighted* (1928) by J.B. Priestley.
One Deadly Owner (1974) An episode of the *Thriller* ATV series. Director – Ian Fordyce. Writer and series creator Brian Clemens.
The Others (2001) Written and directed by Alejandro Amenábar.
Repeat Performance (1947) Director – Alfred L. Werker. Screenplay – Walter Bullockand William O'Farrell.
Randall and Hopkirk (Deceased) (1969-71) Creator – Dennis Spooner.
Scooby Doo, Where Are You! (1969-1978) Creators – Joseph Barbera and William Hanna.
The Sixth Sense (1999) Written and directed by M. Night Shyamalan.
Tales from the Crypt (1972) Directed by Freddie Francis. Screenplay – Milton Subotsky. Based on stories from the American bi-monthly horror comics *Tales from the Crypt* and *The Vault of Horror* created by Al Feldstein, Johnny Craig and Bill Gaines, which were published by EC Comics between 1950 and 1955.
Talk to Me (2022) Directed by Danny Philippou and Michael Philippou. Screenplay – Danny Philippou and Bill Hinzman. Based on a concept by Daley Pearson.
Theatre of Blood (1973) Directed by Douglas Hickox. Screenplay – Anthony Greville-Bell, with ideas by Stanley Mann and John Kohn.
The Shining (1980) Directed by Stanley Kubrick. Screenplay by Stanley Kubrick and Diane Johnson. Based on the 1977 horror novel of the same name by Stephen King.
Truly, Madly, Deeply (1990) Written and directed by Anthony Minghella
Under the Shadow (2016) Written and directed by Babak Anvari.
Vertigo (1958) Directed by Alfred Hitchcock. Screenplay – Alec Coppel and Samuel Taylor. Based on the novel *D'entre les morts* by the crime-writing duo Pierre Boileau and Thomas Narcejac.
The Unquiet Dead (2005) An episode in the *Doctor Who* television series. Director Euros Lyn. Writer – Mark Gatiss. Producer – Russell T. Davis.
What Beckoning Ghost (1964) An episode in the *Boris Karloff Presents* series. Director – Ida Lupino. Writers Harold Lawlor and Donald S. Sanford.
When Evil Lurks (2023) Spanish title: *Cuando acecha la maldad*. Written and directed by Demián Rugna.
'*Whistle and I'll Come to You*' (1968) Written and directed by Jonathan Miller. Based on the M.R. James short story '*Oh, Whistle, and I'll Come to You, My Lad*' (1904).

Appendix II

A Yelly Nada in Polari

> 'All slang is metaphor, and all metaphor is poetry. If we paused for a moment to examine the cheapest cant phrases that pass our lips every day, we should find that they were as rich and suggestive as so many sonnets.'
>
> *IN DEFENCE OF SLANG*
>
> *G. K. Chesterton (1874–1936)*

A short history of Polari followed by a glossary of the words and expressions used by the character Billie Blooming in the stories VISITING HATTIE and 'I WAS ONCE A HAUNTED HOUSE'.

POLARI IS A JIGSAW PATCHWORK OF words and phrases that come from diverse sources with varying origins. Whether Polari (from Italian *parlare* 'to talk') should be given the status of a fully fledged language or simply called a lexicon of slang is a continuing academic debate. What Polari is, however, is less interesting than what it represents, why it exists, who used it and how it went on to play a key role in gay culture.

The history of Polari has been traced back to the time of William the Conqueror when many Saxons turned against their invaders and became outlaws. These Saxon rebels developed a secret language the Normans couldn't understand and over the centuries this became known as 'Thieves Cant'. It's thought that several terms from this subcultural world, including *bene* (good), *ken* (house) and *cove* (man), were taken up by those on the fringes of society such as prostitutes, beggars and homosexual men. In the eighteenth century a more direct influence on the language used by gay men came with the arrival of the 'Molly House', a tavern where men of all classes would meet for sex. The lexicon that survives from this period includes phrases for coitus such as '*swive*', '*ride the rump*', '*do the pleasant deed*', plus the term '*trade*' (sex in exchange for money), which survives to this day. The term '*queer ken*', i.e. a bad house or prison, is also thought to come from this Molly House period.

Two later key influences on Polari were Lingua Franca and Romani. Lingua Franca developed as a pidgin language around the various communities of the Mediterranean and offered speakers a simple way of communicating with those who had limited understanding of the other's language. Some of these expressions and phrases were then imported into Polari via continental travellers and sailors who picked up certain words, sometimes with sexual meanings, while going from port to port (and man to man) in the Med. The Romani language influence on Polari mainly came to Britain via circus performers, Punch and Judy street puppeteers ('*Yeute munjare*' – no food, '*Yeute lente*' – no bed, '*Yeute bivare*' – no drink), and fairground showmen. An almost identical Parlyaree has been spoken in fairgrounds since at least the seventh century and is still used today.

In the twentieth century, Yiddish became an influence on Polari (for example, '*meese*' – ugly, from Yiddish *mieskeyt*, meaning 'an ugly person'), as did Cockney rhyming slang and backslang (where the letters of words are reversed, for example, 'hair' becomes '*riah*' and 'face' becomes '*ecaf*', which in Polari was shortened to '*eek*'). And a further twentieth century connection could be said to be American slang which, during World War Two, brought in terms such as '*barkey*' – sailor, '*bevvy*' – drink, '*bod*' – body (particularly of another guy), '*bold*' – outrageous, '*facha*' – face, '*grope*' – feel up. Interestingly many of these terms had their own origin in the language of Sicilian and Italian immigrants who made their homes in America in the late nineteenth and early twentieth century.

In London in the 1940s and 1950s Polari developed variations within itself. The East End was more likely to use Yiddish words and the slang of the fish market, whereas the West End Polari used expressions known within the theatre world. And there was a further influence here in that many gay men worked extensively in the British Merchant Navy as waiters, stewards and entertainers. Theatrical drag shows were popular on ships and these would often be re-staged at The Salisbury pub in St Martins Lane when the crew were back on shore. It's easy to see then how Polari spread into the wider gay subculture. The advantage of a coded language meant that gay men could, to some degree at least, speak of sexual matters in public places, on top of buses or wherever, while the elderly lady with the blue rinse sitting nearby, or indeed the undercover policemen, wouldn't have a clue as to what was being said. And of course Polari was a way of alerting those around you to your own sexuality. With its irony and innuendo, Polari then offered gay men an effective wall of resilience in a world where homosexuality was outlawed and stigmatised.

The history of Polari is curious and fascinating. One particular word that is now considered as Polari was even used by William Shakespeare in both *Henry IV, Part 2* (Shallow: And I may say to you, we knew where the bona robas were and had the best of them all at commandment) and *Henry VI, Part 2* (Dick: What say you of Kent? / Lord Saye: Nothing but this: *'tis bona terra, mala gens.* / Jack Cade: Away with him, away with him! He speaks Latin.) The popular music hall song '*The Daring Young Man on the Flying Trapeze*' ('He'd fly through the air with the greatest of ease, / That daring young man on the flying trapeze') published in 1867, with words by George Leybourne, music by Gaston Lyle, hints at the circus origins of Polari. The lyrics give the name of the trapeze artist in the song as 'Bona Slang', though it was in fact based on a real flying ace called Jules Léotard, who famously gave his name to the one-piece outfit he always wore. But these examples of Polari in print and in the mainstream are rare because Polari was essentially a coded way of speech and only passed down orally. *Oooh Matron.* Polari words, however, clearly existed in the spoken language of particular groups, even if they rarely found their ways into books or newspapers or dictionaries.

All that changed with the BBC radio comedy series *Round the Horne*, starring Kenneth Horne, which was first transmitted in 1965 and ran until 1968. One of the most popular features on the show were the sketches involving Julian and Sandy, a camp theatrical pair (played by Hugh Paddick and Kenneth Williams) whose names were inspired by Julian Slade, who composed the music to *Salad Days* (book and lyrics by Dorothy Reynolds), and Sandy Wilson, who wrote the musical *The Boy Friend*. Julian and Sandy, created by the writing team of Barry Took and Marty Feldman, were out of work actors who while 'resting' took up temporary employment in various businesses, usually based around Chelsea. These enterprises had names such as 'Bona Tours', 'Bona Books' and 'Bona Antiques'. A typical sketch began with a shop bell ringing and Kenneth Horne saying: 'Is anybody there?' The reply: 'Oh hello, I'm Julian and this is my friend Sandy.' These fun loving former chorus boys would then welcome Mr Horne into their establishment saying, 'Oh look, it's Mr Horne! How bona to vada your dolly old eek' or 'What brings you trolling in here?' Suddenly the secret language of gay and theatrical slang was being broadcast to the entire nation on a Sunday lunchtime. And within it was much sexual innuendo. For example, in the 'Bona Law' sketch, Julian says: 'We've got a criminal practice that takes up most of our time,' which, given that gay sex was still illegal, can be taken several ways (if you pardon the expression).

Julian and Sandy probably survived BBC censorship either because the authorities hadn't a clue what they were talking about or didn't want to admit that they understood the gay meaning. Kenneth Williams consciously used camp humour to disarm prejudices in the hope of bringing about more tolerance. And it worked. Radio comedy in the 1960s was listened to by millions and Julian and Sandy became hugely popular with the public. Many academics and critics have now credited this funny and lovable pair with helping to make the British public more accepting of gay men, but as Barry Took and Marty Feldman point out in their foreword to *Bona Book of Julian and Sandy*, Kenneth Horne deserved much credit too because his 'very ordinariness when chatting to them made the characters somehow safe.'

But times were changing anyway, for the Labour government of the 1960s was progressive on social matters and in the Sexual Offences Act of 1967 adult homosexual acts in England and Wales were to some limited extent decriminalised. However, with gay sex more out in the open and the emergence of Gay Lib in the 1970s, and later the very visible activism of Act Up in the 1980s, the need for a gay subcultural language declined. On top of that, many radicals in the gay liberation movement began to view Polari as way past its sell-by date and, worse, actually harmful in perpetuating camp gay stereotypes.

In recent years several Polari words have entered mainstream slang, including hoofer, mince, ogle, scarper, slap (make-up) and trade. The Polari word *naff* was popularised in 1970s when the television sitcom *Porridge*, set in a prison, employed it as a broadcastable alternative to more well known expletives. In the 2000s *zhoosh* (or sometimes *zhuzh*), meaning to improve or smarten up, especially when applied to the way one dresses, became part of the lexicon used in *Queer Eye for the Straight Guy* and it's also a term that's been heard a few times on *RuPaul's Drag Race*. The Church of England was less than impressed though when, in an evening liturgy in Cambridge, God was referred to as Duchess. Even so, a group of gay activists called the Sisters of Perpetual Indulgence have recently created a Polari Bible.

In his essay *In Defence of Slang*, Gilbert Keith Chesterton wrote, 'The world of slang is a kind of topsy-turveydom of poetry, full of blue moons and white elephants, of men losing their heads, and men whose tongues run away with them – a whole chaos of fairy tales.' And, he said, slang was constantly changing and developing, 'Every day a nameless poet weaves some fairy tracery of popular language.' Importantly for Chesterton the most inventive slang comes not from the upper classes but from ordinary working people, 'Nothing is more startling than the contrast between the heavy, formal, lifeless slang of the man-about-town and the light, living, and flexible slang of the coster.' It's unlikely that Chesterton ever encountered Polari or was even aware of it, yet his observations on slang do seem to fit Polari's history and inventiveness.

In a book of ghost stories it somehow feels appropriate that the spirit of Polari has found an afterlife in the character of Billie Blooming. In *Visiting Hattie* and *'I Was Once a Haunted House'* Billie speaks a form of Polari that also includes numerous Lingua Franca terms. How he came to know or use these expressions is never explained. Perhaps Billie had a Romani heritage or maybe he travelled a lot round the Mediterranean or worked in the Merchant Navy or was once a Punch and Judy performer. But none of that matters, for Billie speaks the way he does because that's how he has chosen to present himself to the world. It's just about possible to follow his meaning even if you don't always understand some of the specific words and terms. However, for the record, here is a glossary, which includes not only Polari and Lingua Franca but also some gay slang.

Ajax – Nearby (probably from a shortening of adjacent).
Anima – Soul (from Lingua Franca).
Arthur and Martha – Arthur is the partner who takes the active role, whereas Martha is the partner who takes the passive role. To say you don't know if you're Arthur or Martha can also mean you are unsure as to your sexuality.
Auntie or *y'Auntie* – A self referential term often used by an older gay man (also *y'Mother* or *Mother*).
Attacca – Attack (from Lingua Franca).
Aunt nells – Ears. '*Aunt nell*' can also mean to listen.
Aunt Nell fakes or *danglers* – Earrings (when Billie says 'Pin back your *aunt nells*' or 'Pin back your *danglers*' he means 'listen carefully'.)
Barbaro – Savage (from Lingua Franca).
Bear – Large or hairy or overtly masculine man (from gay slang).
Bestai – Beastly (from Lingua Franca).
Bene – Well, in good health.
Betty Bracelets – The police (also '*Lilly Law*').
Bijou – Small (from the French for jewel or trinket. *Bijou*, however, is a word that can be traced back to Breton, a Celtic language, where *bizou* means 'ring'.)
Bod – Body, especially one that is attractive (from gay slang).
Bold – Daring or outrageous.
Bona – Good or attractive (from the Italian – *buono*)

Bona Nochy – Goodnight (from the Italian – *buona notte*).
Bonaroo – Wonderful / excellent.
Botega – Shop (from Lingua Franca).
Bisogno – Needful (from Lingua Franca).
Butch – Masculine.
Cackle – Gossip.
Carts/Cartso – Penis.
Cativitá – Evil (from Lingua Franca).
Cassa – Box or container (from Lingua Franca)
Charper – To seek or go in search of something or someone.
Cod – Not very good.
Conoscir – To know (from Lingua Franca).
Contentar – Satisfy (from Lingua Franca).
Crimper – Hairdresser.
Crudel – Cruel.
Demandar – Ask for (from Lingua Franca).
Dinari – Money (from Latin *denarii*. In the British pre-decimal currency of pounds, shillings and pence, 'd' was the letter that represented the penny or pence.)
Dish – An attractive male. *Dish* can also mean arse.
Dizzy – Scatterbrained.
Dolly – Pretty, nice, pleasant.
Dona – Woman.
Drag – Clothes, particularly women's clothes.
Dropped the soap – A mistake leading to surprising consequences.
Duchess Gloria! – Good Heavens! or Good God!
Ecaf – Face (from backslang).
Eek – Face (an abbreviation of ecaf).
Fabbola – Fable (from Lingua Franca).
Faked the facha – Put on make-up (where *facha* – or sometimes *fatcha* – means face). To *fake the facha* can also mean 'to shave one's face'.
Fantabulosa! – Wonderful!
Favola – Story (from Lingua Franca).
Feely – Young or child (from the Italian *figlio*, for son).
Finir – Finish (from Lingua Franca).
Fortini or *fortuna* – Beautiful.
Furba – Deceitful (from Lingua Franca).
Gildy – Fancy, elegant, lavish, sumptuous, usually referring to clothes or decor.
Glad rags – Clothes or outfit, from theatrical gay slang, particularly drag.
Heartface – A term of endearment.
Hold my pearls! – An expression of surprise.
Hoofer – Dancer, especially in musical theatre.
Jarry – Food, also *mangarie* (from the Italian *mangiare*, meaning 'to eat'.).
Lallies – Legs.
Larder – The bulging crotch in a man's trousers.

Latty or *lattie* – Room, house or flat.
Lilly Law or just *Lilly* – The Police (also *Betty Bracelets*).
Lills – Hands.
Lucoddy – Body.
Luppers – Fingers.
Lungo – Long (from Lingua Franca).
Manly Alice – A good looking guy, often referring to a straight man.
Mangarie – Food, also *jarry* (from Italian *mangiare* or Lingua Franca *mangiaria* meaning 'meal').
Moltisimo or *Molto* – Very much or very strong (from Italian).
Naff – Bad, drab, dull.
Nanti – Not, no.
Nelly yada – Talk or gossip.
Nishta – Nothing, no.
Noche or *nochy* – Night (from the Spanish *noche* and Italian *notte*).
Nuovo – New (from Lingua Franca).
Obes – Ears.
Ogle – To look (*oglefakes* means spectacles).
Ogles – Eyes (also *orbs*)
Omi – Man.
Omi-Polone – Effeminate man, or homosexual.
Oro – Gold (from Lingua Franca).
Osservar – Observe (from Lingua Franca).
Parlay or *Parlyaree* – Speak, talk or chat.
Palone / Polone / polony – Woman.
Perque – Why (from Lingua Franca).
Pianto – Tears (from Lingua Franca).
Pieno – Full of (from Lingua Franca).
Potento – Powerful (from Lingua Franca).
Pots – Teeth.
Punizzion – Punishment (from Lingua Franca).
Rabia – Rage or anger (from Lingua Franca).
Ravagiar – Ravage (from Lingua Franca).
Regalo – Gift or present (from Lingua Franca).
Riah/Riha – Hair (from backslang).
Riah Shusher / Zhoosher – Hairdresser. Also *crimper*.
Riguardar – To observe (from Lingua Franca).
Rispectar – Respect (from Lingua Franca).
Savvy – Understand (from the Portuguese or Spanish *saber* meaning 'to know').
Scarper – To run off (from Italian *scappare*, 'to escape').
Schlepp – Travelling, often referring to an arduous or tedious journey (from Yiddish). *Schlepp* is used extensively in theatre talk as an expression for touring.
Screech – To speak.
Shyker / shyckle – Wig (from the Yiddish *sheitel*). Also *Irish*, from the rhyming slang 'Irish jig'/'wig'.
Sentir or *sentar* – To hear, as in to understand (from Lingua Franca).

Slap – Make-up (from theatre slang).
Sling backs – Shoes.
Solamente – Only (from Lingua Franca).
Sparkle – Spirit.
Stimps – Legs.
Strillers – Piano.
Sweetheart – A term of endearment.
Thews – Thighs.
Tristo – Sad (from Lingua Franca).
Troll – To walk about.
Tutto – Everything (from Lingua Franca).
Vada/*Varda* – See (from Italian *vedere*).
Vellaco – Villain (from Lingua Franca).
Vivo – Alive (from Lingua Franca).
Vogue – Cigarette (probably from Lingua Franca *fogus* meaning fire or smoke). '*Vogue me up*' means light me a cigarette.
Vera (Lynn) – Gin (from the rhyming slang).
Yew – Eyes (from the French *yeux*).
Yorno – Day (from Lingua Franca).
Zhoosh or *zhuzh* – To style, tart up or make glamorous in some way. *Zhooshy* means showy.

In the preparation of this short essay and in the compilation of the glossary I would like to acknowledge my reliance on and indebtedness to *A Glossary of Lingua Franca* (2003) by Alan D. Corré; *Fantabulosa: A Dictionary of Polari and Gay Slang* (2004) by Paul Baker; *Bona Book of Julian and Sandy* (1976) by Barry Took and Marty Feldman; and *In the Life* (2019) by Christopher Bryant.

Alternative spellings and pronunciations of Polari include *Parlare*, *Parlary*, *Palare*, *Palarie* and *Palari*.

Appendix III

Two Lectures from the Claverley Manor Conference Centre symposium 'The Ghosts of Many Worlds'

THAT MOST PECULIAR TALE I TOLD, concerning the events during the conference held by The Society of Paranormal and Psychic Investigation at Claverley Manor, was, in certain respects, incomplete. You may remember, dear Reader, that the conference was entitled 'The Ghosts of Many Worlds', and it was called such because of the wide range of speakers who attended, and the contrasting opinions presented. There were writers, clairvoyants, academics, scientists, psychologists, and, if you recall, an unexpected ghost, who was the genesis of my tale.

I learnt so much that day from the lectures that were offered and from the discussions I overheard over coffee, lunch and dinner. I became particularly well versed in the vernacular of the modern literary academic. There was much said about the 'structural device' of the 'textual-narrator' making use of the story-within-a-story or the 'inner-narrator'. According to one speaker, although the narrative aim may be to establish the veracity of the tale, in 'distancing the diegeis' the inner narrative creates the potential for and phenomenon of the 'unreliable narrator'. Henry James, in connection with this technique, was mentioned repeatedly, and his work was even described by one lecturer as 'an onion'. 'For,' he said, 'like all onions, James's stories have no centre, only layers.' A most intelligent observation, I thought.

There was also discussion, at dinner if I remember correctly, of the epistolary ghost tales such as F.G. Loring's *The Tomb of Sarah* and Rhoda Broughton's *The Truth, the Whole Truth, and Nothing but the Truth*. No nonsense about unreliable narrators here, for these stories are based on actual letters and diaries and journals. Or so it is purported.

Fascinating as all the lectures were, I was only able to include in *'I Was Once a Haunted House'* those that were pertinent to the story of my ghost. And nor can I now offer you every word of every lecture and discussion, for I am nearly two hundred years old and my memory is not what it was. Yet, in the furtherance of learning and scholarship, I feel obliged to set out two of the talks from that day that were briefly mentioned in my tale. They are 'Now You See Me, Now You Don't', presented by a gentleman by the name of Mr Miles Morecroft, and 'Transgressional Queer Sex and the Victorian Spook', offered to the assemblage at Claverley Manor by a speaker who called himself/herself/themself Pixie.

First, 'Now You See Me, Now You Don't' with Mr Miles Morecroft.

'WHEN SPEAKING OF THE CHESHIRE CAT in *Alice's Adventures in Wonderland*, Lewis Carroll writes: "This time it vanished quite slowly, beginning with the end of the tail, and ending with the grin, which remained some time after the rest of it had gone." And so what I want to do in this talk is look at, literally, because I have some slides, the physical nature of the Victorian ghost, which, like the Cheshire Cat, ranges from solid and lifelike, through to invisible, with various disembodied body parts along the way.

'Let's begin with the mysterious lady in Charles Dickens's *The Portrait-Painter's Story*, published in *All the Year Round* in September 1861, a journal edited by Dickens himself. The sitter for the portrait is believed by the narrator to be real, only of course the twist –

typical of many tales of the period – is that she is revealed to be a ghost. A curious postscript to the publication of this tale is that Dickens received a letter from a miniaturist, one Thomas Frank Heaphy, claiming that he was that very painter in the story and had written his own version of the tale. Dickens replied assuring Heaphy that he had heard the story told at a friend's house and assumed it was an anonymous piece of lore. Nowadays we would call it an urban myth. Dickens read Heaphy's version and later even published it. After Heaphy died, his widow collected the letters from Dickens to her husband, and published them, alongside Heaphy's original tale, with the title *A Wonderful Ghost Story*. Anyway, here's the illustration from that cover of the artist and his ghost.

'The more general point is that in such narratives the walking dead are always, as with Daniel Defoe's Mrs Veal, 'of substance'. In other words, corporally real. The mysterious lady in Guy de Maupassant's *A Ghost* has manifested herself in order to get her hair combed, and that hair is definitely of substance because, as de Maupassant's narrator informs us, "my dolman" – a sort of Turkish robe – "was covered with long woman's hair which had rolled themselves around the buttons."

'So what else is there along our taxonomy of the ghost? Or "spookometer", as I prefer to call it. Well, to offer a clue, there's the nursery rhyme riddle in *Uncle Cornelius His Story* by George MacDonald: "What makes your eyes so holed?" / "I've lain so long among the mould." Yes, we are now onto corpses that won't stay in their graves. Let's begin with the old lady ghost in Sir Walter Scott's 1828 tale, *The Tapestried Chamber*. "Upon a face which wore the fixed features of a corpse were imprinted the traces of the vilest and most hideous passions which had animated her while she lived." Well, you can't get more Gothic horror than that. More subtle is the decaying carcass in Edith Nesbit's 1905 story *In the Dark*. True, the image of spectrality in this tale is not exactly a corpse, but since it is described as being harder than those alive – "more like a stone thing"– we can deduce perhaps that the process of *rigor mortis* has at least begun. Decay though is well under way in Perceval Landon's *Thurnley Abbey*, because when the ghost, if you can call it that, appears, as you can see from this illustration of the period, it does so swathed in a rotten and tattered veiling, and has a visage "not entirely that of a skull, though the eyes and the flesh of the face were totally gone." In Amelia Edwards's tale *The Phantom Coach* the putrefaction is contagious because it's even spread to the coach itself: "The sashes splintered at the touch. The leather fittings were crusted over with mould, and literally rotting from the woodwork." And it's worth noting here the description of the medical skeleton in Jerome K. Jerome's *The Man of Science* where "those empty sockets in that grinning head... seemed to be drawing him towards them."

'At least that skeleton had all his bones, but what about when there are only parts of you that do the haunting? A bit like Lewis Carroll's Cheshire Cat, whose grin remained some time after the rest of its body had gone. Ah! And there *is* the Cheshire Cat in his full splendour in this famous John Tenniel drawing. Anyway, what we are moving onto now is the partial ghost in my spookometer. I'm thinking here particularly of little Margaret in Arthur Quiller-Couch's *A Pair of Hands*, and the title is essentially a spoiler as to which limbs we're talking about. But remember, even though some of the body is missing, we're still in the world of the corporeal. As the tenant at Tesillack in Quiller-Couch's tale observes: "...just a pair of small hand and the wrists, and after that – nothing. They were moving briskly – washing themselves clean. I saw the water trickle and splash over them – not through them – but just as it would on real hands." Little Margaret, we are told, was taken by diphtheria, aged seven, but death doesn't seem to stop her doing all the household chores. Of course, we would take a dim view of such things nowadays, but maybe Elizabeth Barrett Browning's campaign against child labour never reached beyond the grave.

'Anyway, ghostly disembodied limbs, solid or otherwise, now bring us to the vexed issue of whether footfalls – or footsteps as we would call them now – can be seen and heard. I say vexed because Victorian ghosts tend to be a bit fickle in this area. There are visible ghosts that can walk side-by-side with the living, but leave no footprints, as in this illustration from Elizabeth Gaskell's *The Old Nurse's Tale*, yet there are those spirits who remain unseen, as in

Edward Bulwer-Lytton's *The House and the Brain*, who are still able to leave a physical trace. As Bulwer-Lytton's narrator tells us, "I saw, just before me, the print of a foot suddenly form itself." And this takes us on to the half-way house of the nebulous and the insubstantial.

'For the ill-defined, there's the snowdrift in *The Captain of the 'Polestar'*, which may or may not have taken the shape of a woman – a clever bit of pencil work there from the artist – and for the see-through and translucent, I give you Mary Louisa Molesworth's *The Story of the Rippling Train*: "He came towards the library, and seeing the door open walked in, and I, still gazing, saw his figure pass through that of the woman in the doorway as you may walk through a wreath of mist or smoke." At last a ghost who can walk through walls! And talking of walls, our final stop-off on the spookometer before we consider complete invisibility is the shadow on the wall in Tom Hood's *The Shadow of a Shade*: 'There was something always at his side, which none could see, but which cast a shadow."

'It's often said that the written word is fundamentally visual in that, as with radio drama, you create the pictures your head. And what this means is that there are few truly invisible ghosts in Victorian supernatural fiction. An exception can be found in Fitz James O'Brien's *What was it?* And what a "what" it was! The narrator writes, "I shudder now as I think of that awful moment. I saw nothing! Yes; I had one arm firmly clasped round a breathing, panting, corporeal shape, my other hand gripped with all its strength a throat as warm, as apparently fleshy, as my own." Creepy. But even this exception isn't really an exception because the entity is then tied down and given chloroform. Later the lifeless body, which they can feel but not see, is covered with plaster and from the mould a figure is made that looked "capable of feeding on human flesh." Other speakers I know are due to talk about the ghosts of Edwardian fiction becoming more psychological than real, but the point I want to make is that Gothic terror needs a physical spectre, be it corporeal or imagined in the mind. And it's that visual nature of the ghost that is the key to the Victorian supernatural tale.'

THE SECOND TALK I WOULD LIKE to offer you, dear Reader, comes from Pixie, whom I remember vividly, for he/she/they were dressed in a one-piece outfit made up of harlequin diamonds of pink and purple, with a lacing of gold thread. And I say 'he/she/they', not in ignorance of English grammar, but because this person, being 'poly-sexual', had selected these appellations as their pronouns. As I have previously observed, it was a most diverting talk. However, it occurred to me, as I listened to this and the many other lectures presented, that the more writers of fiction leave out of their stories, the more academics tend to put in. This was certainly the case with Pixie's observations in his/her/their talk entitled 'Transgressional Queer Sex and the Victorian Spook'.

'OFTEN READING NINETEENTH CENTURY SUPERNATURAL FICTION you think, "Blimey, what's going on here?" Take Sheridan Le Fanu's *The Strange Event in the Life of Schalken the Painter*. A girl is pimped for gold to an evil masochist who is either a devil or a corpse. Take your pick, demonic slavery or necrophilia. I mean, it has to be one or the other.

'Yes, I know most Victorian ghost stories are more subtle than the tales of Le Fanu, but that doesn't stop the characters in them from being sexually transgressive if you know how and where to look. And what I'm talking about here is what I call "reading the lust lines". Here's an obvious example: "She loved as fiercely and rashly as such wild and untamed natures do," which is how the supposed sexual and insatiable animal needs of one woman are described in *The Story of Clifford House*. No one knows who wrote the story but it first appeared in *The Mistletoe Bough* in 1878, a Christmas annual edited by, and with contributions from, Mary Elizabeth Braddon, founder of what became known as "sensational" fiction. Personally, I think the evidence points to Braddon writing those words herself.

'In queer stories, however, the code is more veiled, but usually there is enough in the lust lines to identify the nature of the character of the sexual outsider or transgressor. In Algernon Blackword's *The*

Kit-Bag, Johnson, the ghost seer of the tale, is referred to as having "a delicate face like a girl's" – clearly suggesting he's queer. Of course the idea that it's "the queer" who sees ghosts goes way back to Reginald Scot's *The Discovery of Witchcraft*, published in 1584, where witchcraft is directly associated with "women and effeminate men", and where the seeing of spirits proceeds "from a cowardly nature and complexion, or from an effeminate and fond bringing up." Which reminds me of that old joke, "My mother made me a homosexual." "Really? Do you think if I asked nicely she'd make me one?"

'Anyhow, where does this tradition of the queer ghost seer leave the heterosexual male ghost seer in a Victorian spook story? In Sir Walter Scott's *The Tapestried Chamber,* merely seeing a ghost leads General Browne to say, "I was ashamed of myself as a man and a soldier." Tom in Sheridan Le Fanu's *An Account of Some Strange Disturbances in Aungier Street* goes even further and says that his encounter with a ghost "unmanned him". Seeing a spook literally de-sexes Tom's masculine identity. There's more I could say on that subject, both personally and professionally, but the text I want to concentrate on today is Francis Marion Crawford's *The Upper Berth*, first published in 1886.

'Running through the whole narrative is the dread of sexual contagion that comes as a result of men having to share rooms. And M.R. James fans will understand this conceit from the many queer readings of his classic tale *'Oh, Whistle, and I'll Come to You, My Lad'*. In this story, Parkins, one of James's crusty old closeted bachelors – let's be honest, that's basically James himself – is uncomfortable about sharing a holiday – and we infer a room and most definitely a bed – with a colleague. However, in blowing a mysterious whistle he's found near a beach, the M.R., or Montague Rhodes's stand-in, conjures up some sort of supernatural entity that spends the night under the sheets of the adjacent bed and even takes on a face of crumpled linen. But of course it doesn't just lie there – 'With formidable quickness, it moved into the middle of the room, and, as it groped and waved, one corner of its draperies swept across Parkins' face. He could not – though he knew how perilous a sound was – he could not keep back a cry of disgust, and this gave the searcher an instant clue. It leapt towards him upon the instant, and the next moment he was half-way through the window backwards, uttering cry upon cry at the utmost pitch of his voice, and the linen face was thrust close into his own.' Here the supernatural can be read, as in many of James's ghost stories, as his own sexually repressed subconscious coming alive in spook form. And I've mentioned '*Oh, Whistle, and I'll Come to You, My Lad*' because in *The Upper Berth* what we're specifically dealing with is having to share a state room on a transatlantic crossing on the *Kamtschatka*. And as it turns out it's more than the room, or indeed the upper berth, that is shared.

'*The Upper Berth* is a first person narrative but with an after dinner story-within-a-story framework of an inner-narrator. The overseeing textual narrator of the narrative, never named, describes the after dinner inner-narrator, Brisbane, as strong and above average in size and having 'those gifts which chiefly attract the attentions of men.' Hmm. And I should add here that it is just men in this tale, because no woman is ever even mentioned. No wonder it was a favourite of M.R. James.

'But where does our overseeing narrator place Brisbane on the masculinity spectrum? Well, he says that Brisbane's 'muscular hands appeared to possess a peculiar skill in breaking walnuts without the assistance of the ordinary cracker.' Well, that's an unmanning castration image if ever there was one, and that, I'd suggest, puts Brisbane firmly in the sexually dominant role. Incidentally, I personally never use the terms "top" or "bottom" because I believe they reinforce the social class prejudice inherent in the patriarchy.

'Let's then have a look at how the tale begins. The narrative opens with the line 'Somebody asked for the cigars,' from the overseeing textual narrator. Cigars, it should be noted, are mentioned no fewer than nine times, and, I'd argue, they function essentially as symbols of oral-centric phallic desire. And here you might also include the phallic pipe, smoked by the ship's doctor, who, Brisbane says, as he tells his after dinner tale, had a "healthy look about him which was rather attractive." I bet it was. But the point I wish to stress here is that within this tale, oral-centred sex, signified by the need and constant reference to the cigar and the pipe, is coded as perfectly acceptable and even to be encouraged. However, the problem comes when two other phallic signifiers are confronted by a different and more threatening kind of orifice, but I'll consider those in a moment. Anyway, 'Somebody asked for the cigars' soon becomes 'Everybody called for cigars', and once all the men at the dinner have their cigars in their mouths, Brisbane, our inner-narrator, can begin his story.

'Brisbane tells us that on his crossing on the *Kamtschatka* he was allocated the bottom berth and when he goes to the state room he sees that in the upper berth there has been deposited "a neat-folded rug, with a stick and umbrella." Wow! Two phallic signifiers. Double helping! So what sort of guy is this? Well, Brisbane soon tells us what he thinks of him when at last he encounters the stranger. And this is how Brisbane describes his room mate: "He had about him, I thought, an air of rather dubious fashion; the sort of man you might see in Wall Street, without being able precisely to say what he was doing there – the sort of man who frequents the Café Anglais, who always seems to be alone and who drinks champagne; you might meet him on a racecourse, but he would never appear to be doing anything there either. A little over-dressed – a little odd." Let's leave aside the stranger for a moment and ask what do these observations tell us about Brisbane? Well, I'd say that our inner-narrator, whether he knows it or not, is telling us that he has spent a lot of his spare time walking up and down Wall Street and staring at single men in cafés. How do we know this? Because that's the social context of the comparator. But what is our double-penis guy doing in these places? Well, I'd say these none-too-subtle references to him being a lone figure who's a little over-dressed and hanging around without any perceivable purpose is code for sexual availability. Cruising, in other words. And since it's the financial distract, where buying and selling of a commodity is the way of things, I'd go as far as to suggest that's a lust line code for soliciting. But how does Brisbane feel about this guy? Well, he says that he did not care "to make his acquaintance". Window shopping is fine, honey, but don't touch!

'Anyhow, Brisbane falls asleep but is then awoken by a noise coming from the upper berth. The stranger jumps down, exits the room and annoyingly leaves the door open. Brisbane gets up to shut the door, returns to his own berth and goes back to sleep. And it's after this that the tale gets a bit weird, because Brisbane is awoken again, this time by "a disagreeable sensation of cold". Guess what? The porthole in the state room is open and hooked back. Of course it is! Later Brisbane discovers that his berth companion has gone and jumped overboard. In fact, it's revealed that on the last three trips all the men who slept in that upper berth went overboard.

'Okay, so what's going on here? Well, what I'm suggesting is that the upper berth is code the active role in rectal sex – remember the double phallic images of the umbrella and the stick? – and that the bottom berth and the open porthole represents the passive role in rectal sex. Let's not forget here that buggery, within the Victorian mindset, is the ultimate sexual transgression that must be punished by a judicial death sentence. Or, as in this story, suicide. Going overboard indeed.

'Now in Queer Studies we have what we call "sticky words", because these words have associations and connections attached to them in a sticky way. In other words, a secondary meaning. And "bottom" and "went overboard" are certainly words with strong relational sexual and social contexts. And it's these words which, you might say, since this is a ghost story, haunt Crawford's tale.

'And talking of haunting, the drowned man doesn't entirely disappear from the story because, as Brisbane tells us, "his face rose very distinctly before me as I undressed, and I even went so far as to draw back the curtains of the upper berth, as though to persuade myself that he was actually gone." Methinks the lady doth protest too much! Anyway, this is where the supernatural part of the story really takes off because the damp smell returns and that porthole mysteriously keeps on opening all by itself and can't be closed. What a surprise! And at the sight of the open porthole "a sort of creeping horror began to take possession of me which I never felt before, nor wish to feel again." "Porthole" in this story is another of those sticky words and it clearly operates as a signifier of penetrative rectal fears. Brisbane even tries to keep the porthole shut with his cane, but "the strong wood snapped suddenly and I fell upon the couch." I don't think we need Freud to tell us what that means, for what we have here is Brisbane's own masculinity being unmanned and de-sexed in his symbolic and metaphorical castration.

'But Brisbane can't help his curiosity and, like Toto in *The Wizard of Oz*, this results in him literally pulling back the curtains. Not only pulling them back but "thrusting in my hands to discover if there were any one there". And what does he find in the upper berth? "I laid hold of something that had the shape of man's arm, but was smooth, wet, and icy cold. But suddenly, as I pulled, the creature sprang forward against me, a clammy oozy mass, as it seemed to me, heavy and wet, yet endowed with a sort of supernatural strength." I bet it was!

'The captain of the *Kamtschatka* then joins Brisbane in the state room to keep watch and it's then that Brisbane is attacked once more by the entity in the upper berth: "I wrestled with the dead thing; it thrust itself upon me and forced me back and nearly broke my arms; it wound its corpse's arms about my neck, the living death, and overpowered me." And then it goes for the captain, who "fell forward upon his face, with an inarticulate cry of horror. The thing paused an instant, seeming to hover over his prostrate body, and I could have screamed again for very fright, I but had no voice left." No need to interpret beneath the lust lines here – porno more like – because they really are staring you in the face!

'Anyway, the drowned "thing" escapes and it seemed, says Brisbane, that the creature "made its exit though the open porthole, though how that was possible, considering the smallness of the aperture, is more than one can say." Well, I know exactly how it's possible. But that's another story altogether!'

Acknowledgements

Many thanks to Sonia Beldom, Fiorenz Bolgna, Jack Bowman, Simon Ellinas, George Grimes, Barry Gurney, Mark Mander, Marcus Prince, Carolyn Scott-Jeffs, Sam Supple, Paul Smith, Kate Somerby, Julia Tarnoky, Jo Thackery, Adam Trembath and Tim Wallers for their advice and encouragement. Thanks to my family, especially Doreen, Jordan and Scott, for their unceasing support. Thanks as well to Rory Bremner, the Reverend Simon Buckley, Matthew Cuss, Iain Dale, Christian Dion, Dick Fiddy, James Dreyfus, Neal Foster, John Henderson, Jenny Lecoat, Alistair McGowan, Helen Lederer, Jonny Maitland, Jessica Martin, Andy Merriman, Nigel Nelson, William Palmer, Robert Ross, Graham Seed, Denise Silvey, Ian Talbot and Arabella Weir for agreeing to read a tale or two and offering thoughtful comments. Thanks too to Ed Clarke for the Latin, and Julie Scattergood for the French and German, as well as her forensic proof reading skills. Not forgetting Matthew Cuss, Andy De Emmony, John Henderson, Jamie Lennox and Sue Spenceley-Burch for their very welcome advice on the screenplay. Thanks as well to Rachel Adams, Collette Nicolle and David Nicolle for invaluable comments and corrections.

Scott Brooker would like to add his own acknowledgements to the above. First of all, many thanks to Steve for the opportunity to do the colouring-in for his magnum opus. Thanks also to my wife Lucy and daughters, Ruby and Ivy, for their invaluable help in posing for some of the pictures, and to Roger Law for his hopelessly biased encouragement. Thanks as well to Steve's neighbour Stevie Kotey for the use of his face – he's the angel on the left in the Christmas scene. Thanks to John Merrell for access to his superb Austin A40 Somerset and to Richard Luck of Coach House Antiques, Hastings, for letting me adapt his Laughing Sailor into the Laughing Policeman image. Special thanks to the Rose & Crown, London N16, which features on the cover and elsewhere in The Gallery. And lastly a big thank you to Tiffany Vernon and Aaran Eccles for posing so wholeheartedly for *The Ghost Light*!

A particular thank you from both of us to Liam Simms MA, Fellow of the Society of Antiquaries, and Cambridge University Library for their kind permission in our using an image of M.R. James from a photograph in the collection of Cambridge University Library MS Add. 7637.

Finally, a big thank you to our publishers, Scratching Shed, and Phil Caplan and Tony Hannan for their support and faith in the project. A special thanks as well to our wonderful story editor Gemma Ross for her guidance, counselling and invigorating encouragement.

Ghost Story Publications

There are many ghost story collections in print such as *The Oxford Book of Victorian Ghost Stories* selected by Michael Cox and R.A. Gilbert, *Classic Victorian & Edwardian Ghost Stories* compiled by Rex Collings, and *The Penguin Book of Ghost Stories: From Elizabeth Gaskell to Ambrose Bierce* edited by Michael Newton, and all have excellent introductions.

The British Library have recently brought out themed collections such as *Weird Woods: Tales from the Haunted Forests of Britain* edited by John Miller, *Chill Tidings: Dark Tales of the Christmas Season* edited by Tanya Kirk, and *The Weird Tales of William Hope Hodgson* edited by Xavier Aldana Reyes, again all have useful introductions.

If you are new to the ghost tale I'd suggest a good starting point would be Roald Dahl's *Book of Ghost Stories*, not his own stories but rather a collection of his favourite tales by other authors. As you'd expect Dahl offers a fascinating introduction with his own insightful and often idiosyncratic views on ghost stories.

Well-known ghost story writers such as E.F. Benson, M.R. James, Sir Arthur Conan Doyle, Charles Dickens, Sheridan Le Fanu and H.R. Wakefield all still have their work in print. However, collections such as *When Churchyards Yawn* and *The Ghost Story Book* edited by Lady Cynthia Asquith, although no longer in print, are readily available via second hand bookshops and specialist online retailers.

I'd say the best modern writer on the ghost tale is M. Grant Kellermeyer. His annotated editions are extraordinarily detailed and his knowledge and critical analysis of the ghost tale and its literary and social history is unsurpassed. Here I would like to acknowledge that his website www.oldstyletales.com and his publications have proved invaluable in providing me with an insight into the lives of so many ghost story writers and the psychology behind their work.

Roger Clarke's *A Natural History Ghosts: 500 Years of Hunting For Proof* concerns, as the title suggests, the sightings of supposed real ghosts. Although it is not about the literary ghost story tradition, its tales of hauntings are fascinating to read and often have parallels with their fictional counterparts.

FINIS.